Que Será Syrah

POUR DECISIONS

PG Forte

Chapultepec Press

About this title...

They may be keeping secrets and telling lies, but a little white wine never hurt anyone.

ALLEGRA

It's not every day that you inherit one-third of a winery. I should be on top of the world, floating on Cloud Wine, as they say. Instead, don't you just know it? I'm about to make one of the biggest mistakes of my life. And that's saying something. My family has always viewed me as something of a screw-up, not always fairly. But in this case? They're not only dead right about me messing things up; they don't even know the half of it. Yet.

Complicating my quest to redeem myself, earn my sisters' respect, and help them turn our winery into a straight fire success, is my low-key relationship with Sheriff's Deputy Clay Romero. Sure, there are risks involved in sleeping with the enemy, but 'what's meant to be will find a way,' right? And whether Clay believes it or not, I know we're fated. With a capital F.

CLAY

We're Capital F somethin' all right; but I don't think it's fate. Ever since Legs (AKA Allegra Martinelli) blew back into town, I've been flirting with disaster. Literally. I doubt that woman's ever met a rule that she didn't want to at least bend. And, as luck would have it, it's my job to try and stop her. I love my job, and I think I love her. But there's not enough wine in Napa to convince me that I'll be able to hang on to them both.

Legs keeps likening us to Romeo and Juliet. And as I keep trying to remind her; that kind of story tends not to end well. I'm sure there are exceptions, but are we gonna be one of them? I guess we'll find out.

This book is dedicated to Kate Davies and Kelly Jamieson, because just like Allegra wouldn't be able to manage without her sisters, this series wouldn't even exist without you.

And to my daughter and nieces. I wish I had a winery for you all to run. I know you'd kill it.

And to the memory of my cousins Bob, Joe, and Fred. Hey, I'm not saying you guys were Lambros, or anything. But you kind of were.

Link to Playlist

https://tinyurl.com/QueSeraSyrahPlaylist

Prologue

Allegra

"C'mon, c'mon," I mutter impatiently as I frown at my phone, which is taking *forever* to connect. "Let's do this already! I can't miss this call!" I'm reaching for my glass of Albariño, hoping the wine might calm my nerves when—thank you, Jesus! —my sisters' faces appear on the phone's small screen.

"Hey, Bee! And Rosy Posey," I say in greeting forgetting, until I register her slight grimace, how much Rosa's always hated that nickname. "Sorry I couldn't make it back," I find myself babbling. "How are you holding up, Rosy?"

"I'm fine," Rosa says. "I'm sorry you two couldn't be here, either."

I squirm uncomfortably. "You know how it is. I'll try to be there for the memorial."

Full disclosure? I am totally lying right now. Having been forced to attend my father's and grandfather's funerals at far too young an age, I'm *really* not anxious to go through another family grief circus.

"You've got time," Rosa says, continuing to push. "We

3

won't hold it until after harvest season at least. But you really should be here for it, Allegra. After everything Nonna did for us. Pay our respects."

My lips fold in. "Sure. Of course. I'll see what I can do." *After* harvest season? Fuck me, that's like...six months away. How am I gonna avoid going back with that kind of lead time? I'm going to have to get creative.

Rosa's eyes flicker away from the screen as someone clears his throat—our Uncle Geno, I'm betting. And then I do pick up my glass, wishing I'd thought to order something a whole lot stronger. I'd somehow forgotten that I was going to have to deal with my entire family on this call. My sisters. My cousins. My uncle. Ugh.

"Where are you this week, Legs?" Bianca asks curiously. "Is that Greece?"

"Gibraltar," I say relieved to have moved on to a cheerier topic. I don't mean to flex, but who wouldn't want to be me right now? My life is fire. I turn my phone to pan around the square, showing off the picturesque scene around me, feeling as proud as if I'd actually had something to do with it. It's just after sunset here, but there's probably enough light for them to see all the al fresco restaurants and wine bars that line Casemates Square; the ones that have been slowly filling with patrons as I've waited for this meeting to start. "I might actually get some time to look around before I move on."

"That's so cool."

I nod eagerly. "It really is." It's both cool and highly unusual. One of the things they don't make clear to you when you sign up to work on board a cruise ship is how little free time you'll have. Not that I mind all that much. I'd rather keep busy, anyway. Besides, I absolutely *love* my job. The ship I work on has one of the only floating wineries in the world. How cool is that?

I'm about to explain how I came to have this unexpected holiday—how a pod of orcas had attacked yet another hapless yacht (boo-hoo) the remains of which have yet to be towed out of the harbor—when my sisters' faces disappear and I find myself staring at an all too familiar conference room. My stomach roils with remembered distress. It hasn't changed at all.

"Excuse me," I hear Rosa say, no doubt addressing Nonna's lawyer, Jimmy Davenport. And—as per usual—her placating tone rakes over my nerves. "I know this is a little unorthodox..."

"But so are we!" I can't help joking.

"Sorry, sir." Rosa's sigh comes through loud and clear. "You know my sisters, Bianca and Allegra..."

"Quite well," he answers, side-eyeing the screen, clocking my eyeroll. James Davenport has been the family lawyer for as long as any of us can remember, and my grandmother's "admirer" for a lot longer than that. Of course, he knows me!

I wave back, forcing a smile. "Hi, Jimmy!"

Someone laughs—one of my cousins, I assume. Whoever he is, he cuts it off immediately covering the sound with an unconvincing cough. So, yeah...clearly *not* my uncle.

"As I was saying, *Mr. Davenport*," Rosa continues seriously. "Bianca and Allegra are both out of the country, but they wanted to participate in the reading as well."

"That's fine," he responds as he adjusts his glasses. "As long as you don't disrupt the proceedings."

"Yes, sir," Bianca answers promptly, clearly missing the fact that no one would *ever* suggest such a thing in connection with her. Oh, no; that little warning was entirely for my benefit.

"Of course not!" I answer, butter not melting in my mouth. "It'll be just like I'm there in the room."

"*That's* what I'm afraid of," he says, with just a hint of a smile. "Just—be appropriate, please."

5

"Oh, yes, sir," I reply, mimicking my sisters' good-girl tones as I mime zipping my lips closed.

"Thank you." Jimmy looks around the room then asks, "Is anyone else joining us virtually? Your mother, perhaps?"

Rosa's voice is quiet. "No, sir."

I grit my teeth and say nothing. Even from thousands of miles away, I can feel my uncle's disapproval, my sisters' disappointment, my cousins' discomfort. And yep, that's Mama for you. Even when she's not around, even when she's off doing her own thing, minding her own business, not actively saying or doing anything offensive, she still manages to get on everyone's nerves. It's like a gift... Or no, more like a curse, I suppose. And I very much suspect it makes up the main part of her legacy to me.

"Thank you all for being here," Jimmy says. "I know this is a sad and difficult time for the whole family." He swallows hard and I'm reminded again how close he and Nonna were. After a brief pause, he clears his voice and tries again. "Your mother, mother-in-law and grandmother was a remarkable woman."

As he pauses—obviously needing a moment—I feel tears sting my eyes. He's hurting, too.

"She will be greatly missed," Jimmy continues. "She also lived a full life, loved her family, and had very specific thoughts about her will and what would happen after she passed. Her greatest desire was that you remain a family, supporting each other, regardless of what's in these papers."

Fat chance of that, I think as I lean forward, biting my lip, heart pounding with a combination of anticipation and dread. Nonna and I had had so many conversations about what she wanted, what she'd planned to do, her dreams for the future. And I know Jimmy had warned her at the time that the family would likely experience strife no matter what she decided. But that was so long ago. Had she changed her mind since then?

Had we—no. had *I*—let her down one time too many? I'm afraid to find out.

"In regard to Belmonte Winery," Jimmy continues.

My left leg starts bouncing, as it does when I'm stressed. Let's go, I think; get on with it.

Clearing his voice yet again, he begins to read. "'Geno, you have been a faithful steward of the family winery, and I trust you to keep that tradition strong for future generations. All holdings from your father, and his father before him, are passed down to you. I have every hope that your sons, my beloved grandsons, will carry on that tradition on the land bequeathed to your lineage. I love you all.'"

"Thank you, James," Geno says. I hear a rustle of sound; his chair being pushed back from the table as he starts to rise. "I know how hard—"

"We're not finished," the lawyer interjects.

Now, my heart *seriously* shifts gears and begins pounding even faster. I cross my fingers and hold my breath. This is it. *Shit...shit...shit...shit...*

"Excuse me?" Geno sounds confused but still polite. I mentally place a bet with myself about how quickly that will change—and into what. Five minutes, tops; and eye-bulging fury. "You've gone over everything—the accounts, the financials, the properties..."

"One property," Davenport tells him. "Belmonte Winery." There's another, longish pause before he continues. "These are the final wishes of Maria Carmela Bianchi Lamberti, in her own words. 'My dearest children and grandchildren. I love you all and wish I could have remained with you forever, in our little patch of heaven on earth. I have loved every moment together, and wish you all nothing but peace, prosperity, and happiness.

"As you know, when I married my sainted Leo, I brought

my family birthright, Caparelli Vineyards, with me. It had been passed down to me by my mother, God rest her soul. And though I allowed my sainted Leo to run both wineries as one, it has remained my birthright throughout our marriage and beyond.

"Geno, when you took over for your father, you continued to treat them as one entity, as agreed upon previously. But now, in my twilight years, I wish to rebuild the tradition started by my mother and pass Caparelli Vineyards on to the next generation of wine-making women in our family. My dear daughter, Caprice, has chosen to live and work overseas with her second husband, and has shown no interest in Caparelli for many years. Therefore, I leave my vines, my property, and my birthright to my three granddaughters, Rosa, Bianca, and Allegra, to carry on the proud matriarchal tradition of Caparelli. I also leave a modest bank account to provide some cushion should they choose to bring Caparelli back from disuse. I hope with all my heart that they do. My darlings, I wish you all well in your new adventure.'"

Yes! I think wildly, clapping a hand to my mouth to hold back the sob that wants to erupt. But I can't control the tears that track down my face. *She did it. She did it!* She didn't forget. She didn't take back her promise. I didn't disappoint her so badly that she changed her mind.

"What the hell is that?" Uncle Geno demands. And I mentally pat myself on the back because, yep. Called it.

"Your mother's last will and testament. It is quite legal, and she was of sound mind and body when she wrote it. There will be no point in challenging it."

"But it makes no sense!" Geno protests. "Caparelli and Belmonte have been combined for decades! Caparelli can't exist on its own." I hear his chair squeak and imagine him turning toward Rosa. "You agree with me, right? You've been working for the family for years. You see how the two are intertwined.

"Besides," he continues—not waiting for an answer. "There's no way you'll be able to get it up and running on your own in time to save the grapes."

"She's not on her own," Bianca snaps—sounding steely and defiant. And I find myself nodding frantically in agreement.

"Excuse me?" Uncle Geno frowns.

"She's right," I agree loudly—then quickly glance around at the tables around me, embarrassed by the fact that I'm practically shouting. "There are three of us. She's not on her own."

"Whatever," he responds dismissively. "It's not like *you'll* be doing much from your little European vacation. Just like your mother."

I hear a gasp—Rosa, I'm guessing. And, just like that, I see red—oh, not on my own behalf, or my mother's. I know Mama's shortcomings—and my own—and I've made my peace with them. I'm also no stranger to Geno's manipulative bluster. But for Rosa, who's always gone out of her way for the family, that must have hurt like hell.

"Belmonte needs the grapes," Geno continues in wheedling tones. "We have plans for them. And if you don't allow us to harvest and use them, they'll rot on the vine."

"Then we'll turn 'em into raisins," I shoot back, employing maximum snark, and ignoring the fact that—yes, yes, I know. We all know—they're the wrong kind of grapes, blah, blah, blah. But I can't risk my sisters falling for this shit. "We can make a profit that way."

"Allegra!" Rosa gasps again. And I can't tell if she's shocked or amused. I hope she's amused. I hope she and Bianca are feeling as gleeful and giddy as I am. And maybe Bianca is, although, from the way she's biting her lip and looking stunned, it's more likely she's still considering her options. But Rosa's the

9

one who's stuck dealing with Geno—the one who's been stuck dealing with him for most of the past decade, so...yeah, she's probably not feeling all that gleeful at the moment.

"Our arrangement has worked just fine for decades." Geno again. I bite back a sigh. It's not nice to kick someone when they're down—that's what Nonna would have said. Geno was her son. She loved him, too. I'm trying hard to keep all of that in mind, and to hold my tongue—for her sake. But Jesus! He just *will not* let it go!

"We've even honored the history of Caparelli vineyards," he's insisting now, "through our Carleo Cabernet."

I count to ten. And then to twenty. It doesn't help. The Carleo is named after my grandparents—Carmela and Leo. It's a blend—much like the word itself—that's made with mostly Caparelli grapes. I loved my Papa too, but in what way does naming a wine after *him* honor the Caparelli legacy? Or my grandmother? Or her mother, or her mother's mother, all those generations of gifted winemakers who never got the credit they deserved—mostly because they were women?

It doesn't; that's all. It just *doesn't*.

"There's no reason to fix what isn't broken," Geno says, totally unaware of his male privilege—no surprise there—or how his words are landing with me. Rosa glances nervously at the screen and I find myself holding my breath once again, praying that neither she nor Bianca are buying into this bullshit.

"I think...I'll have to talk to my sisters about it," Rosa says, and I breathe out a sigh of relief. *Okay, good. We haven't lost her...yet.*

"But—"

"Yes," another voice—Bianca—insists firmly. "We have to discuss our options. All of them."

"Girls!" Geno snaps. "I must insist—"

"Nope." I say with a laugh that sounds only a little unhinged. "Pretty sure you don't get to insist *anything*. Andiamo, sorelle mie let's go discuss our options."

"We'll be in touch about the financials," Rosa says, sounding confident, professional—like a badass, winery-owning *boss!*

The screen goes dark. None of us speak during the long, long walk to Rosa's car. Until finally, both my sisters' faces appear on the screen, looking different shades of stunned. And I can no longer contain myself. "I have just one thing to say," I tell them as I raise my empty glass in a little toast. "Holy. Shit."

"I KNOW WHAT WE'LL DO," NICO SAYS CONFIDENTLY. "We'll get married. Tomorrow morning. First thing."

My head is pillowed on my arms, and I don't much feel like raising it off the table, but I open an eye and slant a gaze in his direction. "Huh? Wah?"

He's smiling excitedly; that cute little dimple making an enticing appearance. "It's genius, no? It solves everything."

Okay, so...it's late. Like, really late. Hours after my phone conference with my sisters ended with promises that we'd all keep our minds open, think about our options and talk again soon. The square is bustling with people and noise and, as with so many conversations between two people who are only partially fluent in each other's native tongue, communication with Nico is occasionally problematic. So, I'm not sure I've heard him correctly.

No. Scratch that. I *am* sure. I couldn't *possibly* have heard him correctly.

I sit up reluctantly, squinting a little as I attempt to bring his face into focus, and try again. "What did you say?"

My head is reeling. Not surprising really, since I'm more than a little drunk—as who wouldn't be in my situation? It's not every day that you learn you've inherited an award-winning winery. And yeah, okay; it's a been a minute. Years, in fact. But so what? It still freaking counts, you know? Especially since— *hello?*—have I mentioned that it's in freaking Napa?

It's also not every day that you're forced to confront the fact that you've fucked up. Again. Royally. Unforgivably. That you'd waited too long to go home. That your Nonna is *gone.* That you didn't get to say goodbye. That you'll *never* get to say goodbye, or I'm sorry, or...or anything anymore! There's no way to walk this back. Not now, not ever.

But all of that is very much beside the point.

"Marriage," Nico says, enunciating clearly (yet, somehow, still giving total Princess Bride). "Will solve everything."

"Bruh. D'you really think so?"

It's not that I'm unilaterally opposed to the idea of fake marrying someone for the sake of a green card. Desperate times make for strange bedfellows, or however the saying goes. And I like Nico—I do. We're colleagues, shipmates, fuckbuddies, friends. But I'd thought we both understood the strictly temporary nature of our situationship. We're short timers. I don't even think of him as my *work* husband! There's not a chance in hell—

"Hear me out," Nico says smoothly disrupting the flow of my thoughts. "What's the biggest problem you have right now? Your sisters, correct?"

"Uh...no? Whatever gave you that idea?" I mean, obviously, it had to be something *I* said. But I have sooo many problems right now. Rosa and Bianca barely make the list. "Honestly, I think my uncle's a much bigger problem."

Nico waves my objections away. "No, he's not. You heard what that lawyer fellow said, the will is valid. There's nothing your uncle can do to stop you inheriting."

"Well. We'll see about that." I'm not *at all* certain that's true. Experience has proved that betting against my uncle is *never* smart money. He has a history of causing problems—within the family and without. He's wealthy, influential, and used to getting his own way. But that's not what makes me frown. "Wait. How do *you* know what my Nonna's lawyer said? You weren't here when I was talking to them, were you?"

"Your sisters are the real threat. If they decide to join forces against you, what will you do? They can outvote you anytime they want. And if you're there on your own? Just think of the disadvantage you'll be at, the precariousness of your position. They could gang up on you, pressure you into doing whatever they want. Ignore you. You know they won't give your ideas the attention they deserve. I can tell from how you speak of them that they don't respect you as they ought. They can't possibly appreciate everything you bring to the table."

Well. That part *is* true. Maybe it would have been different if I were *just* the baby of the family, but I'm also the black sheep, the slacker, the girl least likely to succeed. My sisters both chose the straight and narrow, college-classroom-to-corporate-office pipeline. Which—don't get me wrong—is definitely the smart thing to do if you've got the brains, the grades, and the abilities to pull it off. Not to mention that it's extremely useful (if not an actual requirement) if your end-goal is to make world-class wine or run a world-class winery. But I knew that was never going to work for me, so I took a different route. I focused on the hospitality aspect of the business and got my training on-the-job. And then kept the whole thing secret, for a variety of reasons.

"Of course they don't appreciate it. But that's not *their*

fault; I never told either of them about my plans. They have no idea what I've been doing since I left home."

Reasons. Like I said.

"That may be true, but by the time they figure it out—if they even bother trying—it might be too late. You might have lost your inheritance. What if they decide to give in to your uncle's wishes?"

"Ugh," I groan. "I don't want to think about this anymore." I reach for the wine bottle, only to discover that it's empty. Just as well, I suppose. But then Nico flags down a passing server and orders another. And I know I should stop him, but I've passed the point of rational thought and have no fucks left to give.

More wine? Sure. Bring it on.

"I know my sisters," I say, returning to the subject because now that the lid's been torn off the box, my worries and fears are all tumbling out. "They'd *never* do that."

But wouldn't they? When I spoke with them earlier, Rosa seemed daunted by the prospect of our going it alone, which is reasonable, considering she's the only one currently at ground zero. While Bianca seemed reluctant to leave her cushy job in Argentina—helping to make wine for an already established (and currently award-winning) high-end winery— to head up what's basically a struggling start-up. And I can't blame them.

But that's just another reason that I need to get home as soon as possible.

"Your grandmother left that winery to *you*, Allegra." Nico's voice is gentle as he fills my glass yet again with more of the sparkling Blanc de Blanc Cava blend that we've been enjoying for several hours too long if the tears of remorse and self-pity that have started to flood my eyes are anything to go by. He sounds sweet and caring and kind—and I've always been a sucker for anyone who takes my side in a fight. It's not like there have been a lot of them.

"She left it to the *three* of us," I correct, in an attempt to be fair. And, even more, in an attempt to sound like I don't really care. My voice has started to sound wobbly, and I hate that. The only thing worse than feeling vulnerable is *appearing* vulnerable.

"It's *your* legacy. You owe it to yourself—you owe it to *her*—to fight for it."

"Why are we talking about this? You don't know *anything* about my family. I'm not at war with my sisters. And it's their legacy too. They have just as much of a right to decide what happens to it as I do."

Which is the real fucking problem, isn't it? That worries me far more than I thought it would. I'd assumed they'd be as excited as I was. I'd assumed they also remembered Nonna talking about it. Nico smirks as he tops off our glasses—like he knows what I'm thinking. "It's funny, isn't it, how you were the only one who wasn't surprised by the bequest? Why do you suppose your grandmother never mentioned it to anyone else?"

I scowl at him. "Nico—what the hell? That was a private conversation. You had no fucking business listening in. Do I do that to you?"

In point of fact, I absolutely would, if the situation arose. Eavesdropping is a necessary life skill.

"A private conversation held at high volume in a very public place," he replies with a shrug. "It's hardly my fault that I overheard you. I'm sure half the city knows of it by now. Not that anyone cares, of course."

"It sounds like *you* care," I tell him.

"*Così così*," he says with a flip of his hand. "I do and I don't. You're my friend, so obviously I care what happens to you. But beyond that, it's nothing to do with me. I just thought we might be able to help each other out. But if you're not interested in what I have to say…"

"I know how it would help *you* out," I tell him—pulling no punches in true in vino veritas fashion. "But I don't see how our getting married would do anything to improve *my* situation."

"But of course it would! It would even the odds. Two of them, two of us; they'd have to at least listen to what you have to say. They'd have to take you seriously, to treat you like a grown-up, rather than a spoiled child."

"Maybe," I say, although I'm pretty sure he's wrong. Our family roles were cemented in place years ago—right along with our nicknames. I'm not sure there's anything that would set us free of them. Aside from power tools and explosives. "But my sisters were already teenagers when we were left in my grandmother's care. So of course, I spent more time with her than they did. If she spoke more about her plans for the winery to me than to them, or if they don't remember it as clearly as I do, that's only natural." Or maybe they'd written it off as one more empty promise. Mama taught us *all* about those.

Nico starts talking again and I'm sort of listening. But the wine is dulling my thought processes and, honestly? I've got more pressing concerns.

What will it be like to return home after all this time? And can I even call it that, now that Nonna's gone? Without the one person who loved and supported me unconditionally, it's just a house. 'Home is the place where, if you have to go there, they have to take you in.' Someone said that; I have no idea who it was. But they're wrong. I already tested out that theory. I'd just turned eighteen when I'd shown up on Mama's doorstep and… well, it sucked. Which is what makes Nico's plan so tempting.

In fact, the more I think about going home with a husband *and a plan*, the more I like it. It's a little like that scene from Pride and Prejudice, you know? The one where Lydia insists on going ahead of Jane because she's a married lady and Jane isn't?

And yes; *I know*, all right? Lydia was an idiot—the liveliest, loneliest, *youngest* sister of them all. But that doesn't mean that Jane and Elizabeth hadn't spent *years* disrespecting her, or that her whole family hadn't viewed her as nothing more than an empty-headed party girl her whole life long. Just sayin'

Still, I know better than to make any life-altering decisions while drunk. It never works out. I've tested that theory, too. So, I'mma take everything under advisement, for now. I'm sure Jimmy would approve of that strategy. And I'll wait until morning before I attempt to reach a conclusion. Probably.

Chapter 1

Clay

SIX MONTHS LATER…

There are days when I love what I do. Days when I get a real sense of pride and satisfaction from my job. Days when the reasons why I joined the sheriff's department here in Napa—because I wanted to give back to the community that raised me, wanted to make a difference in the lives of the ordinary people who live and work in the valley, wanted to be the kind of hero that I so badly needed back when I was a teenager —are brought forcefully to mind. Today, however, is not that kind of day.

It's October, shortly after the local wineries have harvested this year's grapes, and the late afternoon sunshine is gilding the vineyards along both sides of Highway Twenty-nine, making all the gold-to-russet leaves glow in a way that's…almost magical.

No, not 'like fire'—is that what you thought I was about to say? I wasn't. Because, trust me, there is *nothing* magical about that.

But it's not the weather, or the scenery, or the slight but never impossible chance of a wildfire breaking out that's put me in a mood. None of those are what has me second-guessing my career choice. No, that is entirely down to my current posting.

Six months ago, I was assigned to the tiny Oak Creek Canyon satellite office. Ever since then, a huge chunk of my time has been taken up with mediating an on-going family feud between a bunch of wealthy, entitled, wastes-of-air winery owners. Technically, it's all part of the job. A big part actually, because Napa *is* wine, no matter what nearby Sonoma has to say about the subject. And I do still believe that most of the winery owners here care deeply about what's best for the valley —since it coincides so neatly with what's best for them. But you'd never know it from the way some of them act.

See, I grew up poor in some of the rougher parts of the valley. And yes, contrary to widely held public opinion, Napa does have its rough parts. So, I know exactly how people like the Martinellis and the Lambertis view people like me. It's not flattering. But that's okay; I don't think much of most of them either. I'm as frustrated with their snobbery and pettiness as I am with the plethora of rules and regulations that govern wine production in the county—rules that they seem content to either flout or manipulate for their own selfish gains. Enforcing those laws is *absolutely* in my job description. But all the same, this was not the work I signed up for.

If I had my way, I'd shut down all their nepo-baby play-grounds ASAP, and force them all to restructure their businesses, maybe turn them into co-ops owned and operated by the people who actually work the land. So that everyone can benefit, instead of just the privileged few. But, as I said, wine is big business here in the valley—as everyone from my boss, to the Agricultural Commissioner, to the Department of Alcohol Beverage Control agrees. And the Golden Rule is in full effect.

Which is to say that he who grows the grapes (or who owns the land on which they're grown, to be more exact) makes the rules. And I have as much chance of challenging that reality as I have of...well, owning a winery myself someday.

Honestly, I'm not sure how much longer I can stick it out. I'm not even sure how much longer I should try. I don't like the idea of quitting; and I have no idea what else I could do for work, if I did. But, if I'm not actually being useful or helping people, then what the hell is the point?

Luckily, my shift is finally over, because I am more than ready to call it a day and head home. Or maybe not. Home's been a little on the quiet side since my last girlfriend and I called it quits. Maybe I'll head downtown for a drink and to see what else I feel like picking up there—dinner, a game of pool, a warm body. I've got the day off tomorrow, so I might as well make a night of it.

But then, just as the idea is taking hold, another thought intrudes. Oh, fucking hell. I totally forgot that I'd switched shifts with Garcia; something about a doctor's appointment for one of her kids. That means tomorrow is just another workday for me, filled with problems and paperwork, and probably (with the way my luck is running? absolutely) more bullshit out-of-compliance charges to investigate. Which in turn means more snobby rich dudes giving me attitude, acting like *I'm* the one who's inconveniencing *them* and— "What the fu—? Jesus!" I yank the wheel hard to avoid a collision with a little red sports car that takes a turn too fast, goes barreling through the intersection, and then zips on by, headed up the valley, back the way I came.

My temper flares. But, for just one instant, I hold myself in check. Technically, my shift is over. In fact, I'm already late to clock out. This does *not* have to be my problem; I could let this one slide, pretend I didn't see anything and assume someone else will both see and stop the speeder somewhere down the line—probably before they get much farther in all likelihood, and hopefully before anyone gets hurt.

And if that's not the case? Shit. The guilt will eat me alive. I'll never be able to look at myself in the mirror again.

Giving into the inevitable, I hang a quick huey and head off in pursuit. Several vehicles have already gotten between us, but they quickly pull off to the side as soon I turn on my overheads. When I get behind the highballer, I flash my brights, signaling that they should pull over as well.

The car—an older Caddy XLR—slows as we approach a busy intersection, and I assume the driver is searching for a safe place to stop. I can't help noticing that the registration tags are a couple of months overdue. Which just figures, doesn't it? The prospect of additional paperwork really makes my day. My already fucked up evening is about to become even more fucked, and I have only myself to blame.

But then, in the next instant, the car speeds up again. "Oh no, you don't," I growl as it flies through the intersection just as the yellow light turns to red, forcing me to employ my sirens as I run the light.

I grab the mike for the bullhorn, advising the driver that, "This is the Sheriff's Department. Pull your car over to the side of the road. Now!"

This time, finally, I've gotten their attention. After we've both come to a stop, I exit my vehicle (still fuming) only to find that the driver, female, Caucasian, mid-twenties, has done the same. She's dressed to match her car, wearing open-toed shoes that show off her red-painted toenails, fitted white slacks, a red, off-the-shoulder top that stops just below her midriff and a puzzled expression as she stands on the shoulder of the road, looking like a movie poster for a mid-century Spaghetti Western. Her hands are fisted on her hips. Her gaze is glued to the front of my SUV. A red and white polka-dot scarf holds her long hair off her face. But the ends of the scarf and the bulk of her mane snap and flutter in the wind kicked up by passing traffic—like Venus in that Botticelli painting. Something about that association tickles my memory, but I push it to the back of my mind.

"Get back in your car," I instruct, frowning as I approach.

Venus ignores me. Why am I not surprised? Goddesses never listen to mortal men. "It's pink," she says as she finally transfers her gaze to my face. "Why is it pink?"

"What?"

"Your truck," she explains, pointing at it. Then her eyes narrow in suspicion. "Hey. Are you *really* with the Sheriff's Department?"

"Yes." For the record, I'm driving a department standard, black and white SUV. The grill, however, *is* currently wrapped in bright, pink vinyl, so I take her point. "It's October."

"The *Napa* Sheriff's Department? Really? Pink?"

It's all I can do not to roll my eyes at her continued obsession. "Affirmative. Now, are you getting back in your car, or am I placing you under arrest?"

"You're arresting me?" she asks, eyes widening in dismay.

"That's entirely up to you," I say, slanting a meaningful look at her car.

"Okay, okay." She raises her hands in a gesture of surrender and flashes me a smile. "I'm going. Sheesh."

Just before she turns away, I'm struck with an unwelcome realization. I know that smile. And, somewhere in time, I've seen those eyes—dancing in amusement, dark with heat. *Where the fuck do I know you from?* I wonder, staring hard at her as she slides back into the driver's seat. Since we appear to be approximately the same age, the most likely answer is that we went to school together at some point. My memories, however, are suggesting otherwise. They're suggesting something decid-edly *not* classroom related. But she doesn't seem to recognize me, so I should probably just let it drop.

"So, what's October got to do with anything?" she asks.

This time, it takes me a moment to make the connection. "Oh. Breast Cancer Awareness Month."

"For real?" she says again, craning her neck to glance at my truck. "Wow. That's a lot cooler than I was expecting." She holds up her phone and asks, "Is it okay if I get a picture?"

"No," I tell her—and then annoy myself by relenting almost immediately at the first hint of a pout. "There are some shots on the department's Facebook page. You can probably download one from there."

"Yeah? Are you in any of them?"

That twinkle in her eyes is something that (under a lot of other circumstances) I might find hard to resist. "No," I reply, taking care to keep my voice level and my expression neutral.

"Pity," she murmurs as her gaze slides over me, as her smile peeks out again, tempting me to play.

Right. Time to shut this down for real. "I'm gonna need to see your license, registration, and proof of insurance."

I don't miss the way her mouth tightens as she reaches for the glove box. "Okay so, here's the story," she says, and once again I feel my temper start to rise.

"There's a story?" Of course, there fucking is. I am fresh off the "I Can Explain Everything, Officer" Oak Creek Canyon Winery Summer Tour, where nearly every day found someone with more money than morals coming at me with some tragic tale about how they were being maligned, or persecuted, or misunderstood. And no, it doesn't help that a lot of the times they were right. Because, even when I did eventually side with them, they still acted like I was the one at fault for simply doing my job.

"Well, you see..."

"No paperwork?" I say, hazarding a guess.

"What?" She frowns. "Oh no, no, no. Nothing like that. I mean, I think it's all here. It should be. But, as I'm trying to explain, I just bought this car. I mean, literally. I picked it up in Oakland less than half an hour ago. So, obviously I haven't had a chance to register it yet. Also, I don't have the insurance paperwork, but I have several days to get that, don't I? That's what they told me."

"Mm," reply, noncommittally. Technically, she's right. But Oakland to Napa in under half an hour? Yeah, that means she's been speeding the whole way here. "You do know that the speed limit on most of twenty-nine is fifty miles an hour, right?"

She winces in response. "Um...yeah, I guess I was forgetting that. Sorry. I've been living in Europe for the past few years. They don't even have speed limits there."

"Uh-huh," I mutter without much interest. I don't know if that's true, and I don't much care. I'm more concerned with sorting through the folder of paperwork she's handed me. Bill of sale—dated today, as stated—check. Expired registration—already noted—check. Maintenance records—I don't need those. And okay; I'm surprised to note that everything seems to be in order. I *could* cite her for the tags or leave it for the DMV to sort out (they will anyway). That just leaves the speeding charge, but the easiest thing would be to do us both a favor and let her off with a warning.

"I'll still need to see your license," I remind her, handing back the folder.

"Oh...right." As she twists around to reach into the back seat, her shirt rides up baring several more inches of smooth, bare, suntanned skin. I try not stare as she spends a long moment digging around for something out of sight, but I can't exactly take my eyes off her either, can I? Granted, it doesn't seem likely, but she *could* be reaching for a gun. So...I end up staring, all the same. Which is not exactly a hardship. She's beautiful, which I already knew. And I'm pretty sure I'm going to let her go with a warning and a favorable first impression of me in the event we ever do run into each other again. Spoiler alert: I'm hoping we do.

The late afternoon sun is warm and dry, the air is dusty; and in my full uniform, I've begun to sweat by the time she finally emerges with a backpack, which she then searches through for nearly a minute, before—finally! –handing me a booklet, about the size of a passport. "Here you go."

I look at it blankly. "What the hell is this?"

"International Driver's License," she replies with a smile that I'm pretty certain is one-hundred-percent pure bluff. I've got one of my own, so I know it well. "It's for driving internationally. And, like I said, I've been traveling, so..."

"Yeah well, unfortunately, the State of California does not recognize it for driving here."

"What? Why not? I mean, I got it in California, right before I left. How can they not recognize it?"

"I don't make the rules," I tell her, which (given how often I've had to say *that* lately) I'm starting to think I ought to get tattooed on my forehead. "And anyway—" I take a quick glance inside to confirm my suspicions. Yep, just as I thought. "It's expired. So, what else you got?"

"I uh..." She looks a little panicked, and that draws an exasperated sigh from my throat.

"You do have a valid license, don't you?" Because if she doesn't, we're both screwed—and not in a good way.

"Of course! I mean, I would have had to, right?" She waves at the booklet in my hand and adds, "They wouldn't have given me that without one."

"Great. Then I'll need to see it."

She heaves a big sigh, causing her breasts to rise, pushing against the neckline of her blouse like twin waves surging against a jetty, which I do appreciate (inappropriate, I know, but unavoidable, all the same); then she looks at me entreatingly. "Look, Romeo..."

My thoughts stall out. What the fuck did she just call me? Romeo? That was unwarranted. I may be thinking inappropriate thoughts, but my actions have been one-hundred percent professional. Fuck if I know why she thinks baiting me like that is gonna help her case. And if that's her idea of flirting? Well, all I can say is it's missed the mark by several miles.

"...mentioned that I've been traveling, right? So, yes, I have a current one. At least I'm pretty sure I do. But obviously my family wouldn't have been able to send it to me, since they didn't know where I'd be."

"Unfortunately, Napa County has a zero-tolerance policy when it comes to driving without a license," I inform her. "Now, I'm gonna ask you once again. Do you have a license on you, or not?"

She reaches into her bag once more and comes out with a familiar looking laminated card. "I have this," she says in a small voice that contains an even smaller (and entirely baseless) amount of hope because...

"This is expired."

"I know that. But like I just explained..."

Whatever else she says is lost on me, due to the rush of blood to my face. *¡Venga!* I recognize the name on the license: Allegra Martinelli, youngest member of the family that's helped to make my last few months a living hell—and me the laughingstock of the entire department. But that's not the worst of it. Thanks to the several-years-old-now picture on her license, I now remember *exactly* where and when I know her from.

She's been playing you, hombre, my inner voice taunts me. *She clocked you from the start. That's why she called you Romeo.* Sonofabitch.

"I'll need the keys to your car," I tell her, interrupting whatever she's saying and holding out a hand.

"Okay?" she mutters, reaching into the console and handing me her fob. "What happens now?"

"Now we wait for the tow truck to get here," I tell her as I head back to my vehicle to call for one.

"The *tow* truck? Why?"

"I'm impounding your vehicle."

"What? No. You can't!" She slides from her seat and starts after me. "Please! I—"

"*You* will stay with your car," I order, as I stop and pivot to glare at her. "Or I *will* place you under arrest."

"Bu-but what do I do now?" she asks as she sinks exhaustedly onto the seat. "You aren't going to j-just l-leave me here, are you?"

I'm tempted to tell her that turn around is fair play, but I refuse to give her the satisfaction of knowing that I know that she knows that I...you know what? It doesn't matter.

"I will give you a ride to the station," I say instead. "You can call someone and have them pick you up there, after you—or they—pay the fees."

"But I can't— Th-there's no one. I..."

But that's definitely a lie. I know she has family, and that her family has money, so... "I guess we'll find out, won't we?"

"Romeo, please," she begs, rising out of her seat. "Can't we just—"

"Do *not* call me that!" I say as I level a finger in her direction. "And stay with your car—or else."

Chapter 2

Allegra

"I don't understand," my sister Rosa says—not for the first time. "It's not that we're not happy to see you and all. I mean, of course we are! But how are you even here?"

"Well, see, there're these things called airplanes," I tell her wearily. "You may have heard of them."

"Very funny," Rosa glares at me from the rear-view mirror.

Bianca, sitting catty-corner in the passenger seat, like she's afraid to completely turn her back on me, shakes her head. "Really, Legs. I think we deserve a better answer than that! You've been promising for months that you were coming home, and—"

"Oh, stop exaggerating," I groan. "It hasn't been that long."

"No, she's right," Rosa says. "It *has* been months. I remember because the first time was at the will reading—all the way back in April. We talked about holding Nonna's memorial after the harvest and you said you'd be here."

I hadn't. But what's the point in arguing? People remember what they want to remember. "Yeah well, there you go. It's after harvest, and here I am."

"Yes, except that every time we asked you since then about when you'd be back, you just said, soon," Bianca reminds me. She's a scientist. They're relentless when it comes to facts.

"Well, I'm *sorry*," I tell her. "But I had things to do." Embarrassing things that I will never, *ever* divulge to either of my sisters. "I got here as soon as I could. And I'm here now, aren't I? So, why are we still talking about this?"

"I just don't understand why you wouldn't tell us you were coming," Rosa says. "We could have gotten things ready for you."

"Maybe I wanted to surprise you; you ever think of that?"

"Well, you did that," Bianca says, smiling ironically. "When Rosa told me we had to go and bail you out of jail I was *definitely* surprised."

Okay, so maybe *that part* was my fault. But bail is what the officer I first spoke to at the station called the money she said I'd need in order to get my car released. And I guess by the time I got Rosa on the phone, I had started freaking out and wasn't as clear I might have been. My bad.

"We could have picked you up at the airport," Rosa insists. "And avoided...all of this."

"I didn't want to inconvenience anyone," I say before I can think better of it, and then wince when it hits me how stupid that must sound. Bianca's lips roll in. She's trying hard not to laugh, and I guess I can't blame her. "Yeah, yeah. Say less." I rest my head against the seat back and close my eyes. "It just seemed simpler to buy a car, that's all. And it would have worked out fine, too, if only that Romeo dude hadn't been such a jerk about my license being expired."

There's a moment of silence, then Bianca asks, "Who?"

"Romeo," I repeat opening my eyes to find Bianca looking confused and Rosa shooting me puzzled looks in the rearview. "You know. The cop who busted me?" If anything, they look even more confused, bordering on alarmed—like I'd halluci-nated the whole thing, which I know damn well I haven't. "Oh, come on! What is this? He was at the station—I know you both saw him. About six-foot-two, dark hair, square chin, nice guns?" Nice eyes, too, which is something I noticed only *after* we got to the station, and he removed his shades. They reminded me of someone, but I can't think who.

Rosa and Bianca share a wordless look then Rosa asks, "Are you... You're not talking about Deputy *Romero,* are you?"

"No, I— Wait, *what?*"

"Deputy Romero," Bianca says. "He's the only deputy I saw there that matches your description."

"And it was definitely his signature on the citation," Rosa agreed.

"Nooo," I groan, and begin smacking my head against the headrest repeatedly as the implication hits home. "No, no, no, no, no." I've obviously been in the service industry for far too long. He doesn't tend bar or wait tables, he's a sheriff's deputy; so, of course he wouldn't have had his *first* name on his name tag. What the hell was I thinking? "Don't tell me that. Shit!"

"Hold up a minute," Bianca says. "Are you saying you called him Romeo? To his face?"

"Yes," I mumble, feeling my face flame. I hate appearing foolish, probably something to do with being the youngest child, always one step (or more) behind.

"Repeatedly?"

"Unnh," I groan again; I don't want to think about it. "Prob-ably? I don't recall."

"Wow. I'd've loved to have seen his face."

"Right?"

My sisters nod in agreement with one another.

I glare at them both. "No," I say. "You wouldn't have." And, since I'm the one who has actually seen said face, I figure I'm also the only person in this car who actually knows what she's talking about. "Are you *certain* his name is Romero?" I have to ask. I mean...yes, the late afternoon sun was in my eyes, my eyeglass prescription may not be up-to-date, I'm vaguely dyslexic, and I was trying not to stare *too* obviously at his chest, but it's always possible that I was right, and my sisters are wrong, isn't it? "Maybe you're the ones who got it wrong."

"Allegra," Rosa protests, "Of course, we didn't! He spent so much time out at Caparelli this summer I was starting to think we should charge him rent."

"He did? Why?"

"All part of Geno's brilliant scheme to run us out of business. He—"

"Or someone," Bianca quickly interjects. "Who may or may not have been acting on Geno's behalf."

"Riiiight," Rosa corrects herself, deploying sarcasm at about the same skill level that Serena uses when wielding a racquet. "Some person or persons unknown, for reasons that may have been wholly unrelated to our uncle's attempt to regain control of Caparelli, repeatedly called the station to lodge bogus complaints against us, sabotaged our operations, and stole equipment that by sheerest coincidence just happened to end up at Belmonte. *Quelle surprise.*"

They both sound like they've been talking to lawyers. Probably the same lawyer; and I'll bet I can guess which one. This also sounds like exactly the type of family acrimony Nonna had been hoping to prevent by keeping her plans a secret. Much good that did her. I imagine I, too, will be meeting with Jimmy Davenport in the not-so-distant future. More joy; someone else I can disappoint.

"I still don't see what this has to do with Deputy Romero," I say, only stumbling a little over the second (wholly unnecessary) R. "Why was the Sheriff's Department getting involved in our family drama?"

"I told you. Mostly it was because of all the anonymous calls they received claiming that we were out of compliance."

"It seems there are only a handful of deputies assigned to the Oak Creek Canyon station," Bianca explains. "Because it's so small. And according to Miles, they all work twelve-hour shifts—either day or night. So, Romero, who works the day shift, caught most of the complaints. He hasn't been too happy with any of us."

"Terrific," I mumble, feeling unaccountably angry. If I'd have been here sooner, could I have done anything to prevent this mess from happening? Doubtful. I've never had much luck influencing any of my family. But I could have tried. And perhaps, I could at least have prevented my family from alienating Deputy (Extra R) Romero. "So, you're saying *that's* why he was such a hard ass? My car got impounded because you'd all spent the summer pissing off the local heat?" Which, now that I think about it, makes perfect sense; because it seemed like we were getting along great, at first.

My sisters share another long-suffering glance, reminding me yet again exactly why I wanted my own car. So that I could do my own thing and not have to put up with all this Judgy Mcjudgerson bullshit.

"As I understand it," Rosa says dryly, "Your car got impounded because you were driving without a valid license. Are you saying that's *not* what happened?"

"Not to mention all the other charges that he could have filed but didn't," Bianca adds. "Like the speeding and the expired tags, and...wasn't there more?"

"You mean the 'reckless driving' charge?" Rosa asks, shooting me a look in the mirror. I don't know how to interpret that remark. Is that supposed to be snarky or rude? Is she intentionally referencing my tattoo, or has she forgotten all about that by now? She's smiling, so maybe she thinks she's being funny. But the jet lag is catching up with me and I've used my last spoon.

"Right. Got it. I guess we're thinking it was *my* fault. As usual."

"Well...yes, Allegra," Bianca responds, a little more bluntly than usual. "I don't know who else you think is to blame."

"Honestly, it sounds to me like he went easy on you," Rosa says. "Maybe you should be thanking us for softening him up, or something?"

"Whatever," I grumble. Then I close my eyes and pretend to sleep.

"Anyway, I wouldn't sweat it if I were you," Rosa continues. "Romeo's a much nicer nickname than any of the ones *we'd* come up with for him. He should be happy."

Right, I think; *he looked real happy.* I'm tempted to ask my sisters if either of them happens to know what the deputy's *actual* first name is, but I'm supposed to be sleeping, so I don't. No one says anything for a while, but eventually my sisters go back to quietly discussing my actions. And, eventually, same as always, they conclude that this whole situation is just so typical of me. Which would probably hurt more if it wasn't also accurate.

My family has always viewed me as a screw-up. And sometimes they've been wrong. In this case, however, not only are they correct, but they don't even know the half of it.

All the same, Rosa is one hundred percent incorrect about at least one thing; there's nothing "soft" about Deputy Hard-Ass-Extra-R Romero. *I wish I knew who you remind me of,* I think. And then I really do fall asleep.

Que Será Syrah

Clay

By the time I finally get home from work, going out is just about the farthest thing from my mind. So, I place an order for tacos, allow myself one beer (it's a work night, but I deserve it) and kick back on my couch. I try channel surfing, but nothing catches my interest. My thoughts keep drifting into the past, back to a certain party I'd attended, down by the river, the summer I'd turned eighteen...

I can't recall now how we'd even found out about it. I know that I'd gotten a ride there with some friends and I imagine one of them had heard about it from someone else— who may have heard about it from someone else again. That's how those things usually worked.

Other than the guys I came with, I didn't know anyone there—they mostly looked like prep-school types to me, which was something that I very much was not. I'm also pretty sure we were trespassing on private property, because if we'd been on public land, the place would have been crawling with cops. Instead, it was just a bunch of kids—maybe three dozen in total, maybe four, maybe less than that. It was hard to tell exactly. We were outside at night and there wasn't a lot of light to be had. People kept slipping away in groups of twos or threes, disappearing into the trees, or into the bushes that lined the dusty dirt paths, or into the backseats of nearby cars.

There was music coming from somewhere not too far in the

distance (I had no idea from where. Perhaps a local festival? Or a house party?) and people were dancing. There was wine—a lot of wine, and not all of it labeled—because, again, it appeared that quite a few of the kids present had ties to wineries, and ready access to Napa's most famous and ubiquitous commodity. There was some beer as well, and a few bottles of stronger stuff. Weed was only mostly legal, at that point. Not that it would have mattered, since we were all under twenty-one, as far as I could tell. But it was enough of a gray area that it was a safe bet that no one was going to come out and investigate the smell like they probably would have done a few years earlier.

The theme of the party was Midsummer. I do remember that, because someone (or maybe several someones?) had strung solar-powered twinkle lights all through the manzanitas that clustered around the riverbanks, prompting several of the girls to remark that it looked like fairyland, to which someone else (usually a guy, trying to sound knowledgeable) would respond that it was meant to, and then mumble something vague about Shakespeare.

My man-card was still pretty new at that point, so I wouldn't have been caught dead saying anything about fairyland myself, but that didn't stop me from thinking it, too.

I'd managed to snag one of the few bottles of beer and between that and the zaza I was feeling pleasantly crossfaded as I headed down a path that seemed to wander alongside the riverbank. And that's when I saw her. She was humming to herself, dancing in the shallows, with her hands above her head and a bottle of wine clutched in one of them. Her hair was long and loose, curling nearly to her waist. It swayed from side to side following the movement of her head.

She was not exactly dressed to impress, in cut-off jeans and a graphic T. But I was impressed, all the same. Her legs were long, and the shorts were cut *very* short and the T-shirt hugged her breasts in a way that made the slogan stretched across her chest a little difficult to decipher; but I managed. "Sonoma Makes Wine," I read silently. "Napa Makes Auto-Parts." Wow. I figured it took a lot of guts to wear that shirt here in the heart of wine country. Either guts, or civic pride, perhaps? "Are you from Sonoma?"

Her eyes shot open. "No?" she said, sounding slightly confused. "Are *you* from Sonoma?"

"No, I'm from here," I said, then added. "I mean, I'm from Clear Lake originally, but yeah, I'm...I'm local."

"Clear Lake," she repeated as she tilted her head to the side. "I've heard of it. It sounds pretty."

I shook my head. "It's not."

"So, why were you asking about Sonoma if neither of us are from there?"

"It's on your shirt," I replied, gesturing at her chest.

She glanced down at herself and giggled. "Oh. That. Yeah, it's great, isn't it? I thought it was funny. Also, it pissed off my uncle, so..."

"So, that's a good thing?"

"Uh...yes! Obviously."

Except, of course, that since I had no idea who her uncle was, it had not been obvious. Nor did I care.

"He takes himself way too seriously," she explained. But then she frowned and added, "Except, as it turns out, it also pissed off my cousins. And that was sucky. I definitely didn't mean for that to happen. But it's too late now. I'm committed, so...I can't just back down." She sighed and tipped the bottle to her mouth, dropping her head back, losing her balance as she did, and stumbling just a little.

"Hey! Um...why don't you come out of the water before you fall?" I suggested, feeling a little worried as I suddenly remembered that a girl had drowned a few years ago, not that far from here, at a similar party.

Her eyes met mine. "Why don't you come *in* the water," she challenged. "We can fall together."

Yeah, that wasn't happening. I glanced around and noticed that there was a grass-covered berm a few feet back from the riverbank. I hitched myself up to sit on it and counteroffered, "I think if either of us is gonna fall, we should do it here. It's softer. Come and check it out."

She studied me for a moment. Then she sighed and began picking her way over and around the rocks that lay beneath the water. *She's like Venus*, I thought, when she finally emerged, barefoot and smiling triumphantly.

She bent to scoop up a pair of sandals, then came and seated herself beside me. For a moment she gazed into the distance, her lower lip protruding in a small pout that I found fascinating. "I really wanted to dance tonight," she said, at last. "But I guess no one else wants to, after all."

She sounded sad, and I wanted to rectify that. I'd opened my mouth to tell her that people *were* dancing. That, if she just followed the path back to where I'd come from, she'd see them for herself. But selfishly, I didn't. I wanted her to stay here with me, rather than seek out better company elsewhere. "It's good music," I said instead. "I can see why you'd want to dance to it."

"Yep," she replied, popping the p in a way that suggested I'd hit upon another sore point. "It is."

"Where's it coming from—do you know?"

"Mm-hm. Sure do."

Okay then. Clearly there was a story there as well. "So, what's your name?" I asked, in an effort to change the subject.

"Legs," she answered, which of course prompted me to look at hers.

"Ah. Okay. I can see why that'd be the case, as well."

"What? Oh. No. Not those," she held up the bottle and waved it in the air. "Legs like these."

"Huh?" I looked at her blankly. She gazed back at me expectantly.

When it became clear I had no idea what she was talking about, she glanced at the bottle, as though to double-check that it was still there. "Oh," she said, sounding slightly startled. "I guess you really can't see them through the glass, can you? Okay, never mind."

She lifted the bottle to her lips once again, and my gaze got caught on the way her lips pursed around the glass, the way her throat moved as she swallowed. "What are you drinking?" I couldn't help asking.

"Wine," she replied, frowning at me, as though I'd asked a trick question.

"Yeah, I know. I meant what kind?"

"*Gooood* wine," she drawled, drawing the first word out provocatively. Then her expression changed and giggling slightly, she began to sing.

I recognized the melody right off. It's an old song about a kid at camp writing letters to his parents at home. I vaguely recalled hearing it back when I was a kid myself, probably part of some cartoon. But the words she sang were new to me...

"*Is it Sauterne? Is it Riesling? Sauvi-B can be so pleasing. Is it special, for entertaining? Or just a wine to drink whenever it's not raining?*"

"What?"

"Because it doesn't rain much here—get it? So, it's an everyday wine."

"Yeah, but—"

"Shh, there's more." Clasping a hand to her chest and shaking the bottle dramatically, she launched into the chorus. "*Decant me, I hate my bottle. Can't you see? I taste like rubble.*

Let me breathe before you try to share me with your friends and family."

"Ah. That's the wine talking," I joked, earning myself an approving smile.

"Very good," she said as she angled her body to face me, singing the next chorus while gazing deep into my eyes. *"Is it Malbec? Or a Cab-Franc? Is it juicy, with a good rank? Do I need to keep explaining? If you decant your wine your guests won't be complaining."*

"Who's complaining?" I asked, a little breathlessly. I'd gotten caught in her gaze. I wanted to pull her into my arms and kiss her. I wanted to fall back into the grass with her and touch her everywhere. But I also wanted her to keep looking at me the way she was doing, with that smile, and those eyes...

"No one is," she answered. "That's just the way the song goes."

I found myself lost in confusion. "Huh?"

"Complaining. It rhymes with explaining. Also raining, and entertaining. It's not about anyone in particular. It's just something I do for fun."

"So, you wrote that yourself?"

"Not the melody, just the words. Well, most of them. I have a collaborator. Sometimes we bounce ideas back and forth."

I felt a spike of jealousy. "Oh, yeah? What's his name?"

She pulled back, pouting again. "Why do you assume it's a guy? Because women can't write song lyrics? Really?"

"What? No, I...I don't think that. I was actually hoping it *was* another woman."

"Oh," she said, looking slightly confused. "Well, good." She started to lift the bottle again, then changed her mind and held it out toward me. "Here. Did you want some?"

I lifted my beer bottle in a small toast. "Thanks. Think I'll stick with beer, though."

"Beer? Blech!" She doubled over, pretending to be sick. Then she grabbed hold of my arm and lifted it so that she could peer at the label on my bottle. "Blech! Blech! Blech! Are you kidding? It's not even *craft* beer! And you call yourself a local?"

"Yeah. 'Cause I am." After a moment, I nodded at the bottle in her hand. "You know, you still didn't answer your own question. Is it a Sauterne?"

"What, *this*?" She shook her head. "Nooo. Of course, not. We don't make Sauterne. That just fit the music. This is... hmm...I can't remember." She took another drink and rolled the wine around in her mouth, looking pensive. "Okay, let's see. Lemon...nutmeg...maybe nectarine. Full bodied and...ooh, buttery. Yeah, that's gotta be Chardonnay, but..."

She leaned closer, peering at the bottle, angling it to read the label in the nearly non-existent light. "Oh. Well. This is embarrassing."

"What's that?"

"It's my family's wine."

"And that's not good?"

"Well, no. I mean, it *was*. Once. But it's past its peak. So no, not as good as I was expecting it to be."

"You've been drinking out of that bottle for a while now," I couldn't help but point out. "Couldn't you tell it was bad without the label?"

She shrugged. "I didn't say it was bad. Also, it would obviously taste better in a glass. Plus, it's not chilled, so I figured there were reasons why it didn't taste as good as it should. But until I read the label, I didn't realize that it's been in the bottle for *five* years."

"What difference does that make?"

"All the difference. Chardonnay is meant to be drunk within a few years of bottling." She shook her head and said,

"Rookie mistake. Next time I steal a case of wine I'll be sure to check the vintage."

"Wait. You stole an *entire case?*" You didn't have to know much about wine to know that a whole case of expensive wine was no small thing to lose. "Who from? Aren't you afraid you'll get in trouble?"

"Oh, they'll never notice," she assured me casually and, I couldn't help but think, naïvely. "Or even care, most likely, given that it's so old. Who were they going to sell it to, at this point? I may have even done them a favor by saving them the trouble of having to get it hauled away. Besides, it's my party, isn't it? So, I had to supply *something* to get us started."

"This is *your* party?"

"Yeah. Birthday and graduation." She nodded, looking so sad that I clamped down hard on the inevitable next question, *then why are you out here all by yourself, while everyone else is back up the trail, enjoying themselves without you?* It was clear that she didn't need the reminder—especially when she raised her bottle in a toast and said, "Happy Birth-a-gration to me."

"So...the lights in the trees—that was you?"

She leaned back on her elbows, stared up at the branches and nodded again. "Yeah, that was me."

"You did a good job," I told her and was rewarded when her eyes lit up and she smiled. "Everyone's saying it looks like fairyland."

"Yeah? Do you like it?"

"I do." Then, taking a chance, I reached over and took the bottle from her. She gave it up willingly, which I took as a good sign. "You know what else I'd like?" I asked as I set both our drinks aside then turned back to face her.

She glanced up at me, smiling in anticipation. "What?"

"This." I leaned down, cupped her face in my hand and kissed her. She tasted of summer, of wine and flowers and sunshine, the last of which made no sense at all, since we were kissing in the dead of night under a full moon. But it was what it was and everything about that kiss felt right to me. I hadn't kissed a ton of girls at that point, but I'd kissed enough to know this was something special.

I levered myself on top of her, loving the way her long legs immediately wrapped my hips to hold me in place. She'd tunneled her fingers into my hair and deepened the kiss, lips moving under mine, tongue slipping out to tentatively brush against my own. When I sucked her tongue into my mouth she groaned and began grinding against me, rubbing herself against my thigh.

I slid a hand up under her shirt, gliding over skin that felt impossibly warm and smooth. The barely-there bra she wore was made of thin, stretchy material; it presented no barrier. I pushed it, and her T-shirt, out of my way, shoving them both above her breasts. I palmed a tit, squeezing softly, loving the feel of the hard little point of her nipple poking into my hand, the soft whimper that fell from her lips.

"So sweet," I said, settling my weight on my elbows. "Gotta taste 'em." But when I glanced at her face, seeking permission, I was startled by the flush on her cheeks, the agonized expression and half-closed eyes. And all at once, I realized she was still moving against me, faster now, more urgently, while her nails dug into my shoulders, hard enough that they'd leave crescent-shaped indentations that I'd spend days hiding. "Damn, are you gonna come like this?" It was not what I planned to ask, and the question pretty much answered itself. "Yeah, you are." I'd gotten girls off before, but never like this. "No, no, don't stop," I begged as her rhythm faltered, and embarrassment added more color to her face. "You go and get it, take what you need to get yourself off. I want you coming so sweet, giving it all up for me."

When she continued to hesitate, I leaned down and swiped my tongue across one tight bud. And then again, and again, until her hips had picked up their pace again. One of her heels was digging into my back, the other was planted on the ground, providing leverage. I had my hands on both tits now, cupping them firmly as my mouth alternated between them, lavishing them both with attention, all the while murmuring encouragement. "That's it. That's it. All for me. Let me have it."

When I felt her start to come, I lunged forward, sinking my teeth into the muscle where her neck met her shoulder, sucking and biting, marking her for my own while she shuddered beneath me.

Eventually, I raised my head to meet her gaze. "That was fucking hot," I told her. "Let's see if it was a good for you as it looked." I slipped a finger up the leg of her shorts—no great distance—found her clit and ghosted a light touch over it, chuckling when she uttered a small "eep," and flinched away from the contact.

"Too soon?" I asked, not surprised when she nodded. My hand itched to touch her again anyway; to touch her again and again and watch her dance against my fingers. I knew I could make it feel good, but she'd as good as said no, and I had to respect that. We didn't know each other hardly at all, so she had no reason to trust me to play and not hurt her.

Ignoring temptation, I moved my finger lower, slipping into her wet heat. "God, you're so wet," I groaned, barely able to hear myself speak over the rush of my blood, loud in my ears. "I want to be inside you."

She nodded. "Yes, I want that too."

"Yeah?" I asked, checking in with her. "You sure? Not too soon for that?"

She shook her head. "No. Please. Now."

Well, that worked for me. I sat up, hands going to the

buttons of my jeans. Watching as she did the same—then getting distracted as she shimmied to get her shorts off...

All at once, however, she stopped, eyes going wide with something that was not lust. Something that looked a lot like dismay. And then I did the same as the distant roar I'd been hearing for the past few minutes grew louder, resolving itself into the sound of engines, racing towards us, coming closer.

"Oh, shit," she muttered, the words barely audible, as she pulled her shorts back up and scrambled to hide beneath the bushes, pulling me down with her. In another instant, fairyland faded beneath the blaze of headlights as maybe half a dozen ATVs hove into sight. We hunkered down where we were, saying nothing, barely even breathing, as they flew past us, headed toward the clearing where most of the party was taking place.

As soon as they'd disappeared around the bend, she went into motion. Pulling her clothes together and jamming her feet into her sandals, muttering, "Shit, shit, shit," beneath her breath. "Fucking hell. What are *they* doing here? Damn it. It's just like them to pull something like this. I fucking hate them."

"You know those guys?" I asked.

"Unfortunately, I do," she said as she slid to her feet and grabbed my hand. "They're my cousins. C'mon. This way."

Her cousins? "Wait. Where are we going?" I asked, balking a little as she tried to lead me down the same path her cousins had just come from. What if there were more of them? What if they decided to circle back?

She paused and looked over her shoulder at me. "Do you trust me, or not?"

"I...don't know. Should I?"

"Yes! Because I know what I'm doing. Now...Oh. Shit." She turned to face me. "Wait. Did you drive here? You didn't, did

you? Because if you've got a car back there, that's gonna compli-
cate everything."

"No. No car. I got a ride with some friends. But—"

"Okay, good. I mean, sorry about your friends, but come on.
I know a way out."

She took me along a path that ran through the bushes, probably originally made by deer coming down to drink at the river.
And then over a small footbridge that I would never have found
on my own. Wending our way through fields of grapevines, we
eventually emerged onto Silverado Trail.

I glanced around me, trying to get my bearings. I didn't
know this part of Napa well at all, but it was quiet, cool, and
dark. And, best of all, no one was chasing us. The fog had rolled
in. The stars were hidden—as were we. "I think we got away," I
said, and my voice sounded unnaturally loud.

"Yeah, we're good," she agreed, almost whispering. "They
won't think to look for me here. And if they do, well, it won't
matter. Will it?"

I had no idea. But that's not the part that snagged my attention. "Wait. Is *that* what that was? You think they were out
there looking for *you*? Was it because of the wine? Or...?"

"Nah," she replied. "Stop tripping. They barely remember
I exist. Plus, I already told you; they won't care about the wine.
They're just all miserable and can't stand the idea that someone
else might be having fun when they're not."

I had a pretty good idea that she was wrong on at least two
of those counts, but what did I really know? "So, what now?" I
asked. I was hoping she'd suggest some place we could go to
continue where we'd left off. Perhaps a barn we could sneak
into, or a bedroom window I could climb through, or a car... *A
car would be real good,* I thought, suddenly remembering that I
was miles from home, without any means of transportation. If
she had a car, we could park somewhere secluded and finish

what we'd started. And then afterwards, she could maybe drop me off at home.

I was not surprised, however, when she shrugged and said, "Well, the party's over now. And since we made it this far. I guess we should call it a night. No sense in pushing our luck." Then her eyes grew wide. "Oh, shit. I didn't think. Will you be all right? Can you get home from here?"

"Yeah, sure. 'Course," I said, as though the prospect of having to walk for several miles with no jacket and the temperatures dropping was no big deal. "I'll be fine."

"Okay," she said, taking me at my word—which both pleased and irritated me. She bit her lip. "Well, I...I hope I see you again?"

"Me, too," I told her. "Even though I doubt your family will be too happy if they ever find out about...well, us." Admittedly, I knew next to nothing about her family. But everything I did know—that they made wine, drove around on expensive toys, probably owned the land we'd been partying on, and seemed a lot more protective of their little princess than she seemed to realize—suggested they wouldn't welcome her involvement with anyone who hadn't been born with a trust fund under his pillow and a gold-plated spoon in his mouth.

She laughed. "They're never happy about anything. But it's okay. We just won't let them find out, right? We'll be like Romeo and Juliet."

"Yeah, that didn't end too well," I felt obliged to point out.

"Well, maybe not," she agreed. "But it'll be different for us. We'll make our own ending." Then she held out her hand. "Here. Give me your phone; let me give you my number."

But when I pulled it out, my phone was dead. "Shit." I stared at it in dismay. Now, I couldn't even call for a ride if I wanted to. "What about yours?"

"I don't have it with me," she said, looking disappointed. "I think my uncle has figured out some way to track it, so I always leave it home whenever I don't want the family to know where I am."

Yep. Just like I thought. Super protective family. The absolute last thing I needed. "Okay, well..."

"Oh, I know!" she said brightening up. "This is genius, actually. My uncle is always after me and my sisters to take part in the Fourth of July parade—and I always say no, because it's lame, and afterwards his friends always grill me about my plans for the future, and I never know what to tell them. But this year I'll say yes, which will make him happy and earn me all the brownie points. And then you can find me at the end of the route, and we can get lost in the crowd. What do you think?"

I thought it was pretty goofy, as plans go. But I didn't have an alternative. So, I took her by the shoulders and said, "I will find you! No matter how long it takes. You stay alive!"

She dissolved into giggles. "Omigod, I love that movie! I used to watch it with my Nonna. I cried so hard every time. But I thought we'd agreed we were going to be Romeo and Juliet?"

"I told you," I said, pulling her close for a goodnight kiss. "I don't like the way their story ends."

"And I told you," she replied, just before her lips met mine. "We'll make our own."

OF COURSE, THINGS RARELY WORK OUT THE WAY YOU WANT them to, and this was no exception. As it happened, my mom was going through one of her rare responsible phases. She threw a fit when I finally wandered in, shortly before dawn, then smashed my phone when I tried to show her that it was dead, that it wasn't my fault that I hadn't returned her panicked calls from hours earlier. Then she grounded me for the rest of the month, which was laughable on several counts. It was the first time she'd ever tried such a thing, the month was already almost over, and my social life was (at that point) all but non-existent. My friends were mostly angry with me for having bailed on them at the party. They had zero interest in helping me track down a girl whose real name I'd never learned, and who, in their minds, had set them up to get caught.

I *did* go to the parade on the Fourth of July. Or, rather, I went to *a* parade—the one that was held in downtown Napa. But it occurred to me (a little too late to make a difference) that nearly every little town up and down the valley hosted their own. We'd never specified which one she'd be at, but obviously she hadn't meant that one, since she never showed.

I continued to look for her throughout the summer, and to ask everyone I met if they knew anything about a girl who called herself Legs, and eventually there were some rumors. I heard that she'd left town or fled the country. One person told me that he'd heard she'd eloped.

I didn't know what to believe, but one thing was obvious; if she *was* still in Napa, she was keeping a very low profile.

Then, in October, a series of fires broke out in Napa and Sonoma. And after that, everything else seem massively unimportant.

Chapter 3

Allegra

S pend any amount of time with winemakers and you'll
hear the term terroir mentioned, usually with a certain
amount of hushed reverence. Basically, terroir refers to the
various environmental factors that might influence or affect the
growing grapes. Ideally, it's what allows the grapes to become
the fullest expression of themselves.

When I wake up on the morning after my arrival, I know
immediately where I am. It's as though, from the depths of my
soul, I can recognize my own terroir. From the cool, soft air slipping in through my open window—bringing with it the familiar
sound of bird song and the equally familiar mélange of
fragrances rising up from the earth—to the same familiar views
I'd grown up with, everything looks, sounds, smells and feels
like home. And I am quite sure that, before too many more
hours have passed, I'll be able to say that it tastes like home, as
well.

This is the place that shaped me, that made me who I am.
It's impossible not to imagine that—if only I could run down-

stairs fast enough, before I'm entirely awake—I'll surprise my Nonna in the kitchen, fixing breakfast.

To be sure, there have been some changes (and mostly not great ones) in my immediate vicinity. My room looks nothing like it did when I left it. In the years since I've been gone, someone has removed my belongings and most of the furniture, taken down all my posters, and painted everything—walls, ceiling, doors and trim—a dull, dreary white. Blech.

Fun Fact: Before Napa was known around the world for wine, it was best known (at least within the state itself) for its psychiatric hospital. Back in the day, if you'd said that someone had "gone to Napa" it carried very different implications than it does today. This room, with its sparse furnishings and uninspired color scheme, is deffo giving those vintage Napa vibes.

Earlier in the summer, Rosa's (very much ex) boyfriend Jake Wright had been staying here, helping out with the grapes. It's been over ten years since I've seen Jake, and I was really hoping he'd still be here when I got back, but it looks like I've missed him, too. And given that *this* was the room Rosa chose to put him in, I can't say I'm too surprised. Although, on the other hand, now that the harvest is in, there was probably not that much for him to do here, anyway.

But it's depressing, you know? I always had a sort of thing for Jake. It was never an "I want to bone my sister's boyfriend" kind of thing. More of an, "I wish we could be family" type of deal, mixed in with a healthy dose of envy.

Jake's parents owned the vineyard right next door, and they were *real* parents. Unlike some other people I could name who were too busy getting themselves killed in a freak sailboat accident or running off to Italy with the guy they might have been (definitely was) cheating with to actually be there for their daughters when they needed them.

Which sounds unfair, I know; but as a kid, that's how it felt.

And who knows how much of it was true? I heard the Wrights sold their place, recently, and moved away. Which—yay for us —meant Jake was free to lend a hand at Caparelli this summer, but which probably sucked for him.

There is one good thing about this room, however; it doesn't encourage laziness. I'm not inspired to lie in bed and reminisce, which I'm especially grateful for this morning. I was too tired last night to go over all my plans for Caparelli's future with my sisters, but there's no time like the present (or so they say—I can't honestly say I've ever noticed it making a difference) so I jump out of bed, wash and dress and head downstairs.

The first person I see when I enter the kitchen is the last person I'm expecting. Jake is standing at the counter, pouring coffee into an insulated thermos. "Omigod, Jake!" I rush over and give him a hug. "I can't believe you're still here. I thought I'd missed you."

"Hey there, Legs," he says as he hugs me back. "It's good to see you, too. I hear you had some excitement last night."

"Oh, let's not talk about that." I wave my hands dismissively. "I like the beard, by the way. But how are you still here? I figured you'd bail at the earliest opportunity. Which reminds me, *where* are you staying? I didn't kick you out of my room, did I?"

"I uh..." He glances at Rosa who comes to stand beside him.

"You didn't kick him out," my sister says, and I feel my eyes bug out as she slips her hand in Jake's. "We're in Nonna's old room. I hope you don't mind. But neither you nor Bee were here, and with two of us—"

"You're back together?" I'm so excited, I'm practically squealing. "Really? That's so great!"

"Wait'll you hear the rest of the story," Bianca says, from

the breakfast table where she's finishing a bowl of yoghurt, berries, and granola.

"The rest?" I turn back to Rosa, very much *not* reassured by the blush on her cheeks. "What does she mean?"

"Well, y'see, Jake and I got married after—"

"You *what?*" I want to believe that I sound happy for them, but judging by the expressions on both their faces, I haven't fooled anyone. I can't believe they didn't include me. My usual feeling of not really belonging, of always existing on the periphery of everyone else's life crashes over me. "Married? This summer? Without telling me?" What the actual fuck?

"No," Rosa says, shooting an annoyed glance at Bianca, who's carried her dishes to the sink. "That's not what I meant."

Bianca smiles back at her. "Don't look at me like that. You know I reacted pretty much the same way when I found out."

Jake nods. "And that was still better than your uncle's reaction."

"Geno knows, too?" I glare at Jake. This is just getting better and better. "Are you saying I'm the *last* person to find out about this?"

Rosa sighs. "Legs, it's not what you think. Look, do you remember how, right after high school, I went on that senior class trip with a bunch of my friends?"

"Yeah, so?"

"Well, I kind of made a detour. I didn't actually go."

"You?" I stare at my sister in amazement. I'm not sure why we've suddenly digressed into ancient history land, but the idea of teenage Rosa finding a way to slip the leash of family responsibilities—even for a couple of days—is giving me life. Even though, "You do know that the whole point of senior ditch day is that it's supposed to happen before graduation, right? So, what'd you do instead?" But then something else occurs to me.

"Wait, wait, wait. That was right before you guys broke up. Was that why?"

I definitely remember that part. Because no one seemed to know the reason. And if Rosa and Jake, who *anyone* could see were made for each other, couldn't stay together, what hope was there for the rest of us?

Jake shrugs and says, "I guess you could say that."

And at the same time, Rosa shakes her head and says, "No, that's not why."

They side-eye each other and I glare at them both, wishing they'd hurry up and get back on the same page. Eventually, Rosa says, "The two of us snuck off to Vegas and got married."

"Whoa." I stare at my sister in confusion. "But that was like ten years ago."

"Almost ten and a half now," Jake corrects.

"Here." Bianca hands me a cup of coffee. "You might want to sit down for this."

Figuring it's generally wise to take my super smart sister's advice, I retreat to the table and take a seat. The coffee is good —and it does taste like home, even though everything else is feeling uncomfortably foreign. Like I've wandered into an alternate universe. "Okay so, why'd you break up? And how come this is the first I'm hearing about it?"

"The reason you didn't hear about it," Rosa explains, "is because the first person I saw when we got home was Geno. He convinced me not to tell anyone."

"Of course, he did," I mutter, rubbing my temples, as it suddenly hits me; Rosa has stolen my plan. By which, of course, I mean, Nico's plan. Which was briefly mine, as well. Until it wasn't. And which is suddenly sounding like it would have been a really *good* plan. Because right about now, I'm kind of wishing that I, too, had a surprise hubby that I could pull out of a hat. "So, what gun did Geno hold to *your* head?"

Rosa shrugs. "There were a few, actually. Nonna's health being the biggest. She'd been hospitalized while we were gone, and Geno was desperate for us to get the marriage annulled before she got out."

I want to laugh, even though it's not at all funny. "Annulled? Omigod. That's a joke, right?"

"No. Of course, it's not. Why would I joke about something like that?"

"Because it makes no sense, that's why! What grounds did you have to annul your marriage? And what did any of it have to do with Nonna's gallbladder operation?"

"Gallbladder?" Now Rosa looks confused. "He said it was her heart!"

"What?" Bianca turns to stare at Rosa. "No. No, it was her gallbladder. I'm sure of it."

"Of course, you're sure of it!" I snap at Bianca. "Because that's what it was."

"Ye-es," Bianca replies hesitantly. "Probably. Unless *we* were the ones he was lying to."

I feel my mouth drop open. "Fuck. I hadn't thought of that."

"He really is a bastard, isn't he?" Rosa (who almost never swears) says furiously. "Well, besides *that* guilt trip, he also told me I was being ungrateful, irresponsible, impulsive. I was set to start college in the fall, and he reminded me that my tuition had already been paid and that we wouldn't be able to get a refund if I decided not to go. He said it would kill Nonna—or, at the very least, cause a relapse, or break her heart all over again; or something equally dire—if she were ever to learn that I was following in Mama's footsteps, dropping out of school and rushing into marriage, just like she did."

"You are *nothing* like Mama," I protest angrily. "And what

did your being married have to do with college, anyway? Married people go to college, don't they?"

Rosa shrugged and shot a rueful look at Jake. "What can I tell you? I was eighteen. It made sense at the time."

"I suppose," I concede, shrugging a little as I remember that, when I was eighteen, I'd also allowed Geno to talk me into doing something stupid. Not quite as stupid as Rosa's breaking up with the boy she'd already been in love with for most of her life, but stupid all the same. "I mean, I guess I can see that. So, when did you get remarried?"

Another look passes between Rosa and Jake. Then Jake says, "We didn't."

"What? But didn't you just say...?"

"We didn't have to get remarried. Because I never filed the paperwork for the annulment. We've been married this whole time."

I blink at him in surprise. "For ten years?"

"Yeah."

I turn to Rosa. "And you didn't know?"

She shakes her head. "Didn't know and didn't believe it when he told me."

"Bruh." I scowl at Jake—who'd just admitted to having held my sister's future hostage for an entire decade. "Not cool. Not cool *at all!* I mean, what the *hell,* Jake?"

Be careful what you wish for, I think to myself as chills wash over me—that eerie sensation that Nonna had always referred to as a goose walking over her grave. Having Jake join the family is exactly what I'd wished for all those years ago. He was the big brother I'd always wanted and the father figure I'd needed after my own father died. Not that there weren't other men in my life. But my uncle was always too absorbed in his own concerns—his reputation in the community, the winery and his sons (in pretty much that order). And he and my cousins always seemed to view me and my sisters as poor relations—the kind of people you pitied and low-key disdained, but for whom you were grudgingly (and super annoyingly) responsible, all the same.

But Jake is nodding. "You're right," he says sheepishly. "It wasn't cool; you're not the first person to mention that. And, for what it's worth, I *have* apologized."

"But it's also *not* your business," Rosa tells me, taking her husband's side over mine, which I guess I should have expected.

Except that it literally *is* my business. Jake's turning up now, just weeks after we'd inherited the winery is giving serious ick. Not to mention the fact that, since Rosa was (technically) already married when Nonna died, doesn't that mean Jake stands a good chance of being awarded fifty percent of her share if they ever do divorce? Which I hope they won't because they really are perfect for each other.

But that's the old me's perspective. I used to be a lot more trusting than I am right now. And speaking as a newly minted cynic, it all sounds super sus. "Fine. Whatever," I tell her, shrugging to show I don't really care—a barefaced lie, but they don't need to know that.

"All right well, I'd love to see how this plays out," Bianca says, slinging a heavy-looking canvas tote over her shoulder and heading for the farm-house's back door. "But I'm already late for work, so—"

"No, wait!" I say, stopping her before she can slip out the door. "Don't go yet. I wanted to go over some of the ideas I had for the winery."

"Sounds great," she replies, not even slowing her steps. "Maybe tonight, or sometime this week, for sure." And she's gone before I can pin her down to anything more specific than that.

"Where's she even going?" I complain to Rosa. "I thought the harvest is in, isn't that what you said yesterday? That the grapes have all been pressed and crushed, etc? Aren't they all fermenting away at the moment?"

"Yes, but—"

"There's still a lot to do," Jake points out. "The numbers still need to be monitored, etc."

"Sure," I agree. "I get that. But does that have to be done rightthisfuckingminute? She couldn't even spare half an hour to talk to me?"

Rosa smiles. "You've met our overachieving sister, haven't you? You thought working at one winery at a time would be enough for her? Oh, no; she's also making wines for Bar Down. That's where she's gone this morning. There's even more work that needs doing over there—blending, bottling..."

"Wait, what? She's making wines for who?"

"Bar Down. The winery formerly known as Take Flight," Jake says, smiling a little sadly.

I stare at him in dismay. "You mean *your*—?"

"My *family's* former winery," he says, finishing my sentence, if not quite the way I would have. "Yes. Exactly."

"When did this happen?" And how come I'm the last to know about this, too?

"Just since August." Rosa frowns at me. "She did tell you, though. Remember? She said she was going to help out over there in exchange for using their lab?"

"Helping them out is one thing. Making wine for them is a whole different thing." It's huge. It's a commitment and a conflict of interest and...oh. Fuck. This has got to be killing Jake. "So, she's in bed with the competition?" I ask him. "Or should I say, 'sleeping with the enemy'?"

To be fair, relations between winery owners in Napa are usually pretty good. Usually. But nothing about this situation is as usual, and I can't help wondering just how hostile things may have gotten around here lately.

"You shouldn't say either one," Rosa scolds. "Not if you're going to be saying it in front of Bee."

"Although it is literally accurate," Jake jokes.

Which earns him a stern look from my sister and a gravely toned, "Not helping."

"What do you mean literal?" I ask, no doubt looking as puzzled as I feel. Because they can't mean what I think they mean. Can they?

Rosa turns her frown on me. "Do we really need to spell that out for you?"

"I mean...yes?"

She stares at me for a moment and then says, "Okay, hold on a minute." She shoves a hand through the heavy mass of her hair and peers at me through narrowed eyes. "I assumed that Bianca had already told you about Jansen; is that not the case? Are you saying that was just a really poor, random word choice, on your part?"

"I have no idea," I say, feeling totally at sea. "Who's Jansen?" If this is jet lag, I might need to go back to bed for the rest of the week.

"Jansen Beck," Rosa replies.

"The hockey player?"

"Former hockey player," Jake clarifies. "Current winery owner."

"You follow hockey?" Rosa asks, looking totally mystified. "Since when?"

"I wouldn't say I follow it, exactly. But I know his name. He plays—or I guess I mean played—for some team out of Long Beach, didn't he?"

When you're on an international cruise ship, someone is always talking about sports. You pick up a lot of gossip. Which, now that I'm thinking about it, had included the tidbit about Jansen Beck's plan to retire from hockey and buy a winery in Napa. I guess it stuck with me because I was always on the lookout for any news from home. But then the other shoe drops. "Okay. Now I remember. She did mention him, didn't she? I think she said he still has all his teeth?"

Rosa smirks. "As I recall, she said she 'thought' he did. But only after you asked."

"Right." I nod, and slurp down another mouthful of coffee. I really need the caffeine to start kicking in. "It's all coming back to me now. But are you saying he and Bianca—"

"Are seeing each other," Rosa says quickly, before either Jake or I can say something cruder, I suppose. "Yes, that's what we're saying. We don't talk about beds or sleeping."

"Or sex," Jake teases. "Or Bruno."

"Or boxed wine?" I suggest, apropos of absolutely nothing.

"You mean cardbordeaux," Jake fake scolds me.

"Or *anything* that's not our business," Rosa says, looking low-key disgusted with us both. But once again, how is this *not* my business? Because if Bianca is hooking up with the owner of the winery next door—a winery that Jake already has emotional ties to—wouldn't the next logical step be for the four of them to form a partnership and run the two wineries together?

After all, it's what Papa did with Belmonte and Capparelli —what Geno still wants to do. But it would leave little old lone wolf me very much on the outside.

It would also explain why Geno's been having a menty b. I think I might join him.

"So then, what am *I* here for?" I demand because holy cluster crush, this is worse than I thought.

"What do you mean?" Rosa asks, looking innocently perplexed.

"What do I—?" *Cazzo!* I rein in my temper and try again.

"Look, all summer long, every time we chatted, you and Bee have been all 'where ya at?' always comin' at me, wanting me to hurry back, and *for what?* I'm here now, and I have *no idea* what I'm even supposed to be doing. And it doesn't sound like you do, either."

Rosa sighs. "I don't know, Allegra. But I don't have time for this aggro. Jake and I have to get to work now, too. So, why don't you just focus on getting your own stuff squared away, and I guess, like Bianca said, we can get together later and discuss our plans. All right?"

"Yeah, sure," I lie again. "No worries." And maybe in the meantime, I'll visit my uncle and get his side of the story.

IN THE END, I DON'T GO TO SEE GENO. I DECIDE TO POKE around Caparelli instead, to see what's been done, and what still needs doing. Which—talk about depressing—holy shit!

First of all, there's no tasting room to speak of. Which, considering I'd been counting on claiming that as my domain, the place where my talents would really be able to shine, puts a huge crimp in my plans.

The room that used to be Caparelli's tasting room (way, way, way back in the day) has good bones—including a terra-cotta tiled floor, a turn-of-the-last-century oak bar and built-in wine racks, high, raftered ceilings, and three sets of double glass doors that open onto an unkempt (but possibly redeemable) brick terrace at the side of the house.

It's obviously been decades since it's been used for anything other than storage, however, and the place needs to be dusted, swept for cobwebs, and scrubbed from floor to ceiling.

Including the windows, which are so caked with grime you can't even see through them.

After that, it will need to be painted. And furnished. And lit—preferably with something other than the bare bulbs that are currently hanging out of the ceiling.

And, yeah, I get why this wasn't Rosa's first priority, or Bianca's either, obviously. Until you actually have wine to sell, you don't really need an attractive room for people to taste it in. And I know money's been tight, and other expenditures might have appeared more urgent, but I'm worried they're going to tell me there's no budget (or plans) for it at all.

And I can't even say with any certainty that they're wrong. Financially, it might make sense for us to start out selling direct to restaurants, to wine stores and distributors, or even online, but that doesn't exactly play to my strengths. And if you eliminate all the things I'm good at right off the bat, how am I ever going to start pulling my weight?

One bright spot on my tour of the winery is the wine cave, which is looking better than I expected. And I'm briefly optimistic that I can make that work in my favor. Someone's obviously put money into it recently, updating the lighting and purchasing pricey French oak barrels. If I can talk Bianca into letting me use the space for tastings and occasional events—by promising not to get in her way and to not to let the public get too close to her equipment—it could be a win-win.

At least, that's where my thoughts are headed until I talk to a couple of the cellar rats and learn where the money that went into fixing it up came from. Jansen Freaking Beck, that's who.

Sheesh. I haven't even met the man and already I'm feeling hostile towards him—and twice as panicked as before. I'm going to lose everything if I'm not careful, and if I don't start proving my worth immediately. And there are only so many ways for me to do that.

So, I pivot again. I suborn one of the interns into driving me over to Napa (the city, that is) so I can get my license sorted and pick up my car. Then I run a few errands.

It's while I'm browsing through all the antique stores on Second Street that I catch sight of Deputy Romero seated at a window table in a small, sidewalk café, having an early lunch with another deputy—who also looks somewhat familiar. Before I can stop to reconsider, I'm crossing the road and pulling open the door to the restaurant.

The lunch rush hasn't started yet, so I'm seated immediately, albeit at a small, dark table toward the back. After ordering—fish tacos (something I haven't had in *ages*!) and a locally produced hard kombucha—I make my way to the front of the restaurant.

He looks up as I approach. Our eyes meet and...I can't interpret the look that crosses his face, but his eyes definitely go dark and my pulse speeds up in response.

"Ms. Martinelli," he says in a voice that's all gravel and smoke and...mmm. Yum. I hadn't noticed *that* the other day. "Something I can do for you?"

"Hmm?" I'm momentarily distracted by the question because, *yes, please.* I'm sure there are *many* things I'd like him to do for me. "Oh! No. Sorry. I just...it *is* Deputy Romero, isn't it?"

He frowns at that. "I believe we already established that, didn't we?"

I sigh. "No, unfortunately, we did not. My sisters told me that was your name. And of course, I was hoping they were wrong. Which, if you know anything about my family, how likely was that to be the case, right?"

"I'm not following," he replies cautiously, which makes me want to kick myself.

Of course, he's not following me. I'm babbling like an idiot.

Pull yourself together, I order myself. "Sorry," I say again, which irritates me even more. I'm generally *not* the kind of person who goes around apologizing for every little thing. But something about this guy has me rattled. Which—annoying as fuck, to be sure—also has the potential to be really, really good. In the right circumstances. "I have dyslexic tendencies," I tell him, hurrying into speech before I make even more of a mess of things. "Which is not a big deal normally, but it does means that occasionally, especially when I'm tired, my eyes sorta cross and I don't always read things correctly."

"I'm very sorry to hear that."

"No, it's fine. What I'm trying to say is that, when I looked at your name tag the other day, I really did think it said Romeo. So, that was why I—"

I break off, startled by the muffled snort of laughter coming from Romero's companion. "Romeo?"

Shit. Did I just make things worse?

Romero shoots the other man a quelling look, then turns his attention back to me. "You were saying?" he asks. His tone is polite, but I swear I can see a small smile flickering at one corner of his mouth.

"Oh, just that's why I started calling you...that. I wasn't trying to be funny, or rude, or...or whatever else you might have thought. I just...wanted you to know. That's all."

"Ah. Well, thank you," he says. And now I *know* I'm imagining things because, if anything, he looks a little disappointed. "And can I assume you got everything straightened out with the DMV as well?"

"Oh, my license. Yes." I feel myself blushing a little. "That's all taken care of. Thank you for that, by the way."

"For what?" he asks, looking startled and wary again.

"For only charging me with an infraction. You did me a favor." I've read up on the subject. The choice was his. He

64

could have written it up as a misdemeanor, if he'd really wanted to be a dick. And while the infraction fine was hefty enough, the misdemeanor charge carried an even bigger fine, a court appearance, and the possibility of six months in jail. Ack!

He smiles wryly. "You're welcome. But considering I'd also have had to appear in court for anything other than an infraction, I'm pretty sure I did myself a favor, as well."

"Even so, I'd like to buy you a drink. To say thank you."

"I appreciate that. But unfortunately, I'm on duty at the moment, so..."

"Oh. Right. Maybe another time?"

"Perhaps."

"All right. Well, I'll let you get back to your lunch." I start to turn away and then think better of it. "My name's Allegra," I say in the instant before I remember that "But you already know that don't you?"

"I do."

"Right. Well, Legs, then. People call me Legs."

He nods solemnly. "I'll keep that in mind."

I do turn away then. I make it all the way back to my table before it hits me that he still hasn't told me his name. "Fuck," I mutter beneath my breath as I resume my seat. My food's arrived and it looks and smells amazing. But all I can think about is, *what the hell do I call him?* For someone who doesn't want to be called Romeo, he's sure doing his best to channel Montague's heir. "What's in a fucking name, for real."

Chapter 4

Clay

"So. You and Allegra Martinelli," Miles Raymond muses, gaze tracking Legs as she returns to her table. "Man, I did not see that coming."

"You still haven't," I reply, struggling to keep my temper in check. He's getting married in five days. Shouldn't he be keeping his eyes to himself? "Because there is no 'me and Allegra Martinelli'. She was a traffic stop. End of story." And I hope to hell I'm doing a better job of convincing him of that than I am myself.

"Better be—for your sake. Because, given the amount of time you've spent investigating her family this summer, I'm pretty sure the department would view it as a clear case of conflict of interest if the two of you were to get together."

"I'm aware," I tell him, taking a bite of my burger. It's Kobe beef, which is typical for the bougie restaurants in downtown Napa—one of the many reasons I rarely eat here. Although I have to admit, it does taste pretty good.

"I know *you're* aware of department policy," Miles says, "But is she?"

"I doubt it. Why should she be?"

I can understand Miles's concern. His fiancée is besties with one of Allegra's sisters. I think she might even be a member of their wedding party. When things started to heat up this summer, he requested to be reassigned out of Oak Creek Canyon rather than run the risk of violating policy.

"And anyway, she's been out of the country for the last several years. So, whatever's been going on around here, she was probably unaware of it."

"Yeah well, Bianca—her sister—had been gone even longer. That didn't stop you from suspecting her."

"*I* didn't suspect anyone," I point out. "I didn't invent those false complaints. I'm just the jackass who got stuck following up on them. And trust me, if we start getting anonymous calls about Legs over there, I'll be following up on those as well—no matter what you think."

"Well, I think that's a lot more likely to happen than you realize," Miles says, looking troubled. "I mean look, we all got up to no good, now and again, back when we were teenagers. That's par for the course. And Allegra was a few years younger than me—more like your age—so all I really know about her is what I remember hearing at the time. But she had a reputation for being on the wild side, even then."

"Somehow that doesn't surprise me in the slightest," I say, just barely managing to repress a smile. Because yeah, that tracks with the Legs I remember. "But I don't get why you're so concerned. I turned down her offer of a drink, didn't I?"

"Yeah. This time."

I nod and shrug, acknowledging the truth in that implication. Because yeah—even knowing it's a bad idea, on another day, I might decide differently. "I doubt it's going to be a problem," I tell Miles. "I cited her for driving without a license; I impounded the car she'd just bought; I embarrassed her in front of her sisters and stuck her with a hefty fine. So, I'm pretty sure she hates me right now."

Miles shakes his head. "Jesus, Clay. No wonder you're still single."

"Meaning what exactly?"

"Meaning that, in my experience, women rarely offer to buy drinks for men they hate—unless they're trying to get something out of them."

"You might be right," I admit. "Or then again, maybe you've just been hanging out with the wrong women."

Allegra

By the time I'm finished with my lunch, the deputies are gone. Monty—my new nickname for Deputy Nameless, short for Montague, obvs—shot one of those smoldering looks in my direction right before he left. The veiled smile. The hot gaze. The nearly imperceptible nod of his head. Even from across a crowded restaurant, I could feel the BDE. And it made up—if only a little—for the lack of encouragement I've been getting from him otherwise. There's something between us, I'm almost sure of it. I have no idea what, exactly, but it feels hot and dangerous and damn near irresistible.

After splurging on dessert—because how do you say no to lavender Crème Brûlée? – I go back to running errands. I pick up cleaning supplies, painting supplies, and enough snack food to feed an entire stadium of tailgaters. Then make a quick detour to nearby Solano County to hit a big consignment furniture warehouse and arrange for a few pieces to be delivered.

When I get back home, I grab a few of the padawans (who, to quote Prince, are doing something close to nothing—as far as I can tell) and put them to work. Within no time at all they've got the boxes moved out of the tasting room, and the barrels moved in. Then we're scrubbing floors and polishing woodwork; stringing lights along the ceiling; painting the walls a soft, cypress green that will highlight everything I need it to (the oak, the tiles, the wine); and washing the original Caparelli-logoed wine glasses that I've unearthed from behind the bar—one of the two lucky finds I've made here today.

The food is a big draw (as I knew it would be) and soon my army of hive workers has tripled, and then quadrupled in size. It's a party now. And, to make things even more fun for them, I take a few minutes to teach them the words to a couple of the songs Nonna and I made up years ago.

The next thing you know, we're all singing as we work. It's like a scene out of a freaking movie musical. And just as I'm wishing my family could see me now, my sisters and Jake show up with another man. Judging by his build, I'm guessing this is the hockey player.

"I suppose we should have known who was behind the mutiny," Jake says, looking equal parts resigned, exasperated, and fond. "Legs, what's going on? You Shanghaied my interns."

"I think you mean *our* interns, don't you, bro-in-law?" I correct, and yeah, okay, that might have come out sounding a tad snarkier than I meant it to. "Aren't they doing a great job?" I gesture at the room around us and then focus on the unfamiliar face, "And you must be Jansen?"

"Guilty," he says with a slow sexy smile that's almost as

good as one of Monty's. And which (were he not involved with my sister) I might even have found tempting. Rawr.

"This is my younger sister Allegra," Bianca tells him. Then turning to me she asks, "Legs? Are those *my* barrels?"

"Maybe?" I say, casting a quick glance at the trio of sixty-gallon barrels that I've repurposed into bistro tables. "I mean, it's not like anyone was using them." I shoot another glance at her boyfriend and add, "And I've seen the wine cave, by the way, so don't pretend you don't have plenty more—even newer than these."

"That's not the point."

"Well, I don't know why not." I shrug and then turn to Rosa who's been staring fixedly at the wall behind the bar in a way that's making me antsy. "Do you like the paint? It's lime-wash. No chemical smell, so it shouldn't affect anyone's wine tasting experience. And supposedly you never have to clean it. Although, I'm not sure what the FDA will have to say about that. Do you know?"

"Where did you get that?" she asks instead, turning her frown on me.

"The paint? At the hardware store in Napa. Why?"

"No, not the paint." She points at the metal Caparelli sign that I'd hung up earlier. "That sign. It's just like the one we've got hanging in the kitchen."

"It *is* the one from the kitchen," I tell her, "That's where I got it. I think it works much better out here, don't you?"

"Legs!"

"What?"

"It was a gift," she tells me. "A tenth anniversary wedding gift from Jake to me. And no, actually; I thought it was perfect right where I had it."

"What do you mean 'it was a gift'? You told me you found it in storage?"

"I found it," Jake explains. "While I was searching through my mom's storage unit. I think she must have picked it up while she was antiquing."

"Well, I don't know why either of you should have had it," I tell him. "It's obviously Caparelli property—and you know my Nonna would never have gotten rid of it. But I guess if Rosa really wants to keep it in the kitchen, that's her call."

"Gee, thanks so much," Rosa says, her Serena level sarcasm on full display, yet again. "If you're sure it's not too much of an inconvenience?"

"Well, it is, actually," I can't help but point out. "I mean, here I am, trying to put this whole tasting room together with *no* budget whatsoever and you've got this perfect piece of memorabilia just lying around being wasted. And instead of using it in a way that makes sense, you want to hide it in the kitchen, where no one can see it except us."

"Anniversary present," Rosa enunciates slowly. "From my husband."

Who you didn't even know you had, I think to myself. *Who ghosted you for an entire decade.* But I guess we're just ignoring all of that now. So instead, I say, "Tasting Room. No budget."

Rosa sighs. "I know. I heard you. And I like what you've done. Really—it looks terrific. But don't you think it's a little premature? Not to mention that maybe you should have talked to us about it first?"

Oh, like you and Bee talked to me about everything you did this summer? Or anything you did? I think to myself. "I *tried* to talk to you. This morning. But no one had time. And no, it's never too early to start marketing. That's doubly true if you're right about Geno and he really is trying to sabotage us."

"He really *is* trying to sabotage us," Jake assures me—which does *nothing* to reassure me that he's a disinterested party. 'We,' Jake? Really? I am so, so screwed.

Before I can even formulate a response, Bianca (who's been looking increasingly distracted) suddenly asks, "What's that they're singing?"

"Singing?" I ask, because sometimes it takes me awhile to process what someone has said.

"That song," Bianca says. "What is it?"

"Oh, that. I call it the Bentonite Slurry Song. I just taught it to them today. It's cute, right?"

"The what now?" Rosa asks.

"Bentonite Slurry," I repeat, blinking in surprise at all the blank stares I'm getting. It's not possible that none of them know what I'm talking about, because even the interns got the gist. I roll my eyes and start to sing, *"If you think that your wine's looking blurry, you should try using bentonite slurry. You should try using bentonite slurry to clear up the grime. Yeasts, and haze, and tannins will scurry when you add that bentonite slurry; when you add that phyllosilicate slurry, to your vats of wine."*

"That actually all makes sense," Bianca murmurs, speaking to Jansen, who's looking perplexed.

"Yeah?" He shoots her a smile. "Guess I'll have to take your word for it."

I frown at them both. "It's about wine, so of course, you should take her word for it," I tell Jansen—not at all happy that he's lightweight dissing my sister's wine expertise. "And of course, it makes sense," I tell Bianca. "I pay attention." Then I launch into the bridge—which is even more accurate, and therefore even more likely to impress her. *"Just three TBs to a pint of H2O is a pretty good ratio. Bring your water to a boil, before you pour the powder in. Then blend it up smoothly.*

"Can't be done 'til you've completed fermentation and moved your wine to a cooler destination. Stir it well but avoid

agitation, and your wine will shine! You'll have glassy, glossy, clear-as-crystal, radiant wine."

"You wrote that?" Rosa asks when I finish.

I nod. "The lyrics, yeah."

"It's really good," Bianca says, as Rosa nods agreement.

"Thanks," I say, shrugging casually and *not* pointing out that their response would have warmed my heart a whole lot more if they could only have managed to look and sound even a little less surprised.

Chapter 5

Allegra

It's two days later and my sisters have finally made time in their schedule to talk with me about our plans for the winery. Money is an issue—which I totally get. There's none coming in, at the moment. And it'll be next Spring—at the very, very earliest—before we have any wine to sell. And that's only if Bianca decides to make a Rosé, which so far she's been reluctant to commit to.

Rosa doesn't like the idea of investing too much (read any) of our money on nonessentials until the winery is earning money back. She's coming off a season of repeated crises and unexpected expenses and that, not surprisingly, has made her cautious.

Bianca doesn't think it's smart to sacrifice the quality of our wines for speed. Our wines—her wines, really—are what we're counting on to make our reputation. And, like they say, you don't get a second chance to make a good first impression.

I don't disagree with either of them, but there have to be at least a few things we can do now to start bringing in money and getting people excited about our brand.

So far, they haven't liked any of the ideas I've suggested.

"How about this," I say. "I read about this winery in Texas that has a rhinoceros on its grounds. And they're starting a rhino preserve there as well—"

"Where on the winery grounds?" Bianca asks, staring at me above the rim of her coffee cup. "I assume they don't keep it in the vineyards?"

"I don't know where, exactly," I say, but then Rosa interrupts.

"Why? What does a rhinoceros have to do with making wine?"

"I don't think it does. I think they have a partnership with a winery in South Africa. Maybe they did an exchange and sent them some longhorns. Are longhorns endangered?"

"They're domestic," Bianca tells me. "So probably not. But aren't we getting off topic? What does any of this have to do with us?"

"I just think it could be cool if we did something like that."

"We are not getting a rhinoceros," Rosa says firmly.

"I didn't mean we should get a rhino—exactly. After all, that's already been done. I was thinking something native to here."

"Like what?" Rosa presses. "Raccoons? Deer?"

"No!" Bianca's mouth drops open. She glares at Rosa. "Deer? Are you kidding?"

"Oh, right," Rosa nods. "Never mind. Bad idea."

"Actually, I was thinking more along the lines of wild mustangs," I tell them. "They're picturesque, American..."

"They're not exactly native to Napa," Rosa says. "So, I'm not getting the connection."

"I don't know, but they have some in Golden Gate Park, so there must be something."

"Strictly speaking," Bianca points out, "Horses aren't even native to the Americas."

"Bison?" I throw out in desperation.

"Also, not native to Napa," Rosa replies.

"I just want to tell you both that I am categorically opposed to the idea of our intentionally bringing any large, voracious herbivores onto the property," Bianca says suddenly. "I don't care where they're from. It's a terrible idea."

"Okay," I say, feeling frustrated. "You know what? Maybe it doesn't even have to be wildlife. Or herbivores. How about a dog rescue?"

"Why?" Bianca whines.

"What kind of dog rescue?" Rosa wants to know.

"Okay, d'you remember that TV show from a few years back," I ask. "The one that had ex-cons caring for pit bulls? What if we—"

"In *Napa*?" They say in tandem, not even letting me finish the thought.

"So, I guess that's a no?"

"Look, people come here to indulge themselves," Rosa points out. "To get spoiled. Not to think about unpleasant facts of life. I think a doggie day spa would be a much better fit. People could drop their dogs off while they're drinking wine, give their pups a chance to get out of the Teslas for a while."

"Why Teslas?" I ask, getting distracted.

"They have a dog setting," Rosa replies with uncharacteristic enthusiasm. "Have you never seen one? You can roll up your windows and walk away and the car will manage the AC to keep the doggos comfortable."

"That is cool," Bianca says. "No pun intended, but how much space will something like that take up? I don't know how big that Texas winery you were talking about is, Legs, but we're a very small winery. We need all the real estate we can get for the vines. I don't see how we can afford to give up the kind of space that a nature preserve, or a dog spa, or a petting zoo would require."

"Petting zoo?" Rosa frowns at her. "Who suggested that?"

"Oh, you don't think she was about to?" Bianca replies. "Please."

I roll my eyes. "Okay, fine. Scratch all the domestic animals then, too. Maybe we could do something with birds—they're already here, so that wouldn't take up any space at all."

"Birds are as bad as deer, aren't they?" Rosa asks.

"Yes!" Bianca gets up and pours herself another cup of coffee. "We really need to end this conversation before I have an anxiety attack."

"No, listen," I tell her. "You'll like this. I'm talking about raptors. If we could entice a mating pair of some type of raptor to build their nest somewhere on the grounds, that would be good, right?"

"Oh." Bianca sits back down and nods. "Okay, yes. That would make a difference."

"Make a difference how?" Rosa asks. "And what are we supposed to be doing with these raptors, anyway?"

"They would actually help keep the rodent population in check," Bianca explains. "And prey on the birds who eat our grapes. It's actually kind of genius."

"And we wouldn't be doing anything," I add. "That's the best part. Other than putting up cameras and livestreaming the footage so everyone can see what they're up to."

"Cameras?"

"Yes," I tell her. "There are raptor cams set up all over California. There are several in the Bay Area that do falcons—Berkeley, San Jose, Alcatraz—and another in San Francisco for ospreys. And there's at least one place in SoCal that monitors barn owls."

"So, all we'd need to do is put up a few cameras and we're done?"

"We probably only need one camera," I tell her, getting excited. "At least to start."

Have I finally hit on something they both actually like and are open to? Halleluiah! "You focus the camera on the nest, so people can watch online as the eggs hatch, and the babies grow up. Once they fledge, all their fans will want to come here to watch them flying around. And, when they're here, we sell them wine. And branded merchandise, or whatever. It's kind of a shame Jake's parents didn't think of that because having birds as brand ambassadors for a winery called Take Flight would have been a perfect fit."

"Oh," Bianca says suddenly. "That's why it sounds so familiar. Jansen's already doing it. So maybe we can ask him for tips?"

"He...what?" I ask as my heart drops.

"Yeah, can you believe it? His vineyard manager suggested it. You should go see it. He bought this state-of-the-art barn owl nest box. It came with its own solar powered, Wi-Fi camera. I don't know if he's streaming it though. He should do that, right?"

"Yeah, totally," I say, crossing another great idea off my list. "I mean, assuming there's anything to stream. But if he's already got a nest box set up, we wouldn't want to put up another one this close."

"Oh, because the birds are territorial, right?"

"Uh-huh." I glance through my list.

"Well, that's disappointing," Rosa observes. "I thought we were onto something there."

I nod agreement. Do I even want to suggest we build a habitat for native butterflies and other pollinators? No, I sure don't. I don't think I can take any more rejection at the moment. I scribble some notes regarding other ideas I need to research—artwork, food trucks, bike tours, picnics. All of which have the advantage that I can get started now and don't have to wait for Spring.

"So, are we done?" Rosa asks. "Or was there something else you wanted to discuss?"

"Two things actually," I say. "Bee, have you given any more thought to the idea of hosting barrel tastings over the winter? I know it's premature, but almost no one does it, so it will be unique."

"I guess it'll be okay," she tells me. "But only occasionally. It can't become a regular thing. And I'd want to be on hand to supervise. It's not that I don't trust you, but..."

"I know. The wine is your baby." I nod politely, and refrain from pointing out that in my last steady job I conducted barrel tastings all on my own, *without* supervision. All. The. Time. "What about the Rosé?"

Rosa's eyebrows rise. "Do we have a Rosé?" she asks Bianca. "We don't, do we?"

Bianca shakes her head. "Not at this point. But Legs wants me to release a blend in the Spring and...I'm thinking about it." She turns to me and adds, "I can't make a decision on that until I see how everything's tasting in the Spring."

"All right," I say. "Good enough." But is it really? If she decides against it, it's going to be another year, or maybe two before we have any wines to sell—or taste. And what am I supposed to do until then?

THE MINUTE I WALK THROUGH THE DOOR OF THE GOLDEN Cougar Bar and Grill I'm greeted by a chorus of familiar voices.

"Hey, look who's back!"

"Allegra?"

"Legs! Over here!"

It's Saturday night. My sisters and their plus-ones had all gone off to attend a wedding earlier in the day, leaving me with nothing to do but rattle around the empty house feeling very Kevin McAllister-esque.

Unlike Kevin, however, I'm an adult with access to both money *and* a car so there was no reason for me to stay home alone if I didn't want to, which I very much did not. So, I'd dressed up as much as I could—putting on a light, summer dress that's probably too thin for October, and some rando jacket I'd found hanging in the hall closet—and headed downtown in search of food, companionship, maybe a little adult entertainment, and also to take a break from all the family tension I'd been feeling.

So of course I end up running straight into my cousins. Great. Just perfect.

"Hey, fam," I say, feeling a little wary as I approach their table. "What's up? It's been a minute." I'm honestly not sure what to expect. I haven't seen them in years and, as I recall it, we hadn't exactly parted as friends. Not that I ever thought of them as friends, exactly, anyway. They're all older than me—enough so that it made a difference. Gianni's the youngest and he's the same age as Rosa...or I dunno, maybe a little younger? Still. He's definitely older than Bianca, so...

Not that any of it matters anymore. Apparently. It's all water under a bridge or something like it, at least if the hugs and smiles I'm greeted with are anything to go by.

I join them at their table where they've apparently ordered

"one of everything" off the happy hour bar menu. I mean, seriously? Why not just order a meal?

They've got crab cakes and hot wings, short rib tacos, mac and cheese arancini, grilled artichokes, roasted Mexican street corn riblets, barbecued oysters, caprese salad, shishito peppers, and an entire charcuterie platter including cold cuts, baked brie and an assortment of olives... I'm honestly not sure where they're planning on putting it all. And in a way, I'm doing them a favor by joining their party and taking some of that food off their hands.

I accept a glass of wine from one of the several bottles they're working their way through (it's a decent enough Meritage from a winery whose name I don't immediately recognize) and we catch up. By which I mean that I give them a heavily redacted version of what I've been up to in Europe (Vitto is particularly interested in hearing about my work aboard the cruise ship) and they fill me in on what's been happening since I've been gone, and all the local gossip.

I'm surprised by how much I'm enjoying myself. They're charming and funny and seem genuinely happy to see me. The Cougar is loud and crowded—but not in a rowdy sort of way. Servers bustle about the space, taking orders and delivering delicious looking food. Everything smells amazing; and it tastes even better.

If I'd stayed at home instead of spending the last few years in Europe, this would probably have been my hang-out. Or maybe not. Granted, I can't see all of the room, but from where I'm sitting, I only see a few familiar faces—and most of those are gathered around the table with me.

"So, level with me," I say at last—finally addressing the elephant in the room. "What exactly went on here this summer? I mean, the real story. Because some of the stuff I've heard…" I trail off, leaving the sentence unfinished because I don't know how to finish it.

If you must know, I don't really want to believe half of what I've heard. I'm hoping to learn that my sisters have been exaggerating how bad it's been. Except…I don't really want to think that either. I mean, would you want to learn that your sisters—and business partners—are paranoid and delusional? No, I think not.

Leo shrugs. "I don't know what you've heard but…yeah, it's been rough. Pops… Well. In a nutshell, he hasn't been handling things well."

"No," Vitto agrees. "Not at all.

"I think he felt betrayed," Leo continues. "And, honestly? I think he still does. So, I guess you could say he's been acting out."

"*We're* okay, though," Gianni says, circling his hand in a gesture to encompass the entire table. "I just want to be clear about that. We're not mad at you or your sisters at all."

"Ohhkay?" I reply, feeling the wariness creep back in. Because why would he bother to deny something I hadn't even hinted at?

"I'm just saying," Gianni continues. "Because I think Bianca was worried that was the case. But it's not."

"Good to know."

"But," Vitto adds, "It was a wake-up call; that's for certain. We weren't expecting it."

"For real," Gianni sighs.

"It was a shock. And it's definitely forced us to think more about our own situations, and… I don't know….maybe what we want our futures to look like? And how we can get there?"

"Right," Leo agrees. "Because this ain't it. And if things don't change—"

"Which we know they won't," Gianni insists, as he tops off

my glass. "Because Dad is incapable of letting go of the reins or even loosening his grip on them to even the slightest degree."

"Which...yes, I agree, is very unlikely to happen," Leo continues undeterred. "Which means we all have to make other plans. Because I don't think any of us—" He pauses to look at his brothers for confirmation. "Feel like waiting another ten, twenty, maybe thirty years to start living our own lives, making our own decisions."

"Or for the chance to *finally* inherit a failing winery that could have been saved if we'd have been allowed get involved now," Vitto finishes. "*Before* he runs it entirely into the ground."

"Okay, wait a minute," I say frowning at them. "Is Belmonte in trouble? Because this is the first I'm hearing about it. And I thought you guys *were* involved. Vitto, aren't you making wine for Belmonte?" I'm pretty sure that's what Bianca had said.

"Well, there's involved, and then there's *involved*," Gianni says in answer. "We're all working there, sure. But, as Rosa can tell you, that doesn't mean we're making any of the big decisions. At least, not like you and your sisters are doing at Caparelli."

I shove an arancini in my mouth to keep from blurting out the truth—that no one's letting me make any important decisions either—and immediately get distracted by the creamy, cheesy, crispy goodness. Yum.

"I mean, sure. If you wanna be *technical* about it," Vitto says. "I *do* make most of our wine. But what kind of wine am I making? It's not the kind of wine I want to make; that's for sure. I'm making the wines Dad wants me to make, using only the grapes Dad wants me to use, and I'm only allowed to utilize the methods, equipment, and timelines that he approves of. God only knows what he thinks would happen if he were to give any of us a say in any of it. It's like he thinks he's the only one capable of making good decisions."

"Which would be a lot easier to accept if his decisions were even half as good as he thinks they are," Gianni says—earning himself some serious side-eyes from both brothers. Although I notice they don't disagree.

Leo sighs. "Look, we've talked about this. And no, the winery isn't in trouble—yet. But some of Pops actions this summer have put us in a pretty bad position—with the community, the Sheriff's Department, the Commissioner's Office, the Vintner's Association..."

"Not to mention the ABC," Vitto agrees.

"The problem," Leo continues. "Or one of them, anyway—is that Belmonte was never supposed to be Geno's responsibility. He wasn't groomed for it. He doesn't have a degree in Enology or Viticulture—or anything else that would've helped him. He took over because he had to. And he started making all the decisions because, at the time, there was no one more capable—or willing—to make them.

"I think it's more habit now than anything else. But since that business with Nonna's will...it's like he's lost confidence. Like he thinks he has to prove himself all over again."

I almost ask Leo what he's talking about. Who *was* supposed to be responsible for running the family business if it wasn't Geno? But then I remember. My Uncle Leo—Mama's *older* brother who no one ever talks about. He died when we were all just kids, so long ago that I can't be sure, from this distance, whether the shadowy figure from my memories is him, or someone else.

"And I get it, you know? He feels like he's being disrespected," Leo (that's Cousin Leo, obvs—not my uncle's ghost) says now. "He thinks we should all be more appreciative of the fact that he supported the entire family for all these years, that he's the one who's kept the business going. It also doesn't help that none of us realized, until recently, that he didn't always make the best decisions."

"Speak for yourself," Vitto grumbles.

"Okay fine. But still—it's only in the last few months that we've spoken up about it."

Gianni shakes his head. "Look. I'm not saying you're wrong, Lee, but...what's the reality? Is it that he always made such bad decisions, and we just failed to notice, or is this chronic lapse in judgment something new?"

"Shit. Is this the senile thing again?" Leo scowls at him. "Because I still think that's ageist on your part."

"It's only ageism if I'm wrong," Gianni shoots back. He slants a look in my direction and then says, "And, not for nothing but, given all the other shit he's been pulling, I can't be the only one who finds it strange that Dad hasn't really leaned into the idea that Nonna wasn't of sound mind either when she made her will."

My mouth drops open. "What? No!"

Leo and Vitto say nothing. Gianni studies their expression and then nods—as though they'd confirmed his suspicions. "Uh-huh. Exactly. So, what I'm thinking is that maybe he *is* losing it—and he knows it—and he's trying not to draw attention to that fact. Which is what would happen if he started pointing that particular finger in someone else's direction. You know?"

"What the what?" Vitto glances at me and Leo and says, "Do either of you understand what he just said?"

Leo sighs. "I think what he means is that people in glass houses might wanna think twice before they start throwing stones."

"Exactly," Gianni agrees. "Especially if he's afraid we're

gonna turn around and do the same to him. Which we absolutely should, if that's the case."

I shake my head. "I don't know about the rest of what you just said, Gee, but Geno has to realize no one's going to take that claim seriously. How long was Nonna supposed to be incompetent? She put her plan for Caparelli in place years ago—I think *someone* would have noticed if she'd been losing it for the past ten years."

Three heads swivel in my direction. Three sets of eyes narrow suspiciously.

"What did you say?"

"Ten...*years*? Where'd that come from?"

"Wait, wait, wait, wait wait. Are you saying you knew about this? *Before* the will was read?"

Uh-oh. Did I just say the quiet part out loud? "Uh...maybe? I mean, I didn't know *exactly* what was in her will, but she'd talked about it. Didn't she?"

"Not to us!"

"Let's just be clear, okay? You're saying you weren't surprised to learn she'd left Caparelli to you and your sisters."

"Not completely, no."

"And it never occurred to you to...I dunno...*tell any of us*?"

"Yeah. For real! What the fuck, Legs?"

They're not being particularly quiet. I glance around and notice that at least a few people at nearby tables appear to be listening in on our conversation.

I lean in and lower my voice. "Who did you want me to tell?" I whisper-shout. "I was out of the country until just recently, in case nobody happened to notice. How should I know what conversations you all did or didn't have while I was gone? I figured it was just one of those things that everyone knew, but no one wanted to talk about."

"That's...actually a fair point," Vitto concedes after an

awkward moment of silence. "There are a lot of things like that, aren't there? Things the whole family knows, but which are never discussed."

"You're not wrong," Gianni agrees ruefully.

Even Leo reluctantly nods. "No, you're not. 'We'll never tell' might as well be the family motto."

"We should get matching tattoos," I say, before anyone else can suggest it.

But even as they're agreeing with me, I find myself wondering. How much of what I just said is true? And was that really the *only* reason I never said anything? Memories surface. I remember I was home the day James Davenport came to the house to talk to Nonna about the new will she wanted him to make for her. I remember how he'd argued with her, advocating for greater transparency. And then how he'd questioned *me*, asking what I thought of my grandmother's plan, and which of us had originally suggested the idea...

"JIMMY, STOP BADGERING THE CHILD," NONNA HAD SCOLDED. *"Do you really think I'm so weak-willed, that I don't know my own mind? The decision is mine. And the idea for it was mine. If anyone influenced my decision, it was my son. Allegra had nothing to do with it."*

Jimmy shook his head. "Think about it, Carmela. You do want me 'badgering' her. Because when—God forbid—the time comes, you want me to be able to testify—under oath, if need be —that I spoke with you both and that I was satisfied that you were acting on your own cognizance. And if I predecease you, my successor will need the records I leave behind to make sure your wishes are carried out. Otherwise—"

"Basta," Nonna said fretfully. "No more. Stop it now. I've

made my decision, and that's enough. I don't want to think about this anymore. It's too depressing."

"I know," Jimmy sighed. "This is hard for you. And you've already suffered so much loss. But it's my job to think about these things for you, cara. There's a great deal of money involved, after all. And if you don't think questions of mental soundness and undue influence are going to be raised, you're fooling yourself."

So YEAH, MAYBE THERE HAD BEEN OTHER REASONS WHY I hadn't wanted to talk about it—and why I'm wishing I hadn't said anything about it now. Because *of course* everyone is going to assume that it was my idea, that I'd somehow manipulated Nonna. And maybe I was also afraid that if anyone found out ahead of time that they'd try and talk her out of it.

"For what it's worth," I tell them. "I'm sorry that you were all blindsided. And I understand why Geno in particular would be upset about that. But did he really have to involve the Sheriff's department and file a bunch of sketchy complaints against my sisters? What's up with that? That's low. That doesn't help anyone."

Another silence falls over the cousins—deeper and somehow even more awkward than the ones that came before. And I find myself wondering if I've somehow stepped in it again?

"You probably should know," Leo says at last. "That Geno denies having made those calls."

"Do you believe him?" I ask—this time directing the question at all of them.

No one answers at first. Finally, Leo shrugs and says, "We don't *not* believe him."

I stare blankly at him. What does that even mean?

"Look, someone's obviously been working over-time trying to cause trouble for you and your sisters," he continues. "And we know Geno was responsible for some of it. But the complaints...that doesn't have to be him, too, right? It could be someone else."

"I...guess?" I'm still confused because who else could it be? And I'm about half a second from asking, when I notice the uncomfortable expressions on all three of my cousins' faces, the way they're all very carefully *not* looking at each other. And I change my mind.

I allow the conversational ball to drop, dip a piece of artichoke into some parmesan aioli and spend a few moments stuffing my face while I consider what it all might mean.

Do they suspect each other? Is that what's going on here? Are they trying to protect the guilty party? Or do I have it all wrong again? Maybe Geno was the master mind behind the calls, but someone else actually made them. Could my Aunt Janet be involved?

"All we really know, at this point," Vitto says, picking up the conversational ball. "Is that someone's been causing problems for Caparelli. Which has caused problems for Belmonte, as well. Would Geno really not have thought of that beforehand? It's hard to tell. I suppose it's possible that there never were any calls. Maybe that deputy— Romero, isn't it? —is making the whole thing up, for some reason of his own. But that doesn't seem too likely, either, does it?"

"I dunno about that," Gianni says, shooting a scowl at something—possibly someone—over my shoulder. "You have to admit it's a little weird the way he keeps popping up. Seems like everywhere any of us go, there he is. Why's he gotta keep sticking his nose in where it don't belong? Why can't he just mind his own business and stay out of our way?"

"Theoretically, it *is* his business," Leo says. "He's in law enforcement. If someone's making complaints he has to follow up, doesn't he?"

"Does he?" Gianni claps back. "Why? This shit's been going on for months. He's gotta know by now that someone's just capping on him. Why's he wanna waste time and taxpayer dollars on this shit? Doesn't he have anything better to do than follow us around and harass us?"

Leo, seated next to Gianni, glances across the room and shrugs. "Well, it doesn't look like it, does it?"

"Speaking of which," I say. "Do any of you happen to know his first name?"

"Whose name?" Gianni asks. "Romero's? No. Why?"

"No reason." I shrug. "Just curious."

"Why are we still talking about this?" Vitto asks as he swallows an oyster. "The food's getting cold. We should eat."

"You're the one who brought it up," Leo points out as he starts building a sandwich, layering meat and cheese and peppers on half a baguette.

I reach for a piece of corn. "I just don't see how it helps *any* of us to be on bad terms with the Sheriff's Department."

"Sure," Vitto concedes "Unless the deputy in question is waging some kind of crazy vendetta against our whole family, in which case, all bets are off."

"Oh, come on," I'm surprised by how much I hate that idea —like, really, really hate it. "Aren't you the one who just said that was unlikely? You don't actually believe that? Do you?"

"I don't know why not," Gianni scowls at me. "Personally, I wouldn't put anything past that bastard. You think it was just coincidence that he stopped *you?* That he impounded *your* car?"

"I, uh...don't know?" What I didn't think was that it was common knowledge. Who's been talking about it? And does everyone know?

"It's obviously because you're one of us."

I feel my cheeks grow warm. And maybe that's the wine, but I'm touched by the unspoken assumption that I was not at fault, by the feeling of solidarity, the suggestion that they're on my side.

"I mean, he clearly has it in for us, at this point," Leo says, agreeing with his brothers. "Not that we haven't given him cause."

I shake my head. "I appreciate the support, guys. But— again—don't you think we should at least try and be on good terms with the Sheriff's Department?"

"Why? What's the point?"

"Well, it's like community outreach. Or public relations. Also, it would be a net good for the family if we could get him off our backs."

"So go ahead," Gianni says around a mouthful of chicken wing. "Go ask him his name. If you think it'll make a difference. I mean, I wouldn't bet on it changing anything, but I'll be curious to see how you make out."

"Well, I will." I fork up a bite of crab cake and add, "Next time I run into him."

"Why wait? Do it now."

"Do what now?" I ask in confusion.

"Are you serious?" Leo glares at his brother.

Gianni ignores Leo's scowl, gestures behind me and says, "He's right over there. So, if you really want to talk to him, now's your chance."

I turn my head and, sure enough, Deputy Romero is seated at a 2-top on the other side of the restaurant.

Vitto has turned around in his chair to look as well. "Jesus. Are you kidding me?" He shoots his younger brother a scathing look. "That's a terrible idea."

"Why's that?" Gianni asks, clearly unmoved by his brothers' censure. "We're in a public place with plenty of witnesses. Seems ideal to me."

"Don't do it, Legs," Leo says. "I don't know what you think's gonna happen, but this guy's not Miles, if you know what I mean."

"I have no idea," I tell him. "I barely know Miles. Couldn't pick him out of a line-up if the deed to Caparelli was on the line."

"It means he's not one of us," Vitto explains, which really doesn't clarify anything for me.

Miles is one half of Miles and Millie—the couple whose wedding Rosa and Bianca were both invited to. I vaguely remember Millie, who was one of Bianca's BFFs since...well, forever. But, like I said, I don't know Miles at all—hence why I'm the only Martinelli sister who was *not* invited to their wedding, I suppose.

Which begs the question: Is there an "us" that somehow encompasses Miles and me? Because I think not.

"It'll be fine," I tell them. "Dealing with difficult customers has been a big part of my job for the past several years. And, as it happens, I'm pretty good at it."

Chapter 6

Clay

"Deputy Romero?"

I glance up from my menu to find Legs standing beside my table, smiling winsomely. "Ms. Martinelli. Is there something I can do for you?" I ask, even as my gaze strays involuntarily across the room to the table where, last time I checked, she'd been seated with her cousins. Yes, they're still there. And shooting death glares in my direction—which, frankly, is nothing new.

"Well yes, actually," she replies. "Since you ask. You *could* let me buy you that drink I've been offering. I mean, assuming you're off-duty."

Shit. Of course. I should've figured that was coming. I hesitate for an instant, trying to decide how best to play this. I could lie and say I'm working. Or point out the obvious, that I already have a drink. I could suggest we do it another time or try and convince her that it's really not necessary. But then I see a flash of disappointment hit her eyes.

"It's just a drink, Deputy," she teases. "I'm not offering to have your babies or anything, you know."

"Ah. Well. I'm glad we got *that* out of the way."

"Mm. Although, I would be remiss if I didn't point out that they would likely be very pretty babies."

I can't help but grin. "Oh, no doubt. But don't you think..." I trail off as I realize that this is exactly how this conversation should *not* be going. If Miles were here, I know he'd be urging me to shut it down fast, to 'just say no,' to all of it. But Miles is *not* here. In fact, at this exact moment, Miles is probably happily ensconced in a first-class seat, sipping champagne and toasting his bride as the two of them wing their way to a Hawaiian honeymoon.

So, he has no legs to stand on—pun intended—and I... Well, I've just spent the better part of the day celebrating his wedding, surrounded by a goodly number of happily paired-off couples; including (I couldn't help but notice) both of Allegra's sisters. It's been fucking torture. And if she's spent the day feeling even half as left out and lonely as I have, it would be cruel to turn her down. And unnecessary. And...let's face it, not nearly as much fun as it would be to continue flirting with her for just a few more minutes. I mean...we're both adults. And it's just a drink. What could possibly go wrong?

Well, a lot, apparently, because the next thing you know I find myself saying, "I tell you what. I *will* accept that drink, but *only* if you'll join me for dinner." And yes, thank you, I *have* lost my mind entirely. I mean, clearly, I have.

Accepting a gift of under twenty dollars (ie a drink, while off-duty) falls into what's very much a gray area. Yes, it's frowned upon, but it's exponentially far less problematic than the conflict-of-interest charges I'm positively begging for by asking her on what could very reasonably be misconstrued as a date.

But hey, what's life without a few risks?

"All right," she says, eyes lighting up at my suggestion. "I'd like that." Her cheeks flush pink. She's smiling broadly as she pulls out the chair across from me. And that right there—the look in her eyes, the blush on her face, the smile on her lips—that's all the reward I need.

Out of the corner of my eye, I can't help but notice that her cousins are still scowling at me. But since that seems to be the whole family's default expression where I'm concerned—less Allegra—I pay it no mind. As per usual.

She might not remember much about the night we spent together down by the river, but I do. And, ill-judged or not, I *want* this chance to catch up with the-girl-from-the-party, the-one-who-got-away, and to maybe find out what happened to her that long ago summer. It's one night—no. Hell, no. Not even one night. It's a single meal, a couple of drinks, a few hours at most. All of which will take place in public, with plenty of witnesses to attest to the fact that nothing untoward occurred. After which, she'll go her way, and I'll go mine. No harm, no foul, and—with any luck at all—no unfortunate fallout.

"So, what's good here?" she asks.

"D'you mean to drink?" I ask, having noticed that she'd picked up the drink menu. "If you're talking wine, you probably know more about the subject than I do."

"Probably," she agrees as she lays the menu aside. "But no, I meant to eat. I already know what I'll be drinking. I noticed earlier that they have a Chardonnay from a winery that I've been hearing good things about. It's in the Los Carneros AVA; and I haven't had any wines from there yet, so I'm curious to try it. I'm just not sure what to get to go with it."

"They're known for their burgers," I say as I hand her the dinner menu. "But the barbacoa puffy tacos are outstanding. That's what I'm getting."

"Mmm. That does sound good," she says. "But perhaps not with Chardonnay."

"Well, what does go with Chardonnay?"

"Seafood, poultry, some pasta dishes—anything like that."

"Dungeness crab tostadas?" I suggest.

"Ooh, yes. That sounds perfect. Thank you. I haven't had Dungeness crab in years!"

"Well, good then. Glad I could help."

The server comes to take our order, and I get another Saison. It's called Cuffing Saison, and it's one of their seasonal offerings. Legs chuckles when she hears the name. "I swear, beers, boats, and racehorses have the *best* names," she observes.

"Not wines?"

"Sadly, no. I mean, there are a few that do; but it's not common. I wish more wineries would get behind the cutesy, clever names. But I guess it's just not a big part of the wine-making culture."

"So is Chardonnay your favorite wine?" I ask, as it hits me that that was what she'd been drinking the night we met.

She shakes her head. "No, I wouldn't say that. I don't really have a favorite. Or rather, I don't just have *one* favorite. I like a lot of different wines; it depends on the occasion. What about you—do you only drink beer?"

"Most of the time," I admit. "But, like you, I don't just stick to one type. In fact, that's one of the things I like about craft beers—they're not generic. I can always tell what kind of beer I'm drinking; there's no guesswork involved. And I can choose what I order to match what I'm eating. I guess you'd call that pairing, right?"

Legs grins. "Look at you, all up on the lingo."

"With wine, on the other hand, it's either white or red—I can't tell anything beyond that."

"What? No, that's—"

"Beer is easier. If I order a Saison, I don't expect it to taste like an IPA. If I ask for an IPA, I know it's not gonna taste like a Lager or a Porter or a Pilsner."

"Or a wheat beer," she says. "Or an Altbier, or a Lambic, or a Doppelbock—yeah, I get it. And you're not wrong about that."

I have to admit, I'm surprised. And maybe a little impressed. "For someone who doesn't like beer, you sure seem to know an awful lot about it."

She frowns. "What do you mean? I like beer."

"You do?" I blink at her foolishly while I adjust my thoughts. In my memory I can still hear her pretend-gagging: *blech, blech, blech.*

"Yes. I just don't like *cheap*, generic beer. But, then again, I don't like cheap, generic wine, either. There are a lot of really good craft beers out there. I like cider, too, for that matter. And whiskey, and...a whole bunch of other stuff. Tequila, for example. But this is Napa so...you know...when in Rome?"

I have no idea. So, I shrug and tell a little white lie, "Makes sense."

"Anyway, wines are the same. They don't all taste alike, either." I must look skeptical because she rolls her eyes and says, "Okay, fine. I'll admit that, possibly, especially to the untrained palate, the differences are maybe a little more subtle. But Master Sommeliers are able to distinguish between nearly *every* fine wine *in the entire world* with ridiculous accuracy. *You* could certainly learn to tell more about a wine than simply is it white or red. There are different types of grapes, different blends, different vintages. Have you ever had a vertical flight?"

"I wouldn't know. I have no idea what that even is."

"It's when you try several glasses of what's basically the same wine from the same winery, made from grapes grown on the same vines, but each glass contains a different vintage. It's amazing how just one little factor—in this case how the weather changes from one year to the next—can make such a huge difference in the taste of."

"Interesting. I guess I'll have to take your word for it."

"Well, no. Don't do that. I mean, I'd be happy to show you, if you're actually interested. Although, I'm somewhat hamstrung, at the moment. It'll be a few years before I'll be able to set up that kind of tasting at Caparelli. And Belmonte's out, because apparently my uncle is being a dick. But there are plenty of other wineries around, and if you wanted a tasting buddy, I'd be happy to tag along."

"Thanks. I'll...keep that in mind." I smile as I say it, trying to let her down gently; but, c'mon. She has to know how bad those optics would be, right? Or then again, maybe she doesn't.

"If you think about it, it would be kind of a win-win," she says musingly. "I really ought to be familiarizing myself with what's out there and what's selling right now, anyway. And that could be awkward if I were to go by myself."

"I don't know why," I say in an effort to change the subject. Although since we're still talking about wine, it's probably not enough of a change. "You sound extremely knowledgeable. And even I can tell you're passionate about the subject." And to be honest, I'm not sure if that's a good thing or not. I've known a few people whose lives were ruined by drink. I'm related to most of them. Which, yes, is probably another reason that I tend to stick with beer. "I'm sure any winery owner would be thrilled to have you hanging out in their tasting rooms, talking to people about wine. And whatever awkwardness there might be, it probably wouldn't last beyond the first few sentences."

"Well, thanks," she replies sounding doubtful. "I mean, I *hope* I sound knowledgeable. But I grew up here, you know? I think it would be more surprising if I didn't sound like I knew what I was talking about. But sometimes I wonder if I'm just fooling myself. Because you don't always know what you don't know—if you know what I mean. And I didn't go to school for any of this stuff like my sisters did."

"Hey," I tell her. "Don't sell yourself short. I grew up here too. And dealing with winery owners is a big part of my job, at the moment." A job I'm *clearly* ill-suited for. "And...I don't feel like living here has given me any particular advantage, or inside knowledge—at all. I'm pretty sure I don't know nearly as much about wine or the wine industry as I should."

"You grew up here?" she asks, eyes narrowing as she studies my face a little more intently.

"Yeah, sure. I..." And suddenly I realize I don't want to rehash the same conversation we had five years ago. I don't want to mention Clear Lake, don't want her to make the connection—or worse yet, *not* make the connection. And, mostly, I'm enjoying myself for the first time in months. I don't want things to get weird. "I mean, not entirely. But...well, you know...mostly."

"You don't sound very sure, about that," she says, lips twitching as she grins. "But not to worry. There's an easy way to tell if you count as local. Just answer one question for me. Do you identify as a Napkin—yes or no?"

"Fuck, no." I stare at her, appalled. "Are you kidding me? I can't believe you even asked that."

Legs gurgles with laughter. "And there you have it. Definitive proof."

"Of what?"

"Of your status as a local. Obvs!"

"Why's that? Because I think Napkin is a stupid name for Napa residents?"

"Nooo. Because you've clearly heard the term before, *and* you have strong feelings about it. Your actual opinion *isn't* the deciding factor. There are people who live here who *do* use it to describe themselves, you know."

"Yeah. And you know who they are, right? They're the same people who open bougie restaurants that only tourists eat in."

"Well, yes, that's quite possible. But that just proves my point. They obviously feel *just as strongly* that it's a *good* name for us."

"And what do you think?"

"Oh, I don't count," she says, shrugging it off so quickly, that I find myself frowning.

"I can't imagine that's true. In what way?"

"I've been away too long. I've got the whole, 'absence makes the heart grow fonder' thing going on. I was homesick and learned to appreciate all the stupid little things that used to irritate me. Which, I'd like to think was what my uncle intended when he shipped me off to Italy; although I'm not convinced it was."

Before I can question her further, our server returns with our drinks. Allegra spends the next several moments sniffing and sipping and swirling her wine. She even pulls out her phone to take a picture and make some quick notes.

"Sorry," she says when she notices my surprise. "But I've been thinking of starting a wine blog. We don't have any of our own wine to blog about yet, but I figure maybe I can start off talking about other local wines, as a way to build an audience ahead of time. After all, it's never too soon to start branding."

"If you say so." Lifting my glass in a small toast, I say, "Hey, maybe I should start one, too. I could highlight local beers."

Her eyes are twinkling as she raises them to meet my gaze. "A Napa based beer blog? Wow. You really like to buck the trend, don't you?"

Oh, sweetheart, you don't know the half of it. But that's a dangerous thought, so I keep it to myself.

"You know," she says after a moment. "Here's a thought. There *is* a winery-slash-brewery operating right in downtown Napa. I've been meaning to check it out. Maybe we could go there for our first tasting. Afterwards, we could both blog about it, or do a joint video, or... Oh. Wait a sec." She pauses, her eyes going wide. "What if we did a collab? It could maybe even be a regular feature where we could both talk about the same wine or beer from two different perspectives. Like a 'he said, she said' sort of thing. I bet people would find that interesting."

I'm sure my bosses would find it extremely *interesting*, I think to myself. *And not in a good way.*

Thankfully, it's at this point that our food arrives, and I'm spared the trouble of having to explain that I'd only been joking about the blog. That commenting on specific, local businesses when I should at least be preserving the *appearance* of neutrality is a whole lot more than merely 'bucking the trend'. It'd be more like career suicide.

Allegra snaps a few more pictures, and then we settle in to eat. I have my own version of her "are you a local?" test—a non-verbal one, which she passes by not even hesitating to pick up her tostada with her hands.

"Good?" I ask, amused by the happy little noises she's making.

"So good," she responds between bites. "How's yours?"

"Also good," I say. The meat is perfectly smoked, with just the right amount of heat from the chipotle glaze. The blue corn tortillas are pillowy perfection, and the paper-thin sliced radishes add a note of crispy, spicy freshness. Before I think better of it, I find myself asking, "Wanna bite?"

She's chewing, so she doesn't answer right away, but the calculating look in her eyes makes me wary. *Too intimate, I* think to myself, as she puts down her tostada and carefully wipes her fingers clean. *Too much like a date.*

"On one condition," she says at last, then quickly amends, "Two conditions. *If* I can also try your beer, and *if* you'll try my pairing as well, and let me know what you think."

"Fair enough," I say as I hand her my plate. She pushes hers across the table. We exchange drinks, and dig back in.

The tostada is also excellent. The crab is sweet and buttery, the avocado and crema are offset by fresh green notes from the jalapeno and cilantro—but that's all as I'd expected. The wine, on the other hand, is a revelation. It's got...a weight to it and a creaminess. Almost like a Stout, except that (of course) it tastes nothing at all like a Stout. What it also doesn't taste like is anything at all like my memory of what a typical white wine tastes like. *Cheap. Generic.* Yep, the lady may have a point.

"Well?" she asks, after I've gone back for a second sip. "What do you think?"

"I think you're right," I say as I hand her the glass, and we go back to our original dishes. "I think I *could* learn to tell wines apart."

Not that I will, of course, because...well, I don't know how far I'd get on my own. I'm pretty sure I'd need assistance from someone like her. And that's never going to happen.

In fact, none of the things that she's suggested tonight—not the blogging, or the collaborating, or the hanging out with each other at wineries or breweries or whatever—are ever going to happen. At least not in the foreseeable future.

Still, she's nodding happily. So rather than saying any of that and spoiling the mood, I say the first thing that pops into my head. Typically, it's also about the dumbest move I could make.

"So how *did* you end up going to Europe," I ask. "You said it had something to do with your uncle?"

I don't miss the flicker of pain in her eyes, the way her smile dims ever so slightly at the mention. *This is a mistake*; I tell myself as my heart begins to pound. Am I about to learn the answers to the questions that have plagued me for the past five interminable years, the reasons why she ghosted me without a word? Will dredging up those memories cause her to put two and two together and realize who I am?

And how the hell do I respond to it, if she does?

Chapter 7

Allegra

"You said it had something to do with your uncle?"
It's an innocent sounding question and, yes, I guess I did imply that, didn't I? Still my mood takes a nosedive—and not in a sexy, Post Malone sort of way. "Kind of?" I reply, squirming slightly at the thought. I really don't like thinking about that period of my life. "I mean, he said he'd buy me a ticket if I wanted to visit my mother. She lives in Italy now, with my stepfather and his family. They have a winery there. In Tuscany."

Romero rolls his eyes. "Of course, they do."

"It sounded almost too good to be true. So of course, like an idiot, I jumped at the opportunity."

"Why do you say that?" he asks, tilting his head to the side and regarding me curiously. "That doesn't sound idiotic at all. At eighteen? Who wouldn't make that choice?"

"I guess. Maybe you'd have to know my family better in order to understand how really stupid it was."

"Possibly," he agrees. "And I admit that I don't know your

uncle well at all, but based on what I've observed this past summer, what you've told me, various claims your sisters have made; it does seem a little...out of character?"

"Perhaps," I admit. "But...did I mention it was a one-way ticket?"

"Uh, no." He grins back, ruefully. "You did not. I suppose that does change things, doesn't it?" But a moment later, his expression changes. "Wait. Are you saying he sent you all the way to Europe, completely on your own, with no return ticket? Do you even speak the language? What were you supposed to do over there? How did he expect you to get back?"

"Whoa. Hold on now," I tell him. "It wasn't *that* bad. It's not like he dropped me off on a deserted island. I was staying with family, remember? Mama could certainly have afforded to send me back, if she'd wanted, or if I'd've insisted. But yes, I'm sure Geno was hoping I'd stay gone for a while. I think he viewed it as an easy solution to the problem."

"What problem was that?"

"Well, me, of course. I was always the problem. And I guess, after eight years of dealing with me, he decided he'd had enough."

Romero's lips tighten. He eyes me narrowly, like he wants to say something, but isn't sure how I'll take it. My money's on either pity, or censure, and I don't want either.

"I don't know why we're even talking about this," I say, rushing into speech before he can. "He had a point, after all. Not that I would have agreed, at the time."

"What point was that?"

"Well, I'd just turned eighteen, as you pointed out. But I was not yet twenty-one. So the law was going to treat me like an adult, even though a lot of what I was doing, or wanted to do still wasn't legal. Or should I not be telling you this?"

He shakes his head. "You're fine. That was years ago. So, unless you 'killed a man in Reno,' you're in the clear."

"Good to know," I reply solemnly. "And I will neither confirm nor deny said Reno-cide."

His lips quirk. "Noted."

"Anyway, the reason my uncle was so triggered was because my cousin Leo actually *did* get into some kind of legal trouble when he was about that age. He's the oldest of the cousins. I think Geno feared there'd be a repeat performance, so he tended to overreact with the rest of us. Or at least that's how he was with me and my sisters."

"So did *he* kill a man in Reno?"

"Who, Leo?" I shake my head. "God, no. Can you imagine?" I sip my wine and laugh at the idea until I realize he isn't laughing with me. "Are you serious right now?"

"I don't know," he says in a politely neutral cop voice that immediately grates on my nerves. "You tell me."

"I just did," I snap in response, bristling with family loyalty as I rise to my cousin's defense. "Of course, he didn't." Although, to be honest, I'm responding on instinct. I *don't* actually know what kind of trouble Leo had gotten into. I remember the tears, and the raised voices, and the parade of cop cars coming and going down Belmonte's wide drive, but if I ever knew the details, I've forgotten them now.

In all likelihood, that was one of those family secrets—like the ones my cousins and I had talked about earlier. Given my age at the time, I was probably shielded from the drama. But it's also possible that I just didn't care. My own life was chaotic enough to keep me wrapped up in my own concerns—especially after my father died.

That hit me hard. It changed everything. Not just for me, of course. We were all affected. And I'm not saying it was a relief when Mama finally up and ran away with Sergio. But, in retrospect, given her own behavior at the time and my outsized feelings of culpability, it kind of was.

"Anyway," I continue, determined to wrap up the conversation, which has drifted so far off course, I can barely remember where we were headed. "Long story short. My grandmother was against my going. She and my uncle argued about it, but in the end...what can I say? I hadn't seen my mother in several years, at that point, and...I really wanted to go."

But that's another memory I'd rather not revisit. Sitting cross-legged on the porch, right below the open window, straining to hear what was being said. The rapid patter of their voices—speaking in Italian, too quickly and too quietly, for me to easily interpret their words. My uncle's anger. My grandmother's pain. My own, deep-set certainty that I would never stop messing up, that I would always find a way to hurt the people I cared about most.

And all at once, I'm blinking back tears, crying for the grief-stricken teenager I no longer am.

"Hey. What's wrong?" Romero asks, his voice concerned as he reaches across the table to cover my hand with his. "I didn't mean to upset you."

I shake my head. "You didn't. I just... I guess I wish now that I'd chosen otherwise. Because that was the last time I ever saw my grandmother. And...and she's gone now and I... hate that our last words to one another in person were spoken in anger."

"I'm sorry for your loss," he says. The words are trite and standard, but he sounds sincere, as though he too has known grief, and can recognize it in others.

But I don't deserve his sympathy. Not for this. "It was my own fault," I say, slipping my hand away, attempting to shrug it off. "I could have done things differently, come back sooner, not gone at all, but...I didn't, so..."

"So, were you with your mom all this time?" he asks, clearly hoping to shift our conversation into a more positive direction. "That must have been nice?"

"Oh. No." I shake my head. "Nonna was right about that. That didn't work out. At. All. I clashed with my new step-family almost immediately. And Mama...well, she'll never change. But I guess there are some lessons you need to learn for yourself." It's not that my mother is intentionally cruel or uncaring. But she's incapable of being the mother that I wanted her to be. "I was only there for about a month before I decided I'd be better off on my own."

I nod to myself as I take another sip of wine. I'm pleased with the way that sounds—not traumatic at all. If only the reality had been the same...

In the beginning, Mama had seemed thrilled to have me there. As had Sergio. And yes, it went to my head. How could it not?

Suddenly, after years of being ignored, I was being show-ered with gifts, lavished with attention, heaped with praise. And I was all too willing to forgive and forget. Who cared that my mother had made the decision to move halfway around the world, to leave me and my sisters behind? Or that she'd been emotionally absent for most of our lives? She was doting on me now and I was there for it.

And maybe it was inevitable that Sergio's children by his previous marriage—Bettina, Massimo, and Elettra—would resent the shit out of me. But I also know my behavior didn't help.

On the other hand, it wasn't *all* my fault, either. See, no one ever troubled to guard their tongues when I was present, because it was well-established that I couldn't speak Italian worth *un cavolo*, as the Italians would say. But I'd grown up eavesdropping. And just because I struggled to find the words necessary to speak Italian, with any kind of fluidity, that didn't mean I couldn't understand a lot of what was being said. And what I quickly learned was that while my stepfamily didn't like *me* very much, they absolutely *loathed* my mother.

La opportunista was one of their nicknames for her: the opportunist. Which, sad to say, they weren't completely wrong about. The three of them (six if you counted the spouses, seven if you added in my new step-grandmama) spoke openly about what they could do to prevent Mama from gaining control of their family's businesses and finances. How they might use *me* to somehow drive a wedge between Mama and Sergio. What none of us knew, at that point (well, Mama knew, and Sergio of course) was that that ship had already sailed.

But I was young, ignorant, reckless, hot tempered, and firmly on my mother's side. And I, too, could concoct elaborate plots, and avenge supposed wrongs, and embark on wrong-headed missions.

Having made up my mind that I would prove that my mother was *not* the only gold-digging, cheat within the Di Stefano family circle, I set my sights on the tomato.

But I'm getting ahead of myself.

What you need to know is that we were all living together, at the time—albeit in a mansion so large that it made the Belmonte estate look like a condo. And, when I say all, I mean Mama and Sergio; Sergio's widowed mother, Dona Lucia; Massimo and his wife (who were expecting their first child); Bettina, her husband (and their three daughters). and Elletra and her boyfriend, Timoteo. Or Tomato, as I liked to call him— as much for the sound of his name as for his very round face.

Which, yes, had a pronounced, and unfortunate tendency to grow red whenever he got excited or annoyed. Or, for example, when someone purposely, and repeatedly mispronounced his name.

And while I'm not particularly proud about what happened next, I don't think it should have surprised anyone, either.

As I've said, the family did not like me. Timoteo was the only member of my generation, who did not look on me with disdain. And, yes, I quickly realized that he was a total cascamorto (Italian for flirt). Of course, I did! He complimented my appearance and said outrageously romantic things. He tried to help me with my Italian—even after I'd intentionally butchered his name. And he attempted to proposition me whenever Elettra was out of earshot.

And, yes, I should have heeded the warning. But I was lonely—Mama and Sergio having quickly grown tired of the novelty of having a gauche American relative constantly under-foot—and Timoteo was kind.

And so one thing led to another, as those things usually do, and it didn't take long before he and I were discovered passion-ately limonare, which...doesn't translate into anything sensible, so don't even worry about it.

My mother was very understanding when I tried to apolo-gize. "No, no. Don't be silly," she said, brushing my explana-tions aside. "Really, when you think about it, you did us all a favor."

"I think so, too," I answered meekly. "Maybe it's better for Elettra to find out now what he's like, before she marries him."

"Oh, we all know what he's like. And Sergio was never going to allow his daughter to marry that man, anyway." Mama waved a hand dismissively. "But now he has an excuse, and someone else to be the bad guy."

"Me," I guessed, feeling sour. Because I really should have seen the writing on the wall. I should have known what was coming next. "So, I guess I should leave?"

"Well, of course," my mother said. "That's inevitable. But it's been lovely having you here and getting to know you again. I've missed you."

"I've missed you, too," I replied. "We all have." Then I add, impulsively, "Come back to Napa with me! You don't have to stay here. They all hate you. You have to know that!"

"Oh, I do." Her eyes danced with amusement as she shot me that grin—the one that's so terrifyingly like my own. "Of course, I know that. It's hilarious, isn't it?"

"What? No! How is that funny? They think you're here to steal their inheritance, that all you care about is getting your hands on Sergio's money."

"I know," she repeated, patiently. "And that's *why* it's funny. He and I have no illusions. He married me to maintain control, to keep *them* from ousting *him*. They don't know it yet, but he's put nearly everything they care so much about in my name. They won't get a penny if they try to act against us."

I gaped at her as she smiled serenely. "But..."

"So, you see," she continued. "I have no reason to ever go back to Napa. Why would I? Just so I can argue with my brother? No. I have everything I could ever want right here."

But she wouldn't have me, and she wouldn't have my sisters, and I guess I should already have known how little that mattered to her.

"So where did you go?" the deputy asks, shaking me from my stupor.

"What?"

"Afterwards. If you didn't stay with your mother, and you didn't come home...?"

"Oh. No, of course I couldn't go home, at that point. If I didn't even stay for the summer? Then everyone would have known that I was wrong, and Nonna was right, and that Geno had played us all; so...I stayed."

"Stayed where?" he asks, looking confused. "And how? You couldn't work there, could you? How'd you support yourself."

I shrug. "Oh, everywhere. Just Europe in general. I moved around a lot. And as it happens, I have dual citizenship through my dad, so I never have to worry about visas, and working anywhere in the EU isn't a problem, either. So..."

"Lucky."

"I know. I'm not sure if Geno realized that was the case. Or maybe that was part of what he was counting on? Anyway, who knows? Maybe I'll get around to asking him sometime."

"So, what kind of work did you do?"

"Different things. Whatever sounded interesting. The first job I got was at a winery. The timing was perfect; it was getting close to the end of summer, and I knew vineyards can always use extra hands during harvest. Also, as you've pointed out, I can sound knowledgeable enough in the short term, so getting hired wasn't all that difficult."

Romero frowns. "I meant that as a compliment," he says in protest. "I don't know why you're twisting it into some sort of criticism."

"Because it works either way, doesn't it?" I ask. "And anyway, harvesting grapes is harder than you might think— especially since summer in some of these places is so much hotter than it is in Napa. So, I decided I'd try my hand at other things."

"Such as?"

"Well, I worked in hostels for a while—I'd stay for a few weeks at a time, and then I'd move on. That was great, because it meant I got to travel a lot. I could go wherever I wanted to go, and basically stay there for free. I managed to save a ton of money. And if I didn't get along with someone—a boss, or my co-workers, or whoever—I could be gone before it became a problem."

"Did that happen a lot?"

I feel myself blush. "Maybe. At first. Not so much later on. And it honed my customer service and hospitality skills, which comes in surprisingly handy running a tasting room. I worked for several tour companies, too: leading all sorts of tours— walking tours, bike tours, ghost walks, pub crawls. Those were probably the most fun—short shifts, big tips, no supervisors looking over your shoulder, everyone loves you."

"Sounds nice."

"Yeah. It was," I say, as I'm hit by a wave of nostalgia. Running my own show, having everyone love me, that was the dream right there. I sure don't have that now, and I miss it. "Eventually, I got hired to work on a cruise ship. That's what I was doing when I got the call about my grandmother."

"And now you're back here."

"Yep. Trying to help my sisters get Caparelli up and running—much to my uncle's dismay."

"Yeah. So I've noticed. What's up with that, anyway?"

I shrug again. "Who the hell knows? I guess he was hoping we'd fold, that we'd decide it was too much work and put every-thing back in his hands."

"And what about your cousins?"

"What about them?"

"Well, you all seemed to be getting along earlier tonight. Weren't they also dismayed?"

"Good question," I mutter. "I'm not altogether certain. I mean, they *claim* that they understand what Nonna was trying to accomplish, that it was her decision, and that they all wish us luck. But I guess I'm skeptical by nature, or something, because

I'm finding that a little hard to believe. But, apparently, they've been really supportive so far, so...I dunno maybe I'm wrong."

"Well, maybe. Or maybe not."

I frown at that. "What?"

He leans in close, lowering his voice to say, "Don't look now, but your fan club appears to be looking pretty annoyed, at the moment." He tilts his head toward the table where my cousins are seated. "So, if it's not *you* they're annoyed with, should I be concerned that it's me?"

I immediately turn to look—which he should have known I'd do. I mean, that whole, 'don't look now,' thing never works, does it? I give my cousins a little wave and a thumbs up—eliciting eye rolls and head shakes in response—before turning back to grin at my dinner companion. "I think they're just being protective. Which, honestly? Is kind of nice for a change."

"If you say so."

"Well yeah," I reply, in annoyance. "I just did, didn't I?"

He shrugs in response. "What can I say? Maybe I'm skeptical, too, but those expressions don't exactly say 'protective' to me. They look more like a prelude to violence."

"Oh, I wouldn't worry," I tell him. Then, hearing the echo of my mother's lack of interest in that response, I lean in close. "They're just concerned, that's all. They didn't want me to come over here to talk to you." I stop, for a moment, to reconsider. "Actually, that's not completely true. Gianni's the one who suggested I talk to you. It was the other two who didn't like the idea. But that's just because they all think you have a grudge against the family. So, are they right?"

"Well, that's a loaded question, isn't it? I'm not exactly sure what you—or they—mean by that," he tells me. "I know I ended up wasting a lot of time, this summer, following up on mostly bogus claims about your sisters' winery not being in compliance. And then even more time following up on charges that *they* had leveled against your uncle. And that wasn't fun either, but—"

"What do you mean 'my sisters' winery'?" I interrupt, as all my insecurities are triggered. "Caparelli is *my* winery, too, you know."

Chapter 8

Clay

Legs scowls at me. "Caparelli is *my* winery, too, you know." And, oh boy, there you have it. I crash back to earth so abruptly it's painful. The very rich really *are* different. They wander around Europe for years on end with no visible means of support, avoiding the wildfires that repeatedly displaced the rest of us, falling in and out of jobs on a whim. Until, out of nowhere, wineries are dropped into their laps.

"I guess I was forgetting about that," I admit. I'm pretty sure it was intentional. Because that's just one more reason why we shouldn't be doing this, why I shouldn't be enjoying her company as much as I am, and why we should both do our utmost to steer very clear of each other from this point forward.

"I think there's been a lot of that going around," she mutters darkly.

"A lot of what—forgetfulness?"

"Nothing. It doesn't matter."

"Right. Well. The thing is, it's easy for me to forget about your family connections," I tell her. "Because I've been enjoying your company. But your family, on the other hand, they've been nothing but a major pain in my butt."

She laughs at that. "They really are, aren't they? I thought I was the only one who felt that way about them."

"Not hardly," I say as I lift my glass. "To families."

"To families," she responds touching her glass to mine. "Can't live with them, can't live without 'em."

And we both drink to that even though, honestly, I think I've been doing just fine without mine. And given everything she's told me of her recent history, I would have thought she felt the same about hers.

"But, seriously," she says. "You really *don't* have to worry about my sisters, you know. Or my brother-in-law, Jake. The three of them know this business inside and out. They were brought up with it; it's in their blood. I know that sounds like a line out of a movie."

"Just a little."

"But it's true, all the same. They're good, law-abiding people. They're ethical. They're all serious about making Caparelli a success and wouldn't do anything to jeopardize that."

It's a nice thought, if somewhat biased, and I don't miss the fact that she didn't include herself in that defense. But clearly, someone does *not* agree with her assessment. *Or* someone doesn't care about the facts and has either an ulterior motive, or an actual grudge against the Martinelli clan. "What about your cousins? Do you think they could be the ones calling in the complaints?"

"I actually asked them that. They all insisted that they don't know who's doing it."

"Do you believe them?"

"I think I do. Mostly because I think they're too smart to do something like that in the first place. But also...it just seems so petty. You know?"

I nod in a noncommittal sort of way; but I'm not sure I agree with that. There's a lot of money involved, a lot of potential fines, a lot of unpleasant consequences. None of that says petty to me. "Well, I appreciate the insight," I tell her, in as diplomatic a fashion as I can manage. "And if you learn anything more, I hope you'll share it with me. But it's still my job to follow up on all the complaints I receive. So..."

"I know." She smiles ruefully. "It's frustrating all the way around. But don't you think it's in everyone's best interests if we can all at least accept that we're on the same side?"

"I hear you. But I think that sounds..." My voice trails off. Far-fetched, unlikely naïve, and possibly completely without merit. "Very tolerant of you," I say at last.

Legs blinks in surprise. "Not really. Not unless it turns out that my cousins are right about you."

"In what way?" I'm startled into asking.

"Well, one school of thought says that the only reason you stopped me and impounded my car is because of who I am, because of the family connection."

For an instant, I'm struck speechless. Because that's uncomfortably close to the truth. "I stopped you because of how you were driving," I say, focusing on the first half of her accusation. "I was worried you'd cause an accident. I had no idea who you were at that point."

"I know," she sighs. "My sisters keep reminding me of that, too."

"Well, you brought it up," I point out as I pick up my last taco and take a big bite. Legs finishes her wine and asks our server for some sparkling water. We both agree to take a look at the dessert menu and then move on to other topics.

"You know," Legs says somewhat hesitantly, scratching at

the tablecloth with the edge of her thumbnail—an odd sort of tell, and an unfortunate one, since it immediately has me remembering what her nails felt like digging into my skin. "It feels weird having to bring this up at this point, but I still don't know what your name is."

"Not that weird. It's probably a good thing," I say, which is also unfortunate, because of course she asks the obvious question.

"Oh? Why's that?"

"Ah, you know. I don't really like my name, so why would I want to share it?"

Unfortunately, I can't remember if I told her my name the night we met. There'd have been no reason not to—then. Now...maybe I don't want her to connect the dots. Maybe I'm hoping that she's thought about me, over the years, as much as I've thought about her. Which is unlikely as fuck, seeing as she apparently had no reservations about jetting off to Europe, just days later, and ghosting me. Maybe I'd rather stay a mystery.

But she's eyeing me with sympathy now and nodding her head. "Yeah, I get that. It's the same for me and my sisters. None of us like our names. That's how we ended up giving each other nicknames that we use more than our actual names. Well, not Rosa, so much, but Bee and I for sure do."

"It's not the same," I tell her. "And anyway, I think Allegra's a beautiful name."

"Thank you. It's okay on its own, I guess. But paired with Martinelli, it's just too much. Too many ells, and people are forever misspelling it. But I suspect you're deflecting. Which is cool, and all. But there has to be *something* I can call you other than Deputy."

"Well, sure," I say, finding a brief respite in my beer. "I mean, if Deputy's too long, you could always just call me Sir."

The look of shock and outrage that sweeps over her face,

has me laughing. "Kidding," I say as I hold up my hands in a gesture of peace. "But, you know, most people just use my last name."

Her lips roll in and it occurs to me that suggesting she's 'most people' might not sit well with her, either. But after a moment she nods and shrugs and I'm fool enough to think I've dodged that bullet. Our server returns and we order—decaf coffee and pumpkin flan for her, a French apple tart with a locally produced Cheddar cheese, and another beer for me.

Once we're alone again, Legs takes a sip of sparkling water and says, "So, fine. I guess I'll just go on calling you Romero—like everyone else does." She smiles sweetly and adds, "And I'm *sure* I'll remember to use that second R *most* of the time."

I laugh and bury my head in my hands. "I should have seen that coming, shouldn't I?"

"Yes. Probably. You don't seem unintelligent, after all."

Right. That, too. But mostly because she could never, ever be like 'most people'. Whatever was I thinking? "Fine. You win. My name is Clay. Happy now?"

"Ecstatic," she assures me. She's quiet for a moment. I watch as her eyes drift to the right, as though she's imagining—as I suddenly am—how my name would sound emerging from her lips in a whisper, or a shout, or a mindless, repetitive chant. I belatedly slam the lid on all that conjecture when I realize that all the scenarios I'm imagining are sexual in nature. From the flush on her cheeks, I wonder if she was doing the same.

"I don't know why you don't like your name," she says, hurrying into speech. "I- I think it's a good name. It's solid, easy to remember; it's short... Ohhh." She leans in suddenly, her eyes wide as she covers one of my hands with hers. "Is that the problem? Is it short for something long and horrible?"

"Like what?" I ask, distracted by the press of her hands on mine, by the internal struggle that's demanding that I move—

either turn my hand to grasp hers, or pull my hand away. Neither seems optimal, so I force myself to not react.

"Well, I don't know," she's saying. "Claymore? Or...whatever else it's short for. Clayville? Claybourgh? Claynaught?"

"God, no. It's not short for *anything.*" I solve my hand problem by sitting back in my chair, folding my arms and glaring with mock outrage. "Claynaught? Really? That's just obnoxious."

She grins unrepentantly back at me. "So then, I guess it's gotta be spelled weird."

"It's spelled just like it sounds. How else would you even spell it?"

Legs rolls her eyes. "Well, that's what *I'm* asking. Maybe it's spelled with a K. Or with an E, like in Hey. Or with an E-I. Or an E-I-G-H. Or—"

"Or an E-I-E-I-O? No. It's just Clay. Just C-L-A-Y. Okay?"

"Okay, Just Clay," she replies, and let the record show that, this time, she does *not* roll her eyes. But it's a close thing. I can tell she wants to. "So, let me see if I've got this straight. You're saying that you were gifted, I presume at birth, with an entirely unobjectionable, perfectly serviceable, *one* syllable, easily spellable name. Which, I might add, when combined with your last name, gives you a total of only four syllables. Which is the same number of syllables in just my last name alone. So, unless you have a couple of obscenely long middle names...?"

"No middle name," I assure her, and just barely stop myself from asking what kind of name she would consider obscene—because, of course, she had to go *there.*

"Lucky you," she says, grimacing slightly. "I have three. You can have one of them, if you'd like."

"Thanks," I tell her, just as our desserts arrive. "But I don't think so." And I do *not* spend the next few minutes, while our water glasses are refilled and our silverware is replaced, imagining scenarios that would involve the two of us giving or taking each other's names. Because that would be stupid. All the same, and perhaps even more surprisingly, that's also a close thing.

"So, then what exactly are you complaining about?" she asks, startling me, just as I've dug my fork into my apple tart.

"Complaining?" My gaze shifts—from her face to my plate, then back to her face again. "I wasn't. What do you mean?"

"No. Not the pie. I'm still trying to understand about your name. Why don't you like it?"

"Why is this so important to you?" I ask, putting down my fork and resting my arms on the table. "You can't possibly find it that interesting."

"I don't know why you'd say that." She shrugs. "But, after all, this is just basic getting to know you conversation."

"Exactly. It's basic. So..."

Her cheeks turn red as she toys with her flan. "What can I say? I find you interesting. But obviously sharing makes you uncomfortable. So then, let's talk about something else. Do you follow any specific type of sports? My family really hasn't until recently. Now we're all learning about hockey, thanks to Bee's relationship with Jansen Beck. So, that's been different."

I'm being a dick. I'm letting her carry the whole conversation, then giving her shit about it. "I guess what bugs me most about my name is what it represents, where it comes from, how I got it."

"Really?" She perks up right away. "Is it an old family name? Like, do you have a rich uncle and your parents were hoping that if they named you after him he'd leave you all his money when he dies?"

"As if." I roll my eyes, pick up my fork and finally get a mouthful of apple tart. Which is delicious, by the way. Rich, crispy crust, paper-thin, sweet-tart apple filling, offset by the sharp, vaguely yeasty taste of cheese. "You must be thinking of yourself. Because I have zero rich relatives—either living or dead."

"Okay, then...was it the last name of the doctor who delivered you? And before you say no one does that—yes, they do. I grew up with a girl that happened to. She always said that her mom picked it to piss off her dad. See, her mom went into labor while her father was on the golf course. By the time he got to the hospital, Cameron had already been born."

"I'm starting to think you know a lot of people with unusual stories," I observe.

She nods. "I know. It is surprising, isn't it? But I think that's because most people feel comfortable telling me about themselves. Present company excepted. You don't want me to know anything about you."

"That's not fair," I tell her, even though I'm pretty sure I'm lying.

"We'll see." She looks at me thoughtfully for a moment then says, "In that case, my money is on it being either the street where your parents' first house was located, or the name of a beloved family pet. You know, like the dog in Indiana Jones?"

"He wasn't named after the dog," I'm forced to point out. "He just called himself that because he didn't like his given name."

"Aha! That's it, isn't it?"

"What? No!" I'm startled into replying. "That doesn't even make sense. Why would I give myself a name I don't like to take the place of another name that I also don't like?" I take refuge again in my beer glass, steeling myself, because I know I'm about to give her another 'fun story' to add to her collection.

"Well, I don't know. That's what I'm trying to find out."

"Fine," I say at last, giving up, like I should have known I would. "So, the first thing you should know is that my mom's a little cray cray."

She pauses with a spoonful of flan partway to her mouth and blinks at me in surprise. "Well, sure. Isn't everyone's?"

"What? No, of course not."

"If you say so," she replies, not bothering to hide her skepticism. Then her grin turns sly, and she adds, "But that's like, just your opinion, man."

I frown. "Is that another movie quote?" I'm pretty sure it is. The words—and more importantly, her delivery of them—are tickling something in the back of my memory.

She favors me with a smile of approval, and a quick nod. "Yes, it is."

"Gonna tell me which one?"

"Maybe. But only *after* you explain about your name. Don't think you're gonna get away with distracting me with movie conversations."

"Wouldn't dream of it," I reply, even though, yeah, I was hoping. "So, my mom was big into Astrology. Maybe still is. I dunno. She named me Clay because I'm a Virgo."

Allegra's brow furrows. "But isn't Virgo the virgin? What does Clay have to do with— Oh, wait. Is this a Biblical reference? That's clever."

"Huh?"

"Sure. Isn't it? You know, 'cause Adam and Eve were the original virgins, and Adam was made from clay."

"Oh. No, it's nothing to do with that." It occurs to me that Legs and my mom would probably get along great—which is basically equal parts heartwarming and ball-shrivelingly terrifying. Don't get me wrong, I love my mother. I mean, of course I do; she's Mom, you know? But she's complicated and far from perfect, and the same goes for my relationship with her. It makes me wonder if that's not part of why I feel so attracted to Allegra Martinelli.

Not in a weird way, and you can fuck right off if you think that's what I'm saying. But because there's something familiar about her particular brand of crazy, something comfortable and comforting.

In a very strange, and otherwise inexplicable way, I feel at home with her. It's like she's someone I can talk to. Someone who I know won't judge me. Someone who sees me for who and what I am—except that she doesn't. Does she?

She has no idea who I am. She doesn't remember how we met. Which means the entire idea that we vibe with each other is a product of my own imagination.

"Virgo's an earth sign," I explain in an effort to get my mind off its weird tangent and our conversation onto safer ground. "It's also what they call mutable. So, one of its characteristics, supposedly, is that it's changeable, moldable—"

"Oh, like clay!" she says, catching on. Then she pauses. Eyeing me critically she asks, "Is that accurate? I mean, do *you* think that describes you? Because that's not the impression I get."

I shrug. I'm not really sure how to answer that because, no, I never thought of myself that way, either. Although, on the other hand, I don't like to think of myself as rigid or inflexible, either. "Who's to say? Like you said, I was assigned that name at birth. So, it's more of an interpretation of a concept than it is a character description."

"I get that," she says, nodding thoughtfully. "You know though, now that you've explained it, I think it's really—"

"I have siblings," I say, intentionally cutting her off. I don't want to know how she'd finish that particular sentence. I've heard most of the variations. My mother is either brilliant, a genius, laughable, dumb, or legit in need of a 5150—the common term for a California law that allows people, who appear mentally unhinged, to be detained for a psych eval.

"Oh?"

"Twins. They're Pisces. She named them Rain and River."

"I like it." Legs grins at me. "I don't think there's anything wrong with any of those names."

"It could be worse," I tell her. "Mom always said she wished I'd been a Taurus—fixed earth—because then she could have named me Rocky, and we'd all have had the same initials."

"Not a fan of the movies?"

"Not a fan of the alliteration," I say with a grimace. "Rocky Romero? No. I don't think so."

She laughs then, a joyous, infectious sound that causes my heart to clench and leaves me feeling like the envious woman in the Harry Met Sally diner scene. I want what she's having.

"Omigod," she says, suddenly sober. "*That's* why you over-reacted to me calling you Romeo. I'd wondered."

"I did *not* overreact," I'm stung into responding. I mean, I did, of course. But that wasn't why.

"Dude! You so did. You impounded my *car!*"

I shake my head. "I don't make the rules. Napa County has a zero-tolerance policy when it comes to—"

"Yeah, yeah. So you said," she interrupts, rolling her eyes. "I remember."

Of course she does. *Take that, Miles,* I think to myself, feeling disappointed even though I *knew* she had to resent that, at least a little.

"I'm sure there's gotta be a way around it," she says, and I can only shrug in response.

What answer could I give her, after all? Because of course, she's going to think there are loopholes to every law, or that some laws don't apply to her. That's what I've come to expect of the very rich. And of course, she's right—I probably could have thought of some other way of handling it. But I reacted rashly. Something my mom would likely attribute to my Aries rising sign...

"You're Earth and Fire, Clay," she used to say with tiresome regularity after the fires that un-homed us in 2017 *and* 2018. "That's your nature. Which means this is *nothing* you can't handle. There's a reason we put clay the kiln. It hardens it, makes it stronger, less likely to bend or melt."

Which generally caused the twins to exchange glances and say things like, "I think you mean, more likely to crack under pressure, don't you, Mom?"

And while I knew that they all meant well, that my mother was attempting to offer comfort, that my siblings were trying, in their bumbling, adolescent way, to defend me, I can't say that any of it landed well. And I wasn't overly upset when Mom decided to move them all down to Cabo following the lockdown.

"Anyway, you're not the only victim of poor parental decisions," Legs says now, breaking what had become an awkward silence. "My sisters and I were named for *wine*. How cliché is that?"

"I don't follow?" I reply, as grateful for the change of subject as I am perplexed. "Named for wine...how?"

"Well, it's obvious. Rossa, or Rosso, is red in Italian. Vino rosso is how you say red wine. Vino Bianco is white wine."

That explained her sisters' names. "What's Allegra mean?"

"It means my parents weren't as clever as they thought they were. Also, they sucked at thinking ahead."

"What?"

"They never anticipated having a third daughter, so..."

"I'm not following."

"Well, what were the choices, once red and white wine were covered?"

"Rosé?" I suggest, and then stopped, stymied. "Oh."

"Exactly," she says, propping her head on her hand and looking glum. "Far too close to Rosa."

"So then...?"

"Lively," she answers. "Allegro means lively. A nod to sparkling wine, because of the carbonation." She rolls her eyes and continues, "Not that we ever made a sparkling wine. The closest we ever came to anything like that were the small batches of Pét-Nat that my Nonna used to make every year, just to keep her hand in. I guess I should be grateful that my parents weren't more literal because the Italian word for sparkling wine is Spumante. Can you imagine?"

I can't help but grimace. "That's even worse than Rocky."

"Uh-huh. So much worse."

"All the same," I say—stupidly, because I feel like I'm channeling my mom, and that rarely works out. "You were named for Champagne, which is kinda cool, no?" It also fits her to a T. She *is* lively. Also bubbly, sparkling, irresistible and generally priced beyond my reach. "Isn't that the best wine?"

"Not exactly." She shakes her head. "Plus, I'd've had to be born in France for that to apply. At best, I'm just a sparkling disappointment."

"What? No."

"Yes. Absolutely. They were hoping for a boy."

"Well then, that's their loss."

"Thank you. But, you know, even Champagne shouldn't be called Champagne—that's just more male entitlement."

"How's that?" I ask.

"Well, sure. There's this cute little town in France, Limoux; I worked there for awhile. They claim that's where the first sparkling wines were made. The stories vary—as they do—with one school of thought saying monks first made it in the monastery there. And that they taught the procedure to Dom

Perignon. But the story the locals tell involve a married couple who they say invented the technique together. But then, when they split up, the husband took the recipe to the Champagne district, and claimed to have come up with it himself. And then insisted that, since his was the original, everyone else had to just call their versions sparkling wine. And that totally figures because women were the original brewers and vintners—and cooks, for that matter—but once anything becomes high profile, men insist on taking the credit and awarding themselves Michelin Stars and Grand Cru awards."

"I'm sure you're right," I tell her, then steer us back to safer topics by asking how she's enjoying her dessert.

We have a bit of a tussle when the bill comes. I hand my credit card to our server without thinking anything of it until Legs frowns at me.

"What are you doing?"

"Paying for dinner?" I respond, feeling mystified.

"But I was buying you a drink, remember? Although, at this point, I think I should probably buy you several."

Oh. That. "Thanks but...let's not and say we did, okay?" I joke, even though she isn't laughing. "Seriously. It's like I told you the other day, that's really not necessary."

"I *know* it's not necessary. It wouldn't be much of a gesture if I didn't have a choice. But—"

"Look, this has been nice. I've appreciated the company and the conversation. So, why can't we just leave it at that?"

"Well thank you," she says, giving in a lot more quickly than I thought she would. "I really enjoy your company, too."

I smile and nod, thinking, *it would have been nice to enjoy more of it.* Thinking, *if only we'd met again under different circumstances.* Thinking, *perhaps, in another lifetime...*

Which is when she hits me with, "So, I guess I'll just pay for dinner next time?"

Shit. "I don't think that will be possible."

"What? Why not?"

"Well, for one thing... Look, your cousins weren't completely wrong. Not that I have a grudge against your family —I don't mean that, exactly. But while your family is under investigation, it would be a conflict of interest for us to see each other."

"I don't know why. Haven't we already covered this? I wasn't even in the country when most of it happened."

"Still. Don't you think your family might see it as a betrayal —you siding with the enemy? You already said they warned you away from me."

"Yes. They did. Does it look like I listened to them?"

"Well, maybe you should."

"I don't think so."

"Legs, I..."

"I am *not* my family, Clay. Any more than you are yours. And I think we're both old enough to decide for ourselves who we want to spend time with."

"Well, my *department* might disagree with that assessment," I tell her. "Maintaining personal contact with someone I met as a result of an investigation is also frowned upon."

She stares at me then for a long moment without speaking. Then she gathers her things and gets to her feet. "Fine," she says, just as our server returns with my credit card and the receipt for me to sign. "I get it. For the record though, I'm a big girl. You could have just said you weren't interested in seeing me again. You didn't have to lie and make up bullshit excuses."

"Legs, wait," I say. "I didn't— They're not—" But she's gone, threading her way between tables, waving to her cousins from a distance. From the corner of my eye, I can see them turn to scowl at me again as I settle up with my server. "Yeah, yeah," I grumble beneath my breath. "I'm not happy about it either."

Chapter 9

Clay

I exit the restaurant onto Laurel—Oak Creek Canyon's main street—and glance around. It's Saturday night, which means there's a decent amount of foot traffic, but I quickly spot Legs standing beside her car, digging for something in her purse (her keys I assume) as I break into a quick jog. "Allegra, wait."

"No," she says, removing her hand, with the key fob, from her bag just as I reach her side. "Go away."

"Please," I say pressing my palm against the car's door to keep it from opening. "Just hold on a minute. You can't just—"

"I can't just...what?" she snaps, then her expression changes. "No. Oh, no, you don't," she says angrily. "I am *not* drunk, damn you. You had even more to drink than I did. So, don't you *dare* try and say that I can't drive or I'm gonna call in a citizen's complaint on *you!*"

"What? No! That's not— I wasn't—" I shake my head. "Would you give me a chance to explain? Please?"

"You mean give you a chance to lie some more? No. Thank you. I've already bagged my quota on liars for this season. Actually, I think I've exceeded it. So, if you don't mind—"

"I'm not lying," I insist, although—technically, I suppose I am. A bit.

"Oh, really? So then explain this: Miles Raymond is a deputy, too, is he not? Right here in Napa? You do know him, don't you?"

I nod. "Yes, of course I do."

"Of course, you do," she mimics. "Great. So, then you probably also know that he got married today—yes?"

"I was there. I was one of his groomsmen, in fact."

"Okay, well good. So, then you know who else was there, don't you? My sisters! So, if there are all these rules, and regulations, and conflict of interest clauses, and you're all so untouchable, or sacrosanct, or whatever word you want to use, then how come he can socialize with them, but you can't go on a second date with me?"

"Because it's an entirely different situation, that's why."

"How so?"

"Well...there are several reasons," I tell her. "For one thing, as far as I can tell, he's known your family for years, right?"

"Maybe. Sort of."

"For another, why do you think he transferred out of Oak Creek Canyon in the first place? It was for this very reason, so that he wouldn't get stuck investigating his friends, or having to recuse himself, or whatever. Also, if I understand the situation, your sisters are Millie's friends, primarily. Miles just gets them by association."

"Close," she says, crossing her arms and glaring at me—much as her cousins had been doing. "Bianca and Millie are friends. And Miles has been hanging out with Jansen, so I guess they're friends, too. But Millie only gets Rosa by association and Jake by...I don't even know. What's another step out from that? Default?"

"I have no idea," I admit. "But you see my point? There are degrees of connectedness, and—"

"And my connection to your investigation is very slight—we're barely acquainted. Ships passing in the night."

"I'm investigating a series of potential crimes that have been happening at *your* winery—remember that part? You were very clear about being one third of Caparelli. Which means you're up to your ears in connectedness. Your ship ain't passing anything. It's docked and anchored."

"Bullshit." She leans her shoulder against her car, as though she's settling in to fight. "I was in Europe the whole time this nonsense was going on. In fact, I haven't been back home in about five years. So, whatever's been going on here—and I'd bet every last penny in my bank account it's nothing worth investigating, I haven't been part of it.

"Plus," she says, lifting a finger to keep me still when she senses that I'm about to interrupt and point out that she would still be responsible, still be involved, still be off-limits. "No, listen. You wanna know the truth? Technically, it's not even mine yet. I mean, yes, it was left to me, and ultimately it will be mine, but there's a shit-ton of paperwork I need to sign first. And I haven't gotten around to doing that yet, so...at this point, minimal connection. Association level connection—if that."

"It doesn't matter," I say wearily.

"No, of course it doesn't. Because you're not interested. Which I get. So, why don't you move out of the way and let me get into my car now so I can go home?"

"You're wrong about that," I tell her. "And I can prove it."

"Really? What? What can you prove?"

"I can prove that if things were different, I would definitely want to go out with you."

"Oh, you cannot. That's ridiculous."

"It's not and I can."

"All right, go ahead then. This should be good."

"The thing is, I haven't been completely honest with you."

"Noooo?" she mutters, blinking quickly as she glances away. "I can't believe it. What a shocker."

"The thing is, that traffic stop was not the first time we met."

She looks at me blankly for a moment—clearly this was not what she'd been expecting me to say. Then her scowl returns. "Oh, nice try Romero," she says rolling the second R dramatically. So that, even though she's not saying Romeo, we both know that's what she means. And not as a compliment. "But that's ancient history, so you can fuck right off."

"What exactly do you think I'm talking about?"

"My sketchy past, what else?"

"Okay, then, no. That's not it."

"Look, we both agreed that barring any dead guys in Nevada—which, sorry to disappoint you, but there aren't any—I'm in the clear. That was years ago; so, statute of limitations, or whatever it's called. Whatever I did, or whatever you think I might have done, is in the past. Plus, I was a minor, at the time. So—"

"Are you freaking kidding me?" I ask, losing my temper just a little. "That's not what I'm talking about either. Five years ago, I was *also* a minor. And probably getting into even more trouble than you were." Although, come to think of it, that might not be true. I never stole a crate of wine, that's for sure.

"Okay. Cool. Good for you," she says with a shrug. "So, then what *are* you talking about? And make it fast. I want to go home."

"There was a party. I think it was something to do with Midsummer? Down by the river. There were lights in the trees, and music playing, and you were dancing all by yourself, and—"

"Yeah. I remember. So, what are you saying—that you had some kind of vision? Are you a psychic, or something?"

"Am I what? No! I'm saying I was there!"

"You were..." She trails off, and gazes at me searchingly. "You know, I actually don't remember much about that night, but..." Her eyes widen abruptly. "Omigod. No way. *You* were the boy with the beer?"

"I was...what?" *The boy with the beer?* I stare at her in disbelief. "*That's* how you've been thinking about me, all this time?" It's safe to say I'm a little underwhelmed. "That's what stuck in your memory—the fact that I was drinking beer?"

She laughs then, soft and warm. "I didn't say that's *all* I remembered about you."

"I would hope not," I say. And yes, it comes out sounding sulkier than I'd like. I'm feeling more like the hapless, blundering boy I'd been back then than I could ever have believed. Teetering on the edge of a serious crush, desperate to impress the pretty girl who'd come apart in my arms.

"How did you want me to remember you?" she asks. Then her smile falters. "Oh, shit. Now I get it. *That's* why you got so mad when I called you Romeo. You thought that I knew who you were and was making fun of you."

I nod, chagrined. "Something along those lines, I suppose."

"I hurt your feelings," she says—catching on a little more quickly than I'd have liked. "I'm so sorry. I can't believe I didn't recognize you."

"It's okay," I mumble. "Like you said, it's ancient history."

"Hmm." She shoots me a look. "More like unfinished business, if I'm remembering correctly." And damned if my body doesn't agree.

I clear my throat. "Listen, Legs—Allegra, I mean. I—"

"Oh, no," she says sliding closer, twining her arms around my neck. "No excuses—save those for someone else.

You've just made it *very* clear that we did not meet 'in the course of an investigation.' You and I have been acquainted for years and years—just like Miles and my sisters. More so, in fact. Which means we're golden. And like I said, I haven't stepped foot on Belmonte property in years and I was in Europe when you began investigating Caparelli. So..."

"Yes, I know all of that. However, I doubt anyone else will see it that way. Especially since I'm guessing neither of us wants to explain the circumstances under which we met."

"I wouldn't mind," she says after giving the matter a second's thought. "Statute of Limitations, remember?"

"Well, I'd mind. I am *not* going to tell my bosses that the reason dating you wouldn't be a conflict of interests is because we met as teenagers during the course of breaking multiple laws."

I try to sound firm, but I feel like the fact that my hands have settled—all too comfortably—around her waist somewhat diminishes the effect.

Legs smiles at me knowingly. "Yeah, no. That doesn't sound good, does it? We'll have to think of something else."

"Or we could not. We could just forget it ever happened and go on with our lives."

"Yeah, right." She rolls her eyes, as though I'd been making a joke that was too stupid to even laugh at. But then I guess she realizes I'm being serious. She bites her lip and asks, "Is that *really* what you want to do?"

"Of course it's not," I say, trying not to focus on her mouth, on how much I want to kiss her, to taste her again. "But it is what it is."

"Is it, though?" Her eyes are agleam with mischief. Her lips are curved in a knowing, secretive smile.

I know a challenge when I see one and I can't keep from

groaning. "Legs, c'mon." Because yes; it is. It has to be. "Be reasonable."

"So, how long have you known?" she asks, abruptly changing the subject. "About us, I mean. Tell the truth; did you *really* recognize me right away?"

"Not immediately. It wasn't until I saw the picture on your license," I say, not mentioning the vague, but instant recognition her smile had evoked. "Also, your name—Legs, Allegra. That's when it all made sense."

Mm," she murmurs. "So, you know what I think."

"Nope. Not a clue."

"We'll just have to be each other's sneaky links until you finish your investigation. Who knows? It might even be fun."

"I'm not sure about that," I say, still trying hard not to stare at her mouth, still failing miserably. "And, what about you? Aren't you worried at all about your family finding out?"

"No. I told you. I don't care what they think—not about something like that. Besides, it's always been inevitable that your people and mine would be against our hooking up."

"How d'you figure that?"

"It's what *you* told me."

"What? When?"

"Five years ago. You said then that my family wouldn't approve of you. And you're right! We've got the whole, '*my only love, sprung from my only hate*,' thing going on."

She's quoting Shakespeare again and I groan in despair. "You're doing it again, aren't you?"

"I'm not doing anything," she says shaking her head and gazing at me pityingly. "It's this thing; it's bigger than both of us. Do you really think it was just coincidence that I called you Romeo when you pulled me over?"

"You said it was dyslexia," I remind her.

"It was. And jet lag, and sleep depro. But it was also fate."

"Oh, fuck me. For real? You think we're *fated?*"

"Well, yes," she replies, looking surprised. "Duh. Of course, we are. What would you call it?"

"Uh, I dunno. A really terrible idea?"

There's a slight pause, and then she smiles, "Yes. Don't you love those?"

Between the pause, the wicked smile, the expectant gleam in her eyes, there's only one conclusion I can draw. "Let me guess," I say as I roll my eyes. "Another movie line?"

"See?" she says, smiling even more brilliantly. "You know me so well."

And maybe I'm just looking for an excuse at this point. But it really *is* starting to feel like fate and I'm tired of fighting it. So, I give into the inevitable and do what I've wanted to do for far too long. I draw her close. "Maybe," I murmur as I lower my face to hers. "But not as well as I'm going to."

And then I kiss her. And it's...Jesus Christ. It's fucking earth shattering, is what it is. It's life changing, soul-searing. It's everything I remember—and more. The taste of her lips, the feel of her body pressed against my own, her breasts, her butt, her hair, her scent—they're all so familiar, shockingly so. Familiar and perfect and irresistible. She's everything I've been missing, everything I've been longing for—without even realizing that was the case—for five long years. Five and change, but really, who's counting?

I bend her over my arm, tugging at her hair to expose her neck. I run my tongue up the length of it before returning to her mouth, losing myself in her kiss once again, content to dive in and drown there. She whimpers and sighs, clutching at me with her fingers, hooking one leg around my thigh. The world around us disappears.

Eventually, the need to breathe reasserts itself. I pull my

mouth away from hers and straighten up—but I continue to keep my hold on her.

Sighing, she lets her leg slide to the ground. Eyes still closed she murmurs, "What's in a name? That which we call a rose...would smell as sweet."

I huff out a laugh. "Your obsession with that play is starting to concern me."

"*That play*," she replies mockingly, as her eyes meet mine. "You can't even say its name, can you? Why? It's not Hamlet, you know."

"Hamlet?" I feel myself frown; even I know *that's* wrong. "No, that's not the play that people are superstitious—" I stop mid-sentence. "You know what? Never mind. We're getting sidetracked. All I'm saying is that Romeo and Juliet is *not* a love story." That's a hill to die on—or, preferably, to *not* die on.

"You don't think so? Tell that to the Swifties."

"It's a three-day relationship that results in six deaths."

"So? What's your point?"

"It doesn't end well—that's my point. Don't you think we should at least try and find something a little more hopeful to model our relationship on?"

She rolls her eyes. "Sure. Who says we can't? We can be the Romeo and Juliet from the Taylor Swift song, that doesn't end so badly, does it?"

"I don't know," I answer cautiously. "How does it end?"

"Really? You don't know that either? How's that possible?"

"Guess I've never been much of a fan," I tell her.

She leans in close again, smiling as she goes up on her toes —taking the initiative to kiss me this time—as she murmurs, "Well then, I'm clearly going to have to broaden your horizons. But for right now, listen up; it's simple. *Just say yes.*"

Chapter 10

Allegra

We're on each other instantly. From the moment we get inside his apartment, even as Clay is turning towards me, after locking his door, we're already reaching for one another. His mouth is hot and demanding on mine as he crowds me against the wall. I brace my hands on his shoulders, give a little hop, and climb him like a tree, wrapping my legs around his hips, angling my face, deepening our kiss. He slides his capable hands beneath me to help support my weight. But my dress is short and I'm nearly naked under it, so the result of this seemingly chivalrous gesture is that his hands are all over my ass, palms cradling my bare cheeks in a way that makes me shudder with heat.

I'd packed light when I left Europe to come home; and I didn't bring a lot of clothes—have I mentioned this? And this dress, while pretty, had seemed a little too summery when I'd first put it on. Not to mention a little too casual for a Saturday night, even in downtown Oak Creek. I'd second, third, and fourth guessed my decision while I was getting ready, nearly taking it off several times. But there weren't a lot of options. And right now? I'm so, so happy with my choice.

My attempts to grind against him draw a rough chuckle from Clay's throat. I'm already close to unraveling, and I'm pretty sure he knows it. His fingers slip beneath the edges of my thong to tease and caress me, coming tauntingly close to where I want to feel his touch, only *juuust* missing the mark. Which leaves me whimpering with need.

The taste of his mouth is a revelation. Memories from that night on the river—that I'd thought had been drowned by a case of wine and held under by the weight of years—come bobbing to the surface. The way he smelled and tasted, the sound of his voice, the heat of his skin, it's all coming back to me now. I was shocked tonight when he explained who he was, when I finally realized why he'd seemed so oddly familiar when we— quote/unquote—first met a week ago.

I still can't believe that I did not instantly recognize him when he pulled me over. And yes, I'm sure jet lag had something to do with it, but if he hadn't told me, would I ever have put two and two together? I can't be sure.

Learning that he hadn't immediately connected the dots, either, only makes things worse. Were it not for the serendipitous circumstance of my having an out-of-date picture on my license, we might have *never* figured things out! Which only fuels my sense of urgency. We came so close—too close!—to losing each other forever. I need him now!

I wrench my mouth away from his long enough to gasp, "Take me to bed. I want you naked." *I want you in me.* "Now!"

"Mmph," he mumbles, his response lost as I seal his mouth once more. I assume we're in agreement, however, since he immediately hefts me more fully into his arms, pivots away from the wall and lurches through his apartment until we reach his bedroom.

I'm breathing hard as I get my legs under me, and so is he. We disengage reluctantly, each of us taking a single step back, away from one another. An extremely shaky step, on my part. I'm lightheaded, probably from lack of oxygen, and so concerned that my knees are about to give out, that I quickly lower myself to the bed—and then watch transfixed as he quickly toes out of his shoes, peels off his shirt, and begins to undo his pants.

He's lean and sleekly muscled. His chest is lightly furred, his abdomen is bisected by a narrow strip of dark hair that runs from his sternum to his groin. There's so much yumminess there, that I can't stop myself from staring. Damn. My mouth is watering. My hands are itching. I want to lick him all over, touch him everywhere.

"What are you doing?" he asks, as his hands stall on the fly of his jeans.

Reluctantly, I raise my gaze to his face, only to find him eyeing me critically. "What?" I'm surprised into asking. Does he not like that I'm staring? He doesn't seem like the shy type. "I wasn't doing anything."

"Exactly."

"Huh?"

He gestures at me impatiently. "You, too: naked, now. Strip."

"Oh. Right." I can't keep from grinning as I hurry to comply, kicking off my own shoes, pulling my dress off over my head, unclasping my bra. I love that he's as eager as I am.

Or maybe even more eager. Because, before either of us have removed our underwear—black boxer briefs on his part, a lacy thong (as previously mentioned) on mine—he joins me on the bed. Rolling me into his arms, surrounding me with his heat. His lips find mine and we're kissing again, hands roving everywhere, skimming over each other's bodies, stoking the fires that—swear to God—feel like they've been smoldering for years.

I moan in appreciation when he pushes my thong aside and slides his finger over my pussy.

"You're so wet," he murmurs between kisses. "Do you always respond this quickly? Or is this just for me?"

"Do I...?" I blink in confusion. I can only assume he's talking about the night we met, but unfortunately, I can't remember all that much about it. "Why? Is that what you remember?"

"Mm-hm," he says as his thumb strokes over my clit, again and again. My legs open wider all on their own. He's not wrong. I'm desperate, needy, so hot for his touch that I can't keep from moaning. *There. Right there. More.*

"So?" he prompts. "What's the answer?"

I shake my head. "Stop asking questions that require me to think. Or at least save them until later. Right now, unless the answer is: yes, there, now, more, or harder—I don't know, and I really don't care."

A sexy grin spreads across Clay's face. His chuckle is deep and wicked. And his touch—deliberately missing the mark now, circling my clit with light, feathery touches that dance on the edge between frustrating and fun—reduces me to whimpers.

"So impatient," he murmurs teasingly. "I guess some things never change."

I glare at him through narrowed eyes. "Are you...criticizing me?"

"Oh, hell no," he assures me, turning serious for a moment. "Absolutely not. In fact, that's one of the things I always kinda loved about you."

Loved? That's a loaded word. And not one I feel like

dealing with, at the moment. I do my best to disarm it by asking, "D'you know what *I'd* love?"

Clay stills. Maybe he's hearing it too, now. His eyes are wary as his gaze meets mine. "No. What?"

"Less talk," I respond, as I buck my hips and wriggle against his hand. "More action."

"Fair enough," he replies with a nod, as his smile comes glimmering back. "I can do that." Then, pushing himself away from me, he moves down the bed. He slides my thong off, then clasps my thighs in those talented hands of his, spreading them wide. Then he lowers his face to my pussy and—holy mother of Merlot.

Obviously, this is not the first time I've had someone pay me lip service, but comparatively speaking...it might as well be. There's already no comparison. His mouth might already have ruined me for anyone else's. And he's just getting started!

"Clay!" his name emerges part squeal, part squawk as his lips latch onto my clit, sucking with just the right amount of pressure, immediately siphoning off part of my brain. His tongue lashes my sensitive flesh and quickly reduces me to a babbling mess, keening all the answers I'd previously listed as acceptable, "Yes, there, now, more, harder. *Pleeease!*"

At some point, although honestly, I couldn't say exactly when it happened, his fingers have joined in on the fun. They stroke inside me again and again, and it's so, so good.

My fingers are in his hair, digging into his scalp as I writhe beneath him. Eventually however, I'm distracted by my breasts.

What started out as a tingling sensation has now become a full-on throb. But Clay's busy elsewhere and I definitely want him to stay on task, so I take matters into my own hands, cupping and squeezing my girls, then tugging at my nipples. I twist and I pinch, increasing the pressure as the heat rises within me until I'm arching my back keening with need, drawing Clay's attention upward. His breath hitches. His fingers tighten on me. His eyes grow wide and then he groans—long, low, heartfelt. And that little bit—just the addition of his breath, vibrating against my skin, the bite of his nails into sensitive flesh, the naked desire I can hear in his voice, and see in his gaze—that's all it takes to send me tumbling over the edge. I cry out as I come, almost sobbing with pleasure,

Clay lingers for a moment, breathing me in, easing me through multiple aftershocks—which is nice and all, don't get me wrong—but I'm not ready yet for slow and gentle. What I really want right now is *more*. More heat, more passion, more everything. I want him sliding inside me, pounding my pussy, hard and fast and mindless. I want my name on his lips as my body squeezes and tightens around him. I want a long, hot, heart racing, hard breathing, mind bending fuck.

"Stop," I groan as I pull on his hair and tug at his shoulders, urging him upwards. "Come *here*."

But when he finally slides up beside me, I can tell that he has himself firmly in control. Instead of looking half-crazed like I want him, he's sporting a smug grin that, okay, yes, fine. He totally fucking deserves to be wearing that look. But does it have to be now? I'm not ready for this to be over. I want something to look smug about, too.

As he dips his head to kiss me, I hold him off. "Condom. Now. Hurry."

"Shh," he replies, still angling for a kiss. "It's okay. There's no rush."

I push him back again. Harder this time. Eyes narrowing as I ask, "Hold up. You *do* have protection, don't you?" Because Romeo, or not, if he thinks he can somehow manipulate me into going without a condom, he can damn well think again.

"It's not a problem. We're good," he says. Denied my mouth he alters course. His lips graze my neck, causing an all-body flush to sweep over me, heating my cheeks as memories from last time rise to the surface yet again. *We've been here before. I remember this part. Oh, God!*

But I can't let myself get distracted. "That's not an answer!"

"Chill," Clay says as he rolls onto his side. "Give me a little credit." He props himself up on an elbow and smiles down at me with a somewhat exasperated expression. "You really think I can't figure out for myself that I need a condom?"

"And yet. I'm hearing a lot of words, but none of them are yes."

"Yes, all right? I have plenty of condoms. Promise. I just… we don't need them yet, do we?"

"We do if we're gonna fuck," I point out.

Clay nods in agreement. "No cap. I just figured we could take our time, play around a little first. We have all night, don't we?"

"Ohhh, now I get it," I say. "You're an edger."

"I'm what?"

"Someone who likes to edge. That's when—"

"Jesus, I know what edging is," Clay says, rolling his eyes. "And let me guess; you're not a fan?"

"I didn't say that, exactly," I reply, although…fine; he's not altogether wrong. Orgasm denial has never been my go-to kink. Sure, it can be hot, every now and again. Tormenting each other over the course of endless hours, delaying satisfaction, channeling your frustration into the growing realization that's all leading (eventually) to one, huge, mind-blowing, mega-orgasm that'll leave you both wrung out and shattered.

But is that really so much better than using that same time to enjoy multiple orgasms? Jury's still out, as far as I'm concerned; but overall, I'm thinking not.

"You didn't have to say it," Clay tells me. "It's written all over your face. But that's not what this is about."

"No?" I eye him curiously. "Then what is it?"

"It's just..." He pauses and sighs. "Look, I'm a realist, you know? And hope is a liar. So, I try real hard to stay grounded, to focus on the things I can see and touch, and count on. If someone had asked me a month ago, whether I thought I'd ever see you again, I'd have said no, probably not. Because what were the odds? If we hadn't run into each other even once in five years? It seemed massively unlikely."

"To be fair, we were on two different continents. That lowered the odds a little bit."

"True, but I didn't know that was the case. The point is, I'd be totes lying if I said I'd never thought about the possibility. That I never hoped, or wondered, or dreamed about our paths crossing once again. But I really wasn't expecting it."

I nod, aware of the sting of tears in my eyes, the shakiness of the smile that trembles on my lips. "Same."

"Yeah, but like I said, even knowing how unlikely it was to ever happen, I still had a really clear idea in my head about how I wanted it to go, what I wanted to do if we were ever to hook up again."

"And?"

"And now, tonight, this first time that I finally get to make love to you, I want to do things right. I want to be buried deep inside you when I come. And I want to feel you climaxing around me when it happens."

"Not seeing a problem," I say, my voice faint, breathless, my pussy clenching at the thought. "I'm totally on board with that scenario."

Clay flashes me a grin. "Good to know. Except, right now... I'm so damn hot for you, I don't think I'd even last five minutes.

And I don't imagine you're ready to come again that quickly, are you?"

"Probably not," I admit. "But why does it have to be all or nothing? Why can't we—"

"Nothing?" he repeats in mocking tones as he slides a hand between my legs, fingers brushing lightly over my sensitive clit. "Really? That's all this was to you?"

"Stop it." I push his hand away. "Not for *me*, I'm talking about *you*."

"Oh, trust me," he says, raising his hand to his mouth, licking between his fingers and sucking loudly. "It wasn't 'nothing' for me, either. That's something else I've been dreaming for years; how you'd taste, how it would feel to have you come on my tongue, what you'd sound like, how you'd look..."

"Oh." His words are making me so hot I have to bite my lip to keep from whimpering, to keep from begging him to do it again. I clear my throat and try again. "It um... It sorta sounds like I was the subject of a lot of fantasies?"

Clay laughs at that, a short, surprised bark. Then he rolls to his back and stares at the ceiling. "You have *no* idea. On the other hand, *everything* about you was a fantasy, anyway—from start to finish." He eyes me somewhat ruefully. "I'm pretty sure that's still the case."

"You think?" I roll onto my side, splay a hand across his chest, loving the way his chest hair tickles my palm. "'Cause I'm pretty sure I'm as real as you are. Just a girl, standing in front of a boy..." I let me voice trail off, since the rest of the quote would put us in dangerous territory. "Etc, etc."

"Oh, sure. Just a girl. Ordinary as fuck, right?"

"I didn't say *that*."

"Just a sexy, rich, untouchable girl, who lives in a castle on top of a hill, and who just so happened to be standing in front of the fancy sports car she bought on a whim. Totally normal. I run into women like that every day."

"What hill?" I demand, ignoring the whim part—I put a lot of thought into that purchase. "Napa's a valley, in case you forgot. The clue's right there in the name."

Clay shakes his head. "I was speaking metaphorically. But there are hills here, too, you know. Like the ones on the way to Lake Berryessa? I used to live out that way. But, I guess maybe you've never been there."

"Of course, I have," I protest. "What're you thinking? You're making me sound like some kind of snob."

"You don't think you're a snob?" he asks, smiling gently—although not enough to completely remove the sting of his words. "I know the world you come from, remember? I've seen your family's wineries. All those big, bougie houses, surrounded by acres of guap. That is where you lived, right? When you were a kid?"

"Sure, some of the time. But..."

"Did you know that, from the hills, you can look out over the whole valley? Sometimes, at night, you'd throw parties, and those houses would blaze with lights, like something out of a fairy tale."

"That was my family—not me. I only ever threw *one* party. And that was the one *you* came to. So...maybe you weren't missing out on as much as you thought."

"Yeah, there was no missing you that night. The enchanted princess, dancing in the moonlight, coming apart in my arms. You were like something out of a fairytale, too, come to think of it. A total fantasy. And then, just like in Cinderella, you disappeared. Only I didn't even have a glass shoe that I could use to track you down."

"Cinderella," I scoff. "Please. That was never our story.

And anyway, why would you have needed a shoe? You knew exactly where I lived. You walked me home, as I recall."

Clay shakes his head. "I guess there really were two of us in that delusionship. That's comforting, in a way."

"Meaning what, exactly?"

"Meaning, if you believed that, you were putting way too much faith in the navigational capabilities of my lust-soaked, half-baked, seventeen-year-old brain. I had *no idea* where I was that night."

"*Seventeen?*"

"I'm not saying I could have *never* found my way back there. But the odds were not in my favor. Given how fried I was, it was a miracle I found my own way home."

"What are you talking about?" I frown, as I sift through my memories, trying to recall the moment; everything we'd said, or done. "Did you not have a ride home? I thought you were eighteen?"

"No, you didn't."

"I'm sorry...what?"

"Neither of us were thinking about anyone's ages back then. Why would we? We were kids. It wasn't an issue."

"I wasn't a kid. I was eighteen."

"Barely," he replies dismissively. I'm startled until I remember that, of course, he's seen my license. Of course, he knows more about me than I do about him.

"Besides," he continues, "my birthday's in August, so what're we even talking about? Two months? That's close enough for that to make no difference either."

"Says the cop."

"Deputy," he corrects teasingly.

"An L.E.O. by any other name," I shoot back at him, widening my eyes, daring him to disagree. "Besides, I thought you were a 'by the book' kind of guy?"

Clay rolls his eyes. "Not always. I try to be. But...well, here we are. So, I'm obviously willing to bend a few pages where you're concerned."

"Hmm. Lucky me," I purr as I stroke down his chest and belly, feathering the lightest of touches across the bulge in his briefs. Full disclosure? I don't entirely hate the idea that he wants me this much, after all this time, and despite all his reservations. Who doesn't want to be irresistible?

"Yeah?" he asks, as he studies my expression. "How lucky? Because you still haven't said—are you spending the night, or do you need to get back?"

"Oh, I'm definitely staying," I promise, bending over him to kiss his lips. "You're not the only one with fantasies to explore, you know. In fact, I think we're going to need more than one night to address even a fraction of them."

"Hell, yeah," he says as he pulls me close, wrapping an arm around me, trapping me against him. "I'm counting on it."

Birds chirp loudly outside the window the next morning, but it's not that that pulls me from sleep. It's the traffic noises filtering in—louder, closer, more constant than usual. I blink my eyes open and find myself alone in an unfamiliar bed, in an unfamiliar bedroom. It takes a moment for my brain to wake up and my memories to unwind. I stretch and twist in the sheets cataloging all the little aches and twinges I'm feeling, smiling as I remember how I acquired them. *Rawr.*

Somewhere close at hand someone is making coffee. It smells delicious, although not quite as delicious as the sheets which smell of sex and Clay.

I do love solving mysteries and connecting dots—as much as I love the spontaneous appearance of anything serendipitous in my life. And last night gave me all those things in spades. I'm thankful now that I never gave beer boy a name in any of the fantasies I've concocted about him over the years. Because I don't think Clay was one that would ever have occurred to me, and that might have led to confusion now. I start to laugh as I remember our conversation, but then the other shoe drops.

He lied to me. He let me believe that the reason he reacted so poorly to being called Romeo was merely due to his dislike of alliteration. He even let me apologize—twice!—for my mistake, all the while withholding the truth about our shared past. It was only after I'd changed the rules of engagement, when I'd gotten the upper hand by walking away, that he'd deigned to tell me the truth. Which is not sitting well with me this morning.

The problem is that I have a type. I tend to be attracted to the kind of man who'll do and say *anything* in order to get what they want—me in their bed, their ring on my finger, etc. And while I know it's not fair to judge Clay based on how men like Nico have behaved, the truth is, I never expect any of them to act like bastards until they do.

And yes, I'm probably overreacting. I'm easily triggered by lies and manipulation. But you know what they say—just because you're paranoid, that doesn't mean there's no one out to get you.

I'm pondering all of this—and trying to decide whether to get up, get dressed, get out of here while I can—when the bedroom door opens, and Clay appears. He's dressed in a pair of black boxer briefs similar to the ones he was wearing last night—and nothing else. His hair is tousled, he hasn't shaved and, all things considered, he's even more mouthwateringly yummy looking than he was last night. He's also bearing two steaming mugs—which ups his attractiveness level by several points.

I sniff the air hopefully. "Coffee?"

"Mm-hm," he says, smiling as he hands me one then sits beside me. "Good morning. How'd you sleep?"

"What sleep?" I demand mockingly. "As I recall, you kept me up most of the night."

"Guilty as charged," he responds as his smile shifts into something wicked. "But, as I recall, you weren't complaining."

"No cap," I say, as I sip my coffee. It tastes as good as it smells, and he's made it light and sweet, exactly the way I like it —further triggering my earlier suspicions. "Hey. How'd you know how I take my coffee?"

Clay's eyebrows rise. "You ordered some at dinner last night. I watched you fix it."

"And you remembered?"

"It *was* only last night. If I'd remembered from five years ago, that would be something. But a span of only several hours? That's well within my capabilities."

"Still. You must be very observant."

Clay shrugs. "I suppose. It kinda goes with the job, you know?" He eyes me curiously for a moment then asks, "Is everything all right?"

"Yes, of course," I answer immediately. Then I sigh and shake my head. "I don't know. Probably not."

"Okay. Wanna tell me what's going on?"

"Great question. I don't know. What are we doing here?"

"Well, I was thinking breakfast, but then I realized I probably need to shop. I can offer you eggs, or avocado toast, but that's about it."

"No, I mean *us*," I tell him. "Is this it? Are we 'one and done'?"

His face goes blank—that kind of non-expression that's like a closed door. "Is that what you want?"

"Why are you asking me? *I'm* not the one who was making excuses last night for why we shouldn't be together. Are you saying something's changed since then? That maybe your excuses no longer apply?"

"Yes and no," he admits with a sigh. He takes a big gulp of coffee—which he drinks black, by the way—like my mood this morning. "First of all, they weren't excuses, they were reasons. Valid reasons. And of course, they still apply. That part hasn't changed."

"So, that's it then. We scratched the itch, found closure from five years ago, and now you're calling it quits?"

"Can I finish?" His eyes are troubled as his gaze bores into mine. "Because no. That's not what I'm saying at all."

"What then?"

"Obviously, *some* other things have changed. What we did last night...well, that's a bell we can't un-ring, isn't it? Not that I'd want to, even if we could."

"Me either. But..."

"I'm not willing to go back to pretending that there's nothing between us, or that I don't want you. I don't think that was working very well, anyway."

My head is reeling. My hands are shaking so hard I have to use both of them to hold my mug. "Really? You seemed to be doing okay with it."

"Yeah, no. I really wasn't."

"So then where does that—"

"I don't want to wait until our situation changes, or until I'm no longer investigating you and your family. Who knows how long that might take?"

"Hopefully not too much longer," I say. "I thought things

had gotten better?" I know Bianca talked to Geno. If it really was him behind all the sabotage, surely, he's backed off by now.

"I don't know. And I don't care."

"You don't care?" I repeat in surprise. "Since when? I mean, who even *are* you?"

"At this point? I have no idea," Clay murmurs. His eyes are hooded. His gaze is locked on my mouth as he gently frames my face with his free hand, and drags his thumb, back and forth, across my bottom lip. "But as long as you're all right with keeping things on the DL until we can be together without ruining both our lives and outraging everyone we know, then I'm all in. Screw the consequences. You're not the only one who can make bad decisions."

I let my tongue flick out to tease his thumb. "Well, just for the record, you're definitely the best bad decision *I've* ever made."

"Same," Clay says as he presses a too-chaste kiss to my lips, distracting me just long enough to pluck the mug from my unresisting hands.

"Hey, wait," I protest, as he gets to his feet and swiftly makes room for both mugs on the night table. "I wasn't finished with that."

"I'll make you a fresh cup," he promises, stripping out of his briefs. His eyes are gleaming with heat and intent. "Later."

"How much later?" I tease, falling back onto the pillows, welcoming him into my arms as he slips between the sheets and covers my body with his own. "Because I thought we were going to have breakfast? Didn't you say something about eggs and toast?"

"I did. But breakfast is just gonna have to wait. It's important to follow the proper procedures, you know, when dealing with emergency situations. There's a whole hierarchy of priorities to take into account, protocols and standards that need to be rigorously adhered to."

"This all sounds very official, officer, but aren't you supposed to state the nature of your emergency?"

"Nope. You already did that."

"I...what?"

"You're the one who brought up the topic of itches that might need scratched. Aren't you still feeling itchy?"

"Oh, I am," I murmur between kisses. "Very much so. But what about you?"

"Like I just broke out in a full-body rash."

Chapter 11

Allegra

It's late afternoon when I finally return home. I follow the murmur of voices to the living room, expecting to see Rosa and Jake. Instead, I find Bianca and Jansen cuddled together on the couch, looking very cute and coupley. Jansen's dog quickly uncurls himself from beside them, and comes prancing up to greet me.

"Oops. Sorry," I say, coming to an abrupt halt just inside the room. "I didn't know you all were in here."

"Oh, hey. You're back!" Bianca turns to smile at me. "We're watching movies. Come join us." Then her eyes widen. Her gaze flickers over me and she asks. "Is that...my jacket you're wearing?"

Uh-oh. I tug the collar closer to my neck, to hide the hickeys I'm not ready to explain. "It, uh... I dunno. M-maybe?" I stammer a little, feeling sheepish and defensive. "It was cold last night, and this was in the closet."

"Legs..."

"But hey, at least I didn't lose it, right? Or spill anything on it?" I crouch down to pet the dog, wishing I'd had the sense to ditch the jacket as soon as I came in. But then again, I needed something to hide the marks on my neck. "I'm going clothes shopping this week, so it won't happen again."

"It's fine," my sister replies quickly—although it sure doesn't seem like that's the case, now does it? Otherwise, why are we still talking about it? "Just, you know, maybe ask before-hand, okay?"

"I said I wasn't going to do it again," I reply, straightening up. "Besides, you weren't here to ask, were you?" Of course she wasn't. My sisters went off to play with their friends, leaving me behind. Just. Like. Always.

Bee's mouth falls open, but before she can recover enough to point out that I'm acting like a brat—I know I am, all right? Being back here has me falling into all the old, familiar patterns, childhood habits that I can't seem to break—I hurry into speech. "How'd the wedding go, anyway?" I ask, in hopes of changing the subject.

Before Bee can answer, Rosa emerges from the kitchen. She's carrying two large bowls piled with popcorn—one sweet, one savory, if I had to make a guess—and is followed closely by Jake who's toting two six-packs of beer.

"Okay, popcorn's ready, pizzas are ordered—"

"Beer's cold," Jake interjects, holding them aloft.

"So, let's do this," Rosa finishes, just moments before she catches sight of me. "Oh, Allegra. You're here." Her gaze runs over me, in much the same way as Bianca's did. But if she recognizes the jacket, she doesn't mention it. She does heave a relieved sigh, however. "I was starting to worry. Where've you been?"

I bite back the snarky reply— 'sorry, Mom. Didn't realize I needed to check in with you'—as it tries to slip out. Because, even at my brattiest, that's *not* the kind of thing I can say to either of my sisters. I mean, yes, it's ridiculous for Rosa to worry about me, a grown woman, now that I'm home. Especially since, during most of the last five years, she rarely even knew what *country* I was in. But all the same, it's too low a blow. That kind of line really hits different when your mother flat-out abandoned you. "There was nothing for you to worry about. I went out to dinner, ran into an old friend," I say instead. "We ended up back at his place. Then it got late and..." *Oh, shit. What the fuck am I doing?*

Damn my sleep deficient brain, that is *not* a door I want to open right now. "So, what movie are you watching?" I ask—deflecting yet again.

"I believe it's called Bottle Jock," Jansen says, drawing a muffled laugh from Bianca.

"You mean...Bottle *Shock?*" I correct—and okay, yes. I admit it. This time I let a little *too much* of my frustrated snarkiness bleed into my tone. But he's not my sister, not a client, practically a stranger, so that makes him fair game.

Judging by Bianca's frown, she disagrees. "He knows that," she tells me, giving Jansen's thigh a quick, reassuring pat. "He was just being funny. It was a joke."

"Well, how was I supposed to know?" I answer. Grasping for a witty response, I find only, "I thought maybe you guys were watching porn. That sounds like it could be a porn film, doesn't it?"

Jansen barks with laughter. He nudges Bianca and says, "You know, I'm starting to think you were right. Maybe I shoulda gone with that for the winery."

Bianca's cheeks are fiery red. "No, no. I think you made the right choice," she says in stifled tones.

"Why don't we all sit down?" Rosa suggests, shooting me a look that I can't interpret as she slips past me to deposit the bowls on the coffee table, where stacks of napkins, plates, and smaller bowls have already been assembled.

"Beer?" Jake asks, extending one of the six-packs in my direction.

"Thanks," I say as I take one, more or less automatically. I study the label for a moment, then glance around at the others. "Hey, how come nobody's drinking wine?"

Jake pauses in the act of handing out beers and arches a brow. "With popcorn?" He snags two bottles—for himself and Rosa, I assume—then stretches out on one of the oversized lounge chairs that bracket the couch. "What would you even pair with that?"

All eyes turn to Bianca. She twists open her beer and takes a swig. "It depends. What flavor of popcorn are we talking about?"

"Well, today we've got spicy ranch and lavender honey," Rosa tells her, as she hands individual bowls to her and Jansen.

"Ooh, that sounds yummy." Bianca scoots forward to fill her bowl. "Riesling? Or maybe Prosecco?"

"Do we make either of those?" Jansen asks. He glances around the room and adds, "I mean any of us here—in the valley?"

Bianca shakes her head. "Not so much anymore. It used to be pretty popular, but now I think there's less than one-hundred acres planted in Riesling grapes. And that's in all of Napa."

From what I remember from my wine-making lessons of a decade ago, there are reasons for that. The first one being that Riesling grapes are difficult to grow here due to the weather. Something about them needing a longer, cooler growing season than most of the valley can provide? Then there's the issue of the Botrytis cinerea fungus—useful when making sweeter wines like Riesling and Sauterne, deadly if it were to spread to other crops that the state's economy depends upon, such as strawberries. But I'm not sure enough about my facts to show off. Not in front of my sisters. Or even Jake. All of whom have degrees in this sort of stuff. So, I keep silent and let the subject drop.

"Legs, c'mon," Rosa urges, startling me out of my musing. "Pick a seat already. Let's get started."

As I suspected she'd do, Rosa has snuggled up with Jake on the lounge chair, leaving the other chair—isolated on the far side of the room—or the empty space on the couch for me to choose between. Not liking either of those options, I opt to sit on the floor in front of the couch where I can be insulated from all the happy coupledom and still have easy access to the popcorn. I'm shocked when the dog curls up beside me.

"That's Moose, by the way," Bee tells me.

I hide my surprise, because Moose, a mostly Jack Russell with a missing ear, appears to be the least moose-like dog imaginable. *Ohh-kay then.*

"You know, we do *have* wine," Jake says, gesturing at my still unopened bottle. "If you really don't want that beer." Then he turns to Rosa and says, "In fact, why don't you let her try the Carleo. Maybe she can figure out what's wrong with it."

I feel myself frowning. The Carleo was hugely popular, back in the day. It was even rumored that rival vintners—throughout the California wine growing regions—had celebrated for days after Geno announced his decision to stop entering Belmonte's flagship wine in any more contests. He'd been winning with tiresome regularity, and I had it on good authority that it was the organizers of said contests who'd begged him to do so, in an effort to keep submissions from other wineries from dropping away to nothing.

"What's wrong with the Carleo?" I ask now.

"That's what we'd like to know," Bianca says, tossing a piece of popcorn in the air and catching it in her mouth. "It's not what I was expecting, that's for sure."

"Same," Rosa agrees.

"What they mean is that it's not very good," Jake clarifies.

Well, I don't know how *that's* possible. "How'd you even get some—I thought it was a Wine Club exclusive, at this point?"

Rosa shrugs. "The cousins. We had them over for dinner several weeks ago. Just after Bianca got back. They brought several bottles with them."

"That was so fun," Bianca enthuses. "We should definitely do that again. Especially now that Legs is back. You haven't seen them yet, have you?"

"That's a good idea." Rosa nods in agreement. "Let's schedule something."

"I want to hear more about the wine," I say, quickly changing the subject. "Was it corked or something?"

"No, nothing like that," Bianca says. "I'm not saying it's bad, mind you; it was just not great. And yes, it could have been a bad vintage, or just an issue with these particular bottles, but it certainly didn't live up to the hype."

"But, please, whatever you do," Rosa cautions. "Don't tell Vitto we said anything. He's their head winemaker now and... well, you know. I'm sure he tries his best, but..."

"But he's clearly not as talented as your sister," Jake finishes, nodding towards Bianca.

"Hear, hear!" Jansen says, raising his bottle in a toast. Bianca blushes as the others join in. I lift my bottle, remember belatedly that it's still not open, rush to untwist the cap, and end up spilling half the contents on the floor, and over the dog, who beats a quick retreat to the couch.

But hey, at least I manage not to get any beer on Bianca's jacket, so I count that as a win.

While I'm cleaning up the mess, my thoughts circle back to the previous topic. And I find myself saying, "You know I'd *never* repeat anything you said about him to Vitto. Especially now that you asked me not to, but if you have complaints, I bet he'd be glad to hear them. Judging by what he told me, about how Geno keeps hamstringing him, not letting him make wine the way he wants to, etc. I don't know if that counts for much. If he could convince his father that the Belmonte brand is in trouble, he could maybe force Geno into at least letting him *try* to do his own thing."

"Have you actually met our uncle?" Bianca asks skeptically. "He does not react well to criticism. Plus, if it gets back to him that people are trash talking his wine, it'll likely incentivize him. He'll be more determined than ever to get his hands on our grapes."

"I thought he'd given up on that idea?" I ask, feeling low-key dismayed. "Didn't you tell me you talked to him?" Could it be Clay was right, and I was wrong about how long we'll have to keep sneaking around?

Bianca shrugs. "I talked. And maybe he heard me. But whether he'll actually take it to heart is anyone's guess."

"But..."

"Okay, wait. I'm confused," Rosa says, looking puzzled. "When did you talk to Vitto?"

I can't help myself; I freeze for an instant. I stare at my sister like a glazed zombie, while my brain takes its sweet time coming back online. This is why I hate lying. Making up stories on the fly is hard work! The details always trip me up. But this is something even more ironic. I'm actually telling the truth, but I'm still screwing things up!

"Last night," I finally admit. "I went to the Golden Cougar and ran into the Lambros. Apparently, they'd ordered *all* the Napatizers. I figured it was my duty to stay and help them out."

"What did you say?" Rosa squeaks in surprise, as Jake chokes on his drink and Bianca slaps a hand to her mouth—to keep from spewing beer all over the place, I imagine. Only Jansen seems composed, lips quirking into a smile as he waits for me to explain.

"I said I didn't want them ending up in a food coma—why?"

"No. Not that. What did you call them?"

"Napatizers? I'm talking about your standard-issue Napa Valley appetizers. What d'you want me to call them? They were bussin' by the way. Have you been?"

Bianca nods. "Yes. I love the food there."

"Not that either," Rosa says. "Was I hearing things, or did you just refer to our cousins as The Lambros?"

"Yeah? I mean, technically it's short for Lamberti brothers, but tell me they wouldn't totally be driving expensive, Italian sports cars—all day, every day—if Geno wasn't so tightfisted." I shrug and add, "At least, that was my impression five years ago. Have they changed?"

"I don't know," Rosa admits. "But I do know that they stepped up to help us several times over the summer."

"That's true." Bianca nods in agreement. "They did. I don't know what we'd have done without them."

"Well, cool," I say as I shrug and look away, busying myself with the spilled beer again, even though there really isn't anything left to clean. I'm not sure if the unspoken subtext I'm hearing—"*they* were here to help us, but *you* weren't"—is real, or just the product of my own guilty conscience. "Glad to hear it. And I actually had a good time chatting with them last night. You know, a nickname is not *necessarily* a bad thing."

"Can confirm," Jansen agrees, unexpectedly. "That's just what I told Razor."

"Who?" I turn to ask him—just in time to see Bianca roll her eyes in fond amusement.

"He means Miles," she explains. "Jansen gives everyone nicknames. Apparently, it's a hockey thing."

I nod absently, searching for the right tone—amused, casual, disinterested—before adding, "So, speaking of nicknames, or names in general, Gianni happened to notice that Deputy Romero was there, so he dared me to go over and talk to him. And you know me and dares." I roll my eyes, as though I'm amused by my own foibles. "But hey, at least I finally learned what his real name is, so there's that."

"Oh, we did, too!" Bianca says. "I knew there was something I meant to tell you. He was at the wedding. Turns out his name is Clay. But Miles says no one ever calls him that."

"I know," I say as I help myself to more popcorn—quickly stuffing my mouth so more words won't fall out. The story Clay told me about how he and his siblings came by their names and why is so cute! I want to share it with my sisters, but I know I can't.

Rosa is still looking concerned. "So then...who's this mysterious friend you spent the night with," she asks.

"There's no mystery," I reply, twisting the truth just the tiniest bit. "I just reconnected with someone I used to know. *After* I left the restaurant," I add, in case word of this gets back to the cousins, and they start to get ideas. "But come on, you don't want to hear about that now, do you? I thought we were gonna watch this movie?"

Lucky for me, the others agree. And—even luckier—the film had already been queued up. So, within less than a minute, the danger has passed and we're all happily watching Chris Pine in his most relatable (at least from my perspective) role *ever* as the cute but underachieving, cellar-rat-slash-party-boy who ultimately makes something of himself. And maybe, sort of, kinda gets the girl at the end? Hard to say.

It's been a few years since I've seen it, and parts of it are hitting different now. Possibly because I've just been with Clay, who reminds me a lot more of Gustavo than he does Bo.

They're both serious, passionate, impulsive (hello, antenna scene). They've both had to work hard for every achievement. They never had anything handed to them— unlike Bo. Senor Garcia was right about that. Or like me, if I'm honest.

And that cabin scene with Gustavo and Sam? Whew. It's only been a couple of hours since I left Clay's apartment, but that scene has me wanting to break out my phone and start sexting. I don't, of course, because I'm not alone, and that would be weird. But I really want to, all the same.

My sisters keep up a running commentary (that I occasionally contribute to) as we watch the film. And it feels so right, so familiar, so much like old times. I can't stop wondering if Clay has seen it (apparently Jansen had not) and what *he'd* think of it, how *he'd* react. Which ultimately leads to me feeling cranky again, and out of sorts—even after several slices of Divino's pizza—because I can't even imagine what it would be like if he were here, hanging with my sisters and their misters. I mean, it works well enough on paper—they're all friends (or friendly) with Miles, after all. But in real life? I just can't see it. And that makes me sad.

And actually, now that I think of it, the pizza, while delicious, is *also* part of the problem. Everyone's s been great about sharing with me, but I wasn't here when they placed the order, and it shows. Not that I have any real issue with sausage, pepper, and sun-dried tomato pizza. Or with barbecue chicken, bacon, and black olives, either. They're both solid choices. But it's been *years* since I had my absolute favorite toppings, the controversial, much maligned, ham and pineapple. Which is only the best combination ever.

But let me tell you, if you think people on this side of the pond look down on Hawaiian pizza, try ordering one in Europe!

All of which leads me to wonder what kind of pizza Clay would order. For the record, I'm betting on pulled pork and jalapeno with Cotija cheese. Which in turn leads to me missing him, ridiculous as that may be after just one night. But fate is weird like that. Look at Rosa and Jake. They just spent *ten years* apart and yet; to look at them now, you'd never know it.

By the time the movie is over, I'm done. I'm tired of feeling envious, lonely and, seriously out-of-sorts. I'm also just plain tired from lack of sleep. I'm too horny to go to bed alone, even though that's the only option available tonight. I'm also stuffed full of pizza and popcorn, slightly buzzed from one, I mean two...no, make that *three* beers! All of which puts me in serious danger of saying too much, and all the wrong things, if my feet don't hit the stairs rightthefuck now

"Well, I'm out," I announce as I climb to my feet. I pause for a moment, swaying slightly as I adjust to the change in altitude, vaguely aware that my sisters are gazing at me in concern. And frowning.

"What? No! Where are you going?" Bianca asks. "We're about to watch A Walk in the Clouds—your favorite!"

Oh, hell. That *is* my favorite. But I can't right now. This is a movie about a woman returning to her childhood home in Napa. A woman with a secret love life that she's hiding from her overbearing family. I'm already living that particular dream. Less the unwed pregnancy, obvs. "I'm tired," I tell Bianca. "This has been great, but I gotta go to bed."

"But it's peak Keanu," Rosa says—as if I didn't know that! Even though the age gap makes it a little embarrassing to talk about now, my pre-teen-self fangirled *hard* over Neo. "You don't want to miss *that* do you?"

"Seriously," I say—then immediately have to pause for a

jaw-cracking yawn—a real one, but it helps to sell the story. "I can't tonight. But you know what's great about movies? He'll be just as beautiful next time we watch it. And I'll be better able to appreciate it then."

I cross the room to a chorus of people wishing me a good night—in between yawns of their own. Sorry, not sorry. I pause in the doorway to smile at them all. "This was fun," I say. "We should do it again. Soon."

"We should," Rosa agrees. "We can do it next weekend, if you want. And maybe we'll invite the cousins, too."

"The Lambros," I say, just to pull her chain. "Learn it. Use it."

She rolls her eyes and grins in response, shooing me away with a flap of her hand. "Go to bed. You're delirious."

"I know you are, but what am I?" I tease. As I hit the stairs, I'm hugging happiness and contentment to my chest like a soft and squishy, heart-shaped pillow, metaphorically speaking, of course. For the first time in years, I feel like I have a family that loves me and a home where I belong. It's a nice feeling. Add to that this thing with Clay—whatever it is—and life just can't get much better.

Enjoy it while you can, my inner cynic advises. *Nothing this good could last for long.* Like I don't know that. All it would take to have my entire world come crashing down is to have one or more of my secrets come to light.

What happens after that is anyone's guess.

Chapter 12

Clay

T he next week starts off great. Which should probably worry me more than it does because, in theory, starting a relationship with Legs, at this point, is a terrible idea. I'd be lying if I said otherwise. But in practice...I just can't wait to see her again.

I feel more like myself when I'm with her than I have for a very long time. I suppose, in part, that's because she knew the me from before the fires. That Clay Romero doesn't really exist anymore.

And yes, there are others who knew me then and now, but most of them have been changed as well. We've all been touched by fire, by tragedy. We've all let our old selves fall away, and when we interact now, it's with the new, scarred versions of ourselves.

Legs missed out on all that chaos, making her a pure conduit to that earlier, happier, more innocent time. Or so it seems. In all likelihood, that's nothing more than a massive rationalization, on my part, and unfair to her. Am I really suggesting that she's a case of arrested development? That the rest of us have grown and matured, while she has not? I think I am.

Because it's true, isn't it? Money and circumstances have shielded her from a lot of the troubles the rest of us have suffered through.

I think one of the reasons we coddle the rich—beyond the fear of retribution—is because they possess something most of us have lost and dream about someday regaining. A childlike (largely unwarranted) belief that life is good and fair, that people are kind, that things are always working out for them. We're drawn to protect that innocence—in part because we know how bleak the world can be without it. In part because they've even fucking colonized our brains to the point where we think they'd do the same for us.

It's the same instinct that causes us to respond so strongly to babies and puppies and who knows what else. And to prioritize their needs, sometimes even above our own. Unless we're total dicks or hardcore leftists or someone who's been driven to such an extreme that the slogan, "eat the rich" has begun to make sense.

But these are the kinds of philosophical thoughts anyone might have on a gloomy, rainy Tuesday night, after a long day at work, and a challenging workout afterwards. I stare into the depths of my well-stocked refrigerator, and it might as well be empty. I try to eat clean and green, for the most part—so that I can stay in shape and do my job. But nothing in the stack of healthy, high-protein, pre-packaged, prepared meals is appealing to me right now.

There's nothing in here that will fill the emptiness I'm feeling now, or assuage the need that has hollowed me out, because it's not food that I'm craving.

My thoughts keep drifting back to Saturday night, to the meal I shared with Legs, the camaraderie and conversation.

And, yeah, the sex afterwards, too. Because, of course, I'm thinking of that; I can't get it out of my head.

I want to call her. I want to hear her voice, to see her face, to invite her over and fuck her senseless; but it's too soon for that. I have to resist. I can't become that needy, that fast. Nothing good will come of being that dependent on someone else.

The first storm of the season is battering against my windows, shaking the cheap glass so hard it rattles. The beat of the rain is so loud and insistent that I almost miss the knocking at my front door.

"Jesus Christ," I say when I pull it open and find Legs hunched on the front stoop with the collar of her jacket pulled up so that it's partially covering her head. I glance at the street as I take her by the arm and pull her into my house. "I don't see your car. Where'd you park? You couldn't possibly have gotten this wet between here and the curb?"

She shakes her head, ineffectively swiping at her face, with wet hands. "I parked around the block. I was trying to be subtle."

"Trying to die of hypothermia, is more like it," I scold, using the sleeve of my shirt to wipe her face. A useless task, given that her hair is soaked, and water runs in rivulets down her face. "Fucks sake. You look like a drowned rat right now. In fact, I'm pretty sure I've seen some that were drier."

"Thanks?" she says, still blinking water out of her eyes as I help her remove her jacket. "I was going to say, 'you look nice, too' but maybe I won't now."

I stop fussing long enough to grin at her. "If it helps, I meant a very pretty rat." Then I lean in and kiss her. She tastes of rain and wild nights, of coming home to a place of comfort and warmth, but all too soon she's pulling away. Which, now

I'm thinking of it, is exactly like coming home—elusive and fleeting and gone before you know it.

"I'm getting you so wet," she murmurs, plucking at my shirt —which is now plastered to my chest and arms in all the places where our bodies touched.

"Mm. I'm pretty sure that's supposed to be my line," I say, as I dip my head for another kiss.

"Oh, yeah? That sounds promising."

"C'mon," I say as I take hold of her hand. "We need to get you out of those wet clothes."

"Ooh. V-very promising," she replies, stuttering slightly as she starts to shiver.

"Out of your clothes and into a hot shower," I elaborate, as I tug her into my bathroom.

"You know, there are other ways of warming a person up," she points out as she starts to peel off her wet garments.

I turn on the shower and grab a few towels—the thick, bougie ones my last girlfriend left behind—in an effort not to get caught up in staring. "I know that. Which is why, after I toss your wet clothes in the laundry, I'm going to come back here and try some of those, too."

"Even better." She thrusts the sodden pile of clothes my way. "Here. Have at it." Then she steps into my shower, but not before tossing a grin at me over her shoulder. "Just don't keep me waiting too long, okay?"

I make quick work of the laundry, stripping out of my own clothes and adding them as well. Then I join her in the shower, crowding against her from behind. She leans back against me, her eyes closed, the open shampoo bottle held close beneath her nose, squeezing it repeatedly to release more fragrance.

"You know you can't get high from huffing soap—right?" I tease, pulling her close, murmuring into her ear.

"Mm, this smells so good," she replies, as she leans against me. "Like you."

Technically it smells like my ex—Lori. Who, as you may have gathered, has more money and better taste than I do. When she agreed to move in with me, it was with the clear expectation that I'd up my game and accept the long list of subscription services that she considered indispensable—one for hair and skin care products, one for prepackaged dinners, another for cleaning supplies. After she left, I kept most of them in place. Some might say out of laziness.

I'm someone who values stability, order and quality but I don't always know how to achieve it on my own. My mom would no doubt ascribe that to my Virgo nature, and claim it was inevitable. I think it stems from the chaos and uncertainty that marked most of my childhood—but what do I know?

Water rains down on us, courtesy of the waterfall shower (again, courtesy of Lori). An additional expense that I'd initially argued against, it's the one luxury I have yet to regret. After separating Legs from her new squeeze toy, I take hold of her wrists and position her arms so that her hands are now pressed against the shower wall. I collect her hair at the nape of her neck, and bend to kiss her there. Meanwhile my other hand coasts down the length of her spine. Pushing gently against her back, I urge her forward—so that her back arches, her hips cant and her arms are now stretched overhead. Then I nudge her legs apart. It's a standard-size tub, so the spread is not very wide, but it's enough.

The curve of her back is still tempting me. Uncapping the bottle of body wash (same scent as the shampoo she was sniffing) I pour the thick soap down the length of her back, following the line of her spine. When I get to her butt, I use my free hand to spread her cheeks, drizzling some more soap over her crack.

"Tickles," she whimpers, wriggling in place. So, I slide my hand into her hair again, grab a fistful and pull.

Leaning over her back, I whisper in her ear. "Stay still!"

"Unnnh," she moans. "I didn't know we'd be playing Dirty Cop tonight."

I hadn't either. "Are you okay with this?" I ask, feeling a tinge of unease. I know the power dynamic can freak people out sometimes, especially when it's a little too close to reality.

"Yes." The word emerges as a frustrated whine. "Just doooo it. Please."

I'm chuckling as I straighten up and begin to massage her back, using long slow strokes, enjoying the slide of my hands over her warm slick flesh. "I think it's going to become my mission in life to teach you to enjoy edging," I tell her. Knowing how she feels about waiting, I suspect she'll view it as a sexy threat.

"Noooo," she moans. "Not that again. Please, Clay. Not tonight."

"That's what you said last time," I remind her, as I reach around to cup her breasts—massaging them, too, until her nipples are hard and tight. Leaning in close again I tighten my arms around her, sliding one hand up to cover her throat, allowing the other to slip between her legs, finding her clit, stroking over it. "But you can't hold it off forever, you know. Sooner or later...it's coming."

"Coming—yes," she groans. "Make me come, Clay, please."

"I like the way my name sounds on your lips," I tell her— something I never expected to hear myself say. "I want to hear you scream it when you come."

"Claaay," she groans again, this time in frustration, when I release her clit to search for the shower sponge.

"Shhh," I tell her, fractionally increasing the pressure on

her throat, teasing her nipples with the sponge, whispering, "Be a good girl now and maaaybe I'll let you come."

"Cla-ay," she groans again, but this time there's a hint of warning in her tone.

"So good," I murmur as I move the sponge lower, trailing down her abdomen, and then move my hand back between her legs. "Doesn't it feel good, baby? Don't you want more."

"D'y'know what'd feel even better?" she asks, her words slurring with her arousal. "That'd be you inside me." And I can't fucking argue with that.

"Okay, you win," I tell her. Straightening away from her, I grab for the condom I brought into the shower with me. "Are you wet for me?" I ask as I'm suiting up. "Are you ready for me to fuck you now?"

"Am I what?" Legs cranes her neck to look at me over her shoulder. "We are literally standing in a shower, Clay, with water pouring down all around us; what do you think?"

"I think," I say, giving her ass a quick smack. "That you should answer the question."

"Hmm. Well, you know what I think?" she asks, her gaze calculating, her teeth worrying her lip, a smile tugging at her mouth.

"No, what?" I ask, breathless with anticipation, suddenly desperate to hear what she'll say.

"I think...if you really want to know the answer..."

"I really, really do."

"Then you should fuck me and find out!"

I'm chuckling and groaning as I take her advice, as I take hold of her hips and slide deep into her slick heat. I reach for the wall, covering her hands with mine, lacing our fingers together, as I piston my hips, pushing deeper and deeper inside her. Meanwhile, her plush butt provides a counterpressure, pushing back into my hips again and again.

Water continues to pour over us, dripping into our eyes and our open mouths, making everything impossibly slippery, impossibly wet, as our bodies slide against each other...

Then, all at once, she's rising up on her toes, head thrown back, keening as she comes, clenching all around me. And I'm slamming home one final time as I follow her over the edge.

After the tremors have stopped, I wrap my arms around her, holding her against me as we both try to recover our breath. She lets her head rest against my shoulder. And I lower my lips as close as I can get to her ear and whisper. "Say what you want, but one of these days, I *am* going to train you to take what you're given—and like it."

And her lips curve into a sensuous smile. "Oh, yeah? You really think so?"

"I really do."

She nestles against me, laughing softly. "Well, have fun trying."

And I know we both will.

"Okay, I think I figured it out," Legs says a short while later, while we're eating dinner—random bowls that I pulled out of the fridge and heated for us. I have chicken with cilantro rice, she has quinoa with black beans.

"Figured what out?" I ask, glancing up at her. Yes, up. She's seated on my kitchen island—that's right, *on* the island—with her feet planted on the seat of one of my stools, while I sit on the other stool, like a normal person. I'm wearing a tee shirt over sweatpants (yes, they're gray. And yes, I've heard the jokes) she's in my robe, which was another gift from Lori. It's soft and plush, extravagant as fuck and, other than being too big, it suits Legs perfectly.

"I've figured out why I didn't immediately recognize you," she says. "You know, when you pulled me over? It's because you're taller now, broader, and more...I dunno, muscle-y?"

"That's not actually a word," I say as I fork up another piece of chicken. I mean, she's not wrong, but...

Legs rolls her eyes. "So you want to police my grammar now, too? Fine. Have it your way, you've filled out some. Is that better?"

"You know, you *could* just say that I'm bigger now, and harder," I tease.

"Mm, I suppose I *could* do that. Except..." Her gaze drops to my lap. A smile plays on her lips as she sing-songs, "Not right now you're not."

I shake my head, because, yeah, come to think of it, that right there is probably the biggest difference. Even with all the shower action we just indulged in, I'm pretty sure that, at seventeen, I would have gotten it up again by now. I wouldn't have been able to help myself. Not with her sitting right there, naked beneath my robe, looking at me the way she is right now.

"Well, then what do *you* think the reason was?" she asks, misinterpreting my head shake for disagreement.

"I don't know. I'm sure it's a lot of things. I have a different haircut, I was wearing my uniform..." I zone out a little as I think about that, as I remember all the first responders I'd encountered during the fires. All I ever saw were the uniforms —the gear and the masks that obscured their features, the soot and ash that coated and smeared them. I couldn't have picked a single one of those people out of a lineup, not even to save my own life—and how ironic is that?

"Hey." She reaches forward to cup my face. "Where'd you go just now?"

I close my eyes—in part to revel in her touch, in part to gain some space. Are we really going to talk about this? Now?

"Clay?"

Sighing, I open my eyes. "You weren't here during the fires."

"No." Her hand slips from my face as she sits back. She clutches her bowl, looking troubled. "That first year...I didn't even hear about them until weeks later. My grandmother downplayed it. She said there was no reason for me to worry, that I should enjoy myself and stay where I was. But Rosa said it got pretty bad."

I shrug and nod. "It really depended on your circum-stances. Some people weren't affected at all. For others it was a temporary inconvenience." Some people lost everything.

"What about you?"

I shrug again. "I was luckier than some people."

"How so?"

"Well, I didn't die, right? And no one in my family was seri-ously injured. That was the important thing."

"But...?"

"Oh, you know, we were part of the fairground people, if that tells you anything."

She shakes her head. "I don't know what that means."

Right. Of course. "It's nothing. Just a stupid name they had for some of us." I push my bowl aside, take hers from her hand, and then pull her into my lap.

"'Us' who?"

"Just people. Just anyone who was displaced during the fires or who lost their homes. They housed us on the fair-grounds in Calistoga for a few weeks in tents or RVs, or just sacked out on the floors. Hence the name."

"Don't do that," she says, pulling back to frown at me. "Don't act like it doesn't matter when clearly it does."

"What do you know about it?" I ask, smiling gamely. "What makes you think I'm acting?" And yes, by the way, I'm totally acting.

"I know a lot." Her mouth twists into a grimace as she shrugs and looks away. "Because I do that, too. I know the signs. You can't kid a kidder, you know?"

"Yeah." I tug at a lock of her hair, waiting until glances back at me to continue. "I always suspected we had that in common."

"Yep," she says as her lips edge up in the smallest of smiles. "Kindred spirits."

But that might be a bridge or two too far. So, I shrug in response and equivocate. "Maybe. So, what signs have *I* missed? What's something you been pretending about?"

That makes her pause. "Well, let's see..." She gazes up at the ceiling, thinking hard—or so I imagine. Not being a mind reader, I can't say for sure. For all I know, she's taking a moment to make shit up.

"Okay," she says finally. "You know that party I threw—the one where we met? I pretended like it was for midsummer, but it was really more than that. It was a revenge party."

"Okay. Revenge for what? Or was it a who?"

"Both, in a way. See, my uncle was throwing a party the same night."

I nod as a stray bit of memory falls into place. "Ohh-kay. That's where the music was coming from. The music you were dancing to, right?"

"Yeah. Exactly. His party was actually supposed to be— Well, no, that's not true. I *thought* it was supposed to be a party for me—mostly because of the timing. See, I'd just graduated high school. And since he'd thrown parties for both my sisters and all my cousins after *they'd* graduated, I just naturally assumed that was the reason he was having it."

"And it wasn't?" I ask, although the answer is obvious.

"Nooo." She shakes her head sadly. "Absolutely not. I'd gone to see him, a few days before. You know—to ask why I couldn't invite some of my friends? Turns out he was holding a grudge, or trying to teach me a lesson of something. He was angry because I hadn't already chosen a college—like everyone else in the family had done, at that point.

"I said I wanted a gap year. He insisted that was just an excuse, that I'd end up not going back at all."

She stops and shrugs. "Which...he wasn't entirely wrong about. I mean, that *might* not have been my plan up until that point, but once he told me that since I refused to act like a grown up I didn't deserve a party. That he'd decided to throw one for Rosa instead—because she had gone to college, and had just graduated. And that I wasn't even allowed to attend the party, because there would be drinking there, and I was underage, and he didn't trust me to behave myself..." She shrugs and looks away. "Well, you know. School had always been really hard for me, so..."

"That sucks."

She shrugs again. "Yeah. I mean, it probably didn't help that I was wearing my Sonoma T shirt when I went to see him. But he still didn't have to be such a dick about it."

"I remember that shirt." I smile at the thought. "So, you stole a case of wine, and...?"

She nods. "I stole some wine, bought some lights, invited everyone I knew to come and hang out with me. And ended up meeting you. So, all in all, it was a good night."

"Mm," I say as I reposition her on my lap so that she's straddling one of my legs. "As I recall, it was a really hot night. In more ways than one."

"Um...what are we doing?" she asks as I pull the lapels of her robe apart and palm her breasts.

"Recreating one of our greatest hits," I say as I lean in to place a kiss below her ear and begin to work my way down her neck. "I want to watch you come on my leg like you did that night, no hands, only friction." I nip softly at her throat—and then blink in surprise when she pulls away.

"No. Stop."

"I'm sorry," I apologize, immediately pulling away from her, even dropping my hands from her breasts. "I thought you liked that."

"Oh, I do!" she replies—looking almost as dismayed as I feel. "I love it. It's just...we probably shouldn't right? Not if we're trying to keep this discreet. I don't want to have to try and explain *that* again."

I must look puzzled, because she rolls her eyes. "So, you were not wrong about my uncle. He was just a *little bit* annoyed about the wine I stole. But, I might have been okay. There really wasn't anything to connect me to the theft. I mean, as far as anyone in my family knew, I'd spent the entire night alone, sulking in my room. You know?"

"Not really."

"I didn't realize it until my uncle came to question me the next day but—" She waves vaguely at her neck and stares at me, somewhat pointedly.

I stare blankly back, still not getting the message. "But... what?"

"I had love bites on my neck," she replies in a strangely altered tone that I can't quite place, but which sounds oddly familiar, all the same. "My life was in the toilet!"

But then comprehension—or perhaps memory—hits and I remember sucking at her throat while she ground against me. "Oh. Shit. That was me?"

"Yeah, buddy. That was you."

"Okay, but that toilet thing you just said. Was that a line from a movie, or something?"

She nods. "Yes. Of course. Moonstruck." Then she gasps, eyes widening as she asks, "Oh! Do you think that's the reason he decided to send me to Italy? Because of the movie connection?"

"Huh?" I frown—feeling confused again. "What movie connection? I thought you said it was because you wanted to see your mother?"

She eyes me pityingly. "That was *my* reason for wanting to go—and the excuse he used to get me there. *His* reason was because I had obviously fallen in with a bad crowd, and it was only a matter of time before I got into serious trouble."

"Was he right?"

Her lips quirk. "Well, you tell me. You were the 'bad crowd' after all."

Oh, shit. And, suddenly, I want to smack younger me upside the head. "You know, what? I think he may have had a point."

"Really?" She stares at me in disbelief. "Well, I don't think so. And, anyway, I didn't know it at the time, but this was actually a pattern with him. Four years earlier, he'd talked my sister into annulling her marriage. Which...the irony of *that* is just insane."

"Oh?" I ask, but she shakes her head and wriggles suggestively.

"It's not important. Forget him. Now, where were we?"

The change of subject is abrupt, but it doesn't fucking matter. It takes barely an instant for my brain to switch gears—I've been primed for this moment. Waiting for it. Dreaming of it for five, long years.

"Just one sec," I say as I lift her off my lap and set her on her feet. I stand as well, fingers delving into the pocket of my sweats for the condom I'd optimistically placed there. I place it on the counter, where it will be readily accessible if I need it. It's hard to say if I will, at this point. Pun not intended.

Legs eyes the packet with a wicked smile. I shrug and say, "Just in case."

"Oh, yeah?" Her eyes light up. "Well, that sounds like a challenge to me."

"Don't you mean it sounds like a challenge *for* you?" I say as I return her smile.

"Could be, could be," she agrees.

I shove my sweatpants down my legs, then reclaim my seat on the stool. "Climb on," I urge, holding out my hands and helping her to once again straddle my leg.

"Omigod," she whispers, sounding awestruck as she tries an experimental slide. "Yes. Your leg is so hairy. Fuuuck. I'm going to come so fast." Her hands settle on my shoulders, fingers gripping me tight, as she slides forward and back, skin to skin.

"Holy shit," I groan. She feels even better than I imagined she would, even better than I'd remembered it. And the way she looks—with her lower lip caught between her teeth, and her face already flushed. "You're so beautiful," I tell her. "So fucking hot."

"You, too," she says, nodding frantically, already starting to pant. "Plus, you have the best ideas."

"I can't take credit for this one," I tell her. "This was all you."

"I dunno about that," she tells me, her eyes half-closed as she rocks on my leg, finding her rhythm—and stealing my breath in the process. "I think if it were my idea, you'd be touching me more."

"Can I touch your breasts?" I ask in response. It might not be necessary, but having spoiled the mood once already tonight, I'd rather err on the side of clear consent.

She gulps for breath, gasping, "Yes. You can touch me anywhere you want." And oh, fuck, does my dick like that.

"You're killing me," I murmur as I shape her breasts, curving my fingers around the heavy swells, plumping them up, using my thumbs to rub circles over and around the tight peaks.

"Same," she says, as her hips pick up speed and her fingers dig harder into my shoulders. "Same."

Her eyes are squeezed shut now. She's lost in the moment, racing for the finish line, when inspiration strikes me. "Can you do it without hands?"

Her eyes snap open, her rhythm faltering to a stop, as she protests, "But I'm not...?"

"Yeah, you are," I say shrugging my shoulders, drawing her attention. "You're using them here."

"I...don't know," she replies, frowning now, shifting restlessly on my leg. "I don't...think so?"

"Let's try it," I suggest. "Put your hands behind your head."

Her eyes gleam with mischief. "This sounds like more dirty cop talk, to me," she says. But she does as I ask, clasping her hands together, spreading her elbows wide—shoulders back, breasts thrust forward.

I clasp my hands on her hips, supporting her as she begins to move again. Then I dip my head and suck a nipple into my mouth and in less than a minute she's crying out, curling inward, hands clutching my head as she shudders in my arms.

Then I'm rising from my seat once again, carrying her with me. I clear the island with a swipe of my hand, shoving everything to the side. I tip her onto the counter, set a new speed record for gloving up, and then I'm sinking deep inside her for the second time tonight.

Her arms are stretched above her head, my hands encircling her wrists. Her legs are clenched around me, heels digging into my butt.

I stare hard at her neck as I pour everything into her. And in my mind, I'm leaving hella marks.

"So, THE FIRES," LEGS ASKS, A FEW MINUTES LATER, WHILE we're once again cuddled together on the stool, muscles lax, bodies at peace, just reveling in the afterglow. "How bad were they?"

"I told you," I say as a hint of tension begins to creep back in. "It varied. A lot."

"I know. That's what I'm asking. How bad was it for you?"

"Oh, you know..." I take a deep breath and tighten my hold on her. I *don't* want to talk about this. Not just now, I mean I never want to talk about it. I figure that it was enough that I lived through it, enough that I still have nightmares about it. But she asked for honesty, and I owe her that much. "It was bad. That first night... The fucking wind was insane. I heard later it was something like sixty miles an hour, which, Jesus fucking Christ, if that's the equivalent of a category *one* hurricane? I can't even imagine what four or five must be like. I swear, it felt like the whole world was on fire. Our entire neighborhood got destroyed. Not that we knew that, at the time, because you couldn't see shit through all the smoke. The noise was horrific—sirens, explosions, screams, and the constant roar. You know how they say if you're buried in an avalanche, you can't tell which way is up? It was kind of like that, you couldn't tell where anything was. If it weren't for the firefighters and the police who were running from door to door evacuating people. And then herding us in the right direction... And then there was the drive out—walls of flame on both sides of the road, everyone praying and whimpering, scared out of our minds. I just..."

She's hugging me tight, fingers digging into my hair, and

I'm clutching her back. "And then the next year...the same damn thing again. Only, that time, the smoke was blowing down from Paradise—from the Camp Fire—too. The air was thick with ash. It was weeks before you could go outside without a mask, or before anyone could breathe without coughing. And *then*—"

"Omigod," she gulps as she shudders against me. "No. Stop it. There can't have been more?"

"Yep. There sure was. It didn't get as much press, what with the pandemic and all, but in 2020 we got the Glass Fire. At least no one died in that one."

The shaking of her shoulders finally registers. Fuck me, for an insensitive asshole. She's crying. So, I hug her even tighter, murmuring, "Shh, shh. It's okay. It's like with you said about your party; at least something good came of it, right? It helped me decide what I wanted to do with my life. So, that's good, right?"

She pulls back to look at me. "Really? So, you didn't always want to be a deputy?"

I shoot her a disbelieving look. "What, are you kidding? You thought the seventeen-year-old who 'put your life in the toilet' and was ready to fuck you without even telling you his name was a law-abiding kind of guy?"

"Well, when you put it that way..." She smiles, shakily. "But honestly? Yeah. He didn't seem so bad; he was kinda sweet."

"Sweet?" I ask in mock outrage. "Who the hell're you talking about?" I mean...it's mostly mock, and I'm pleased when she giggles in response. "Not me?"

"God save me from men's fragile egos," she murmurs as she rolls her eyes. "And also hot, okay? Hot *and* sweet. And, as I recall, he was also *very* concerned about my little wine theft. So, what does that tell you?"

I open my mouth to point out that a case of wine is not a 'little' theft. But then I stop and reconsider. "Okay," I tell her. "You may have a point. But, to answer your question, no. Even after the fires, deputy was not a no-brainer." I snuggle her against me once more. "I knew I wanted to give back to the community that had saved my life, to maybe someday be a hero to someone else. But becoming a firefighter was flat out never going to happen. I'd've been suicidal within a week. There was no fucking way I could do that on the reg." Just thinking about it makes me shudder. And I have to pause, remind myself to breathe, and shove the memories to the back of my mind once again before I can continue. "Like you, I wasn't the best student, so I figured a career as an EMT was out. I just didn't have the science or math background, you know? And...well, Napa College had a Criminal Justice certificate program, and I liked how that sounded. You know—Justice? It was..."

"Quixotic?" she suggests, teasingly. But she's not wrong.

"Kind of."

"And how's that working out?"

I huff out a laugh. "Well...it's touch and go. I don't like everything I have to do, but up until this Summer, I'd've said it was going pretty good."

"Oh?"

"No offense, but your family kind of sucks."

"Hey. Not all of them," she replies immediately. "Some of us are just trying to make great wine and make our grand-mother proud."

I sigh and shake my head, reminded again of the gap between us—and all the reasons why we're just so totally fucked. "Maybe," I say. "But I thought I was signing up to protect the helpless and serve the community. And lately, I feel more like a hall monitor at a middle school. A snooty, private middle-school full of assholes."

"Wow," she says, shaking her head and staring wide-eyed at me. "Don't hold back, Deputy. Tell me how you really feel about me."

"Not you," I quickly assure her. "Just your family."

"Uh-huh. And did you ever actually go to a school like that?" she asks.

"No," I admit. "But I've met plenty of people who did."

"Well, I did go to one of those schools—for all the good it did me. And I don't even speak to those people anymore. Those are *not* my family."

"Okay. If you say so," I say, just to end this discussion which, anyone can tell, isn't going to lead to anything good. And, somehow, we've both agreed that spending her the night again this soon isn't the best way to conduct a clandestine relationship. So as soon as her clothes are dry, and the rain has stopped, I'm walking her to her car, we're kissing each other goodbye, I'm watching her drive away. And it's still on of the best weeks I've had in a really long time.

But then it's Thursday afternoon, and all it takes is one glance at the evil grin on my dispatcher's face. Just one single glance and my spirits start to sink, and my hopes start to dim. Because, sure enough, a new complaint has just been lodged against Caparelli. And, from the moment I read it, I know in my heart of hearts that this one is probably valid.

Chapter 13

Allegra

There are bees foraging among my grandmother's rose bushes. Which surprised me, when I first heard them. After last week's heavy rains, I figured they'd be holed up in their hives by now, huddling together for warmth, waiting out the winter—even though, in reality, winter is probably still several months away.

I know you've heard people say that California has no seasons, and of course that's a lie. Probably the second biggest one they tell, right after the one about how it never rains here. Or maybe the third. D'you really think we're all hippies? Think again. Sure, most days are pleasant and sunny, and Mediterranean Maritime Mild is the flavor *del día, todos los días*, but there *are* seasons. And it seems I've forgotten a few key facts about them. Like the way that summer can be too cool, winter can be too wet, autumn can be too hot, and spring can seem like one, long, endless fog bank.

Anyway, the bees: I can hear the drone from where I am lying, stretched out in the hammock that has hung between these trees for as long as I've been alive. Longer, probably.

Although now that I think about it, it's probably not the same one, is it?

It's a little embarrassing actually, the fact that I can't recall with any real accuracy what the original one looked like—but there again, that probably wasn't the *original*, original one, either.

It's hard to be the latecomer in a dynastic sort of family. To paraphrase from one of Nonna's favorite movies, if you're gonna be born this late in the game, you're gonna miss out on a few decades of family drama.

Which is not to suggest that I think the past was better. In a lot of ways, it was not. For example, when I was a teenager, I wouldn't have been relaxing in the shade like this. Not on a day like today. No, I'd've been toasting in the sun—or attempting to. Lying on a towel in my swimsuit, working on my tan, or trying to sun-bleach my hair with lemon juice.

Given my Italian heritage, the hair lightening was a clear and obvious L. Unfortunately, so was the tanning.

Working against me there was the fact that Nonna was not a big fan of teenage me lying around in a state of undress while there were workers in the nearby fields. So, it's not like I ever managed to give it a fair try.

Ironically, Nonna may have had a point. I'm pretty sure I'd've freaked the fuck out if I'd attracted unwanted attention for real, but the idea of a sexy someone showing up unexpectedly and overcoming my initial reticence? That was a hot and persistent fantasy.

The idea makes me hot even now...make that *especially* now that I can put a specific face to the fantasy. The idea of Clay joining me here, out in the open, where anyone could see us. Of him demanding that I bring myself off again... I'm so fucking tempted. It's all I can do to keep from touching myself. I reach a hand down, over the side of the hammock, and search blindly for the bottle of sparking rose lemonade that I'd brought out of the house with me.

I uncap the bottle and take a long, satisfying sip and then return it to the grass. The result of all these maneuvers is just what you'd expect. The hammock swings gently, and I'm getting turned on all over again. I wriggle around as I try to get comfortable. And then, just as I'm contemplating whether a cold shower might be in order, the sound of someone (fairly close by, from the sound of it) clearing their throat startles me into opening my eyes.

I lose my breath when I catch sight of Clay standing at the edge of the drive, hat in hand, staring right at me. For a moment, I think I must be dreaming. The heat in his gaze makes me wish I was wearing my swimsuit now—or even less. A sheer, filmy robe? Or, perhaps, nothing at all? I want to invite him to share my hammock...even though I'm not at all convinced it would support our combined weight.

"Hey," I say, smiling at him. "I was just thinking about you. What are you doing here?"

But he doesn't smile back. And that's an answer in itself, isn't it? The fact that he's wearing his uniform, and a sheepish expression lets me know that this is an official visit. He's here as *Deputy* Romero. Which can only mean one thing.

"Oh, no. Are you kidding me?" I ask as I swing my feet to the ground and sit up. "What now? What obscure and ridiculous law are we supposed to have run afoul of this time? Whatever it is, you know it's bullshit, don't you?"

Clay sighs and shakes his head. "I don't think so babe," he says, just as the screen door slams and Rosa appears, striding across the lawn like a mother bear on a rampage. "Ah, fuck," Clay mutters beneath his breath, and I couldn't agree more.

"Deputy Romero," she greets him as soon as we're in earshot. "To what do we owe the pleasure this time?" Which is just so Rosa that I want to laugh. I mean, I can't even count the number of times she came to my defense, or Bee's (even the cousins, a time or two) when we were all kids. And I love her for it.

Except that, A—I'm not her cub (or anyone's cub anymore).

And B—I don't fucking *need* saving. Not this time, anyway.

And C—more than anything, right now, I want Clay and my sisters to *like* each other. And this *really* isn't helping!

"Rosa, I got this," I tell her when she pulls to a stop besides me, folding her arms and squaring off with Clay in a way that— again—would almost be laughable. If I didn't want to cry in frustration.

"It's fine," Rosa brushes my assurances aside. "We do this all the time." She glares at Clay and asks, "So, what's today's problem?"

"As I was just telling your sister," Clay says, with a nod in my direction. "The Sheriff's Office has received a report that you may be in violation of Ordinance 947, which—"

"The Winery Definitions Ordinance." Rosa nods. "Yes. I'm familiar with it. What part are we supposedly violating this time?"

"In this case, the problem involves section eleven, sub-section h, paragraph 2," Clay responds, and if I didn't know him as well as I'm starting to, I might've missed the way the corner of his mouth quirks up—like it does when he's trying not to smile. Rosa stares at him blandly. Clay stares blandly back. And now—hand to God—it looks like they're *both* hiding smiles.

I'm on the verge of asking if they'd like to be alone, when Rosa says, "Refresh my memory. Paragraph 2 has to do with what again?"

"It has to do with the artwork in your tasting room," Clay explains, grimacing apologetically in my direction.

"What artwork?" Rosa asks, as she, too, turns to face me.

"Really?" I'm distracted from my annoyance with Clay—who at least *knew* about the artwork—by my annoyance with my sister, who *should* have known, but clearly didn't. "The installation has been up for nearly a week!" I mean, technically, I'm talking about a work week, which is five days, and today is Thursday, so in actual time, it's been three days since the pictures were hung. But still!

"Perhaps we could go and see it?" Clay suggests, and since no one has a better idea, that's what we do.

"I'm sure I told you," I say to Rosa. "Didn't I? About the deal I made with Vin Vista?"

Rosa shakes her head. "Sorry, Legs. That's not ringing any bells. What's...Vin...what did you call it?"

"Vin Vista. It's one of the galleries in town. We get to display a rotating collection of paintings and artwork. You get to keep your anniversary poster in the kitchen, where you wanted it—right?"

And yes, I'm loading on the guilt, because why not?

"Wait." Just outside the tasting room door, Rosa stops in her tracks. "We *are* allowed to display artwork." She turns to Clay and demands, "Aren't we?"

"Yes," he agrees. "But you can't sell it."

"Well, of course," Rosa says. "But we're not selling artwork. Right?"

They both turn to me. I shrug. "No. I mean, not technically."

"Not...technically?" Rosa repeats. "What exactly does that mean?"

"Oh, just come and see it," I urge as I take hold of her arm and propel her through the door.

"Isn't it great?" I ask, as I spin around, gesturing to the art that decorates the tasting room walls. There are paintings of grapes, glowing in the sunshine. Studies of vines and leaves. Still lifes with wine bottles, or glasses, or barrels. Landscapes— "That one's my favorite," I say, pointing to a street-side view of the valley, with the Vaca mountains clearly visible in the distance.

I sneak a look at Clay and catch him looking back. We share a long look, and I just know we're thinking of that conversation we had about his having lived in those hills. "The gallery has a stack of cards they'll be handing out to direct people here to see the exhibit. And then, while they're here, maybe we'll sell them some wine; or perhaps they'll want to have a snack, or a picnic."

"Yes, but—"

"Oh, and we have a bunch of the gallery's cards on hand, too. So that people who want to see even *more* artwork will know where to go. It's a win/win."

"Great," Rosa says. "Terrific. But we're still not *selling* them—right?"

"Well, how could we? They're not ours to sell, are they? They belong to the gallery. Or maybe to the artists? I don't really know how that works. It's like a consignment arrangement, except the winery doesn't profit from the sale. That's the important part, isn't it?"

But Clay is already shaking his head. "No," he says as he turns from examining one of the exhibit labels. "It's not a matter of whether or not you make a profit. This isn't like the food clause. The ordinance is really clear on artwork, for some reason. You cannot sell it here. Period."

"Wait. Food clause?" Rosa asks, sounding wary. "Why are we talking about that?"

I shrug in response. "'Hell if I know. I don't even know what a food clause is." At that, they both turn identical looks in my direction—made up of maybe one part irritation, three, or four parts concern. "What?"

"I'm talking about the clause that says wineries can't charge the public more for any food item they serve than it costs them to provide said item," Clay explains. "In other words, you can't make a profit from any food that's sold here. I assumed that's what you were referencing when you mentioned profit?"

"I wasn't," I assure him. "But that doesn't apply to food trucks, does it?"

"What food trucks?" Rosa asks. "We haven't talked about food trucks!"

We hadn't talked about paintings either. But I know better than to point that out. "There wasn't any reason to. It's just something I've been thinking about."

"Food trucks are fine, actually," Clay tells us both. "As long as they have permits from the county and are not operating on public property."

"Can we go back to the art for a minute?" Rosa asks, zeroing in on Clay. "You said it can stay—yes? We don't have to take them down, we just can't sell them?"

Clay nods. "That's correct. Ideally, I'd ask that you change the labels to omit the prices. And just refer people back to the gallery if they want more information, but..."

"What?" My mouth drops open. "You want me to redo the cards *and* my arrangement with the gallery? Do you know how much extra work, and time, and hassle that's gonna entail? Not to mention how many sales will be lost if we force people to traipse back and forth across town just to buy a piece of art? Something like thirty-six percent of purchases are impulse buys."

"That's the gallery's problem," Clay says. "What you need to be concerned with is not getting sued by the county."

Rosa gasps. "Sued by—? No! No, no, no. We do not want

that." She turns to me and says, "Look, Legs, maybe we should take them down and send them back. Just to be safe. We can't afford to fight a lawsuit."

"I don't think that'll be necessary," Clay replies quickly. "Just amend the cards. I'll write it up that the artwork is on loan from the gallery and is just being displayed here—that should cover you. And I'll stop by Vin Vista, when I leave here. and make sure that's clear to them, as well."

"Thank you," Rosa says, looking surprised. "That's very considerate."

Meanwhile, I'm gritting my teeth and holding my tongue. I mean, I should be the one talking to the gallery owner—not Clay. Does *he* not trust me to handle things on my own now either? Typical.

Clay shoots me a look that I can't decipher—Anxious? Apologetic? Who fucking knows—and takes his leave. Rosa lingers for a moment.

"That was...surprisingly easy," she says, looking puzzled.

"Do you really think so?" I scoff.

Rosa nods. "I'd almost say suspiciously so. I feel like I'm waiting for another shoe to drop. On the other hand, it doesn't feel like a trap." She frowns abstractly. "Do you think he has a thing for you? Or maybe he just feels bad about impounding your car."

"It's probably awkward for him," I counter. "Since the wedding. I mean, you're all such good friends with Miles, and so is he." None of which is a lie, but my conscience still twinges. Which is something I'll just have to live with, since this is clearly not the time to come clean.

"Maybe." Rosa glances around and sighs reluctantly. "I hate that WDO."

"The what?"

"The Winery Definitions Ordinance. It makes zero sense.

Why shouldn't we be able to sell art? It looks great in here, and you've done a fantastic job. I just wish we had some wine for you to sell, or for the public to sample—or anything."

I nod, and think about mentioning the food trucks again, then think better of it. "Well, talk to Bee," I say, instead. "Convince her to work on something that we can release early. Maybe like a Pet Nat, or a Rosé?"

To my surprise, Rosa shakes her head. "No. Bianca's got the wine on lock. She knows what she's doing with it, and we're not going to second-guess her or do anything to make her think we don't trust her judgment."

She's not wrong, but for a moment I do feel a bit of envy. It's nice to be trusted. "Well, I don't know. Maybe there's some kind of shortcut we could take, some other way we could sell wine now. We could talk to the cousins? We know that at least some of Belmonte's wine was made using our grapes, maybe they'd be willing to let us sell some of that here?"

Rosa shakes her head. "You could try, if you want. Bee and I both talked to Geno, hoping he would do the right thing. But I don't think it even matters at this point. We're just going to run afoul of that stupid ordinance again. As I understand it, it's not enough that the grapes were grown here. The wine would also have to be fermented, or refermented in Caparelli's facilities. And I think that ship has sailed by now."

"Fuck," I mutter—partly in frustration, partly because my phone just buzzed with an 'incoming text' notification, and I'd bet carboys to bocksbeutel that I know who's trying to reach me. It's gotta be one of two people—either Clay or Jimmy. Neither of whom I want to talk to right now. "Well then...what about the wine Bee's making for Jansen?" I suggest. "I mean, I don't know what he's paying her, but maybe she'd be okay with him giving her some of the wine she's making, in lieu of salary? Or at least in part?"

"Same problem, though. It's mostly all fermented by now. Besides, she's making it *there*, not here, so..."

"Details," I say snapping my fingers to show how little I care about those. "I'm sure we can find a way around that. We'll just roll a few barrels down the road, and let it finish fermenting here."

"Oh, sure. That'd be great for the wine," Rosa rolls her eyes. "Do not suggest that to Bee. She'd probably have an aneurysm."

"Well, I wouldn't put it in those terms, if I were talking to her," I point out. But Rosa's not having it.

Let it go, Legs. I know it's tough right now. It is for all of us. But we'll get through it. It'll be okay."

"If you say so," I respond—not at all convinced.

"All right, well...I'm gonna get back to work," she says. Then she glances around once again and adds, "You *are* going to change the labels though, right? The last thing we need is for Romero to think we lied to him."

"I'll handle it," I promise. I don't want to, but I guess I've got no choice.

After Rosa leaves, I stare discontentedly at the paintings for a while, trying to recapture a little of the joy I'd felt while I was hanging them up. The atmosphere is great, peaceful, serene, prosperous—ideal for an art exhibit. Less so for an up-and-coming winery. All I can think about is the money we're not making—and not going to be making—any time soon. Not from paintings, or food trucks, or even wine.

After a moment, I dig out my phone and check my texts. Just as I suspected, Clay left me a message. A really short one:

"Sorry."

"Me, too, Romeo," I sigh sadly. "Me, too."

I almost type that in the chat box, then reconsider. "Et tu,

Brute?" Yeah, that would be even better. Much more pointed—
no pun intended. Or would it? After all, I'd still be sending a
multi-word answer in response to a one-word text. And that
would give him the W.

In the end, I leave the message on read, turn off my notifica-
tions and return my phone to my pocket. And to think, the
week had started off so promising, too.

OVER THE NEXT COUPLE OF DAYS, CLAY AND I DO TALK.
And text. And he apologizes—sort of—for putting a wrench in
all my plans...

"Look, I hear you," he says during one conversation, his
frustration vibrating through the phone. "The WDO is four-
teen pages of crap and nonsense. It's ambiguous, it's inconsis-
tent, and don't even get me started on all the places where it
actually runs counter to the laws of the state! It's a fucking shit
show. I didn't write the damn thing, and I sure as hell don't
agree with most of it. But, barring a court order, *you* still have to
follow it, as best as you can. And it's still my job to make sure
you do that. Which I knew was going to be a problem for us,
sooner or later. I told you going in that it would be."

"It's not a problem," I answer stubbornly, and partially
inaccurately. "I just didn't appreciate being blindsided, that's
all. Oh, and then being tag teamed by you and Rosa? Not cool."

"That was *not* my fault," he insists. And of course, he's
right. It wasn't his fault. It wasn't Rosa's fault. Nope, once again
the fault was all mine.

"If you could just try not to embarrass me anymore in front
of my sisters, that would be great," I tell him.

"I'll try," he promises, which I guess is all the assurance he can give me. It's not enough, but I guess it will have to do.

SUNDAY, WE HAVE DINNER WITH THE LAMBROS. BEE AND Rosa do most of the cooking, moving around Nonna's kitchen in a complicated dance as they boil pasta and stir sauce and assemble the cheeses filling for the stuffed shells. I'm relegated to tearing lettuce for salad and grating a mountain of Parmigiano Reggiano.

It's not that I don't know how to cook, or don't remember how to make Nonna's classic dishes—of course, I do. But it's been years since I've had a kitchen to call my own. So, at the very least, I'm sadly out of practice. "Did you do a lot of cooking in Argentina?" I ask Bee.

"I did, actually," she answers, looking surprised. "Mostly for myself; I found it relaxing, after a long day. But I ate out a lot, too. The food there is amazing. They eat a lot of beef, of course. In fact, they say there's more cattle there than people. You must have cooked, too," she adds. "Didn't you? I mean, Europe! The produce, the fish, the cheese—although I know Nonna always said you shouldn't mix those last two."

"Oh, no one cares about that anymore," I say, happy to sidestep the question. "That's considered a very old fashioned idea now."

"Well, Nonna *was* old," Rosa points out. "And she was born here, so I guess those rules must have been handed down years and years ago."

"Yeah," I agree. "Probably." And then we all fall silent. And I don't know about my sisters, but I'm thinking about our grandmother, and wishing she was here—even if it was just to scold us when we let the pasta water boil over, or for swiping tastes of the cheese filling—yum.

"Raw egg," Bee cautions me as I go back for a second taste.

"Don't care," I respond making a face. And I don't. It tastes so good that at least I'll die happy. "Hey, I could make some bruschetta," I suggest, when a happy thought strikes me. "You know, for appetizers? We have tomatoes and basil, don't we?"

"Yes. But don't you need the oven for that?" Rosa asks. She points at the trays of shells. "These are about ready to go in."

I shrug. "It was just a thought. How about I open some wine? We can have a toast." But before they can answer, the back door opens and the cousins come pouring into the house— a loud and noisy, Italian American flood. And then Jake and Jansen, and Jansen's dog return from testing the barrels, or whatever they were doing. Probably hiding out at Jansen's place, watching the hockey game that I *know* was on today.

And then someone else starts opening bottles and pouring wine, and I'm once again shunted to the sidelines, but at least this time there's a dog to play with. And I start to think that, when I do get my own place, I should get a pet.

Which, of course, leads me to thinking about Clay, and wondering how he feels about animals. Which leads me to wishing—once again—that I could have invited him. Or maybe not. In fact, I'm profoundly grateful for his absence when, over dinner, the discussion gets into legally gray winery practices. And, yet again, the fault is mine. Because I finally get to try the Carleo and...like Bee said, it's not bad wine, but something is definitely off with it.

"I'm really looking forward to seeing what *you* can do with these grapes," Vitto tells Bianca—as he swirls and sniffs and sips and shakes his head. "I'm sure it will be amazing."

"I do have ideas," she says, smiling mysteriously.

I mostly listen while the others talk—eating and drinking and attempting to figure out what I don't like about this wine. It's dark, round, full-bodied. Maybe a little too round for a cabernet. And a little too off-dry, as well. A little too flabby. Of course, Geno might be blending it with something else—a merlot, perhaps (because Sideways isn't entirely wrong about that) or even white zinfandel, although Vitto would have to know if it's something like that. "Do you think Geno's adding a concentrate?" I ask Leo, who's seated beside me.

And maybe I said it a little louder than necessary, because conversation instantly stops and everyone stares at me.

"What?" I ask, glancing around the table. "It's not that uncommon, is it? I thought a lot of wineries did that?"

"Are you looking to throw down, Legs?" Gianni asks—and I'm pretty sure he's joking, although not entirely. "'Cause those are fighting words."

"Unless she's right," Leo points out. "In which case...?"

And then we're all looking at Vitto, who shrugs and says, "I mean, anything's possible. But no winery that wants to keep their reputation intact would even think of doing something like that. Even to suggest it is not good. That kind of talk could ruin a winery. It's only about one step above claiming that someone's been adding wood chips to his chardonnay to give it more of an oaky flavor. Supermarket chains might do things like that but..."

"Unless she's right," Leo repeats.

Vito nods. "Yes. Fine. Unless she's right. I hope she's not but...I just don't know. I'll try and find out."

"It was only an idea," I say again, in a very small voice.

"You said what you thought," Leo say kindly. "That's not wrong. It's just not something that's occurred to us before."

I nod, to show I understand, but it's clear they're having strong thoughts about it now. And not happy ones. And I guess this makes it official. I *am* the family buzzkill.

I feel that even more when Gianni asks Rosa if we've "given

any more thought to the name change idea." Which is the first time I'm hearing anything about it.

Rosa shrugs. "Not really. I think we've tabled that topic for now."

Then she glances inquiringly at Bee who nods in agreement. "Yes. For now." And the conversation moves on to other topics, and no one appears to realize that I'm just sitting here frozen, blindsided once again. Was there a question of a name change? Did I miss a memo? And why does it seem like everyone knows about it but me?

I'm relieved when dinner ends. I only wish the whole night was over with.

While the Lambros and I deal with cleanup, Rosa whips up a big batch of Nonna's zeppoli, and Bee (with an assist from Jansen) puts together a row of boozy affogatos—the ingredients for which were the cousins' contribution to dinner. Coffee, Amaretto, and toasted almond ice cream from a local creamery. It's an adult upgrade on one of our childhood favorites.

When we were little, movie night at Nonna's was a tradition. Whenever our parents were busy, or needed a break, she'd invite us all over. She'd line the living room floor with sleeping bags, and after dinner we'd all gather there. We'd eat zeppoli and ice cream sundaes and watch movies until we fell asleep.

At least, that's how I remembered it. Being the youngest, I always got the best seat in the house—Nonna's lap—albeit for the shortest period of time, since I always fell asleep first. If the others got up to more interesting activities after I fell out, I never heard about it.

Tonight's movie is A Good Year. Russell Crowe—wearing eyeglasses! And speaking French! Not Keanu, but definitely doable. Although that was *not* something I thought about when I saw this as a kid. As a matter of fact, I found it boring and confusing. It's hitting different now, in a lot of ways.

It starts off with a man—Crowe—returning to the winery in France where he went to live after his parents died. His Uncle Henry, the man who raised him, has died as well now—without making a will—and Crowe (or rather, his character—Max) is assumed to have inherited the entire estate, as his uncle's only known relative.

Coming this soon after Nonna's death, I suspect it's hitting different for the others, too. A heavy silence falls over the room as we watch Max explore the now derelict estate.

During the flashback scene (in which a young Max is learning to play tennis. Or, learning to lose at tennis, from the looks of it) Gianni stirs suddenly and says, "Jesus. He's just like dad." And I'm not sure if he means the overbearing, tough-it-out uncle, or the whiny, tantrum throwing kid. Maybe it's both? And I'm all at once caught up in a flashback of my own...

I REMEMBER NONNA TALKING TO JIMMY ABOUT DEATH— the ways in which it impacted people, vs the way it affected families. It might have been in conjunction with her will. Or maybe someone they knew had just died. I don't really know. I was eavesdropping, as per usual, and couldn't ask for details.

"We're always affected by the death of someone close to us," I remember her saying. "Little fractures of the soul. Some people heal quickly, others take a long time, but no one goes back to being *exactly* as they were before."

Jimmy murmured something in response—I couldn't hear what. And Nonna laughed sadly.

"No, because when the *entire* family is affected—when there are multiple fractures, and no one is whole—that's when families shatter. There's no one left to hold the pieces together. So they come apart like an old ceramic bowl when it hits the floor. The pieces fly in all directions, landing who knows where. Maybe one of them ends up under a bureau, where no one ever thinks to look for it. And the more pieces you have, the harder it is to fit them all back together."

"So melodramatic," Jimmy chided. "But that's not inevitable, is it? Not all families react like that."

"No, but I'm afraid mine will," Nonna said, sounding so sad that my heart broke a little for her.

I got to my feet, ready to burst through the door and hug her tight and promise that I had her back, that I'd never let that happen. But before I could take a single step, Jimmy spoke again—this time in a tone I'd never heard him use before. "Cara." Just one word, but that's all it took. Because, in that moment I finally realized that 'Cara' was more than just a nickname. It wasn't a shortened form of the name Carmela; it was *an endearment*. And the way his tongue caressed the word told me something else.

It told me that they weren't just friends.

"Oh, I know, I know," Nonna was saying—when I recovered from my shock. And I think I may have missed part of their conversation while I was grappling with my surprise. "I'm probably being silly. But I know my son. Geno does not handle change well. He never has. He closes in on himself. He focuses all his attention on what's immediately in front of him and lets everything else go. And it's my fault—I know that, too. Well, mine and Leo's. Actually, mostly Leo's, I think—not that I mean to speak ill of the dead. But we had our own pain, he and I; our own grief to deal with. The loss of our child, our firstborn— neither of us handled that well, I'm afraid."

"I don't know how you would," Jimmy replied. "Or how anyone would. You can't blame yourself for that."

"Oh, I know," Nonna agreed. "But we had other children— and they suffered, too. I think we lost sight of that for a while. Geno was saddled with too much responsibility, at too young an age. And then criticized for not being able to deal with everything as well as his brother had. I should have seen what was happening and put my foot down. But..."

Nonna's voice trails off and Jimmy says something else I can't hear. Then Nonna again, "But no! Don't you see? That's precisely the problem. I *won't* be there to advise him. And I doubt there's anyone else he'll listen to. So, I have to do what I can—to protect my girls, mie tre sorelle. I have to make sure that they are not the 'pieces' that get lost when the bowl shatters."

So, I guess, after all, she *was* talking about the will...

By the time we reach the point in the movie where Max is forging letters to ensure that his mysterious cousin (coincidentally, a girl from Napa) can inherit the winery, instead of him, I'm remembering why I'd found it so confusing.

There's the inheritance angle. The love story sub-plot between Max and his childhood friend. The illegal vine sub-plot—because if you think Napa wine laws are convoluted and pointless, France is here to say, "hold my INAO glass!"

There's a strangely contentious winemaker who clearly knows more *about everything* than he's saying. A passive-aggressive dog— "See, Moose?" I whisper to the little dog whose head is resting on my leg. "That's bad. Don't be like that." And, at the end of the day, Max has to give up the winery (and the life he built in London) in order to get the girl. Which, then and now, has always struck me as being massively unfair.

I mean, he's the one with the memories of growing up there, isn't he? He's the person his uncle wanted the winery to go to. But that's not how the movie ends, and that's not how life works out either, most of the time.

As the end credits roll, we fall into a discussion about when we should do this again, and what movie we should watch next time. Since November is right around the corner, Gianni suggests that we aim for a Friendsgiving dinner. Which has an unfortunately quelling effect on all of us, driving home the point that, with Nonna gone, we probably won't be celebrating Thanksgiving together as a family anymore.

It takes me a moment to rally from that, but my sisters bounce back quickly. "Yeah, for sure. The Sunday after should be good for us," Rosa says. And "You'll be back by then too, won't you?" Bee asks Jansen.

"Wouldn't miss it," Jansen says, nodding gamely. Which makes him a keeper in my book.

In a desperate attempt to move the conversation along, I start tossing out suggestions for next month's movie. I lean hard into the old musicals that I remember Nonna having loved, prompting Leo to marvel at my memory. "How do you remember so much?" he says. "You had to have slept through half those movies."

"Sleep learning!" Gianni suggests. "She remembers more than the rest of us do because all those songs went straight into her subconscious mind."

"*Grullo*," Vitto murmurs dismissively—basically calling his brother gullible. "That doesn't work."

"How would you know?" Gianni replies, playfully shoving his brother. At least I think it's supposed to be playful. "Show me *your* research, *carciofo*." And I can't tell if they're about to start fighting or if calling your brother an artichoke is just something brothers do.

Either way, I switch instantly to deflection mode. "That's not why," I tell them. "It's because I had mono in high school and was sick for weeks." It was early in my junior year—while both my sisters were away at college. I was out for so long and fell so far behind that my school enrolled me in their independent study program, and I was basically homeschooled for the remainder of the year.

"Nonna and I spent a lot of that time watching movies together." And re-writing song lyrics. And making grand plans for the future—this future. Now. A future that, by design, did not include her. Funny how I hadn't really recognized that, at the time.

And now I'm blinking back tears and spiraling into depression again, largely unaware of the worried looks the others are casting at one another.

"Hey, you know what?" Rosa says. "We have weeks to decide, we don't have to make up our minds tonight."

"That's true," Leo agrees. "And we need to get going now, anyway. We can talk about that later."

"Or we don't even have to," Vitto suggests. "Why don't you three decide? You have good ideas. And, you know us, we're easy to please."

"Oh, sure," Gianni says with a laugh—that's cut short when Leo smacks him in the back of the head. "I mean, yes. We are. Total pushovers. Love those chick-flicks."

AFTER MY COUSINS LEAVE, I MAKE AN EXCUSE AND SLIP away to quickly text Clay—

"Can I come over?"

He texts back after less than a minute—

"Now? It's kinda late,"

—a response that's giving serious "Don't Call Me" country music vibes, even after he adds a hopeful—

"How about tomorrow?"

"Or not," I mutter discontentedly. Curious, I glance at the time. I'm surprised to realize it's already after eleven. Which *is* late, I guess, when you start work at six.

And even I'll admit that that's a strange thing to envy someone for. Still, I'm managing it. Because I'm *trying* to create a meaningful role for myself here, too. A reason why *I'd* need to roll out of bed every day at o-dark-thirty. And I'm being hamstrung at every turn. Most recently by him.

So maybe I *am* still feeling a little resentful. And maybe he suspects as much. Perhaps getting together tonight really *isn't* a good idea.

"Yeah, maybe. Sorry to bother you."

"Not a bother,"

—he texts back. Which is sweet. And which does put a teeny smile on my face. Still, I'm heading upstairs to sleep alone, in my childhood bedroom. And that's so not where I want to be right now.

Chapter 14

Allegra

I get up the next morning determined to turn things around
—for myself, and for Caparelli. Having grown up on a
winery that was already established, already successful, I think
I may have underestimated the level of difficulty in starting
over from somewhere this close to scratch. Maybe Geno has
been right all along. Maybe we *can't* do this on our own. But
my sisters aren't ready to give up yet, and I refuse to be the
weak link, the screw-up who causes us to fail.

Which means I need to double my efforts. One way or
another, I need to find some way to keep our brand alive and
our name relevant until there's wine to sell.

Since we already have something of a green light in terms
of food trucks, that seems like a logical place to start. But I
immediately run into a problem. The first few trucks I contact
want to know how much business we do here, and what kind of
crowd they can expect. When they learn we're not even open
yet? They lose interest quick.

Which, honestly, I should have expected. Apparently, the

only businesses in Napa that aren't expected to turn a profit are small wineries. Who knew?

Bottom line, I need people—potential customers—in order to attract the food trucks. But, with nothing else to sell, I need food trucks if I want to attract the people. No people, no food trucks. No food trucks, no people. It's a vicious circle taking me nowhere. I need to find a better way.

I drive into town, hoping to get a sense of what brings people to Oak Creek Canyon—other than wine, of course. There must be *something* we can offer that they're not already getting elsewhere.

It's a gorgeous fall day, sunny and warm. The air is fresh, the leaves just starting to turn. It's perfect. Just being here, being home, lifts my spirits. All the same, my first stop is the Rise 'n' Wine for an iced caramel macchiato—just to further boost my morale.

My plan is to start at the tourism board. I've heard they offer winery tours, so they were on my list of places to visit anyway, once we're operational. But that also seems like a logical place to ask questions and find information on what tourists want to do here.

I'm in sight of their building, when I'm distracted by the business directly across the street, by the row of mint-green cruiser bikes lined up in front—shining brightly and enticingly in the sun—and the signs in the windows offering TOURS in big, block letters that might as well be neon, because that's when inspiration strikes.

As I recently told Clay, I worked as a tour guide in several cities throughout Europe. If leading tour groups was the best gig ever, then bike tours were the best of the best! Easier on my feet than walking tours. And easier on my lungs, as well, since you're generally not expected to talk as much.

I can barely wait for a break in the traffic to rush across the street and through the front door of Wheeling in the Vines. Once there, I shamelessly trade on my family's name and reputation—and my own background as a tour guide and former cellar rat—to talk the owner into letting me lead a series of tour-and-tasting events, which will take in several of the wineries along Silverado Trail. Including (obviously) Caparelli.

Eventually, tour-goers will be able to taste our wines, too, of course. But for now, I figure we can provide a place to stop, to give everyone a chance to rest and eat lunch while I regale them with stories of what it was like to grow up on a winery in Oak Creek Canyon. With vineyard dirt under my nails, my clothes and hands perpetually stained purple, and a sommelier's encyclopedic knowledge of wine bred into my soul.

And *yes*! Of course I'm overselling it! Fake it 'til you make it is totally gonna be my motto from here on out. And maybe that kind of blatant manipulation didn't work out too well for Russell Crowe (I mean Max) in that movie the other night, but Napa Girl is the one who ended up with the winery, and that's the energy I intend to channel.

But getting back to the Tour and Pour, as I'm calling my new venture, if our guests haven't already purchased a boxed lunch elsewhere, they'll soon have the opportunity to order from the food trucks that I know will be clamoring for a spot close to our newly refurbished patio.

Which...okay, we don't actually have a patio yet. So that needs to be my next project.

With that in mind, I head to neighboring Vallejo, to my favorite consignment shop, where I'm able to score four, lightly used picnic tables for barely more than the cost of the paint I'll also need to buy in order to spruce them up.

. . .

BACK AT THE WINERY, I ONCE AGAIN REQUISITION A FEW of the interns. Hey, it's been a coupla weeks since the last time. And, seriously, Bee and Jake need to learn to share.

I set my crew to work weeding and washing and otherwise prepping the neglected brick terrace just outside the tasting room. It's convenient to the parking lot, has easy access to the rest room (okay, it's behind the bar, so not ideal) and it also boasts a decent view of the vines. So, what if it's a little crowded with four picnic tables? I figure that will just encourage people to socialize more.

I'm standing back, admiring my work, when my sisters appear. "There you are!" Rosa calls. "We've been looking for you."

"Well, I'm here," I say as I gesture at the tables. "What do you think?"

My sisters look puzzled. "Are we...throwing a party?" Bee asks hesitantly.

"No, it's our new picnic area."

"Um...did we need a new picnic area?" Rosa asks, while Bee whispers sotto voce, "I didn't know we had an old one?"

"Yes," I remind Rosa. "We do if we want food trucks,"

"But...*do* we want food trucks?" Bianca asks, looking even more confused. "I mean...why?"

"Because! I'm trying to create buzz, that's why. I'm trying to get people interested in what we're doing here, so they'll be excited for our opening. So, that they'll buy lots of wine and we can hit the ground running."

Bee nods. "Okay. That makes sense. But if we don't have any foot traffic, what's going to bring in the food trucks?"

I groan internally. I should have figured she'd immediately pick out the weak spot in my plan. I could have saved myself several hours this morning, if I'd talked to her first. Not that anyone ever has time to listen. "I have ideas," I say, hoping I sound half as confident and mysterious as she did last night. "I'm working on it. But you still haven't said—how does it look?"

"It looks great," Rosa replies, a little too quickly. "I just wonder if we need all four tables? It seems a bit..."

"Crowded?" Bianca finishes for her. "Although, that's probably because of all the paint colors. I think it would look better if they were all painted the same."

"One of the darker colors," Rosa agrees. "Because, otherwise, once we start serving wine, they'll be stained in no time. And that'll look—"

"Blah," Bee supplies. "And dingy."

"Mm."

My lips roll in as I try to keep from screaming. Only one of the colors I've chosen is actually dark, and the burgundy shade clashes with the brick. Also, the point of using multiple colors was to disguise the fact that the tables are not all the same size or height, or in the same condition. Mission accomplished there, I guess.

"A dark green would look nice," Bianca offers. "Or maybe a redwood stain?"

Stain? Seriously? Is my sister suggesting I strip the paint off *all four tables*, sand them all down and then *stain* them? "What do either of those have to do with wine?" I ask.

My sisters exchange a look. "What does what have to do with wine?" Rosa asks. "I thought we were talking about paint?"

"Yes! I can't believe you didn't see it," I say as I point to each table in succession. "Sauvignon Blanc, Chardonnay, Cabernet, Rosé. Did you really not get that?"

Two identically confused expressions meet my gaze. "Nope, sorry." "Didn't get it," my sisters say.

Yeah, we are *so* not in sync, I think to myself. "Okay, never mind. So why were you looking for me anyway?"

"Oh! Right!" Bianca says, looking suddenly much more animated. She gestures at the closest table and asks, "Is this dry?"

"Dry enough, I guess," I respond with a shrug. What does it even matter? I'm going to be repainting it, anyway. Or staining the damn thing. Or—I dunno—maybe I'll just chop them up for firewood. So, they can be used for a funeral pyre after I die of annoyance.

I make a mental note to check the county calendar for a list of Burn Ban dates—because the last thing I need is to get tangled up in any more red tape.

"Bianca has something she wants to share with us," Rosa explains.

"Okay. So, this is just an experiment," Bee cautions, taking three small tasting cups from the satchel she's carrying, and then a flip-top bottle half-filled with a murky yellow liquid. "And it's *super*, super premature. So don't expect it to taste like much right now. It's only been fermenting for a handful of weeks."

"Got it," I say, watching as she carefully fills three glasses with something hazy and sparkling. "It's embryonic wine."

"Proto-wine," Rosa agrees, flashing me a grin.

Bianca rolls her eyes. "So, I got to thinking about what you said, Legs, about Nonna and her pét-nat, and— No, this isn't that!" she hurriedly explains, when I start to get excited. "But I've been playing around with this field blend and...I don't know." She hands out the glasses and shrugs. "I think there are some possibilities here. See what you think."

Rosa and I sniff cautiously, smelling grape juice and yeast, wincing as the carbon dioxide hits our noses. It's harsh and overly sweet, bubbly with a hint of funk. But beneath it all...

there is something. Something promising—I think Bee's right about that. Something exciting. Something...familiar.

"What kind of blend did you say this was?" Rosa asks, taking another small, experimental sip.

"A field blend," Bee replies—a nonsense answer that earns her two disbelieving glances.

"Really?" I demand.

"No, what varietals?" Rosa clarifies—unnecessarily, in my opinion. It's inconceivable that Bee didn't know what she meant.

"Just, you know," Bee shrugs nonchalantly—too nonchalantly, if you ask me. "Two of the grapes we harvested at the beginning of the season."

"Bee..."

"Fine. It's a pinot and a chardonnay."

Rosa blinks. "But that's..."

"*Champagne?*" I squeal in delight. "We're making CHAMPAGNE?"

And now I'm the one catching disgusted glances from my sisters.

"Legs," Rosa scolds, reproachfully. "C'mon."

"What?" Bee stares at me, aghast. "No! Of course not!"

"Oh, I know, I know," I brush their protests away. "We aren't allowed to call it that. But...are we?"

Bee's eyes sparkle excitedly. A grin spreads over her face as she nods. "Yes? I...I think so? Maybe?"

"Omigod," I scream. Fetal champagne splashes everywhere as I tackle-hug my sister. Thankfully, Rosa has the presence of mind to grab the glasses out of our hands before they go flying, too. "Bee! I love you! Both of you," I amend, pulling Rosa into our hug. "This is..." I say, my voice breaking. "Omigod."

"Legs?" Rosa puts a hand on my shoulder and tugs, leaning in to see my face. "What's wrong? What's going on?"

I shake my head and sniffle loudly. "Nothing's wrong. This...it means everything."

Bee's eyes widen in alarm. "You know it won't be ready for a while yet, right? And—we still don't know—it might be awful."

"What? No way." I shake my head. "Awful? *Those* grapes? Grown *here*? With *you* calling the shots? Pfft. Of course it won't be awful. I already know, it's going to be exceptional."

"I think so, too," Rosa agrees. "But, Legs, you're looking awfully upset for someone who claims to be happy."

"It's because you *listened* to me," I tell them. "I didn't think *anyone* was listening. And I know I've screwed up, and that you hate all my ideas—"

"What?" Bee asks.

"We listen," Rosa protests. "And of course we don't hate your ideas."

"We don't," Bee agrees. "You have good ideas. Not about paint colors, or pizza toppings, perhaps. But, in general..."

"Wine colors," I snap back with faux annoyance. "Wine. Why don't you get that?"

Bianca lays a hand on Rosa's arm. "Promise me something," she tells her. "If I ever produce a vintage that looks like that—" She nods toward the terrace.

"Fired," Rosa responds, with perfect deadpan. "Immediately."

"Thank you," Bianca replies solemnly.

"Oh, screw you both," I grouse, but without heat, as they pull me in for another three-way hug. For the first time since I got home— No. For the first time since I got the call about Nonna—my heart feels light.

We can do this, I think, as I send my thoughts winging up to heaven. *We will do this. We'll make you proud.*

It's a crazy moment. I feel hopeful and validated, optimistic and invincible. And I blame *everything* that happens after on that feeling. I really should know better by now.

Chapter 15

Clay

One week bleeds into the next and Allegra's the happiest I've ever seen her. She and her sisters have resolved whatever tension there was between them, and she's bursting with ideas to promote the winery. None of which seems to involve breaking laws or contravening the WDO—something that makes my life infinitely easier. Not to mention that a happy Legs is a spectacularly sexy Legs.

Miles is back from his honeymoon; he's walking around with a perpetual grin and an aura of sexual satisfaction. Under normal circumstances, that's the kind of thing guaranteed to make him the butt of some good-natured (for the most part) jokes. But not this week. I'm doing him a solid by giving him cover. So yeah. Too long/didn't read? Life. Is. Good.

I'm so relaxed, that I don't even stress when I get the call about a possible disturbance on Silverado Trail. A group of bikers has been spotted on the road and the fear is that they might slow down traffic, which normally is not the kind of thing the sheriff's department is asked to handle, but I volunteer to check it out all the same.

I'm pretty sure what I'll find when I get there, and I kind of want to see it with my own eyes.

The day is unseasonably warm as I make my way to the coordinates I've been given. The sky is cloudless and blue. The mostly denuded grapevines glitter in the hard sun. Here and there I spy a cluster of desiccated grapes clinging stubbornly to their vines.

If I understand correctly, they've been left there on purpose. Something to do with concentrating flavors, and some kind of rot? I don't know. I've never claimed to know anything about making wine, but that sounds like bullshit to me.

Up ahead, the bike group comes into view, moving slowly, with Legs in the lead. Two wine-bottle-shaped, mylar balloons, attached to the flagpole at the back of her bike, bob along behind her. A wide smile breaks over my face. She appears to be singing, gesturing widely with expansive, theatrical waves of one hand while she steers with the other. And, unexpectedly, I feel my heart constrict in my chest. She looks so joyous, so care-free, so completely in her element. It's intoxicating.

But that's an unfortunate reminder of why I'm here.

There's a possibility the bikers have been drinking, which could pose a problem. In fact, come to think of it, that might be *why* this ended up on my desk (so to speak) in the first place.

Cycling under the influence is a misdemeanor (as per the California Vehicle Code, Section 21200.5). I'm not sure if Legs is aware of that.

I refocus my attention on the group. And...yeah, so far, so good; I see no issues, no reason to be concerned. Everyone's wearing a helmet. They're staying in line and keeping to the side—for the most part. No one appears to be inebriated—an important consideration. No one is wobbling more than usual, or straggling too far behind, or struggling too obviously. Still, my busy brain can't help but catalogue all the possible problems that might crop up, all the myriad factors working for and against them.

Like the weather, for example. It's warm, like I said, which might increase both the need for hydration, and the possibility of heat stroke. On the other hand, visibility is good, so they've got that going for them.

Then there's the road. Despite being narrow and winding, rife with blind curves and hidden driveways, it's also flat and level and well maintained. And—another point in their favor—I know the group is being led by someone who grew up here, who knows the hazards and is familiar with the terrain.

On the other hand, there's the drinking to be considered. Normally, I'd be vociferous in my objections. Driving any kind of vehicle while inebriated? No stars at all. Would not recommend.

But I have inside information. Legs has explained that all the wineries involved have agreed to special abbreviated tastings. That all the bikers are to receive vouchers allowing them to return for full tastings at a discounted price. So, theoretically, it should not be a problem.

A bigger problem, and my main concern at the moment, is the median age of the bikers. They all appear to be on the far side of fifty, which is forcing me to re-evaluate the danger they face from heat stroke, dehydration, slower response times, reduced balance, and possibly, a lower tolerance for alcohol.

I tap my brakes, slowing my speed, widening the space between us, turning on my hazard lights—as a warning to the vehicles behind me. I'mma hang back here and chill, just keeping an eye on things. For safety's sake.

Air flows in through my open windows, carrying the scents of hay, dried leaves, and overripe fruit. The sound of Leg's voice floats in as well, making me smile. The melody is a familiar one, the words are not. And my smile widens when

I realize what I'm hearing; yet another Legs Martinelli original.

"When I was still too young to drink,
I asked my Nonna which should it be?
Would I like white wine, would I like red?
Here's what she said to me:

"Que Será Syrah
You might try a nice Chablis,
Mourvedre, or Pinot Gris,
Que Será Syrah

"Then I grew up and got engaged,
Went to my lover—what would he say?
Champagne, Prosecco, or Sparkling Rosé,
To serve on our wedding day?

"He said... Que Será Syrah
All three sound just great to me,
Or maybe a Pinot Gris?
Que Será Syrah
Or maybe, Chablis?

"Now when my sisters come to me,
I know the questions, before they ask,
Steel vat or barrel, qvevri or cask,
Bottle, or box or flask?

"And I say... Que Será Syrah
Whatever you do; do you
Just pour me a glass, or two,
Que Será Syrah

Que Será Syrah

What will be, Chablis!

She finishes with an enthusiastic flourish, and I find myself wanting to cheer and applaud. Her bike-riding followers clearly feel the same urge. For the next thirty-or-so seconds the ding-ding-ding of a dozen (give or take) bike bells fill the air, flushing birds (and the occasional small mammal) out of the vegetation on both sides of the road.

The raucous noise is not exactly a pleasant sound. And while it's not triggering, per se, it's close enough to alarm bells that my heart rate spikes. I also find myself wondering whether it's loud enough to qualify as a noise violation. An unlikely possibility, but one which—shit!—I do not want to have to address, right now. To distract myself, I run the words to the song she just sang over in my head.

The first and third verses are clearly autobiographical and at least semi-realistic. But it's that second verse that's got me curious.

Was she engaged, at some point? Or, worse yet, married? She's never mentioned having any relationship after she left her mother's house, and I know she moved around a lot. But it seems highly unlikely that she's remained single all this time.

I rarely ever mention my exes, either. Unless I'm asked, or unless something specific comes up. Like it did with my laundry soap, which Legs asked me about after I'd washed and dried her clothes the night of the storm...

"A LAUNDRY SOAP SUBSCRIPTION?" LEGS SOUNDS BEMUSED. *"Wow. I've never heard of that."*

"Neither had I." I briefly consider mentioning the one for the bamboo toilet paper, but the conversation has already gotten weird, so I don't.

"So, what's your girlfriend—sorry, your ex—doing now?" Legs asks, exhibiting none of the jealousy I'm currently suffering from—and all over a potentially fictitious, make-believe boyfriend. Incredible.

I shrug disinterestedly. "All I know is that she moved back to San Francisco. She was always more of a city girl. Napa was a little too rural for her liking."

"You don't keep in touch?"

"No. Why would we?"

"Well, you shared a life, didn't you?"

"No, not really." I think about it for a moment. "It wasn't like that. We were more like rivers in the delta."

"You were what in the what?"

"The San Francisco Bay delta system—you know, all the rivers that flow down from the mountains and funnel into the bay? Her expression remained blank, prompting me to add, "You did go to school here, didn't you? I assumed field trips to the San Francisco Bay Model was part of the normal curriculum?"

"I don't really know. Maybe I was out that day."

"So how do you describe relationships?" I teased.

"Oh, that's easy." Her eyes lit up and she sidled closer, close enough to slide her hands over my shoulders, her fingers twisting in my hair. "I think they're like vines."

"Which? The relationships, or the people in them?"

"Both, actually."

"That sounds confusing," I murmured, vividly aware that our mouths were mere centimeters apart, willing her to close the distance.

"Mm, not really. We're all wrapped up with one another, anyway, aren't we? All tangled in each other's business?"

"Sounds...uncomfortable," I reply, though that's not the word I was thinking.

"Doesn't have to be," she said, and inched even closer.

And I wanted to disagree, but then her lips were on mine, and we never did return to the subject...

IT'S HARD TO BELIEVE WE'VE ONLY KNOWN EACH OTHER for a matter of weeks—but that's all it's been. And I know I can't be falling for her—not this hard, not this soon. Because that's not at all realistic. Except, "Holy shit." I very much suspect that I am. I'm so caught up in my thoughts, still reeling from this new revelation, that I nearly miss the disaster taking place right in front of me.

An older man, one of several who I'd already had my eye on, collapses suddenly, listing slowly to the side before toppling into the street.

I slam on my brakes, bringing my vehicle to a stop and flicking on the overhead lights before exiting the truck. The tour has, predictably, come to a chaotic stop, there are multiple people milling about, huddling 'round the victim. Some even attempt to lift him from the ground—which I quickly put a stop to.

"I'll need everyone to take a step back," I order as, from the corner of my eye, I spy Legs, off her bike and racing towards me. "Let's give this gentleman some room."

"But shouldn't we move him out of the road?" someone asks.

"No," I tell them. "Not until I've assessed his condition." And probably not even then. I've radioed for an ambulance. Moving him will be a determination for the EMT's to make.

"What happened?" Legs demands when she finally reaches me. I'm kneeling beside the fallen biker, checking his pulse, mentally counting the beats. I lift a hand in an obvious request for her to give me a moment, but she continues to pepper me with questions. "Is he all right? Omigod. Did you hit him."

225

"That's what I'm trying to ascertain," I tell her, just before the last part of her question hits home. "Did I what? Hit him? No, of course I didn't!"

As I glance up, scowling at Legs, I notice a woman on the sidelines, aiming her phone in my direction. "Ma'am? No pictures, please."

"Oh, I'm not taking pictures," she replies, her eyes glued to her screen. "This is video."

"No," I snap. "Absolutely not. I need you to stop what you're doing, delete that video, and then put your phone away. And keep it away."

I turn back to Legs. "Look, we need to move all these people off the road. Bikes too. Can you handle that?"

"On it," she says and immediately starts herding people onto the shoulder with surprising efficiency.

"And no pictures!"

After what feels like a long time, but in actuality is no more than a couple of minutes, the man on the ground begins to stir.

"Sir? Can you hear me?" I ask to no avail. Lifting my head again, I scan the crowd until I catch Allegra's eye. "Do you know what his name is?"

"I do," the amateur videographer tells me. "It's Charlie."

Charlie? Yeah, I don't think so. "Last name?"

"Rogers," Allegra supplies.

I do a double take, but she seems serious. *Mr. Rogers? Ohhkay. I think that's even worse.* "Charles? This is Deputy Romero. You've had a slight accident. If you understand what I'm saying, squeeze my hand." A slight frown creases the man's forehead, but his eyes remain closed. And even though I'm sure he can hear me, his hand remains lax.

"No," my informant corrects me. "Not Charles. Good heavens, you'll never get him to answer to that. I told you; it's Charlie."

I mentally shake my head. *Charlie Rogers?* And I thought I had it bad. *Bruh, your parents hated you, didn't they?*

"Ma'am? What's your relationship to...to Mr. Rogers?"

A thread of startled laughter weaves its way through the crowd of bikers. "She's his neighbor," someone shouts.

The woman in question scowls. "No, I'm not. I'm his sister."

"Okay, well, do you want to come over here and try talking to your brother? He might respond more readily to a familiar voice."

She shuffles a few steps closer, reluctantly. She prods his ankle with her foot and says, "Charlie? Cut it out. You're making a scene." When there's (shockingly) still no reply she turns to me. "What now?"

"Try again," I instruct. "Just talk to him as you normally would."

"Get up, you old coot," she says, prodding his ankle once again. If she prods any harder, I'll have to call it a kick—and book her for assault. "You're making us late. We're gonna miss the whole tour."

The surrounding crowd murmurs menacingly at the reminder. Charlie groans theatrically and blinks his eyes open. "Elaine? Is that you?"

"Of course it's me," his sister replies. "Who else would it be?"

"Where am I?"

"Flat on your back in the middle of the road," Elaine tells him.

"Holding the rest of us up," someone else calls out.

"Sir?" I say, trying again. "You fell off your bicycle. How are you feeling now? Does anything hurt?"

"My arm," he replies instantly, lifting said limb, and holding it out for my inspection. "I think it's broken."

Considering the ease with which he's moving it, I very much doubt that his arm is broken. But I check it out all the same. "I think it's just bruised," I finally say.

"Like my ego," Charlie intones mournfully.

"Oh, for Pete's sake," Elaine grumbles. "You're not hurt. Get up!"

"Actually," I tell her. "Since the ambulance is already on its way, I think it's best if he stays where he is for now."

Elaine's mouth drops open. "An ambulance! Who called for that?"

"And how long is it gonna take to get here?" someone else inquires.

"Should be no more than twenty minutes," I reply in an effort to pacify the crowd, but they continue to grumble all the same. "And *I* called for it."

"But that's... Grr!" Elaine growls and kicks her brother's foot again. "Damn it, Charlie. Now look what you've done."

"Ma'am," I say sharply. "Please stop that."

"You're a terrible sister," Charlie says tearfully, as he rocks his head from side to side. "All you care about is getting drunk. I'm nothing but a mule to you, aren't I?"

Mule? Once again, my gaze arrows in on Allegra. "Is he drunk?" I demand.

Her face pales. "N-no. That's not possible. He can't be."

"Of course, he's not drunk," Elaine snaps. "Charlie hates wine. Never touches the stuff. That's why I brought him."

"But..." Legs frowns at Elaine. "He *was* served? I mean, everyone was. At each stop. The pourers collected the tickets. I made sure of it."

"Yes, of course. That doesn't mean he drank them, does it?" Elaine replies. "He got them for me."

Leg's eyes widen even more. "You had double the allotment? But that's completely against the rules! You knew that."

Elaine shrugs. "Well, there are rules, and there are rules, you know. And well-behaved women rarely make history."

"I think you mean, 'scofflaws who admit their crimes in front of an officer are unlikely to make bail,'" a heckler in the crowd calls back.

Elaine shrugs. "I'm not concerned. I know my rights."

Annoyed with the by-play, I wave Allegra over. "Look," I tell her. "I think you should go ahead with the tour. You don't want to keep all these people standing around in the sun any longer than you have to."

"I know. And I don't. But I can't just leave, can I?"

"Yes, you can. In fact, I'm telling you to."

"But..."

"I'll wait here with the Rogerses until the ambulance arrives. You just concentrate on getting these people off the road and out of the sun. All right?"

"What'll happen to their bikes," Legs asks, looking worried. "I'm responsible for those, as well."

"What's gonna happen to my wine?" Elaine demands, looking angry. "That's what I want to know."

I'm getting close to the end of my rope. "You're already looking at a possible misdemeanor," I snap. "So, I suggest you not say anything to further incriminate yourself." I turn to Legs and add. "I'll take care of the bikes. I can load them in my truck and drop them off at the shop after I'm finished for the day."

"Okay," she sighs, looking sad and defeated; triggering the need to hug her, which I obviously can't indulge. "I guess that'll work. Thank you."

"Hey, c'mon. None of that." Rising to my feet. I give her shoulder a quick squeeze. "It's gonna be okay, you know? You're doing great."

"You really think so?" she asks, eyes widening in surprise.

I nod firmly. "I do. You got this. Now get the heck out of here."

"Okay," she says again. She takes a breath and squares her shoulders. "You're the boss." A grateful smile stretches her lips, and I feel my own lips curve in response.

"That's right," I tell her, lowering my voice to just above a whisper. "See that you remember that."

"Yeah, yeah," she mutters softly—for my ears only. "In your dreams, Romeo."

I'm still smiling when, a few minutes later, the tour group departs, with Legs in the lead again, calling out, "All right, everybody; here we go. It's time for another song."

I SUPPOSE IT SHOULDN'T SURPRISE ME (ALTHOUGH, TO BE honest, I *am* surprised—and not happily) but dealing with the Rogeres takes up most of the rest of my workday. Then, after finally getting them settled at the hospital, I have to stop at the station and write up my report. Which means that, by the time I finally get to the bike shop, at the end of a very long day, it's already closed. So, I let my dispatcher know that I probably won't be in, tomorrow, until sometime after noon. Then I drag my weary ass home.

It's not that I planned on seeing Legs tonight, but I have been hoping. So, when the knock comes at my door, I think I know what to expect.

"Hey!" I say, smiling in anticipation as I pull the door open. But pleasure turns almost immediately to concern as I catch sight of her face. "What's wrong?"

Her expression, already stormy, clouds up even more. "Everything. Can I come in?"

"Sure. Of course." I hold the door open so that she can wheel her bike inside. It's the same one she was riding earlier; I recognize the wine bottle balloons. "Where'd you ride from anyway? Downtown?"

She shakes her head. "Caparelli." Her gaze tracks mine and she frowns. Next thing I know she's tearing the balloons from the pole. "You got somewhere I can toss these?"

I hold out my hand. "Here. I'll take 'em. Now, c'mon. Let's get you hydrated."

In the kitchen, I pitch the balloons in the trash, then get her settled at the island. On a stool, this time. I'm not sure if she's suffering from heat exhaustion, but just in case she passes out, I don't want her to fall any further than she has to.

I grab a sports drink from the fridge. When I turn back around, I find her slumped over the counter, head buried in her arms.

"Here." I nudge her arm with the cold glass. "Drink this. It's got electrolytes."

"Thanks." She straightens up and empties half the glass. I move the open bottle to the counter, placing it within her reach. Then take a seat on the second stool.

"So, what's wrong?" I ask again. "What's happened?"

She shrugs listlessly. "Same thing that always happens. I messed up."

I'm about to ask—again—for a more specific answer, when an obvious one occurs to me. "Is it Mr. Rogers?"

Her head whips around as she straightens up and stares at me aghast. "W-hy are you asking *me*? Y-you said *you'd* take care of that?"

"I did." I place a hand over hers and squeeze reassuringly. "He was fine when I left him at the hospital. I mean, relatively so. They said they'd probably keep him there overnight, for observation. He was being treated for low blood sugar and possible heat exhaustion. Apparently, he said his sister hadn't allowed him time for breakfast before the bike tour."

"Oh, thank goodness," she says, sagging on her stool in relief. Then her face darkens again. "That woman..."

"I know." I nod in response. "And I'm sorry if I spooked you. I shouldn't have assumed."

She smiles faintly. "It's okay. Just promise you'll never, ever get spooked again."

"Uhh...what?"

"Never mind." She flaps a hand dismissively. "Just another old movie quote. It's not important."

"You like movies, huh?"

"I used to." She falls silent for a moment, playing with her glass on the counter, sliding it through the condensation from one hand to the other. "Sorry for bursting in on you like this. I felt like I couldn't stay there a minute longer, but I didn't know where else to go."

"No need to apologize," I tell her. "I'm glad you're here."

"Thanks," she says quietly, still sliding her glass around the counter.

I wait a beat, but it's obvious she's not going to tell me what's wrong. And there's no reason she should. We really don't know each other that well, even if it feels like we do. "I was thinking of making some dinner. You want anything?"

She shrugs disinterestedly. "Yeah. Maybe."

Maybe? Terrific. But—maybe—her lack of enthusiasm is contagious, because suddenly, I don't feel like cooking, either. "Or I could order something. Pizza, perhaps?"

She twists her head in my direction and eyes me curiously. "What kind of pizza."

"Whatever you want."

"No, you. What would you order?"

"I'll eat most things," I tell her. "Suggest something."

She considers for a moment. "Pulled pork?"

I nod. "Ai'ight. Cool."

"What about pineapple?"

"A classic. Anything else?"

"You pick this time."

"Hm." I consider the flavor profile. "Maybe...jalapenos?"

"Yes. Perfect." She's definitely perked up now, eyes dancing with excitement. "What about Cotija cheese?"

"Love it. So is that it?"

"Ranch dressing?"

I shoot her a disparaging look. "Well, duh. Obviously."

She sips at her drink and looks around while I place the order. After I disconnect the call, she sighs and says, "I think my sisters wish I'd stayed in Europe."

"I doubt that," I tell her. "I was there when they came to the station to pick you up—remember? As I recall, they seemed pretty happy to see you."

"Well, sure—then. But we hadn't all lived together, under one roof, in nearly ten years. I think they forgot how annoying I am."

"Are you annoying?" I tease as I reach for her, urging her off her stool and onto my lap. "I hadn't noticed."

"I was today," she says, tilting her head to the side as I nuzzle her neck.

"Yeah? In what way?" But she shrugs and, instead of answering, turns her head and presses her lips to mine. And for a long moment, that lasts until the pizza arrives, neither of us talk at all.

Over pizza and beer—two beers apiece, with me justifying the fact that I'm breaking my own workday rule of only having one, by virtue of the fact that I'm off in the morning—I tell her,

"You know, when something's bothering *me*, I often find it helps to talk about it. A burden shared is a burden halved—my mom used to say that a lot."

"Nonna used to say that, too." She dips her pizza in the cup of dressing. "I don't really have anyone to talk to anymore. She was my best friend in a lot of ways."

"Must have been hard to lose her," I say.

Legs nods. "You have no idea. I-I think I went crazy for a while there—after, I mean. I made *so many* stupid decisions."

"But that was only...what? Six months ago?"

"Yeah," she laughs a little at that. "Yeah, it was. Seven now. It's funny; it feels so much longer. So, what do you think? Maybe I'm still not over it?"

"I imagine it takes a while," I say, which...I'm pretty sure is a lie. Because I don't think you ever do get over that kind of loss. You just find ways to live with it. "You should probably give yourself some slack."

"Yeah." She's quiet for another long while—long enough for us to finish the rest of the pizza, a side of chicken wings, and some of those weird cinnamon things that everyone sells now, and no one can seem to agree on a name for.

"Thanks," she says, and I'm distracted by the sight of her licking cinnamon sugar from her lips and from between her fingers, and for seeking out the last few drops of beer, head tilted back, throat working as she swallows, that I lose the plot and forget to answer for a minute.

"Uhh...for what?" I finally ask.

"Oh, I dunno." She shrugs. "Just...for being here? For letting me talk. For not judging me."

I have no answer to that, so I do what I usually do—or maybe what I *always* do. I find a way to deflect. "You know, you don't talk nearly as much as you think you do. For example, I still don't know what happened today that has you so upset."

"True." She's quiet for a moment. Then she looks at me and says, "Can I spend the night?"

I nod slowly. "I was hoping you would."

"And will you take me to bed and let me ride you?"

"Any time you want."

So, I guess there's more than one way to deflect.

TRUE TO HER WORD, SHE DOES RIDE ME—IN THE MORE traditional sense, this time. Straddling my hips, taking me inside. The soft weight of her on my legs, pinning me down, pressing against my sack, pushing me into the bedding, is a kind of claiming. With every downward stroke, she owns me. With every upward glide—well, that's just sweet, sweet torture.

It's all I can do not to grasp her hips and direct her rhythm, like I did the night of the storm. Instead, I palm her breasts, trapping her nipples between my fingers, teasing them in much the same way her teeth trap and tease her bottom lip. And maybe that's a kind of claiming, too.

Afterwards, we spoon together. I brush her hair aside, press a kiss against the back of her neck, and let my fingers wander idly tracing the curving letters that make up her tattoo. And then she does talk, a little, about how the rest of the tour went. There was a bee-sting that required another ambulance be called, but it turned out all right. And I can't shake the feeling that there's something else, something bigger, that she's still not willing to talk about.

"W-r-e-c-k-l-e-s-s," I spell out the letters of her tattoo. "Tell me about this."

She cranes her neck and glances up at me. "What do you want to know about it?"

"Anything. When you got it and why. What it means."

She laughs softly. "Well, that's quite a lot to unpack. Do you want the official story, or the truth?"

"The truth. Always." I don't even have to think about that. "But I'm also curious to know what the 'official story' is and why you even have one."

"Well, Deputy," she says teasingly. "Any official story is basically a cover up. Surely you know that?"

I slide down the bed a little, enough so that I can run my tongue over the letters. "Uh-huh. But why do *you* need one for a bit of ink?"

"Well, first of all, I got it when I was seventeen."

I nod. Of course. I should have guessed. The legal age for tattoos in California is eighteen. No exceptions made for parental consent, like in some other places. "Ah. Gotcha. Let me guess. You were drunk, at a party, and someone in a back-room was playing with his first machine?" I have a couple of tattoos like that, too—not nearly as good as this one, however. Or as big.

When it comes to tattoos, size definitely matters. And I spend a long, long moment wrestling with yet another unexpected flare of jealousy. The tattoo covers maybe a third of her upper back. It would have taken a while, and she'd have probably been topless. Remembering her as she was the night we met and imagining that version of her lying face down on a bed somewhere, a haze of smoke hanging in the air, crowds of teenagers wandering in and out of the room to gawk—that's messing with my brain. Big time.

"A party?" she laughs at that, sounding a little scandalized. "Nooo. Fake ID. A friend of a friend...of a friend? I dunno. There might have been one or two more degrees of separation in there. Anyway, he was just starting out, working as an intern in a big shop down in Oakland. They used to let him practice after hours on anyone he could pull in. Basically, he was working for tips and experience."

"I was gonna say, that's pretty good work for an amateur. Other than the spelling."

"Yeah. That's the bigger reason," she says. "The funny part is that he actually did a spell search before he began. You know, to make sure he was getting it right? I guess he must've looked up wreck and extrapolated from there."

"Ironic."

"Isn't it?" After a moment, she continues. "So, anyway, I think I wanted a tattoo mostly because I didn't have one. And partially because I wasn't *supposed* to have one yet. But I was also *really* tired of people calling me reckless as an insult, or a criticism. So, I take chances—so what? I think that's brave."

"I can see that," I say gently massaging her shoulders, which were growing tense, now that she'd switched over to defense-mode.

"So, that's the actual story. I decided to own my recklessness, to celebrate it as a positive quality. Unfortunately, I ended up proving my critics' point. That's where the official story comes in."

"So, the official story is...?"

She turns and bats her eyes at me. "Isn't it obvious? I'm just really proud of my driving record. *No wrecks.* I am one-hundred-percent wreck-less."

A wide grin threatens to split my face. "And people buy that?"

"You'd be surprised," she mutters darkly. "Plus, I've mostly lived in Europe, since then. Most of the people who've seen it probably didn't realize it was misspelled, or they thought *they* were wrong."

"Well, if it bothers you, you can always get a coverup," I suggest.

"Yeah. I just don't know what I'd cover it with."

"You could always turn the W into a phoenix," I say, tracing over the letter. "Wings, here and there. Body in the middle. Some of the flourishes already look like they could be flames. Maybe add some red and orange to accentuate that?"

"That...could work," she says in awe-struck tones. "In fact, that sounds really pretty. How did you think of that so fast?"

I shrug, not willing to admit the truth. That it wasn't fast at all. That I've been obsessed for years with the idea of getting a phoenix tattoo myself. Ever since the first time fire nearly destroyed my life. "It just came to me."

"Well thank you," she says. Then she cuddles against me, nestling her butt against my groin. She sighs in contentment and closes her eyes. After a moment she murmurs. "I'm so glad you pulled me over, and that my license was expired and...all of it."

I chuckle softly as I pull her close. "Well, I had to. You were being...reckless."

Chapter 16

Allegra

Noah, the owner of Wheeling Through the Vines, is enthusiastic when we drop off the bikes the next morning—and excited to get the next Tour and Pour on the calendar. It seems most of the reviews that have been coming in have been positive, and he's blithely unconcerned about the fact that I'd needed to call *two* separate ambulances. "That's why we make 'em sign releases," he says cheerfully.

Clay is quiet as we walk back to his SUV—and it's a heavy, judgmental silence that rattles my nerves.

"What's wrong?" I ask as he navigates us in the direction of home. "You've been quiet ever since we left the bike shop."

"Ah, it's nothing." He shrugs. "I just hate guys like that."

"Who—Noah? Why? He seemed nice enough."

"Why?" Clay shoots me an annoyed look. "Because he doesn't care *anything at all* about his clients, that's why. As long as they've signed releases and leave five-star reviews, it's all good. So, what if they need an ambulance, or sustain injuries, or get saddled with astronomical medical bills. Let's get the next tour on the books and rake in that guap."

I stare at him, openmouthed. "Those were *my* clients, too, you know. I was the one in charge. Yet you told me I should leave the Rogeres behind; that I was overreacting to Gracie's bee-sting. So, is that what you secretly think of me, too?"

Clay shakes his head. "No. I think you showed a normal amount of concern. And I did *not* say you were overreacting. I told you to stop catastrophizing about it. Either of those situations could have gone sideways; but the time to be aware of that is when you're in the moment. Agonizing about something after the fact, when there's nothing you can do about it? How does that help anyone?"

"Maybe," I say, and then fall into a protracted silence until Clay breaks it by saying, "Okay, I guess now it's your turn."

"What?" I ask, frowning as I try to remember what we were talking about.

"Now you're the one who's gone quiet. I know you're still upset about yesterday. And I know it's about more than just the bee-sting. I wish you'd tell me. Maybe I could help?"

Talking about yesterday is the last thing I want to do. On the other hand, the closer we get to the winery, the more my tension mounts. And he does give good advice. "I don't want you to judge me."

Clay's eyebrows rise. "When have I ever done that?"

"You mean other than the night you pulled me over for speeding? Don't you dare pretend you weren't judging me then!"

"Fair," he says, nodding thoughtfully. "But that's when I didn't know you. I don't think I'd do that now."

"Unless I started driving badly," I suggest.

"Well sure," he says, grinning playfully. "But it's your *driving* that I'd be judging in that case. Not you."

I nod and pretend to agree, but I'm not sure I do. Me, my

driving, my choices, the mistakes I make. Isn't it all the same thing?

"So...yesterday?" he prompts.

"Okay," I say. Then I nod again. It's funny actually, but I meant to tell him all of this last night. It's partly why I went there. But it's embarrassing and I chickened out. I wanted just one night of fun. And yes, one night of not being judged. But we'll be home soon, and my sisters will be there, and I feel like I have to unload on someone before I get there...

My bikers were in good spirits after we left Clay and the Rogeres at the side of the road. It was a little bit shocking, actually. I knew they were all strangers to one another, but all the same, their lack of interest surprised me. We stopped at one more winery, almost directly across from Belmonte, and that was somewhat bittersweet. While the bikers enjoyed their wine—and the herbed almonds the winery had provided to go with—I contemplated the vineyards I'd played in as a child, trying to imagine the winery from Clay's point of view, remembering what he had said about seeing the house from a distance, lit up for parties. I couldn't imagine what it would feel like knowing I did not belong or would not be welcome there. It occurred to me that that was probably part of the reason why I had not yet made time to visit my aunt and uncle. I couldn't be certain of my reception.

Soon, I promised my inner critic; I'll stop by for a visit soon. But it continued to nag at me, even as I gathered my group back together and headed for the next winery on our route: Caparelli...

"But you don't have any wine there," Clay interrupts.

"I know that. That's why I planned it as a rest and lunch spot. And no, before you ask, I did not sell any food. The bike company provided the lunches. Okay?"

"I know you think I'm a hard ass," he replies. "But I'm just trying to protect us both."

A STACK OF BOXED LUNCHES AWAITED US AS WE ROLLED UP Caparelli's drive. As we approached, I tried to do the same as I'd done with Belmonte, viewing it as an outsider would.

The house itself was looking a little bit dingy. The sign in front was faded and chipped, with gilt paint flaking off the letters. I knew that my sisters, Rosa in particular, had expended an enormous amount of time and energy (and as much money as Rosa's frugal soul would allow) just getting it to this point.

That was not a criticism, by the way. I'd seen the books and the accounts. I was aware of the constant juggling act she maintained. I wouldn't take on Rosa's job for the world.

Well, I couldn't anyway. I didn't have the experience. I didn't have the education. I probably didn't even have the smarts for it.

I just wished there was some magic that would restore the whole property to the way that I remembered it. But at least the terrace looked great.

I had taken my sisters' advice. I'd moved one of the tables (the sauvignon blanc; the one I'd painted a pale greenish cream color) down to where the lawn met the vineyard. I knew the field workers often ate their lunches there. They were embarrassingly grateful that I'd thought of them. I felt bad because I really hadn't. I felt even worse when I remembered what Rosa had said about the lighter colors becoming stained.

There was no denying that the three remaining tables fit the space perfectly, however. And even I had to admit that the dark, pearlescent charcoal paint was a perfect choice. Classier, more elegant, more refined than my earlier choices.

As everyone ate, I told them about the winery, the awards we'd won in the past, the exciting new wines we'd soon be releasing, my sister's skill. I'd posted a QRC on the wall, that people could scan if they wanted to be subscribed to our news-letter (still just a concept). And nearly everyone did. I encour-aged people to wander around and thought nothing of it when two of the women stopped to admire one of Nonna's rosebushes...

"Uh-oh," Clay observes.

"Would you stop interrupting," I snap. "I suppose *you* would have known better and warned them to keep their distance?" *And he'd have been right*, my inner critic points out. *It's not like you hadn't noticed the bees when you were out here last week.*

"No, I wouldn't," Clay replies. "It wouldn't have occurred to me at all. I mean, maybe if it had been a school group, I might've thought of it. But a bunch of grown-ass adults? At some point you have to learn to take care of yourself."

"So, you really don't think it was my fault?"

Clay shakes his head. "Did you tell her to go stick her face in a flower? Are we about to get to the part of the story where you confess to having chased her around the vineyard, with a bee in your hand trying to get her stung?"

"No!" I cross my arms and glare at him. "You know I would never do any of that."

"Then I can't think of any reason to blame you."

But I could still blame myself...

. . .

GRACIE HAD SHRIEKED WHEN THE BEE FLEW UP HER NOSE—SO *loud, that I was surprised when I was the only one who came running. By the time I reached her—a handful of seconds, at best —her eyes were already swollen shut and she was having trouble breathing. Thank God her best friend had taken the tour with her, she'd seen this before. She knew where Gracie kept her Epipen, and how to administer it.*

My biggest contribution was calling the ambulance.

No one complained (at least I didn't hear it) while we waited for the ambulance to arrive. Or while the EMTs were assessing Gracie's condition. She was frightened enough that she opted to be transported to the hospital, rather than continue with the tour. Which...really wouldn't have been an option at that point, anyway.

My heart sank a little when I checked the time and realized that we'd missed our time slots at the last two wineries.

It sank even more when I relayed this to the group.

And when I watched their faces fall, and heard the grumbling begin...I may have lost a little of my common sense.

At first, I suggested a tour of the grounds as compensation. But I guess the threat of encountering more bees was making people nervous. Then somebody asked about a barrel tasting, reminding everyone about the story I'd told them over lunch—all about the new, sparkling wine my sister was experimenting with. And about how she'd given us tastes, even though the juice (really, you couldn't call it wine yet) was still in the early fermentation stages. And suddenly, everyone wants to see the wine cave, everyone wants to taste Bianca's version of Champagne...

"LET ME GUESS, YOU TOOK THEM TO SEE THE BARREL room, or whatever it's called?"

"Ha. I wish." I shake my head. "There's almost always someone doing something there. I'm sure I could have found someone willing to give a mini-tour, point out some interesting features, or to talk everyone's ears off explaining the pros and cons of oak vs stainless steel. That would have been the smart thing to do. So of course, I took them to the cave."

"Wait—you have a cave?" Clay asks. "Your *own* cave?"

I have to laugh. "Omigod. The look on your face! Yes, of course, we do. Lots of wineries have them. Stags' Leap, Pine Ridge. Did you know that the one at Palmaz extends for eighteen stories?"

"Are you serious?"

"Mm-hm. Ours isn't anything like that, of course; it's very small. And before Bianca reopened it this summer, it hadn't been used in years. I remember playing in there when I was a kid. Which they probably wouldn't have allowed if they were actively storing or fermenting wine in there."

"Oh? Why's that?"

"Carbon Dioxide. Did you know that most of the fatalities that occur at wineries are due to CO_2 poisoning?"

"I did not," Clay replies, looking amused. Probably more amused than he ought to, given the grim subject. But I guess maybe, when you're in law enforcement, you get used to that kind of thing?

"So, what was the problem with the cave?" Clay asks. "I mean, I'm assuming that's where something happened. Correct me if I'm wrong."

"No, you're not wrong."

THE GATE WAS LOCKED, WHEN WE GOT TO THE CAVE, WHICH I *wasn't expecting. But, because I'd been an especially sneaky kid, I knew where the spare key used to be kept, and—lucky for me—*

no one had ever moved it. Once inside, it took a little fumbling before I found the light switch, which gave me a moment to reflect on how dark and quiet a cave could be.

Last time I'd visited, just after harvest, it had been ablaze with light, and abuzz with activity. Now it was as silent and sunless as midnight in a crypt. And every bit as creepy as I remembered it feeling when I'd played here as a kid. I shivered involuntarily.

"It's so cool in here, isn't it?" I asked brightly to cover my reaction. I flipped on the lights, as quickly as possible. All the while talking too fast about insulation, and geothermal factors, and passive air flow, and on and on.

People were walking around, poking their noses into every-thing. I warned them about straying too far from the entrance, and I tried to keep my patter light and entertaining, but eventu-ally people started asking when they were going to get to taste the wine.

"I'm sorry," I told them. "But I did say it was only a possibil-ity. I was hoping my sister would be here, but since she's not, I'm afraid that's not going to happen today. But be sure to come back in a few months and we'll be delighted to introduce you to all our beautiful wines. And, don't forget, if you sign up for our newsletter, you'll get updates right in your inbox whenever there's news."

I'd just started to urge my troops back towards the exit, when the clatter of boots on brick reached our ears, and the next moment Jake appeared in the doorway, looking harried and annoyed and—when he caught sight of me—some weird mixture of horror and relief.

"Legs, what the hell? Are these the missing bikers?"

"Well, they're bikers," I replied. "But nobody's missing." At which point I remembered that I currently had four fewer clients than I started out with—which had to be what he meant, right? "I mean, no. Sorry, these are the ones who aren't missing."

"They what? Never mind. Doesn't matter. They need to get out." To which I nearly responded: 'what do you think I'm trying to do?' except I didn't get the chance.

Raising his voice, Jake announced, "All right folks, please start heading outside, right away. And if you are with the bike tour, there are a coupla vans outside waiting for you."

"I could have done that," I told him angrily. After all, I'd been herding this particular group of people all day.

"Let's talk about it outside," Jake said sternly.

Which, of course, pissed me off. But before I could respond, a voice towards the back of the cave (where I'd told everyone not to go) called out, "I think I found it! Hey, is this it?" Startled, Jake and I turned toward the sound, and gasped in tandem. One of the more annoying members of my band was draped over a barrel, with his head practically in the bung hole—

"WAIT. IS THAT EVEN POSSIBLE?"

"Not the point. It's hyperbole. But he had is whole nose in the hole—which is *still* not something you want!

"SMELLS WEIRD," HE COMPLAINED. JUST BEFORE HE LAID HIS head on the barrel, with his ear over the bung hole. "I can hear it bubbling!"

"Sir!" Jake yelled, as loud as I've ever heard him. "Stop that! Get off that barrel and out of the cave—now!"

"Okay, okay," the man replied, replacing the bung hole plug—"

. . .

"It's really called that?"

"Clay!"

"Sorry. Go on..."

Jake was so mad he was vibrating. I was pretty angry as well, as the man (I'd thought his name was Dave, but at that point I wasn't sure) sauntered towards us. "But she said she'd let us have a taste," he said, pointing at me.

"You didn't?" Jake growled, turning his anger on me.

"Of course, I didn't," I replied. Then I turned to Dave. "I said maybe, if my sister was here."

"Why? I thought you were the owner? Can't you make any decisions on your own?"

"One of the owners," I said, holding up a finger (no, not that finger). "One!"

Which was when Jake lost it. "That's it. Out. Both of you!" Then he grabbed each of us by an arm and walked us out.

Once we were out in the open, and he'd relocked the gate, Jake seemed a whole lot calmer. Which surprised me. He'd been one of the kids who'd played here with us. I didn't recall his being this nervous back then.

Jake pointed out where the vans were parked in the drive, and directed Dave (or whatever his name was) towards them. Then he turned to me.

"Jesus, Legs. What were you doing in there?"

"Uh...leading a tour?"

"Leading? That was your idea?"

"Well..."

"Did you not notice how quiet it was down there?"

"Bruh. With the way you were shouting? Uh, no!"

"This isn't a joke! One of the CO_2 fans is offline. I had to go all the way to Sacramento for a part; I just got back."

"Oh. Shit."

"Do you know how dangerous that is?"

'No, why?' I wanted to reply. 'Because CO_2 loooves low places and can kill in minutes and we just had an idiot down there opening barrels—which is where the CO_2 lives?' But of course, I didn't. What I said instead was, "How come nobody told me?"

"Why would they? The gate was supposed to be locked. And you don't have any business in the cave, anyway."

Which was—technically—all true, but after Dave's jabs about me not being an owner, it hit badly. "The whole winery is my business, Jake!"

"I didn't mean it that way. None of us have any business in there right now, other than—" He broke off on a groan. *"Oh, shit."*

"What now?"

"Bianca. She's gonna pitch a fit."

"EVERYTHING'S FINE," I INSISTED, YET AGAIN, TRYING TO *sound as soothing as I knew how.* "I know it got a little chaotic, but nothing happened."

"So, you're saying my wine is not contaminated with some random bacteria?" Bianca's sarcasm game was on point. *"You didn't all nearly die? That's a relief."*

"You tell people they can't get a barrel tasting. But then you bring them to the place where the barrels are," Rosa said—not far behind. *"How does that not seem like a bad idea?"*

'Maybe because that's been the script for virtually every barrel room tour I ever led,' I nearly said, which was God's own truth:

'No, I'm so sorry, you won't be able to get a taste.

*Our winemaker is very particular, and these
wines aren't ready to drink yet. But let me
tell you about the oak we use for our
barrels...'*

"Look," I told her, still trying to stay calm. "I had everything
under control. And if Jake hadn't distracted me—

"Are you kidding?" Bianca asked. "If Jake hadn't just
happened to come in when he did—"

Which is when I began to lose my shit. "Oh, he 'just
happened' to come in? Right. I'm so sure."

Rosa frowned. "Okay, time out. What are you implying,
Legs?"

"Isn't it obvious? I feel like someone's always looking over
my shoulder, checking up on me, keeping track of everything
I do."

Bianca's lips compressed, as though she were trying to hold
onto her temper. But apparently it didn't work because the next
words out of her mouth are, "Has it ever occurred to you that,
maybe that's your fault?"

Rosa nodded. "We never know where you are. You rarely
keep us informed. Take today, for example. If we'd known ahead
of time that you were planning something special, maybe one of
us could have been on hand to help out?"

That burned. For so many reasons. Not the least of which
was the assumption that I wouldn't (or maybe shouldn't?) be
making the Tour and Pour a regular event. Close on the heels of
that was my fear that the tour company would feel the same way.
I wanted to scream; 'Today was an exception. I really can do
this. I don't need your help!' But even if I'd screamed it at the
top of my lungs, would any of them listen?

"Reach out if you need help," Rosa is saying when I tune

back in to our conversation. "Or ask one of us if you're unsure about something."

"Tell me something," I said, glaring daggers at my sisters. "When's the last time either of you thought to run something by me? When have any of you asked me for help, or advice on anything?"

Two blank faces stared back at me. And, trust me, I knew those looks. They weren't the abstracted, 'when was that now?' expression people get when they're attempting to activate their really long-term memory (because they know that the memory in question was forever ago). No, these were hard-core, 'why would we ever do something like that?' looks.

"Oh, that's right," I purred sweetly. "Never."

"Legs," Rosa tried to interrupt, but I was on a roll.

"I bet you can't even imagine a scenario like that, can you? When would you ever need help from me? Well, guess what? That goes both ways. I can figure out how to do my own job, too. All. By. Myself. So, I don't need you, or Jake, or anyone else, to babysit me."

Which was when Rosa finally cracked. Honestly, I should have been expecting it. See, Bianca and I had always had hotter tempers. Or shorter fuses. Or whatever metaphor you care to use.

As kids, we'd battled a lot, but our fights were like microbursts; you know, those strong, sudden rainstorms that spring up out of nowhere and dissipate just as quickly?

Rosa was an entirely different animal when it came to her temper. If the three of us were rubber bands—yes, another metaphor—Rosa's was the one that would have stretched the farthest. And then snap back the hardest. So, I really shouldn't have been surprised when she responded to my babysitter dig with, "Well, good! Because none of us have the time to waste on that shit, anyway! So maybe you should stop making it necessary."

. . .

CLAY IS SILENT AS I FINISH MY STORY—WHICH IS FINE. MY breath keeps catching and tears are leaking from my eyes and I'm not sure I'm ready for his reaction anyway. What if he agrees with my sisters? What if he's disappointed in me, or starts pointing out all the mistakes I made? What if I've violated some stupidly obscure rule?

Oh, shit! What if opening the cave while the fan wasn't on is the kind of violation that could get us shut down?

Just a few feet shy of Caparelli's entrance, Clay pulls his vehicle off the road. The truck lurches a little, listing from side to side as we bounce over the grassy verge.

"I am so sorry," he says as he puts the truck in park and turns to face me. "I thought talking about it would help. I didn't mean to make you feel worse."

"You didn't," I say blinking rapidly. But in the battle between me and my tears, the tears have won.

He undoes his seatbelt, and then mine, and then he opens his arms and says, "C'mere," as he reaches for me.

It's awkward hugging over the console, but it feels nice. "I'm sorry," I mumble. "I know I fucked up."

"No, you didn't," Clay says. "Sounds to me like you had a lot thrown at you, all at once. Plus you were operating with limited information. I thought you did pretty good."

"Yeah?" I lift my head to look at him. "So, you're not mad?"

"Well, I am a little bit," he admits. "If I'd known all this last night, I'd've taken the whole day off. We could've gone up to Calistoga and spent a few hours soaking in the hot springs."

"Ohhh, that sounds nice," I reply.

Clay's lips twist. "I know, but it's too late. I already took the morning off; I can't call in now."

"It's the thought that counts?" I suggest, hopefully.

"No," he sighs reluctantly. "It's really not."

But he's wrong. And I'm not even playing. Nice as the hot springs would have been, just knowing he cares enough to think of doing something like that for me? That's all I need. "Raincheck?" I offer, before I think it through.

Clay smiles. His eyes light up as he nods. "Yeah, okay. Sounds good. Maybe sometime next week?"

"Oh, but wait. I'm forgetting. Aren't you afraid that'll blow our cover?"

"Nah, I don't think so," he says. "Most of the people I work with have families; there's not a lot of spa days on their calendars. I think we'll be okay. Besides, you know we're not going to be able to hide this thing forever, right?" His brow furrows as he adds, "Sooner or later, we're gonna have to figure out a way to tell people about us."

"Like an official story?" I tease.

"Yeah. Like that." Clay's gaze flicks to the winery's entrance, and then back to my face. "I still hate the idea of leaving you here. Are you gonna be all right?"

"Of course," I tell him, squaring my shoulders. "I'll be fine."

So, he puts the truck back in gear, and we refasten our seatbelts—because regulations. And we drive the dozen or so feet down the road, and maybe half that distance again up the drive. Then we park and unbuckle again.

"Uh-oh," Clay mutters, glancing out through the windshield. "Want me to stick around for a minute?"

Rosa is pacing on the lawn in front of the house, with her phone at her ear. As soon as she sees us she ends the call and comes running up to meet us.

"Um...sure," I say as I jump from the truck. "Good idea. Maybe she won't yell as loud in front of company."

"I wouldn't bet on it," he says.

Then Rosa is here, yelling, "Allegra, where have you been?

We've been calling all night!" And I guess I have to give this point to Clay.

Clay

"I-I'm s-sorry!" Legs exclaims, stuttering in reaction to her sister's distraught expression. "I didn't have my charger; my phone died. Did something happen?"

"Uh, you tell me," Rosa says, gazing pointedly at my truck. "What's going on?"

"What? Oh!" Allegra's face clears. "No. Nothing. Clay was just nice enough to give me a ride back from the bike shop." Then she catches herself, flashes me an apologetic look and corrects herself. "Sorry. I meant Deputy Romero."

Rosa's eyes narrow. "I'm sorry, where did you say you went last night?"

"Oh, let's not worry about that," Legs says. Her innocent smile wouldn't fool a child. "What's happening here? Everything okay?"

"Well, that depends." Rosa's gaze flickers once again in my direction as she says the last thing I'm expecting. "Your *husband* is here. Anything you want to tell me about what you did last summer?"

Husband? I swallow the word with difficulty. But, if the old saying about how, 'a wink is as good as a nod to a blind man,' is valid, I figure the reverse is true, as well. And the strangled cough that emerges from my mouth is fucking damning.

"I don't have a husband," Allegra snaps. Then she looks at

me and say, "I don't!" And if her sister had suspicions about us before, I figure they've just been confirmed.

So, I lean my arms on the roof of my truck, prop one foot on the running board, and settle in—abandoning all pretense that I'm not hanging on their every word, or that I don't have a vested interest in the outcome. It was a nice little cover story, while it lasted.

"What do you mean—no husband?" Rosa demands. "He showed us the license, and...and visa documents that the two of you had signed. And pictures of the two of you taken all over Europe. Are you saying they're fake?"

I straighten up at that point, no longer amused. Legs shakes her head, as though to clear it. "No, wait. Are you saying *Nico* is here?"

Nico? And just like that, this non-existent husband has a name.

"Yes!" Rosa exclaims, as her hands fly wide, somehow managing to sound simultaneously validated and disappointed, which is a lot to pull off with a single gesture. But then her frown returns. "Well, of course, I mean Nico. Just how many husbands do you have?"

Which is a fucking great question.

"None!" Legs says, but her protest rings hollow. Then she turns to me and repeats it, "None!"

"Well, I don't understand," Rosa says. "Are you saying you're divorced?"

"Of course not," Legs replies. And then she nails that coffin all the way shut. "Do you know how long it takes to get divorced in Europe? Even in Romania it's at least six months."

Annnd I've heard enough. "Ladies." I nod as I swing myself into my truck. "I'll be on my way."

"Clay, wait," Legs begs.

I shake my head and allow myself a single sentence, "Late for work."

But that, as Legs would say, is only the official story. If you want the truth, the real reason I'm leaving is because there's nothing she can say right now that I want to hear. And I don't really trust myself to speak.

Chapter 17

Allegra

As Clay peels out of the drive, tires squealing, I can't shake the feeling that we're not okay. I'd jump in my car and follow him back to town so we can continue this discussion, but he's been nothing but honest with me up until now, so it's hard to justify that level of distrust.

"Just how long has this been going on?" Rosas asks, eyeing me with suspicion. But I'm still in a state of shock and can't even begin to make up an answer.

I'm saved from trying when Bee runs up and tackle-hugs me crying, "I'm sorry. I overreacted yesterday. I didn't mean any of the things I said!"

"No, *I'm* sorry," I tell her. "Your poor wine—omigod! I never would have let that happen if I'd been paying attention—that's all I meant when I said I was distracted!"

"Forget the wine; you could have died!"

Forget the wine? And that's all it takes to start me crying too, both of us spouting nonsense like, "no, no, I'm fine," and, "It doesn't matter, I don't care," and, "please, don't say that," until Rosa's voice breaks through all the noise. "Could we please stay on topic? This is important!"

Bee and I pull apart. But one look at Rosa's face—eyes wet, lower lip trembling—has us both reaching out and dragging her into a three-way embrace. And I give up trying to interpret what any of us are saying.

But like I told Clay earlier, these downbursts don't last very long. Soon we're pulling apart and wiping our eyes. "Let's go inside," Bee suggests. "I need a drink."

Rosa nods. "It's early, but I think we all do."

And I couldn't agree more. "It's wine o'clock somewhere."

So, a short while later, we're curled up in the living room with glasses of the Tempranillo that Vitto's been secretly experimenting with. And shaking our heads at Geno's stupidity in not allowing him more room for self-expression.

"Unfortunately, it's not that uncommon," Rosa says. "Jake's friend Wade is facing the same problem at his place. "His dad won't let go of the reins there, either."

"Speaking of Jake, where is he?" I ask. I need to apologize to him, as well.

Rosa and Bee exchange worried looks. "Oh, um..."

"What?"

"He volunteered to give Nico a tour of the vineyards."

"No!" I sit up so abruptly that my wine nearly spills. "Don't let him anywhere near this place. The whole reason he married me was to get his hands on Caparelli. He's a fucking leach!"

"Hah! So, you *are* married!" Bee says in triumphant tones.

I open my mouth to answer, but Rosa gets there first. "She says she's not."

"Divorced then?"

"I asked that, too. She said there wouldn't have been enough time."

Bee chews on her lip for a moment and then says, "Legs, is this why you stayed away all summer?"

My face heats up and I cover my eyes. I'm so overcome with embarrassment I can barely mumble, "Yes."

"So, you're in the process of getting divorced?" Rosa asks.

"No," I tell her. "Like I keep trying to explain, I can't get divorced because I was never actually married."

"Which I still don't understand."

"Wait," Bee says in muffled tones. She's sitting cross-legged on the couch, eyes closed, head bowed, one hand placed reverently over her heart while a small, Mona Lisa, not-quite-a-smile glimmers on her lips. "I think I do."

We wait, as requested, but when the silence drags on for several seconds, "Bee? What're you doing?" Rosa asks.

"Shh. I'm having a moment."

"What kind of moment?" I ask.

"A transcendent moment of peak, quintessential middle-childness."

"Huh?"

"Normally, it makes me sad, being the invisible middle child all the time. But I'm just feeling *so good* about my life choices right now."

Rosa and I share a look. "Well, that sounds rude," she observes.

"Mm-hm. I totally agree." Then I drain my glass and hold the empty out towards Rosa. She leans in and refills my glass and then tops up her own.

"So, how long do these transcendent moments generally last?" Rosa inquires after another moment.

"Not long," Bee says as she opens her eyes and smiles benevolently on us both. "Sorry. Where were we?"

"I believe you said you knew what was going on?" Rosa says.

"Oh, yes." Bee nods. "It's obvious, isn't it? You both got secretly married and then had the marriages secretly annulled. And now, you and your spouses have all converged here at the same time. It's like...what are the odds?"

"Whatever they are, it doesn't matter," I tell her. "Because that's not what happened."

Rosa agrees, "No, of course, it's not. I did get married, but I only thought it got annulled."

I nod. "Exactly. And I only thought I got married but couldn't get it annulled."

Rosa frowns. "Yeah, about that. I know how much you love keeping secrets, Legs," she says as she pours more wine into Bee's glass. "But you really need to explain yourself."

"I think you owe us that much," Bianca says.

So, I tell them about the day after the will was read, and how Nico had convinced me to go to the Registry of Marriages with him and apply for a license. And how we were married a couple of days later by the captain of the cruise ship we were both working on.

"You worked on a cruise ship?" Rosa asked.

"Yes, but that's not important right now."

And I tell them about how we broke our contracts and quit our jobs, and then spent the next several weeks applying for Nico's visa and assembling the stack of documents we would need to convince Immigration that we were actually a couple.

"And were you?" Bee asks.

"We were friends," I tell her. And then shrug and add, "Well, at least I thought we were."

I explain how we'd moved into an apartment together. And how I'd come home early one day and overheard him talking to someone about how long we'd need to stay married before he could divorce me and take half of what I'd inherited. "So, you see, sometimes eavesdroppers *do* hear things to their advantage."

"That rat bastard," Rosa growls.

"Yeah, and you wanted to put him up here," Bee reminds her.

"What? No. Please tell me he's not staying here?" I beg.

My sisters shake their heads in tandem. "He's not."

"He already had a hotel, down at the Junction."

"Off the Twelve. So, what happened next?"

"Well, next I called Mama and got a referral for the best divorce lawyer in Italy. On Sergio's dime."

My sisters exchange looks. "I feel like there's a story there," Rosa muses.

"Let me guess," Bee says. "It's 'not important right now'?"

"Well, it's not."

"You said you couldn't get the marriage annulled," Rosa asks. "Why was that? It sounds like you would have had ample grounds?"

"You would think," I agree. "But now all the work I'd put into proving that we actually were married was working against me."

"Okay, so?"

So, I tell them about Romania—the 'divorce tourism' capital of the EU. How I holed up there and waited, taking occasional jobs to break the monotony and stave off boredom, until finally, "I guess hiring a stupidly expensive lawyer really does pay off. He dug up proof of Nico's first marriage—"

"Wait, are you saying he wasn't divorced, either?" Rosa guesses.

"No, he was. But since he only got the idea to marry me after he listened in on the call about the will, he wasn't prepared. He was in a hurry to marry me—before I came to my senses and changed my mind, I guess—but he didn't have his divorce paperwork on hand, and there was no way to get it in time. So, he figured the best thing to do was to ignore the question altogether. Which, ultimately, is what invalidated the marriage. It was a technicality, a lie of omission."

"Okay, and?"

"And nothing; that was that. Since Gibraltar was now basically saying the marriage had never actually taken place, Romania couldn't grant me a divorce to dissolve it. My lawyer wished me *"In bocca al lupo,"* and told me to go home and enjoy my life."

"And you really didn't know?" Bee asks.

"What, that he'd been married before? Honestly, I have no idea. He might have mentioned it at some point. But, even if he had, I wouldn't have thought anything of it. As far as I knew, all being divorced meant was that he was free to marry."

"No, I mean you had no idea he was just after your money?"

"I knew the marriage was transactional. But I thought all he wanted a green card."

"And what were you supposed to be getting out of it?" Rosa asks.

"Oh, um..." Shit. 'Protection against the two of you' seems cruel and unnecessary, at this point. But once again I'm saved from answering an awkward question, this time by the arrival of Jake and Nico.

.   .   .

WE HEAR THE BUZZ OF CONVERSATION IN THE HALL, AND then Jake's voice calling, "Hey, Rosa?"

"In here!" she answers, flashing me a worried look.

And then there he is, flanked by Jake and Jansen (whom they apparently picked up, somewhere along the way). Nico Carvahlo is still as cute and charming as I remember him. I hate him on sight.

"Bellissima!" He smiles in greeting as he approaches me—arms wide, like he thinks I'm going to let him hug me. Please!

"Sfigato!" I sneer in response, basically calling him a loser. "What the hell are you doing here?"

"I'm here as we planned," he replies. "To join my beautiful wife and assist her in her new endeavors."

"Save it," I tell him. "I've already told my sisters everything."

Nico's smile seems to freeze. "As you know, my English is not always very good," he protests. "So many voices make for confusion."

Since we're the only two speaking, I take that as a hint. I return his smile with an icy one of my own as I say, "Good idea. Let's go outside."

"Let's cut to the chase, Nico," I say as soon as the front door closes behind us. "What do you want?"

"Only what I'm entitled to under California law."

"You mean half of my assets? That's never gonna happen."

"We'll see." He shrugs and says, "But why so cold? When I learned you'd broken off the divorce proceedings, I naturally assumed you had a change of heart."

"I didn't 'break them off.' The court ruled that our marriage was invalid, making a divorce unnecessary." Not to mention impossible.

"Again; we shall see. It's true that, in my excitement, I may not have filled out our marriage documents correctly. Perhaps I missed seeing the question about prior relationships? I'm hoping your immigration officers will be more sympathetic. We make a very convincing couple, do we not? Everyone says so. We even argue like we're married."

Shame lodges like a stone in my gut. He's not wrong. Even before the whole will business, our friends used to tease us about our bickering.

"Just go away," I tell him. "You're wasting your time. No one wants you here."

"But that's not true, is it? Your charming sister has offered to make me dinner."

"That was before she knew what you were. The only way that'll happen now is if the recipes were copied straight from the Borgia family cookbook."

Nico laughs. "Ah, Allegra. I have missed you."

"Well, I haven't missed you. So, get the hell out of here, and don't come back."

"I understand. You're overwrought. You're not thinking clearly. I'll give you some time to reflect on the situation. Au revoir, bella, I'll look forward to seeing you again soon."

"Yeah, yeah," I grouse. "And I'll make sure that you don't."

But my threats are empty, and we both know it.

I watch from the porch until he leaves—to make sure that he does. But when I turn back towards the house, I realize there's no way I can face my family right now. So, I ease open the door, as silently as I can and slip inside. I can hear the murmur of conversation—talking about me, no doubt. But, for once, I don't want to know what they're saying.

I find my purse, still hanging from the hook by the door where I left it, and slip back outside.

Once I'm in my car, I plug my phone into the charger so I can send a quick text to my sisters.

"I'm sorry. I need a little time alone. I'll be back later."

At least this time, they can't accuse me of disappearing without a word.

Clay

THIS TIME, I'M REALLY NOT EXPECTING THE KNOCK AT MY door.

"What do you want, Legs?" I say, even as I pull the door open, and let her in. "This isn't a good time."

"I just wanted to make sure that we're okay," she tells me. And between the pain on her face, the uncertainty lurking in her eyes—yeah, it's a fucking time warp. A redo of the night before. And I can't help but laugh.

"Okay? Oh, yeah. Sure. Of course, we are." But then reality crashes in and I shake my head. "No, actually, we're not. You need to leave."

"But- but why? What did I do?" She looks so honestly shocked that it actually steadies me. Because she can't possibly be this clueless, right? It has to be an act.

"I don't fuck with married women," I tell her. "I know I haven't exactly provided you with a lot of evidence of it, but I really *do* have a conscience and a code of ethics. You've been stomping all over them, and it has to stop."

"Omigod," she groans, leaning back against the wall and closing her eyes. "Not this again!"

My mouth falls open and I stare at her for what feels like several seconds. "Excuse me?" I mean, I probably should have guessed that someone with her background wouldn't have much use for anyone else's morals, but really?

"What?" She looks confused for an instant then, "Oh! No, I didn't mean you. I meant that I already went through all of this with my sisters, that's all."

And with that she launches into this long-ass story, all about falsehoods and deceit, and people fucking each other over for the sake of a few hundred acres of dirt. And it's so far removed from my own reality that I can't even begin to relate.

"I'm not sure why you thought any of that would help," I tell her when she's finally done.

"I don't know that I did. I was mostly trying to explain that I'm not married. Didn't you say that was a problem?"

"But you thought you were—right?"

"Well, yes; six months ago, immediately after the wedding. But it was never legal, so..."

"Who cares about the legalities?" I say, almost yelling in frustration.

Her eyes widen in alarm. "Uh...you do? Most of the time? What's going on?"

I wish to God I knew. I feel like I'm stumbling through the dark, disoriented by all the unfamiliar noises. I take a breath and my lungs seize up. "Do not make this about me," I gasp.

"Okay, but listen," she says as she starts to pace. "It shouldn't matter what I thought, right? Because ignorance of the law is not a...something, something. Defense against it? I dunno."

"That is not the flex you think it is," I tell her. "All that means is that you're still responsible for the consequences of your actions, whether or not you were aware of them going in."

"Oh." She stops pacing then, looking startled and so

dismayed that, fuck me, I really want to believe that this is just a stellar performance. "Couldn't it just be that I made a mistake?"

"Sure. You mean like with your tattoo, or driving without a license?"

"Okay, yes, all right?" Her face flushed red, she scowls at me. "I don't know why you're being like this, but fine. Maybe I had too much to drink, and I thought it would be fun to get a tattoo. And when he handed me a mirror and asked me to check the stencil, maybe my hair was in the way, and I didn't notice the big, honking 'W' at the front of the word. Lock me up."

"Jesus, Legs. This is not about your tattoo!"

"Then why did you bring it up?"

"Because what I'm trying to say is that this is a pattern with you. When you keep making the same kind of mistake, again and again—"

"But it's not! I got the tattoo because I wanted one—plain and simple. I married Nico for a lot of reasons, mostly because I was upset. My grandmother had just died. I was hurting, and scared, and not thinking clearly. And it just felt so good, in that moment, to have someone who was on my side. It never occurred to me that he only wanted to get his hands on my winery. I thought he was marrying me for a green card!"

"Annnnd we're done. That's all it needed."

"What? Why? People get married for all sorts of reasons, don't they? In fact, I'd argue that most marriages are transactional. Why should one be different from another?"

"Because what you're calling a transaction, is fraud. And that's a bridge too far."

"But you just said—"

"Stop it! It's like you don't take anything seriously, like it's all a big joke to you. And I just can't deal with it anymore! I don't know where I stand on anything, right now; it's like there's nothing but shifting sand beneath my feet. Do you know how much I hate that feeling?"

"Okay yes, I've made mistakes. My crappy tattoo, driving without a license—you're right about all of that. But I don't think it's fair to say that I don't take things seriously or accept responsibility when I mess up. And this thing with Nico, I *am* dealing with it, okay? That's practically all I've done for six months. I'm trying, Clay; I really am. I'm trying *so hard* to turn my life around, and get myself back on track, to make my grandmother proud, and to earn my sisters' respect. Doesn't that count for anything?"

"What about me?"

"What about you? Do you really think I don't want your respect, too? Do you think it's not killing me, having to stand here and listen to you explain all the ways in which I don't measure up to your impossible standards? You really don't need to keep hammering it home. I've been letting people down my whole life, so I'm very familiar with the process at this point."

I shake my head. "No, that's not what I meant. I mean, is that all I am to you—one of the mistakes of your past, something that you want to make amends for? Or is it even worse than that; was I danger to you—to your sisters and your winery? Was I just another threat that had to be neutralized? Is that why you were sleeping with me?"

"You are not seriously asking me that."

"You used your stepsister's fiancé to take her off the board because you perceived her as a threat to your mother."

"Omigod, *that's* what you got from that story? Great."

"And you were willing to marry that dickwad so you could hold your own sisters hostage. So, it's not really a stretch, is it? Keep your friends close and your enemies closer? Protect the bottom line?"

"That's it. I'm outta here."

As she turns towards the door, my protective instincts belatedly kick in. It's my fault that she's upset, and I cannot send her out into the night like this. "Okay, wait. Hold on a minute. Stop."

"What is it now?" Her arms are wrapped around herself, so tightly—as though that's the only thing that's holding her together.

"You're upset," I say, trying to soothe her—badly and, again, belatedly. "Why don't we...sit for a minute. Or, just, I don't know...wait until you're calmer? You shouldn't be driving right now; it isn't safe."

She shakes her head, eyeing me pityingly. "You know what's sad, Clay? Once I would have thought you meant that. That you were actually concerned about my safety. Just like I believed that my uncle had my best interests at heart when he orchestrated my reunion with my mother. Or—ooh, here's a good one. Once upon a time, I thought Nico was a friend who would never dream of betraying me. Now I know better."

"Yeah? So, what do you think you know about me?"

"I think your primary concern right now is how my driving might reflect on you. If I get into an accident when I leave here, it's possible someone might claim it's your fault; that you shouldn't have let me leave, that you should have stopped me somehow."

"That's not—"

"But you know what? You can fuck all the way off, because I'm done with that bullshit."

"Legs!"

"No! No, Clay, you do *not* get to call me that anymore. I told you, way back at the start, that's something my friends call me. And we are *not* friends."

"But—"

"Do you have grounds to stop me? No, you do not." Raising a hand, she begins ticking the points off, finger by finger. "I'm not drunk. I have no violations. My paperwork's in order. My car's not unsafe. So, the only way you're going to keep me from driving right now, Deputy, is if you arrest me."

"I'm not gonna arrest you."

"Good. Because don't think for a minute that I wouldn't have shown up in court to contest the ticket, or that I would-n't've been happy to explain to the judge exactly why I was upset with you in the first place. And while I'm on the subject, don't you dare even think about using any of this as an excuse to come after my sisters for some imaginary infraction. Because that's one thing you should know about me by now. I protect what's mine. And that might not be you anymore, Clay Romero, but it will *always* be them."

Chapter 18

Clay

"So, you and Allegra Martinelli," Miles says—causing me to nearly stumble over my own feet.

I eye him narrowly. "What do you know about that?"

After last night's disastrous encounter, I texted Miles, asking if he'd be willing to meet with me (unofficially) to discuss some problems I'd encountered. He seemed like a logical person to confide in, seeing as he has a foot in both worlds. He knows what I'm up against at work, the risks I've been running. And he knows the family. He texted back, suggesting I join him for his usual early morning run—a five-mile circuit around Oak Creek Park before the sun's fully up. And here we are. I like to think of myself as being in reasonable shape, but if I survive this run, I'll be amazed.

Miles shrugs. "To be honest? Not that much. But Allegra lives with her sister, and Bianca is one of Millie's best friends. So, you do the math."

I add another point to my mental tally—the one where I keep track of how often Millie's name gets dropped into conversations. Usually, it's an amusing diversion. But this morning, it's hard to find the humor in anything. "I think I fucked up."

"How so?" Miles asks, and then, when I don't respond right away, he slants me a glance, then nods. "Oh. It's like that, huh? Well, you can't say I didn't warn you."

Thanks for nothing, I think to myself. But then, over the next mile or so, the whole sorry story comes pouring out. "I thought I had things under control," I tell him. "But then her husband showed up and everything went to shit."

"Yeah. Him I heard about."

"She lied to me, Miles."

"So? Sounds to me like you lied too." Miles waves off my protests. "Nope. Sorry. Doesn't work that way, pal. If you're gonna equate keeping secrets with telling lies—which, I'm not saying you're wrong about that—but then you're both equally to blame. You lied at work; she lied to her family. Same, same—as my wife likes to say."

I tack on another point.

But it's *not* the same. Yes, I lied at work *and* to her family, but she lied *to me*. "*And* she's married." Surely Miles—this year's Mr. Marriage—will understand the gravity of that!

Instead, he shrugs it off. "Are you sure? 'Cause I heard there's some kind of question about that. Apparently, she claims it was never valid?"

"Who cares what she claims? She knew what she was doing. No one forced her into it. It's not like marriage was a hole she fell into by accident." But even as I say it, I see the trap I've sprung on myself. She'd never claimed it was an accident, did she? And the six months she'd wasted trying to extricate herself from it was proof that she had, in fact, taken it seriously.

She acknowledged her mistake. She worked diligently to fix it. And I still gave her grief.

"So, what's the part that's got you butthurt? And please tell me it's not because some asshole was there before you; because that's some seriously toxic shit. You might need years of therapy, if that's the case."

"No, of course that's not it." I eye the distance between here and the edge of the creek bed and consider accidentally-on-purpose bumping him off the trail. We're running alongside Oak Creek, at the moment. It's still swollen from last week's rain and probably cold as hell. It won't hurt him—much —to go for a swim. But it'll make the rest of his run fucking miserable, which (I'm not gonna lie) makes me smile a little bit brighter. But "I'm not *that* big an asshole," I tell him. And I think, as far as commentaries goes, that one covers both scenarios nicely.

"Besides," I can't help pointing out. "If we're talking about her husband, it's not even true."

"What?" This time, it's Miles who breaks stride and falters. I take the opportunity to pull ahead, grinning to myself as I do.

"Fuck yeah, bruh," I call, turning to run backwards for a few paces. "Didn't you know? It was the other way around."

"Do I even want to know what you mean by that?" Miles asks when he catches up. And fuck me, the old guy isn't even breathing hard.

And maybe it's because that night has always been one of my happiest memories, something to pull out and look at whenever life gets grim. Or maybe it's because the sound of the water is bringing it all back, and I think I'd trade my soul for the chance to turn back time for a couple of hours. But I do end up telling him something about the night we met—the abbreviated, G-rated version, obviously.

"You shoulda seen her," I sigh happily, caught up in the memory. "She was ah-*mazing*."

"I can imagine," Miles replies. Adding, when I turn to glare daggers at him, "What? Don't look at me like that. She's too young for me, even if I were still in the market. But I can see the appeal for someone like you."

"Someone like me?"

"Younger, I mean. You guys are about the same age, right?"

"Yeah."

"And you're a little hung up on the financial aspect."

And, much as I'd like to disagree, I really can't. "Fair."

"Based on how you just described her, she probably struck you as the perfect manic pixie dream heiress. How could you resist?"

"Okay, what? That's not a thing."

"Are you sure? Think about it."

And so, I do. Beautiful and quirky, a little on the wild side. Obviously wealthy. "You might be onto something," I finally concede. "I mean, I didn't even know her name or anything about her family. But yeah, I could tell there'd never been a day in her life where she'd had to worry about money—or a lot of other things. I was the one clocking all the exits, making plans for which way I'd run if shit hit the fan." *When* shit hit the fan. Because that was another difference. For her it was maybe a possibility. For me? Dead certainty.

"So, is that the problem? You were attracted to her money, and now that there's a possibility that she might lose some of it—"

"Half of it," I remind him. And myself. "And it's not just the money, it's the winery."

"Right. So, is that it?"

I want to deny it on the spot, but the question deserves consideration. So, I think about it, while cool mist swirls around us and the trail we're on curves deeper into the woods, diverging from the creek for a little while. Because yes, it burns. The idea that someone is willing to hurt her, for no reason other than that he can, to take something that means so much to her—memories, safety, home. That doesn't sit well with me.

"No," I finally decide. "I'm sure that growing up with money helped to make her who she is, but even if she lost it all, that probably wouldn't change much." Unlike someone like Lori, who'd probably find it incredibly hard to cope. Or even my mom—who had money once and is still struggling to adjust to its being gone.

"Okay, that's her. But what about you? I mean, you'd lose access to it, as well. And I don't know how things stand between you, but it seems like her being rich is a hell of a perk."

I fall silent once again. I mean, yeah, sure, there'd be fewer spa days in my future if we were both trying to make ends meet, that's a certainty. But, other than that... "You know, I don't think so. That woman's resourceful as fuck. Even if a fire had taken out the winery, or if her family cut her off tomorrow, I'd bet anything she'd still land on her feet. And I'm doing okay on my own so..."

"So, then what is the problem?"

"Dude, I don't even know." What *am* I upset about? "Maybe it's got something to do with the fact that she didn't trust me enough to confide in me. I mean, how're you even supposed to help someone if they won't tell you when they're in trouble?"

But even as I say it, I know I'm lying.

There's no doubt she's been let down in the past. And, as a result, it's hard getting her to open up. It took her the better part of a day to confide in me about the cave. But in the end, she did it.

And, not twelve hours later, I threw that in her face, as well.

But Miles is shaking his head. And I don't even know why. "What now?" I ask.

"You, my friend, have got a hero complex. Which, sure, many of us do. But did you ever stop to think that maybe she doesn't want your help?"

"Oh, there's no question about that," I say, laughing bitterly. "She's made it abundantly clear that she doesn't."

"Right. So, what did you want her to say? If we're still talking about this thing with the ex, she was probably embarrassed. No one wants to admit they've been gaslit."

But my brain has just started to process something he said earlier. Of course, I have a hero complex. And I don't need to wonder why that is. The men and women who put their lives on the line for people like me? They're #goals. They didn't quit when things got hard, they stuck it out, they pushed through. I can't do less.

I owe it to them—and to the kid that I was, and the kids that might someday depend on someone like me. But it's hard. And deep down, I'm not entirely convinced that I'm up to the challenge.

The sad truth is that it's easier to be a hero when the people who are depending on you are strangers—the nameless, faceless public. There's a reason surgeons won't operate on members of their own family. Because when it's in your home, or in your heart, when it's someone whose survival is critical to *your own* well-being, and the outcome is deeply personal, that's so much more terrifying.

All at once, I'm no longer here, in the cool, damp woods, on a bright clear day, where the loudest sounds are the birds chirping in the trees. I'm somewhere dark and terrifying. Where the air is thick and deafening. And I can't find my way out.

This is the same thing that happened to me last night. *And you call yourself a protector*, my inner voice is scathing, but not wrong. *You're nothing but a fake.* Because I've done the same thing time and again. When someone that I love has a problem and I can't solve it, that makes me angry. When they need something that I can't give them, I find a reason to reject them, before that fact becomes too obvious. And when Allegra came to me last night, asking for nothing more than companionship, and maybe a little reassurance, I projected all of this on her. I told her she had a pattern that needed changing. When all the time, I was the one with the problem.

"Hey. Are you okay?" Miles' voice cuts through the noise in my head. I open my eyes—when had I closed them? —and realize that I'm no longer moving. My steps had ground to a halt at some point, probably several minutes ago, and Miles is now circling back to check on me.

I shake my head. "Damn, I've been an asshole."

Miles' eyes light up. "Oh, you just figured that out now?" And when I nod and pass my hand across my eyes—maybe to clear the dust and sweat from my eyes, maybe not—Miles shrugs and says, "Yeah well, I think probably we all are, from time to time. The question is what are you going to do about it?"

"I don't know. What can I do? I mean, that's why I called you."

"Me? Oh, my man, if I'm your only option? You really are fucked aren't you?"

We run for a while in silence, pushing each other a little harder. After a while, Miles slows his pace, dropping to something closer to a jog I slow with him.

"Well," he says, and if you ask me, he sounds a little reluctant. "If you really want my opinion, I'd suggest you start by helping her get rid of the ex."

I slide a startled glance in his direction. "Define *get rid of.*"

Miles rolls his eyes. "What the fuck do you think it means? He's here fraudulently, isn't he? Or, at least under false pretenses? So, maybe do your job. The law says he should be deported. Ain't no shame in following the law. Most of the time, anyway."

Fuck. Everything in me recoils at the thought. I uncap my water and down half the bottle before I feel calm enough to say, "What makes you say he's here fraudulently? You can't know that for a fact."

"Sure, I can. He pretty much has to be. I mean, either he's here on a CR1 visa—which would only be valid if the marriage is. If that's not the case—there you go. Or he could've come in on a tourist visa, which likely became invalid the minute he started trying to claim her as his spouse, or pressure her for money. Plus, if he's really trying to shake down the family, just to get a piece of the winery—and he's not even entitled to it? That's not right."

"Yeah." The truth is, it's frighteningly easy to get someone deported these days—sometimes for no reason at all. But for someone like me, the grandson and great-grandson of immigrants (who may or may not have entered the country legally themselves) conspiring with one of "those" agencies is roughly akin to spitting on my ancestors' graves.

And no. I don't think my feelings for Legs justifies my acting counter to what either the law, or my own moral code is telling me is right.

"So?"

"I'mma have to think about it."

We run the rest of the way without talking—other than random observations about the weather, or the wildlife, or whether or not I need better shoes. (Spoiler: I do)

Finally, when the parking lot comes back into view, Miles asks how I'm feeling. And, in retrospect, I guess what he was really asking about was the run. But that's not what pops out of my mouth.

"I dunno," I tell him. "But I think, if you'd asked me a year ago, how I thought my life was going, I'd have told you it was going great—other than being a little boring."

"Okay. And?"

"Man, I fucking miss boring right now."

Miles laughs so hard at that, he damn near gives himself a stitch, and ends up practically limping on the way back to the cars.

"It wasn't that funny," I point out when he finally settles down.

"Oh, I know," he agrees. "That's not why I was laughing."

"Why then?"

"It's just...well, it occurred to me, that if what you wanted was a boring life, then you might have picked the wrong girl."

"Oh. Yeah. Don't I know it."

Allegra

IT'S EARLY. THE MORNING FOG HAS YET TO BURN OFF, AND I'm standing in the kitchen, watching the coffee slowly fill the pot and wondering, *is it always this slow?*

There are reasons why I don't do mornings. And why I never get up early, unless I absolutely have to—an early shift at work, for example. Having stayed up too late the night before, is not one of them. And at least at work, I can generally count on being surrounded by a chattering flock of early birds.

There's none of that here. It's too quiet. It's too lonely. There's too much time to think. And morning thoughts? They're too full of regrets and razor-edged sorrows, jagged memories, the sharp sting of loss and...ooh, have I mentioned regrets?

This morning is no different than the rest, in that regard.

It's no surprise that today's regrets should all circle back to Clay. I have no idea what happened last night, or why I couldn't help him. I wanted to. I'll probably always want to. But either I suck at picking the people I want to comfort, or I suck at giving comfort. Or possibly, I just suck.

Rosa, still dressed in a robe, enters the kitchen on a yawn. She pauses when she sees me, and frowns in surprise. "You're up early."

I nod and tell her, "I made the coffee."

Her eyebrows rise. "You know how to make coffee? Sorry, sorry," she adds when I give her a look. "Of course you do."

Full disclosure? I really don't. "First time's the charm," I reply with a shrug. "Isn't that what they say?"

Rosa looks startled. "What?"

"Beginner's luck?"

Rosa's gaze travels to the pot, which is still slooowly filling. When it gradually turns dubious (her gaze, not the pot, obvs) I rush to reassure her. "I'm sure it'll be fine."

I wave Rosa away when she attempts to help, "I've got this. You look tired. Go sit down." And I start setting out mugs, one for Rosa, one for me, from Nonna's quirky, eclectic collection of vintage mugs. I pause with a third mug in my hand. "Will Jake want coffee?"

Rosa eyes the coffee maker again and answers, "Maaaybe?" So, I set down the third, and then another for Bee. And that's all of us.

Over cream, sugar, spoons, I reflect on the fact that Bee and I should shortly be thinking of migrating, finding our own nests, so that Rosa and Jake can fill this one with their own small brood. I think what most infuriates me about Geno's interference in Rosa's life is those ten lost years.

"Those are some pretty heavy sighs for such a beautiful morning," Rosa observes.

I turn to her. "Is it? Beautiful, I mean?"

Rosa's smile dims. "Oh, sorry. You're probably still upset about yesterday, huh?"

I blink. She can't know about Clay, so... "Oh, you mean because of Nico? Nah, he's a pest, but I'm sure we can find a way to get rid of him."

"Oh, good," Rosa says, perking up, looking so relieved that my own mood plummets. Because I'm not nearly as confident as I know I sounded.

The coffee is finally done. I fill two mugs and carry them to the table, where Rosa and I doctor them to our liking. Or as close as we can get. "Not bad," my sister tells me. She's a terrible liar, by the way.

"Mmm," I murmur in response.

"Hey, do you remember the tea parties?" Rosa suddenly asks. And I don't take offense even though it's pretty obvious what's sparked *that* memory.

"With the espresso cups and demitasse spoons?" I reply.

"Yes! And the cookie cutter sandwiches and tiny cakes," Rosa adds.

"And the musical teapot!" we both exclaim.

Nonna's tea-parties were legendary, even though the tea was so weak it barely stained the milk. Cue the comparison to this morning's coffee. And also, cue the return of my earlier regrets.

Really, mornings suck. I don't know why everyone doesn't avoid them.

"Have you and Jake talked about having kids?" I ask.

Rosa blushes. "Well, yes. But, you know, there are things to consider."

"I promise I'll move out as soon as you say the word," I tell her. And then immediately wish I could call the words back. Do I want to leave home, now that I'm finally back? Hell, no.

Rosa laughs. "I said we're considering it. There's no need for anyone to start packing their bags. And besides, maybe Jake and I will be the ones to leave."

"What? No." I wave towards the window, gesturing in the direction of Bar Down. "You can't leave. This is your land, Jake's land...at least it should have been."

"Coulda, shoulda, woulda," Rosa says. We both sip our coffee, and I find myself wishing I'd thought to make toast as well.

"Well, anyway, you're going to be a great mom someday," I tell her. "You'll have lots of kids and when you start to throw tea parties for them, you have to promise to invite me."

Rosa sighs. "A 'great mom,' I wonder if I will be."

"You don't think so?"

"Well, we didn't have much of a role model, did we? And as Bee pointed out yesterday, you and I share some similarities with her."

My mouth drops open. "When did she say *that?*"

"Oh, you know, with both of us eloping, secret marriages, running off to... Well, just running off, I guess."

"Running off to Europe?" I say, completing the sentence the way I know she meant it.

"Well, I never made it that far, but sure. It's a pattern, isn't it?"

I flinch at the word, which... Seriously, if I never have to hear it again, that'd be great. "No, no, no." Shaking my head, I scowl at my sister. "You are nothing at all like Mama. And I don't believe for an instant that that's what Bee meant."

Rosa shrugs. "You don't know that. You were so young when she left us, how could you?"

My shoulders are tense. I think about that toast again, or maybe scrambled eggs—that can't be hard to figure out, right? Or maybe going out for a run. I haven't taken even one exercise class since I've been back, and I'm feeling it! But Rosa is serious about what she's saying, and that's Geno's fault, too. Well, mostly Mama's of course, but not entirely.

"Didn't anyone ever tell you where I went when I left home after high school?" I ask. "Didn't you ever wonder?"

Rosa stares at me in surprise. "You went to Europe, didn't you?"

"I meant specifically."

"No?" she says, shaking her head, looking so worried that, there's definitely no turning back now. So, I grit my teeth and tell her about Geno's manipulations, and the fun times I had in Mama's house. Oh, not that last conversation she and I had, the one about how she has everything she needs there. I'm taking that one. To. The. Grave.

"Huh. So, Geno screwed you over at eighteen as well?" Rosa says when I'm finished. "That's so weird. Whatever we do, we can't tell Bee."

"Bruh, I know! Can you imagine?"

"Can't tell me what?" Bee asks, showing up right on schedule, looking low-key offended.

"There's coffee," I say to distract her.

She looks at the pot, eyebrows raised. "Is there?"

"Allegra made it," Rosa says loyally. "It was her first time. It's very good."

Bee shrugs, and pours herself a cup and joins us at the table, barely grimacing as she takes her first sip. "So, what is it I'm not supposed to know?"

Rosa and I share a look. "Legs was just telling me about the summer she turned eighteen. Apparently, she didn't just go to Europe. Geno sent her to live with Mama."

"Oh?" Bee says, then I guess the caffeine kicks in because her eyebrows shoot up and, "Oh! Oh, shit. How'd that go?"

Rosa grimaces—and this time I'm pretty sure it's not the coffee—and says, "Oh, you know. About as well as you'd expect."

And Bee's mouth tightens, and she shakes her head. "Shit. I'm sorry, Legs. That sucks."

"Oh. No. It wasn't that bad," I say. And I launch into the story once more, this time hitting all the, this-could-have-been-funny-if-it-had-happened-to-someone-else parts a little bit harder. And by the time I finish telling it, they're both howling with laughter and replaying all the greatest hits.

"Madone. No, no, no! It's Timoteo. Ti-mo-TEO"
    "Sì. I know. That's what I said: Tom-AH-toe."
    "Non ne posso più!"

"I can't believe there's yet *another* thing the two of you share," Bee says. "It was funny, at first. But now, I think I'm starting to get a complex."

"Aw, are you getting a complex, Bee?" I ask. "Please. Don't even start. My whole life's been a complex."

"It makes you wonder, doesn't it," Rosa says. (And what I'm wondering is whether or not she's intentionally changing the subject.) "What made Mama and Geno the way they are, when Nonna wasn't like that at all. It can't be parenting, right?"

So, I tell them what Nonna had said about how death, about the way it changes people.

Rosa nods. "Hm. Yeah, I can see that. It makes sense."

"Little fractures of the soul," Bianca repeats dreamily. "I like that."

"Bruh," I say as I shoot her a look. "That's a little dark, don't ya think?"

Bee's cheeks flush red. "I mean, I don't like it, like it. But it's a good line."

"Like it, like it," I snort in response. "What are you, twelve?"

"Well, that would make you what? Ten?" she shoots back. "So, you tell me."

And I stick my tongue out at her, just for fun. And she does it back to me

And then Rosa rolls her eyes and says, "On second thought, maybe I won't have kids."

And Bee laughs and says, "Maybe you feel like you already do?"

And it feels so good to laugh and tease each other. But eventually, of course, it has to end.

"Okay, well," I say as I get to my feet. "I'd better go and get ready for the day. I have some errands to run."

Rosa glances up and asks, "Do you need any help?"

And at the same time Bee offers, "Would you like some company?"

And then Rosa says, "You're not alone, you know."

"Or, at least, you don't have to be," Bee adds.

And all I can think about is last night, and Clay. And yes, I really am alone, I think. But I smile and say, "No thanks, I've got this."

And I'm still smiling as I leave the room. But honestly? This is *why* I don't do mornings.

Chapter 19

Allegra

"Allegra! Well, this is a nice surprise," my Aunt Janet greets me with a hug as I enter my uncle's office at Belmonte, where apparently time never passes. If Nonna's hammock was an office, it would look and feel like this. Well, not as stuffy and formal as this, but otherwise, samesies.

"You look like you got a little bit of a tan," my aunt observes. "Did you have a nice vacation?" I have not seen the woman in five years, yet she's speaking as though I'd only been gone a few weeks. "Is the jet lag very bad?" Or make that days.

"*Che cosa*," my uncle (who clearly suffers from no such delusion) complains. "What jet lag? She's fine. She's been back for weeks." The subtext—that this is the first time I've bothered to see him in all that time—is made clear in the discontented expression he's wearing. Or maybe he's still mad at me for the raisin remark I made during our phone call back in April? Hard to know.

"How've you been, Uncle Geno?" I ask as I plop myself into one of the chairs in front of his desk (while my aunt lowers herself gracefully into the other one). "It's been a while, huh?" Because two can play the subtext game.

My uncle gives the kind of shrug that Italian infants begin practicing when they're still sleeping in bassinettes. Vague and elaborate, it's a gesture that can mean so many things—I'm fine. So what? Who's asking? Go fuck yourself –Or nothing at all.

"We've been a little worried about your sisters, dear," my aunt leans in to confide. "But hopefully, now that you're back, you can convince them to do the right thing?"

Since she doesn't spell out what 'the right thing' would be, I take the liberty of interpreting it as I please. "Oh, I will," I say brightly. "I promise."

Janet is pleased with my response. Geno...not so much. My uncle may be many things, slow-witted isn't one of them. "They cannot run a winery all on their own," he insists. "In Napa, of all places!"

"Is it unusually difficult here?" It's Aunt Janet who asks the question. Yes, I'm surprised as well.

Geno fixes her with a look which, like the shrug, could have many meanings. Janet flushes. "Well, I don't understand why it would be," she protests. "It's America. You don't even have to speak Italian."

"Or French," I say, nodding in agreement. "Or Spanish. Or Portuguese. German...Hungarian...Greek, of course...I think that's it."

Geno's nostrils flare. "No. That is not why. It is because it is so very small, a mere forty-five thousand acres. And the grapes grown here are the best in the world. To see even a fraction of them go to waste— Bah, it makes me furious."

See what I mean about the raisin remark? Yeah, he's still pissed.

"But they're not going to waste," I say, hope rising (phoenix-like) in my chest. Is he serious? Could it be this simple? Can I actually get through to him (and yes, 'do what neither of my sisters could')? "Bianca's wines are already winning awards. And she was using *Argentinean* grapes. (Yes, all right? *I know.*) Imagine what she'll be able to do with *Napa* grapes! She'll make you so proud, Uncle Geno."

"Vitto is making wine now, too," Aunt Janet says as her gaze flickers nervously between us. "I think his wines are very good."

"I've heard that," I say, mentally crossing my fingers and praying that I don't say the wrong thing. "Everyone says he's very talented."

Aunt Janet beams proudly. Uncle Geno shrugs again. "All these things he wants to try. Everything new, new, new. New equipment, new methods, new varietals, new blends, new barrels. Even new corks," He leans forward, really getting into it now, looking animated for the first time since I sat down. "Do you know what wine has won more awards, over the course of more seasons than any other?"

"The Carleo?" I ask, flashing my best customer service smile.

"The Carleo," Geno affirms. "And who do you think makes the Carleo?"

"Oh, everyone knows that you do, Uncle Geno."

"Sì. I make the Carleo." Then he sits back in his chair, so fiercely proud of what he's accomplished, and in that moment, epiphany slips its silken dagger under my ribs and into my heart.

And I see beyond the pride. I see fear and vulnerability and pain. I see an unloved child. I see myself. And I fucking hate it.

I was going to try and ferret out his secret—what is it that's making the Carleo so blah. I was going to try to convince him to support Bianca and Vitto—the next generation of Lamberti/Martinelli winemakers. I even thought he might have some ideas for how we might be rid of Nico.

And maybe one of these days I'll try again. But, for now, I've lost my taste for the game.

Shortly after, I take my leave of my aunt and uncle. I check the time when I get back to my car and consider breaking for lunch before my next stop. But eventually, I decide against it. Losing my lunch is a distinct possibility; and I'd rather not risk it.

"Allegra," Jimmy sounds surprised when his assistant ushers me into his office. "This is unexpected. I assume this has to do with your grandmother's um, bequest to you?" He stumbles over the last few words, his voice breaking ever so slightly. And in that moment his grief is so painfully obvious that it brings tears to *my* eyes. Or maybe that's my own grief?

"I'm so sorry," I say. "I-I should have called ahead." The sound of my voice is unexpected too. It emerges as something soft and sad. I force it into something closer to its normal range as I finish with a jaunty, "But hey! You know me."

His lips curve in a small, but unmistakable smile as he presses a button on the intercom that connects him with the outer office—I swear, it must be an antique. He's probably been using the exact same one since the nineties... The eighties? Longer maybe? —and requests my grandmother's file. Then he sits back and folds his hands and says, "Yes. I do know you. Quite well. Possibly better than you think."

Which...really doesn't help calm my nerves at all. *Maybe not, Jimmy*, I think to myself; *maybe not.*

I clear my throat and try again. "Actually, there were a couple of things I wanted to discuss with you."

Jimmy nods, his expression serene, his voice admirably under control. "Oh, of course. And how thoughtless of me not to offer my congratulations. I did speak with your sister, yesterday. So, has this to do with your recent, er, marriage? Will we be drafting a will today, as well?"

"No!" This time I'm mortified to have almost shouted the word. "No, definitely not." And then, of course, the whole wretched story comes tumbling out yet again—with only one small pause to allow Jimmy's assistant to deliver the requested file. And apparently Clay was right about this, too. It does get easier with repetition.

"Well, this is all very troubling," Jimmy says when I'm finally done.

"I know," I say in a very small voice. "What can I do?"

And now it's his turn to embark on a long, and convoluted —and painful! —dissertation on all the ways that the situation might conceivably play out, none of them good, and all of which, basically, come down to the same unpalatable conclusion.

I really have screwed the pooch on this one. It's probable my sisters will pay the biggest price. And teams of lawyers and multiple judges will likely be picking at the remains of my grandmother's estate, for a very long time. We'd have been better off letting Geno have it.

"Of course, there are always exceptions," Jimmy says carefully. "Unexpected circumstances..."

"Miracles?" I joke.

Jimmy smiles. "Wouldn't that be nice?"

"But, seriously. There must be something?"

"Yes, of course. The case is not entirely hopeless. If we can prove that the marriage was never valid, without exposing you to prosecution in the process, that is, and if your husband—" he breaks off, possibly due to my instinctive flinch, checks his notes, and then corrects himself, "I'm so sorry, if Mr. Carvahlo can be persuaded to be reasonable, to accept a settlement of some kind—"

"What if I stayed married to him?" I ask, grasping at straws. "Would that be better? If so, I'm willing to take one for team, if you think it would help. Although obviously we'd have to get it in writing, because I wouldn't trust him otherwise. Not that I trust him now. But perhaps the prospect of a green card *and* a small settlement... No?"

I break off when Jimmy begins to shake his head. "No. No. That would be...completely unacceptable. Under no circumstances should you put *that,* or anything remotely like it, into writing. That would almost certainly be perceived as proof of fraud or attempted fraud on your part."

"Oh. Right," I sigh. "Of course." This is what I get for attempting to think on a mostly empty stomach. I really should have eaten more for breakfast. Or maybe not skipped lunch. I wonder what Jimmy would say if I suggested we order something in?

"Also," Jimmy continues, unaware of the direction my thoughts have taken, "If I might remind you, according to what you've told me, you are not currently married to Mr. Carvahlo. Nor were you ever actually married to him. And nor does it appear that Mr. Carvahlo would wish to remain married to you —were he actually married to you; which he is not—for any longer than necessary. Was that not what you told me?"

"Yes," I sigh. "I was forgetting about that, too."

"Understandable. I'm sure this is all very distressing for you."

And for you, I think, feeling a stab of guilt. *God he must hate this. And me.*

"Now, the first thing we need to do is to have you sign these papers and actually accept your grandmother's bequest. Because, otherwise, there's really nothing to talk about."

Hmm. A thought has begun nudging at the back of my brain, causing me to zone out and miss some of what Jimmy is saying.

"...and while it's true that I drafted them myself," he continues. "I would still encourage you to read through the document before signing it."

"Jimmy," I say, slowly, still wrapping my brain around a new idea still taking shape within my brain. "What if I didn't sign that?"

"What? Oh, no, no, no. As I explained, leaving the estate in limbo is not in you or your sisters' best interests. I don't wish to place blame, but this really should have been attended to last April."

"Yeah, no. Sorry. That's not what I meant. What I *should* have said is, what if I didn't accept the bequest? Or, what if I transferred my share—or whatever it's called—to someone else? My Uncle Geno, perhaps. Or maybe one of my cousins. Or perhaps all three of them? Would something like that be possible?"

"Well...ye-es. I see what you're saying. There would be ramifications, to be sure. And I would want to be very clear about that. But theoretically, it would be possible, I suppose."

"Great," I sigh. "Let's talk about it then. But first, would it be possible to get something to eat?"

Chapter 20

Allegra

Reaction sets in immediately. By the time I get to my car, my hands are shaking so hard, I almost can't drive. Even just opening the door, fastening my seatbelt, and putting the car in gear is problematic. All of which is just *sooo* ironic. The contrast between last night, when Clay was so worried about whether I was safe to drive. And now, when I'm actually having difficulty—drifting out of my lane from time to time, nearly missing stop signs that have been in place my entire life, braking too late when lights unexpectedly turn red, and then failing to notice when they finally turn green again. And there's no one to notice or care at all.

Well, that's not completely true, is it? I'm sure Jimmy's a little worried about me right now. And probably more than a little disappointed. I could read it in the set of his mouth, hear it in the way he cleared his voice—repeatedly—as he unnecessarily tapped the papers I'd signed into order...

. . .

"SO THAT'S THAT?" I ASKED, CLUTCHING THE ARMS OF THE chair so hard that my nails dug into the leather, leaving little crescent shaped marks that I could only hope would go unnoticed. I don't know why I'd even asked the question. I already knew the answer, didn't I? I'd walked in here today fully prepared to sign my life away, if need be; and I'd done it. I was just having a little trouble accepting it.

I shifted restlessly in my seat, anxious to leave, wondering, why am I here? It was done. It was over. There was no going back.

Oblivious to my rising panic, Jimmy spent the next few moments squaring the papers until they lined up perfectly with each other. And then arranging them on his desktop so that they were perpendicular to the edge—all prior to sliding them into an envelope, which probably undid all that work in an instant. And through it all, I sat there and watched, still in that same state of disbelieving panic.

To be honest, I felt kind of bad for him. For having put him in this position, forcing him to do something he so clearly did not want to do.

Same, bro; same, I thought to myself.

I could tell he felt like he was letting my grandmother down. I could see it. I could feel it. I recognized it instinctively. Because that's how I was feeling, too.

Finally, after another long moment, he raised his eyes and fixed his gaze on me. "Yes," he said in answer to my question. "That, as they say, is that." But then he leaned forward and folded his hands on top of the envelope, and added, "I think we both know that this is not what your grandmother would have wanted, not in the slightest. All the same, I do think she'd have been proud of you right now. For having had the courage to prioritize your family's well-being above your own."

"Th-thank you," I said as my throat closed up and tears began to obscure my vision. "I hope you're right."

"I hope so, too."

ANYWAY, I DO MAKE IT HOME, EVENTUALLY. STILL IN ONE piece and without killing anyone in the process. Yay me. But even as I park my car, I feel myself moving into a new stage of grief—anger.

That anger's at full steam as I grab my purse and Jimmy's envelope off the front passenger seat, swing myself out of the car and slam the door shut. I stride toward the house, under the startled gazes of my sisters and Jake who are gathered in a worried-looking knot on the front porch.

"Is he here?" I demand when I get close enough to be heard without raising my voice. "Have you seen him?"

"Legs...where have you been?" Rosa asks. "You *can't* keep disappearing like this. We need to be able to get in touch with you."

"Why?" I ask as I cross the porch. I plop myself down on the porch swing, toss my purse and the envelope on the bench seat beside me and regard my family's faces. "What did I miss? Has something happened?"

"No. Nothing. But that's not the point."

"Okay, well..." I struggle to find the right words, finally settling on, "I had some business to attend to. Now that's done, so I'm looking for Nico. He's not here, is he?"

"No," Bee answers. "We thought he was with you. That's why we were worried."

I frown. "Well, I don't know why you'd think that." Then, pointing at the open bottle chilling in the ice bucket I ask, "What're we drinking."

"Goldfinch," Jake replies, naming an award-winning Take

Flight Chardonnay blend from a few years back. And I don't think I'm imagining the faint hint of sorrow in his voice. "Would you like a glass?"

"Please."

"The reason we were concerned," Jake says when he brings me my wine. "Is because you weren't answering your phone and apparently, your— I mean, Nico—has checked out of his hotel. So..."

"Mm," I reply, not really listening. "I know. I just came from there." The wine is lovely. Pale gold in color, very bright nose. Lemon zest, dried apricot, bitter almond, wet stone. If this were my family's wine, and I knew there'd be no more of it, I'd be inclined to hoard every last bottle. But you can't really do that with Chardonnay, which (like so many things in life) doesn't age well, and is best served within a few years of bottling.

And it occurs to me that Jake and I are in similar boats, right now. That, down the road, he might be a good mentor for me, someone to show me the ropes. But then his words finally register. "Wait. How did you know that Nico had checked out?"

"Well, when we couldn't reach you..."

"Of course, we checked!" Rosa glares at me.

"Why? What did you think we were going to do?" I glance around, meeting blank faces. "Run off to Reno to get re-hitched? Really?"

"No. Not that." She shakes her head. "We didn't know what to think. Except that...that maybe he had hurt you?"

A snarky, 'sorry to disappoint,' is already lined up on my tongue, when the hint of a tremor in my sister's voice cuts through my own self-pity. "Oh. No. Sorry, Rosy-posey, I'm fine. I promise. I'm just frustrated that no one seems to know where he's gone. I've been looking forward to finally kicking his gold-digging butt out of here."

"Can you do that?" Bee asks, eyes widening with interest.

I nod and drain my glass as my anger deserts me, sliding back into panicked denial. *Oh, I can, dear sister. I so can. But at what cost?* I hold out my glass. "This is delicious. Can I get a refill please? Or are you saving it?"

Jake shrugs. "No. Not much point in that, is there?" This time he fills my glass almost to the brim. "Enjoy."

I take a small sip and try again. "So. I just came from seeing Jimmy. Davenport."

"Oh, did he find something?" Rosa asks eagerly. "Is there a plan? When I talked to him yesterday, he didn't sound optimistic at all."

"A plan?" I shake my head and snort derisively. "We don't need no stinking plan."

"Legs!"

"C'mon, now," Jake says frowning. "That's not nice."

"Sorry," I say, flashing a conciliatory smile. Or something that's supposed to be a smile. Another L. "What I mean is, we came up with a solution. That's better than a plan—right?"

"What kind of solution?"

My lips twist, an involuntary reaction that I try to hide by gulping more wine. "We don't really have to talk about this now, do we?"

"I think we should," Rosa says. "Don't you?"

"No. I think we should all have some wine and enjoy this lovely day. Look around you; look where we are! Could life get any better?" I drain my glass, glance up at Jake and say, "Mm. What else d'we got? I don't want to be drinking up all your memories, Jake. They're too precious. You should cherish them."

Jake's eyes widen. "Well...there's always the Carleo," he suggests.

"Perfect!" I tell him. "Bring it on."

Jake exchanges a worried glance with Rosa, then turns and goes into the house. As the screen door slams behind him, my sisters converge on me.

"You know, from a scientific standpoint, alcohol *is* a solution," Bee says as she joins me on the swing. "So, is your solution to just keep drinking until you pass out?"

I'm surprised into laughing. "Yeah, maybe. That's an idea, isn't it?"

"Legs." Rosa has dragged one of the wicker chairs over, so that she's seated on my left, catty-corner to me, on the opposite side from Bee. "Talk to me. What's going on?" And she reaches for my hands and holds them captive, giving serious mother hen.

Once upon a time, back when we were kids, we experienced one of those rare to seriously-kids-this-never-happens-here summer thunderstorms. Some people find that sort of thing exciting. It scared the living shit out of me. Rosa found me in my room, cowering under the bed and coaxed me out. We passed the time until the storm blew itself out, seated cross-legged on the braided rug, facing each other, holding hands just like this, while Rosa told silly stories to distract me.

I'm not sure where Bee was at the time, but given her love of science, she was probably busy somewhere setting up gadgets to measure rainfall and windspeed, and calculating how far away the storm was by counting the seconds between each flash and boom.

I loved my big sisters, and I admired their bravery. So, so much. But sometimes, they were impossible to live up to. I'm not sure that's ever changed.

"Nothing's going on," I tell Rosa now, pasting a brittle smile on my face, slipping one hand free of her grasp to accept my new glass of wine when Jake hands it to me. "We had a problem, now it's fixed."

"But..."

"But nothing." I give the hand I'm still holding a squeeze. "Listen to me. I was the one who made the mistake, so it was my responsibility to solve it. And I did. But I don't particularly want to talk about it right now. *Capisce?*"

I take a sip of wine. It tastes heavy and overly jammy after the bright, crisp taste of Goldfinch. And maybe that's all that's wrong with it. It's basic and old fashioned, and stuck in the past, and our palates have outgrown it. Losing interest, I set my glass down. "You know, it's pretty depressing when you realize that this stuff was made with Caparelli grapes." I turn to Bee and say, "I can't wait to see what you'll do with them."

But my sister isn't listening. Eyes wide, mouth agape, she's leafing frantically through a sheaf of papers and murmuring, "No, no, no, no, no."

Where'd she get those? I wonder, then it hits me. The envelope I brought back from Jimmy's office. "Hey! Those are mine. Give that back!"

"Rosa! You need to see this," Bee says, holding the papers aloft with her far hand, using her left to block my attempts to snatch them back.

"Stop that," I growl. "Give 'em back!" I leap to my feet just as Jake leans forward, both of us reaching for the papers in Bee's hand, and my face collides with the wine bottle dangling from his fingers.

"Ow!" I collapse back onto the swing, clutching my face while Jake hands the papers off to Rosa, and then runs for some ice.

"Oh, Legs," Bee groans. "What have you done?"

And then Rosa, gasps, "Allegra—*no*! You *didn't?*"

"Ow!" I say again, ignoring them both. "Ow, ow, ow." And then, when Jake hands me some ice wrapped in a tea-towel, I scowl and mutter, "Thanks, traitor."

"You're welcome," he says, then he goes to read over Rosa's shoulder. And a moment later, I hear him mutter, "Well, fuck."

Which sums it up nicely, I think.

"WE WILL FIX THIS," ROSA INSISTS, JUST A FEW MOMENTS later, having shifted from Mother Hen to Mama Bear in an impressively short amount of time. "I don't know how yet, or how long it might take us, but..."

"That's right." Bee nods in agreement. "We will."

"Guys," I sigh and shake my head. "Just stop, okay? You can't."

"You have my sword," Jake says teasingly. "For what it's worth." Then he nods towards Rosa and adds, "And her bow."

"Oh, I know this one," Bee says excitedly. "And my axe. Right?"

"Look," I say, ignoring the absurd LOTR by-play. "It's not like this was my first choice. I tried to find another way. And Jimmy tried. But in the end, we both agreed that this was the only way we could ensure that Caparelli stayed in the family. Which is what Nonna would have wanted."

"What Nonna wanted was for the *three of us* to run it," Bee corrects. "All of us. Together."

"Well, two out of three...that's not so bad, is it?"

"This isn't funny, Legs."

Don't I know it.

"Go and talk to Jimmy if you don't believe me, if you still

think there was something else we could have done. But, as he explained it, it's actually pretty simple. The will had been read. The bequest had been made. So, at that point, me signing the papers was mostly a formality. But it was an important one. I'd been holding up the final disposition of the estate, which meant everything was still in limbo. Geno could potentially have swooped in and tried to be reinstated. And Nico could have claimed....anything. He could have said I was attempting to hide my assets. Or that I was committing fraud—and that you were both conspiring with me to do so.

"If he found a judge willing to believe him, he could potentially have ended up with *much more* than the half of my share —that he was *already* not entitled to—that he was asking for. He could have taken part of your shares, too. There was no way I could let that happen."

"But you love Caparelli," Rosa protests. "As much as any of us."

I nod in response. "Yeah. I do. But I love you guys more."

As Rosa crowds beside me on the swing and I'm engulfed in yet another three-way hug, I send up a quick prayer—that the bolts and the chains supporting this swing don't fail.

Sometimes heroes have to walk through fire to protect those they care about; that's something I've heard Clay say. And, given his history, I'm not sure if he means that metaphorically, or not. I'm not feeling particularly heroic at the moment. But I'm definitely feeling singed. So, maybe that's the first step?

Over the murmur of my sisters whispered promises, "We love you, too." And "We *will* fix this," I hear the crunch of car tires on gravel.

"Heads up," Jake remarks. "We've got company."

Nico? I think hopefully as my sisters and I untangle ourselves. I'm so ready to get this over with. But Rosa, turning in her seat to look at the drive, positively growls, "Oh, hell, no. Not this again!" Which is how I know my first guess is wrong.

Then she's off the swing and charging across the porch. "Deputy Romero," she chuffs in warning. "This is really not a good time."

"Sorry, about that, Ma'am," Clay replies. And is it fair that my heart still leaps at the sound of his voice—even now? It so fucking isn't. "But I'm going to need to speak to your sister for a moment."

"Which sister?" Rosa asks, while Jake comes up beside her, silently offering support; and Bee and I share a sisterly eyeroll. Which sister, indeed.

"Allegra," he says, with a nod in my direction.

"Why?" Rosa asks crisply. "What's this about?"

"That's a very good question," I mutter. But then it hits me. And I'm jumping off the swing, once again—this time without braining myself, thankfully. I lean over the porch railing and glare at Clay. "This better not be about my driving again," I say, as my eyes drink in every detail of his appearance. He's in full uniform, standing tall and straight, but overall, he looks like shit. His eyes are heavy, his face looks drawn. *Serves you right*, I think. "And you'd better have proof of whatever it is you're accusing me of, Deputy. Pictures, or it didn't happen. If all you've got is hearsay, my lawyer will see you in court."

As I've been speaking, Clay's face has been slowly turning an unhealthy shade of red. Now he demands, "Who did that to you? Was it Carvalho?"

"What, this?" I touch my face gingerly, wincing a little at the bruising. "Oh. No, that was Jake."

Then Clay glares at Jake, Jake glares at me and, almost too late, I realize my mistake. Oopsies.

"I'm joking," I assure Clay hurriedly. "It was an accident. But that's the *only* accident I've been involved in today. So, again, if that's what you're here about, you're wasting your time."

"Hold up," Clay replies, lifting a hand in warning. "I don't know what you're talking about, and I don't want to. So, stop right there, before you say anything incriminatory. That's *not* why I'm here. It's about your ex."

"My...what?" I snarl, all at once seeing red because; this again? "Are you talking about Nico?"

"Unless you have another one?"

Oh no, he did not. I scoop up the papers from the chair where Rosa left them. Then I storm across the porch.

"Allegra." Rosa stops me at the top of the stairs. "Are you sure you're okay?"

"Never better," I lie as I stomp down the stairs and across the lawn. "Here." I slap the papers into Clay's chest. "You can give those to Mr. Carvalho the next time you see him and tell him I hope he roasts in hell."

"I'm sure he is," Clay mutters, looking at the papers in confusion. "What's this?"

"You tell me" I take a step back and cross my arms. "I assume you can read."

He quickly scans through the pages, his scowl deepening with every paragraph. When he's finished, he stares at me, his eyes wide with dismay. "You gave up your winery?"

Ouch. Fuck. I inhale sharply as the blow lands—probably harder than intended. I have to will myself not to cry. "So no, then; apparently you can't read."

"What do you mean? I just—"

"No," I repeat, stepping forward once more. Bending the papers back, I search upside down for the pertinent section, stabbing my finger at the page when I find it. "Look. D'you see what it says here?" I ask, then read it aloud, "'Has not and will not accept the bequest.' So, no. *Clearly,* I did not 'give up' my winery; 'my winery' was only ever a concept. It didn't actually exist. I mean..." I flap a hand to indicate our immediate surroundings. "Obviously, *this* winery exists, but my interest in it was only ever a potentiality, which now is null and void."

"Shit," Clay mutters, looking slightly green. "Are you fucking kidding me?"

"Problem?" I inquire.

"Well, no. But here," he hands me back the papers. "Since I'm no longer in a position to get them to Carvalho, you might as well hold onto them. I suppose you might need them at some point."

"You suppose? Of course, I'll need them! Also, *why* can't you get them to him? I understand he's no longer at his hotel, but I assume the sheriff's department has resources. Can't you find people? Isn't that what you do?"

"Not when they're no longer in our jurisdiction, and Mr. Carvalho was apprehended by ICE earlier today. To the best of my knowledge, he is currently being detained and awaiting deportation back to Portugal. If he's lucky."

"He-he what? How? Why?"

"His visa was revoked, effective immediately, due to the fact that he'd misrepresented the purpose of his visit. The agency may also have received information suggesting that, during his stay here, he was attempting to defraud US citizens —that'd be you and your sisters, by the way; in case that was unclear."

"But..."

"So, he's also been placed on the 'inadmissible aliens' list, which means he won't be allowed back into the country. Probably ever."

"Oh. I see." I take in the grim cast of his mouth, the bleakness in his gaze, the veiled hints about reports being filed. And I take a not-so-giant leap. "So, did you...?"

"What? Make a deal with the devil? You could say that. I took what I knew to my bosses. I explained what's been happening, what I knew about your case, my involvement with you, etc."

"But...didn't that get you in trouble?"

His lips twist into a bitter smile. "What do you think? Of course, it did. I'm getting written up for it. But...consequences, right? I'm not immune, either."

"Clay..."

"No, I'm not looking for sympathy. It could have been worse. And I was tired of all the sneaking around anyway. I'm not built for the shadows as much as I thought."

I stare at him helplessly. "This is a lot to unpack." My glance falls on the papers in my hands, and I feel my insides revolt. Too much wine on an empty stomach, I suppose.

"Tell me about it."

"Yeah, but...Jesus, Clay. I didn't ask you to blow up your life like that. I had things handled."

"Turn it around: *you* didn't have to do what you did, either. You could have left it to me. Should have, in fact. It's my job to protect the members of this community."

"Great. All that efforting, and what did we accomplish? Absolutely nothing."

And I groan so loudly that Rosa calls from the porch. "What's going on, Legs? Is everything okay? D'you need us to call Mr. Davenport?"

I paste on a smile as I turn and wave in her direction. "Nope. No. All good, thank you. Nothing to worry about."

"Liar," Clay chuckles. Then his face grows serious. "Look, I wouldn't say it's all been for nothing. I've done a lot of thinking. Figured out some things that I might not have otherwise."

"Like what?"

His gaze flicks to my sisters and Jake—who are all three

gathered at the top of the stairs now, regarding us with varying degrees of suspicion and concern. "D'you think maybe we can do this in private?"

I'm about to say yes—because, last night aside, I'm generally inclined to say yes to him on everything. But I'm tired of hiding in the shadows, as well. I shake my head. "Nah, let's stay where we are. I think I need my family around me right now."

Clay's eyes widen. "Oh. It's like that, is it? You're saying you want to do this 'in front of God and everyone'?"

His question catches me off-guard. Because no, I hadn't really planned on turning this into a battle of dueling Moonstruck quotes. But if that's what he wants, game on. "Well, you're the one who wanted to stop hiding. Here's your chance."

Clay takes a deep breath, in and out. "Okay, here goes. I love you, Allegra Martinelli. Which...I'm guessing you already knew that?"

"I had an inkling." My lips are twitching, my smile trying its damnedest to break free. "Or at least I thought I did, up until last night."

Clay winces. "Yeah, I know. That was my baggage, and I projected it onto you. And I am so fucking sorry."

"That was some pretty heavy baggage," I say softly.

Clay nods. "I know. That's why it's especially unfair that I unloaded on you."

"I don't mind sharing burdens, Clay, as long as I know that that's what's going on. I just don't like being blindsided."

"I remember."

Meanwhile, up on the porch, I can hear my sisters whispering. First Bee, "I don't understand. Did I miss something? What's going on?"

Then Rosa's bemused response, "I have. No. Freaking. Clue."

"So, was there anything else you wanted to tell me?" I ask Clay.

And he nods. And then, still speaking to me alone, ignoring the chorus, he says, "You know, living here in Napa, even people like me get to hearing a lot about wine. And, God knows, *you* talk about it all the time. And drink enough of it. So, I'm sure you're familiar with that one quote they're always dragging out; something about 'wine is sunlight held together by water'?"

"Maybe? I might have heard of it," I tease. Because seriously, who hasn't?

"Yeah well, I never knew what that meant until the night I saw you dancing in the water, with a bottle of wine in your hand. I thought you fucking outshone the sun."

"Well, it was dark," I feel compelled to point out. "So, that bar was set pretty low."

"And then there's that other one—and I know you know this one. It's the one from the sign, when you first drive in? About wine being bottled poetry? That one reminds me of you, as well. Only, with you it's all song lyrics and movie quotes, rather than poetry, which—same, same—according to Miles."

I blink in confusion. "I'm not sure how these metaphors are supposed to work, but wouldn't that make me the bottle, rather than the wine?"

"Not the point. Thing is, you're a lot like this place. You feel like home to me. You're all the things I love about Napa, along with a few that I hate. But I don't think I'd want it any other way."

What? My mouth falls open. "I'm sorry. There are things you *hate* about me?"

"Well, you *are* part of the one percent, aren't you?" Then he glances at the papers in my hand and shrugs. "Okay, maybe not anymore. But no, that's not what I'm trying to say, either. I wouldn't want you to be any other way, or anything other than what you are."

"Oh..."

"Because for one, you're perfect. Or perfectly imperfect—you know what I mean. But also, I've realized that it's not about the ways that we're alike, or how we're different. We're all like pieces of a puzzle. We're not supposed to be the same. No one cares what the individual pieces look like, or how they're shaped, right? What matters is whether or not they fit together."

"So, are you saying that you think you and I fit?"

"Yeah, don't you?"

I smile at him. "Of course, I do. But you mentioned Miles, a minute ago. And I still don't understand what he's got to do with anything?"

"Nothing, really. Other than he's so fucking in love with his wife that he can't stop talking about her. Dude drags her name into practically every conversation. It's annoying as fuck. At least, I used to think it was. But now, I'm not so sure."

"Really?"

"These last couple of days have mostly sucked. You and I were fighting. I came way too close to ending my career. And I bent my own code of ethics so far off plumb for you, that it all but flatlined. But at least this." He gestures at the space between us, "is out in the open now. So, I'm happy about that. I mean, assuming there still *is* an us?"

We'd been drifting closer together as we spoke, as though drawn together by some gravitational force that neither of us could resist. Or like a giant, invisible hand was quietly nudging two very reluctant puzzle pieces into place. Now I take a step closer, all on my own. I slide my arms over his shoulders and smile at him, teary eyed. "I think that's a safe assumption, Clay Romero—Romeo. Because I love you, too."

Then Bee squeals in excitement. *"What* did she say?"

And Rosa gasps. "Legs...you *love* him?"

And a deep chuckle vibrates in Clay's chest. "Jesus Christ. This family." He looks at me, and I at him. "Well, go on," he urges. "You might as well. You know you want to."

And then neither of us can keep from grinning as I shout back, "Yes Ma. I love him awful." And in a softer voice, I add, "I really do, you know. Even if your version of an apology is about as cheesy as a 90s Romcom."

"But you love those cheesy Romcoms," he reminds me. And he's not wrong.

Somewhere in the background, I hear Rosa murmur confusedly, "Did she just call me Ma?"

And an equally confused Bee murmurs back, "I...think so?"

And an even *more* confused sounding Jake inquires, "Jesus. Just how hard did she hit her head, anyway?"

Clay shakes his head in amusement. Raising his voice, he calls out, "You can all relax. She's quoting old movies. She's fine."

And I smile and say, "You know me so well."

He nods. He tightens his hold on me, gathers me close, and murmurs, "That I do; but not as well as I'm going to." And then his lips meet mine and...

Okay, look. I know I said it before but, whew. This man can kiss!

Epilogue

Allegra

SOME MONTHS LATER...

"It's another beautiful day in wine country," I read from the latest article that supposedly mentions Caparelli somewhere in its uber-flowery depths. "Where every day is another glass of endless possibilities and... Omigod, what *is* this crap?" I glare at my screen. "When do we get to the part about the winery? What are they even trying to say?"

Clay, who's been shadowing my footsteps a little more closely than usual, shoots me a glance from his place on the hammock. "What's the matter, babe? You're not usually this jumpy. Is this still grand pre-re-opening celebration jitters, or is there something else bothering you?"

"I don't know," I admit reluctantly. "I might be a little nervous."

"No reason to be." He smiles bracingly. "You've got this. There are only two things you have to do today, stand beside your sisters and smile."

"I know. It just feels weird."

I've been surprisingly happy, these last few months, flitting around the edges of my sisters' lives, staying in my lane, accepting my limited responsibilities. The feeling that I have to fight *all the time* for the recognition and attention I deserve—gah!—that's mostly gone now, and I don't miss the pressure of it at all.

Still. The lead up to today's re-opening has been hard. To be shunted aside (not just today, but all the time lately). To not be allowed to involve myself in any of the preparations. To not even be consulted on the super-secret name change...

And why is that, by the way? Are they that afraid that I'll screw things up again? That I'll pitch a fit if it turns out they've chosen something stupid? Or maybe that I'll leak the new name to the news? Which...why does it even *have* to be a secret?

And now, to top it off, I'm expected to stand there—on a stage (they say it isn't, but I know better). To smile and pretend, to act like Caparelli is still partly mine, when in reality it's not?

I suppose this is how Jake must feel all the time. Except that it really isn't. He's said it himself. Even if his family had managed to hold on to Take Flight, he still would have had to decide which winery he wanted to live on. And I held my tongue when he said it, and didn't point out that he and Rosa could easily have joined the two wineries together and run them as one. But now Bee's moved in with Jansen, so in a way, it's like she and Jake have simply swapped houses, and no one's lost anything. No one but me.

An alarm starts to ring on Clay's phone, spiking my nerves. "We could just not go," I suggest. "Who's even gonna notice?"

"Well, your sisters, for two."

"Ah, they'll be fine. We could go back to your apartment and tell everyone we lost track of time."

"*Our* apartment," he corrects. "And no, we're not gonna do that either. C'mon." He holds out a hand. "We gotta go."

Reluctantly, I take his hand, and we wander back up the path. "Thank you, by the way," I murmur softly.

"For what?" he asks looking all at once wary. "What is it you think I did?"

"For taking time off so you could be here today."

At that he laughs. "You're kidding, right? Not that I wouldn't want to be here for you, but they pretty much *had* to give me the time off for this. It would've been a conflict of interest if I were here today in an official capacity."

"No, it wouldn't," I protest. "Because I just work here now. It's actually got nothing to do with either one of us."

His lips roll in and he shakes his head, but before I can tell him that no amount of head shaking will change those facts, my sisters converge upon us.

"Oh, good; there you are," Rosa sighs in relief. "I was starting to worry."

"About what?" I reply, eyeing her sharply, feeling a stab of guilt. "Where'd you think I'd gone?"

"Thank you, Clay," Bee interrupts brightly as she steps forward. She slips her arm through mine and begins to draw me away. "We can take it from here."

She looks super excited, and I transfer my frown from Rosa's face to hers. "Okay. What's going on? You look like you know something?"

"Me? No." Bee blinks innocently. "Of course, not. What would I know?"

"Yes you." Glancing over my shoulder, I see that Clay's been buttonholed by Rosa. If I didn't know better, I'd swear they were arguing. "You *and* Rosa. You're both being *so weird* right now."

Bee shrugs. "Well, I don't know what to tell you."

"For starters, you can tell me why you look like someone

with a secret. Like you know something that no one else—Omigod!" I dig in my heels and pull her to a stop. "Is that it? Did you hear back from the committee? Did you get the award?"

Biting her lip, Bee glances around, making sure no one can hear, before whispering, "Nothing's been announced yet, and I don't know the exact results but..."

"Yes, and...?" I urge impatiently.

"Well, don't quote me, but I heard we made the short list, so at the very least we're one of the finalists..."

I squeal and give her a hug. "Oh, you *so* got it. I know you did; your wines are amazing."

That's no lie. The single biggest reason why Caparelli's re-opening has been such an incredible success is our wines; they're already winning awards. "Nonna would be so proud of you!"

"She'd be proud of you, too," Bee replies, eyeing me strangely. Or maybe not so strangely; my nose is suddenly sniffly and I think I might cry. But I know she's right. Because the *second biggest reason* for our success is the fabulous branding I've done, the sensational buzz I've created (today's overblown article aside) that's all been me. And it's all about to be at least partially *undone* now, thanks to this stupid decision to rename the winery.

Don't fix what isn't broken, right? I mean, seriously; who does that? What the hell are they even thinking?

I remember the day I'd first found out about the name change. How I'd walked into Rosa's office annoyed because the order I'd placed for new Caparelli-branded glasses had been cancelled without my knowing.

Those original glasses (the ones I'd unearthed the first day I was back) are kind of sacred, you know? I get teary eyed thinking about how Nonna actually handled those glasses, drank from them, probably washed them—right there in the same, small sink behind the bar that I use.

I didn't want to wait until they'd all been broken to buy more. Or to settle for generic glasses, even if that does make better sense from an economic standpoint. I wanted to take a few out of circulation, to put them away for safekeeping. But that's hard to do when there are already days when we're so busy we run out multiple times, and people have to wait for another load to be washed...

"WHY CAN'T I ORDER NEW GLASSES?" I ASK AS I BURST through the office door, only to find both of my sisters intently studying something on Rosa's computer, something they clearly don't want me to see—judging by their startled expressions and the way Rosa immediately closes the screen.

I frown suspiciously. "What are you looking at?"

"Crop reports," Rosa answers immediately.

"Oh, it's just the latest numbers from the, um—" Bee says at the same time. She shoots Rosa a disbelieving look and finishes lamely, "Crop reports."

I roll my eyes. "Fine. Don't tell me." I drop into a chair near the desk and say, "Now, about the glasses, we're running low."

"Just hold off on buying any new branded ones," Rosa says soothingly. "Okay?"

"For how long?"

"Not long. Just until after the grand re-opening."

"But that's like... Six weeks?"

"That's not so long, is it?" Bee asks hopefully.

"We just have some additional expenses, at the moment," Rosa says.

"So, this is about money?"

"Well, no. Not exactly."

"So, do you need me to find some sponsors for the event? 'Cause I could do that."

"No." My sisters exchange a look. "No, I don't think that'll be necessary."

"No? Well, then here's a thought; maybe we shouldn't be throwing a party for ourselves if we can't even afford essentials like glassware. What'll you want me to cut back on next? Coasters? Bar napkins?"

"Actually." Rosa takes a deep breath before dropping the hammer, "I'd hold off on ordering any new branded supplies for the time being."

"What?"

"She means anything with a logo," Bee says helpfully. Well. I mean, I'm sure she thinks she's being helpful.

"Lemme get this straight," I say to Bee. "You're saying it's okay if I start serving your wine in Solo cups?"

She jerks back as though I'd slapped her. "Oh, that's just rude."

"Look, Legs," Rosa says, speaking slowly, in that same, super-soothing voice that's doing nothing to calm my nerves. "Don't get upset, okay?"

"A little late for that," I murmur. Then the seriousness in their expressions register and I feel the blood drain from my face. "Oh, God. What is it? What's wrong? Has something happened?"

"No, no, it's nothing bad," Rosa insists hurriedly. "It's just that I know you don't like change—and I get that. Because tradition is important to me, as well. But..."

Bee rolls her eyes. "Ay, boludo. We're changing the name of the winery, okay? It's gonna be great. You'll like it."

My mouth drops open. I close it again. Then I squeeze my eyes shut as I try to process what's happening.

"Legs," Rosa says again, using her softest Mama Bear voice.

315

"No." I hold up one hand. "Not. Now. Just...give me a minute." Christie got the winery; Max got the girl. Christie got the winery; Max got the girl. *As a mantra, it kind of sucks, but at least it's more effective than Kate's 'little stone cottage' from French Kiss.*

"I suppose you had to do that?" Rosa whispers vehemently.

"Yes," Bee whispers back. "I did. Because once the two of you get to talking about tradition, you never stop. And swear to God, if I have to sit through even one more of those conversations, I'm moving back to Argentina. Inmediatamente!"

Which, FYI, is the emptiest threat in the whole entire world. And we all know it.

"Okay," I say after a moment. "So...what's the new name gonna be?"

They glance quickly at one another then, "It's a secret," Bee says.

"It's a surprise," Rosa says—*at the exact same time.*

"You're not even gonna tell me what it is?" I demand, voice rising into screech territory at the end.

"Of course, we will," Rosa promises. "At the grand re-opening."

"It'll be so good," Bee assures me.

"Trust us," *they both say.*

Which, if you ask me, is expecting a fucking lot from someone with my history.

THERE'S A SMALL CROWD MILLING ABOUT IN FRONT OF THE winery—not the general public, but nearly everyone we know. The Lambros are here—although neither Uncle Geno nor Aunt Janet were able to make it. I see Jimmy Davenport; and my sisters' friends, Sasha, Millie and Ana. Even Jake's buddy, Wade, and a few of our old teachers, like Mrs. Gerstenmayer have come out to cheer us on. And nearly everyone has a glass of wine. Servers circulate through the crowd, filling and refilling as necessary.

Bee leads me to the small, elevated platform (it's a stage, okay?) where a podium has been set up. I see that the new sign has also been erected and affixed in place, just in front of the house—and not too close to the road because, if you can believe it, Napa has restrictions about that, as well. My gaze goes there immediately, but it's swathed in drapes, awaiting its unveiling—with a couple of interns standing guard to make sure that doesn't happen prematurely.

"How about a hint?" I ask Bee, as we both accept glasses.

"No hints," Rosa says sternly as she joins us. She has wine now, too, I see.

I scan the crowd again until my gaze finds Clay, standing with Jansen, Miles, Logan and Jake—they all have glasses, too. "Just how much wine are we handing out today, anyway?" I ask. "It seems like a lot."

"Oh, we're not," Bee says. "This is all from Jansen's cellar."

I feel myself frown. "But that's not made here. Isn't that gonna be a problem?"

Bee shakes her head. "I talked to Clay. He said that only applies if we're selling or marketing it. Besides, I'm the one who made it, right? I figure that has to count for something."

"I'm pretty sure it doesn't. The county doesn't give a flying fruitcake about what any of us think."

Rosa nudges me with her elbow. "I'm sorry, weren't you the one who suggested rolling barrels from one winery to another as a way to circumvent the fermentation rule?"

"Ugh. No." Bee's expression turns pained. "Don't do that. That'd be awful. Anyway, we needed wine for the toast. But you're right, we don't really have enough yet of our own. And Jansen wanted to contribute something, anyway, so..."

"I still don't understand why we even have to have a toast," I grouse.

"Because we're celebrating!" my sisters insist. "It's a party."

They look excited. Must be nice to be them, I think. "One hint," I urge again.

"No!" They say (in unison this time) and then they laugh.

"But, why?" I whine in frustration and, let's face it, fear. All the attention this event has drawn, all the anticipation that's been building—it's all fun and games until someone gets hurt. What happens if they've chosen a name that nobody likes? Or one that's already in use elsewhere—have they even thought about that? Or what if they've picked the wrong font for the sign-slash-logo? What if, after spending a fortune on rebranding, we end up on one of those viral #FontFail lists? Like the ones where the 'cl' in click looks like a 'd' or the 'li' in flick looks like a 'u'? It could happen.

"I don't know why you wouldn't even let me put together a focus group," I complain. I understand that it's not my winery, not my decision. But at least I could have helped.

"Well, we did have a kind of focus group," Bee says.

"You did?"

"No, not really," Rosa says. "It was totally informal. We just did a little brainstorming with the cousins. And Jake, of course."

"And Jansen," Bee adds.

"Are you saying..." I pause to catch my breath. And maybe to keep from screaming. "That I'm the last to know—*again*?" I glare at Rosa. "Like when I came home and found out that you and Jake were *married*?"

"Oh! Please. Like *you* can talk," she retorts, as her cheeks flush red.

Bee laughs. "Face it, ladies, you both suck. And when Jansen and I get married, I'm not telling either one of you."

Rosa and I share a look. "Bee? Did you say...when?"

"She did," I say, nodding excitedly. "She definitely did."

"If!" Bee corrects quickly. "I meant if!" But, judging by the flush on her cheeks, I'd bet anything that what she really meant was *when*. And that by *when*, what she really means is *soon*.

We're startled, just then, by a blast of feedback from the sound system. "Sorry!" Jake says, looking sheepish. "Sorry, everyone. But if I could just have your attention?"

I gasp for breath. Oh, shit. It's time. And I'm about to start hyperventilating. There's a burst of applause as Rosa approaches the podium. Bee and I clasp hands as our sister starts to address the crowd. But my head is too filled with noise and memories, and I find it hard to focus on anything that's being said. I think back over the past year. The rumors, the scandals, the legal battles. Relationships made and lost. Laughter, tears, and really good wine. Nonna would have loved it. And hated it.

"So, thank you all, so much, for being here," Rosa says— clearly coming to the end of her speech. "And for celebrating with my sisters and me..." She turns and waves for us to join her.

"C'mon," Bee whispers, pulling me along as she goes to stand beside Rosa. "That's us."

"No," I whisper back. "I shouldn't."

"Yes, you should," she hisses, pushing me in front of her, so that I'm sandwiched between them, no way to escape.

"As we embark on this next step in our journey," Rosa continues, her eyes dancing. "This exciting new adventure, the latest iteration of the Caparelli, Bianchi, Lamberti, Martinelli wine making tradition."

Rosa nods at Jake who signals to the interns standing ready on either side of the sign.

"And now, if you'll all please raise your glasses, I give you...
Le Tre Sorelle Winery!"

A roar goes up from the crowd as people cheer and clink
glasses. Somewhere in the distance I hear someone, I think it's
Leo saying, "Ha! What did I say? I knew that's the one they'd
go with!"

Bee and Rosa are right beside me, squeeing in excitement
as they squeeze my shoulders. "Well? Isn't it great?" they
demand gleefully. "What do you think?"

But I can't think. My mind's a blank. Le tre sorelle. The
three sisters. Nonna's name for us all. The words on the sign
keep blurring as tears flood my eyes and I blink them away. I
have no idea where my wine glass went, but both my hands are
clasped over my mouth in an effort to keep from bawling.

Now Jake and Jansen have joined us on the stage. Everyone's smiling and laughing. Kissing. Toasting. I'm so proud of
my sisters, of everything they've accomplished. And I'm so
happy for them. But I still can't process any of it.

"You all right, babe?" Clay asks. Turning, I find him eyeing
me ruefully. I gaze back at him helplessly, unable to answer.

"Yeah," he says, stepping forward and pulling me into his
arms. "That's what I thought." And that's when I start crying
for real—gulping for a breath I can't seem to catch. "Listen to
me, mia," Clay's voice vibrates in my ear. "You're okay, understand? There's nothing to cry about. It's all gonna work out.
Trust me."

And I nod urgently because I know he's right. Except that
he's not. Le Tre Sorelle. It's the *perfect* name for our winery.
My winery. But it's not that anymore, is it?

The microphone growls as it comes back to life. "It's okay,
folks," Jake assures the crowd. "Nothing to worry about. Those
are happy tears." Which only makes me cry harder.

I burrow my face deeper against Clay's chest. He leans

down and whispers in my ear, "You're getting me sooo wet right now. You know that, right?"

I gulp back a laugh and jab a finger between his ribs because that's so not funny. I mean, it is...just not right now.

"Legs?" Rosa's voice is tentative. She lays a hand on my shoulder and squeezes gently. "What is it? Don't you like the name?"

"I do," I mumble. "It's perfect."

"Then what's wrong?"

"N-n-nothing. It's like Jake said, these are ha-happy tears. I'm just...s-so happy...f-for b-both of you."

"Both? But...no! Legs!"

"Shit!" Bee exclaims, sounds horrified. "I *knew* we should have done things the other way around. Legs, honey, of course we wouldn't— I mean, we'd never—"

"Perhaps I can be of service?" another voice interjects. Jimmy? Oh, fuck. Have I ever mentioned how much I hate looking vulnerable? Well, I do. "Allegra? Could I have your attention for a moment?"

"Oh, hey, Jimmy," I mumble, trying for a normal tone— that's a big L, by the way. Normal has officially left the building. "What's up?"

"I have some paperwork here that needs your signature."

I bite back a curse. What kind of paper—? And then it hits me. I'm being *served? Now?* What fresh hell is this?

I turn in the circle of Clay's arms. Then immediately clamp my hands on his wrists to ensure that he won't let go. "What's this about?"

Jimmy's smile is gentle and understanding. "It's very simple, actually. Your sisters asked me to draw up a partnership agreement, making you all equal partners in the Le Tre Sorelle Winery," he explains, as my mind goes blank again.

"W-w-what?"

"I mean, *Le Tre Sorelle*," Rosa says, and now she's fighting back tears too, turning to Jake for comfort. "*Tre!* The clue's right there in the name! I can't believe you thought we'd...what? Just...*not* include you? Really?"

"Exactly." Bee nods in agreement. "We'd never! I mean, if we *were* gonna do that, we could have picked *any* name."

"I understand Bottle Jock is still available," Jansen says, wrapping his arms around her waist and resting his chin on her head, earning himself an elbow to the gut.

"See? I told you it would be okay," Clay says. "You never listen."

And I nod, and swipe at my tears, because he had. And... "Wait a minute." I twist around to face him. "How long have you known about this?"

Clay's mouth compresses into a tight line. "You're not gonna be weird about this are you?" he asks. "Please don't be weird about this."

"How. Long?"

He glances at Rosa and asks, "What's it been, four or five weeks?"

"Yeah." She nods, dabbing at her tears. "I think. Something like that."

"Well, *of course*, we had to read him in on this," Bianca explains. "We wanted to surprise you."

I'm still glaring at Clay. He's still meeting my gaze, steady and unashamed; the fucking nerve of the man. "So, you've just been *lying* to me for weeks? Is that what you're saying?"

"Yep. I sure have. And you know what that means, right?"

"That you're a *liar*?"

"Well, okay. That too," he concedes. "But also, it means I can never again hold it against you that you lied to me first."

"Oh." I think about that for a beat. "I guess that's true, isn't it?"

"Yep."

Then I start to laugh. "Omigod. We are so fucked, aren't we?"

"And this is a surprise?" Clay asks. "No. Look at how we met."

I think about that. Larceny. Underage drinking. Really hot sex. And a mad dash to freedom, through a midnight vineyard. "I guess you're right. But it works for us."

"It appears to."

"So, what happens next?"

"Well, next you sign the paperwork that your sisters went to all this trouble for. And I spend the rest of my life trying to deal with the fact that you're once again a filthy rich winery owner."

Everyone around us snorts in disbelief. "Well, at least we can guarantee the filthy part," Jake remarks.

"For real," Bee sighs, looking sadly at her nails.

"But wait a minute," I turn to Jimmy and say, "I can't do this can I? What if..."

"I think you'll find that you can," he says. "We've received all the necessary documents from the EU and now have everything we need to prove that your attempted marriage to Nico Carvalho was never legally valid. And also that you were unaware of the deception and were acting in good faith. Which means that Mr. Carvalho has no legal standing whatsoever."

"That's why we couldn't tell you before," Rosa says. "We had to be sure. We were waiting until we were absolutely certain that the winery couldn't be taken away from you again."

"We didn't want to raise your hopes, only to disappoint you," Bee adds.

"And like I told you," Clay points out. "He's never gonna be allowed back in the States, anyway. So, all in all, I think you can safely write him out of the picture. For good, this time."

I spare a thought for Nico. I never thought that *he* was going to turn out to be the villain of the story. We were friends once, after all. And he probably didn't deserve everything he got. But I can't be too sorry for him, either. Because this is what happens when you try to come between me and my sisters.

"So, you're sure?" I ask Jimmy.

"I am."

"All right." I hold out my hand. "Then lemme at 'em."

"Perhaps we might use that podium," he suggests.

We straggle across the stage, the whole group of us, and Jimmy begins laying out papers on the polished faux walnut. He eyes the microphone dubiously and asks, "That's not on, is it?"

Jake taps it to check, then gives a thumbs up. "It's off. You're all clear."

Then I'm staring at the papers that will make me part of le tre sorelle once again. My sisters' signatures are already in place, their names printed neatly under each line. And there at the bottom, an empty line awaits my signature. My name is there, too. All of it. In tiny little letters.

"The whole thing, huh?" I ask as I uncap the pen. "Damn, my hand's already starting to cramp."

"Don't be such a baby," Rosa scolds teasingly.

Clay leans over my shoulder. "What whole thing?" His eyes widen. I swear to God his face pales. "Holy shit."

"Uh-huh," I say, side-eyeing him. "Tell me again how much you hate your cute little one syllable, four letter name?"

"Nope." He shakes his head. "No complaints."

"That's what I thought." Then I put pen to paper and write my name and tie myself to this vineyard, this legacy, this sister-hood. One letter at a time. Allegra Francesca Catarina Viviana Martinelli.

. . .

I've heard it said that grandmothers are angels in disguise. And I don't know if that's true, but if there is a heaven I know my Nonna is smiling down at us all right now and whispering, "*Complimenti, le mie bellissime tre sorelle; brava, brava, brava. Tua nonna vi ama così tanto.*"

Wine Songs

Decant Me
(Sung to the tune of "A Letter from Camp")

Is it Sauterne? Is it Riesling?
Sauvi-B can be so pleasing.
Is it special, for entertaining?
Or just a wine to drink whenever it's not raining?"

Decant me, I hate my bottle. Can't you see? I taste like rubble.
Let me breathe before you try to share me with your friends
and family.

Decant me—for just an hour. It is like a superpower.
New and old wine goes from tasting blah to tasting really, extra
fine.

Is it Malbec? Or a Cab-Franc?
Is it juicy, with a good rank?
Do I need to keep explaining?
If you decant your wine your guests won't be complaining.

We Don't Talk About Boxes
(Sung to the tune of "We Don't Talk About Bruno")

We don't talk about boxes, oh no, no. We don't talk about boxes.
It was a Wednesday, or maybe a Thursday, but there wasn't a
cloud in the sky.
Rosa walked in with a mischievous grin.

"I did what?"
"Are you singing this song now, or am I?"
"Sorry, Allegra, please go on!"

She smiles and tells me, "Look what came!"
Apparently, she feels no shame.
But all at once my temper flames—
But anyway, we don't talk about boxes. No, no, no. We don't
talk about boxes!

The Bentonite Slurry Song
(Sung to the tune of "Surrey with the Fringe on Top")

If you think that your wine's looking blurry,
You should try using bentonite slurry,
You should try using bentonite slurry,

Wine Songs

To clear up the grime.

Yeasts, and haze, and tannins will scurry
When you add that bentonite slurry,
When you add that phyllosilicate slurry,
To your vats of wine.

Just three TBs to a pint of H_2O,
Is a pretty good ratio.
Bring your water to a boil, before you pour the powder in,
Then blend it up smoothly.

Can't be done 'til you've completed fermentation,
And moved your wine to a cooler destination,
Stir it well, but avoid agitation,
And your wine will shine!
You'll have glassy, glossy, clear-as-crystal, radiant wine.

No Wines but Rosé
(Sung to the tune of "No Day but Today")

There's no more red, there's no more white,
We've drunk them all, should we call it a day?
No! Hold your glass, there's still one flight.
No wines but Rosé!

I know you've heard (for I have too)
Reject, eject, white zinfandel is dreck!

Wine Songs

But don't discount La Méthode Saignée.
No wines but Rosé!

Might be too late to macerate,
To press, or bleed—but blend we may.
What do you say?

No time for Cabs, or Chardonnay,
We need cash now—c'mon, let's seize the day!
No Chenin Blanc, no Viognier,
No wines but Rosé!

I am a Pricey Bottle of a California Meritage
(Sung to the tune of "I am the very Model of a Modern Major
General")

I am a pricey bottle of a California Meritage,
(A word that combines merit in a portmanteau with heritage).
I'm only made from "noble" wines, those vintned from a
Bordeaux vine,
'Cause that is what it takes to make a California Meritage.

You start with two or more of these particular varieties,
Cabernet (Sauvingnon or Franc), St. Macaire or Carménère,
Malbec, Merlot, Petit Verdot, or possibly some Gros Verdot,
For that is what you'll need, you know, for a California
Meritage.

Wine Songs

You have to use the very best of these specific vintages,
Adjusted with a sweet finesse like all the best of marriages,
To best ensure my taste is great, no single grape can dominate,
'Cause otherwise I will not rate as a California Meritage.

I'm known for being robust with a silky-smooth complexity,
I'm good to drink while young but I'm renowned for aging
beautifully,
I'm more than just a simple blend, and that is why I am a
TREND!
And why you pay the big bucks for a California Meritage.

Wouldn't it be Buttery?
(AKA the Chardonnay song)

(Sung to the tune of "Wouldn't it be Loverly")

All I want is a Chardonnay,
Fermented in the modern way,
In French or White Oak kegs,
Oh, wouldn't it be buttery?

Fifteen months barrel aged on lees,
(fine, not gross, if you don't mind, please)
Best served at fifty-five degrees,
Oh, wouldn't it be buttery?

Oh, so buttery with the barest hint of caramel,

Wine Songs

Pair with pasta, fish or cheese, or maybe some bechamel?
Full-bodied with a creamy mouthfeel,
Ya won't get that outta stainless steel!
S'why oak's the beau ideal if you want your Chardonnay
buttery.
Buttery, buttery,
Buttery, buttery.

Que Será Syrah
(Sung to the tune of "Que Será, Será")

When I was still too young to drink,
I asked my grandma which should it be,
Would I like white wine, would I like red?
Here's what she said to me:

Que Será Syrah
You might try a nice Chablis,
Mourvedre, or Pinot Gris,
Que Será Syrah

Then I grew up and got engaged,
Went to my lover—what would he say?
Champagne, Prosecco, or Sparkling Rosé,
To serve on our wedding day?

He said...

Wine Songs

Que Será Syrah
All three sound just great to me,
Or maybe a Pinot Gris?
Que Será Syrah
Or maybe, Chablis?

Now when my sisters come to me,
I know the questions, before they ask,
Steel vat or barrel, qvevri or cask,
Bottle, or box or flask?

And I say...

Que Será Syrah
Whatever you do; do you
Just pour me a glass, or two,
Que Será Syrah
What will be, Chablis!

There is Nothing Like Champagne
(Sung to the tune of "There is Nothing Like a Dame")

There is nothing like Champagne,
Nothing in this world.
There is no wine you can name
That is anything like Champagne.

When you want to make a toast,

Wine Songs

(C'mon, raise a glass!)
Party, celebrate or boast,
Make it Champagne, or else I'll pass.

'Cause nothing tastes like Champagne,
Makes your heart race like Champagne,
Nothing pops like Champagne,
Or launches yachts like Champagne,
And nothing costs like Champagne,
Says you're a boss like Champagne.

There ain't no drink, be it pink or white,
That'll lift your spirits, give you second life,
Like that mix of four pinots and a chardonnay
Grown in a special terroir mix of limestone, chalk and clay...ay-
ay-ay, ay-ay-ay, ay-ay, ay!

There is nothing like Champagne,
Nothing in this world.
There is no wine you can name
That is anything like Champagne.

MISCELLANEOUS SONG SCRAPS

Crush It (Crush It Real Good!)
(Sung to the tune of "Push It")

Wine Songs

Whew! Napa's sweating today, but then tonight it might just freeze.
C'mon girls, let's show these guys we know this work is just a breeze!
We'll sort those grapes, destem them too, then give that juice a squeeze.
Now crush it, crush it good
(Ah, crush it) crush it real good

How Do You Make a Pitcher of Sangria?
(Sung to the tune of "How Do You Solve a Problem like Maria?")

How do you make a pitcher of sangria?
What do you need besides the perfect wine
(Something that's young and bright and not too oaky)
A cinnamon stick, some fizzy water, a lime?

Plenty of recipes will tell you one thing,
Plenty of them will tell you the reverse.
But where do you set the bar?
Is mango a fruit too far?
Maybe we need an extra bottle to rehearse?
Oh, how do you make a pitcher of sangria?
How do you make that sweet, sweet, summer wine?

Tempranillo
(Sung to the tune of "Oklahoma")

Tempranillo, you're the first to ripen on the vine.
You're the fourth most planted red wine grape, and a top-tier rojo noble nine!
Tempranillo, you're the wine Phoenician traders drank

Wine Songs

As they sailed the Med'terranean 'til the last of the
penteconters sank!
We know that you pair well with meat,
And with aging exhibit fruit and heat.
And when we say, "Hey!
You taste like cherry, fig and suede!"
We're really sayin'
"You're a fine wine, Tempranillo!"
Tempranillo, olé!

Christmas Carols
(I probably won't include these here. I'll save them for the
Christmas story)

We Wish You a Merlot Christmas! (and a Chianti New Year)
(Sung to the tune of "We Wish You a Merry Christmas")

We wish you a Merlot Christmas,
We wish you a Merlot Christmas,
We wish you a Merlot Christmas and a Chianti New Year!
A magnum we'll bring for you and your friends,
We wish you a Merlot Christmas and a Chianti New Year

Oh, Grenache
(sung to the tune of "You're a Mean One Mr. Grinch")

You're a smooth one, oh, Grenache,

Wine Songs

You're so very versatile.
You're licorice, fruit and pepper;
With hints of leather on the nose.
Oh, Grenache!
Three foods I'd choose to pair you with are as follows (please
take notes):
Roast pork, lamb and duck.

Mulled Wine
(Sung to the tune of "My Favorite Things)

Glühwein, bisschopswijn, vin chaud, or caliente,
Glögg, or vin brulé, candola, or quente,
Give me a sec, I'll give you twenty more
Names for that winter drink we all adore!

Just take brandy, and spices, and orange in slices,
A bottle of red, maybe two—who will miss it?
Add cloves and some sugar and heat it all up,
Then when it's done, let me fill up my cup.

When the wind blows and the rain flows,
And my feet feel numb,
Just give me a mug of that sweet winter treat,
And then I won't feel so glum!

Que Será Syrah

Copyright © May 2025 by PG Forte

Digital ISBN: 978-1-880370-87-2

Paperback ISBN: 978-1-880370-89-6

Cover Artist: PG Forte

Published in the United States of America

Chapultepec Press

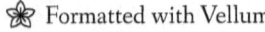 Formatted with Vellum

Acknowledgments

First, of course, I have to acknowledge Kate Davies and Kelly Jamieson for their good humor, excellent writing, and precious friendship. And for helping to keep this dream alive for way longer than any of us thought it would take. Let's write some books about a winery, they said. It'll be fun, they said. Well, they were right!

I'd also like to thank the team at Grape Expectations and the Nevada School of Winemaking, particularly Patty Peters and KJ Howe, for sharing their knowledge and expertise, and for giving me hands on experience making wine. My sister Jane, for sharing the experience with me. And my daughter Chelsea; who still occasionally allows me to read aloud to her— even when she's a continent away.

Very special thanks to Amber Brunkow and everyone at Blank Space Yoga for, yes, keeping me sane-ish.

Finally, I'd like to acknowledge the Cal Falcon community; the Rhinory Winery; and all the First Responders in the Napa, Sonoma and Lake Counties. The impact you had on the communities that were affected by the fires of 2017 and 2018 will never be forgotten.

About the Author

PG Forte inhabits a world only slightly less strange than the ones she creates; filled with serendipity, coincidence, love at first sight and dreams come true.

Originally a Jersey girl, and forever a California girl at heart, she now resides in the beautiful Texas Hill Country where she writes contemporary and paranormal romance in a variety of sub-genres.

To stay in touch with PG and learn more about her books, visit her website, sign up for her newsletter, or join her FB readers group, The Crone's Nest

Pour Decisions

Meet the Martinelli sisters: Rosa, Bianca and Allegra. These partners in wine have just inherited a once-storied winery in the heart of Napa Valley. They're living the dream, right?

Not so fast! Because, as it turns out, not everybody is happy for them. And that includes their Uncle Geno who'd assumed the property would come to him.

There are hoops to jump through, barrels to get over, and a mountain of regulations they'll have to scale. But these sisters are crushing it—and we don't just mean the grapes. They're making wine, falling in love, and working together to restore their inheritance to its former glory, one pour decision at a time.

No Way, Rosé
By Kate Davies

Pour Decisions

Could this be a second chance worth savoring?

ROSA

Don't get me wrong - I'm thrilled that Nonna left her winery to my sisters and me, but I'm terrified, too. With Allegra and Bianca both out of the country, the responsibility falls totally on me - and what if I'm not up to the challenge? Now my ex, Jake Wright, is offering to help out, but that's terrifying in a different way. Working side by side is bringing all those old feelings back to the surface, and I'm falling for him all over again. But does our partnership have a future, or is heartbreak on the horizon?

JAKE

I've been away from our hometown for ten long years. Now I'm back, and working with Rosa is both the best and worst thing that's ever happened to me. We're saving her family winery one day at a time - and giving in to the heat between us one night at a time, too. But I'm afraid this pairing has an expiration date...

Gone With the Wine
By Kelly Jamieson

Where there's a wine, there's a way.

JANSEN

I'm trying to start over after a soul-crushing end to my hockey career and my marriage—so I buy a winery. I have no idea what I'm doing, but at least I have a reason to get out of bed in the morning. I hate asking for help, but when I meet the wine-maker next door, I'm jacked to have an excuse to see her again. She's gorgeous and full of life, with grape juice-stained hands, a sunburnt nose, and long legs in cut-off shorts. But Bianca's not so eager to help a grumpy rich celebrity who thinks he can just buy a winery and become a winemaker.

BIANCA

Holy crap, I've inherited part of the family winery. That should be a dream come true, but I left Napa to get away from my family baggage. I have no choice but to go home and help my sisters get through harvest season, but I'll be making a quick exit back to my rising star wine career in Argentina. Meanwhile, our new neighbor is a tall, dark, and ripped temptation. He needs a winemaker, and I need a laboratory—so we make a business deal. But while we work together picking, crushing, and fermenting, the attraction between us is causing another chemical reaction. And with wine and with life, it's not healthy to keep things bottled up...

Que Será Syrah
By PG Forte

They may be keeping secrets and telling lies, but a little white wine never hurt anyone.

ALLEGRA

It's not every day that you inherit one-third of a winery. I should be on top of the world, floating on Cloud Wine, as they say. Instead, don't you just know it? I'm about to make one of the biggest mistakes of my life. And that's saying something. My family has always viewed me as something of a screw-up, not always fairly. But in this case? They're not only dead right about me messing things up; they don't even know the half of it. Yet.

Complicating my quest to redeem myself, earn my sisters' respect, and help them turn our winery into a straight fire success, is my low-key relationship with Sheriff's Deputy Clay Romero. Sure, there are risks involved in sleeping with the enemy, but 'what's meant to be will find a way,' right? And whether Clay believes it or not, I know we're fated. With a capital F.

CLAY

We're Capital F somethin' all right; but I don't think it's fate. Ever since Legs (AKA Allegra Martinelli) blew back into town, I've been flirting with disaster. Literally. I doubt that woman's ever met a rule that she didn't want to at least bend. And, as luck would have it, it's my job to try and stop her. I love my job, and I think I love her. But there's not enough wine in Napa to convince me that I'll be able to hang on to them both.

Pour Decisions

Legs keeps likening us to Romeo and Juliet. And as I keep trying to remind her; that kind of story tends not to end well. I'm sure there are exceptions, but are we gonna be one of them? I guess we'll find out.

Other Books by PG Forte

Stand Alone Stories

Finders Keepers
Inked Memories
Can't Fight the Moonlight
Fall For You

Angels in the Afterlife

Edge of Heaven
Angel Mine
Christmas Angel

Celtic Legends Stories

Iron
Oak

Children of Night Series

Other Books by PG Forte

In the Dark
Old Sins, Long Shadows
Now Comes the Night
Ashes of the Day
Fallen Embers
To Curse the Darkness
Going Back To Find You
Light Up the Night

Games We Play Series

Truth Or Dare
Never Have I Ever
Two Truths And A Lie
The Name Game
Funnel of Love
Put a Ring Around the Rosie
Giada Mazzi is Living her Best Life

LA Love Lessons Series

Waiting for the Big One
Going to the Chapel
Love, From A to Z
Let Me Count the Ways
Christmasing With You

The Oberon Series

Scent of the Roses
A Sight to Dream Of

Other Books by PG Forte

Sound of a Voice that is Still
A Taste of Honey
Touch of a Vanished Hand
The Spirit of the Place
Visions Before Midnight
Dream Under the Hill
And Shadows Have Their Ending

The Oberon Novellas

Such Fleeting Pleasures
Hungry Heart
Sea Change
I'll be Home for Christmas
Spicy Nick

The Winter Heart Series

This Winter Night
This Winter Heart
Winter World of Love
Winter Of Our Discontent